"A DELICIOUS WHODUNIT!"

People Magazine

The Baked Bean Supper Murders

Virginia Rich

BALLANTINE BOOKS • NEW YORK

Library of Congress Catalog Card Number: 83-70156

ISBN 0-345-31252-X

This edition published by arrangement with E.P. Dutton, Inc.

Manufactured in the United States of America

First Ballantine Books Edition: October 1984
Second Printing: November 1984

To Aunt Ada and Aunt Mary and Aunt Emily, to Aunt Tillie, to Aunt Bernice and Aunt Dorothy and Aunt Louise, and to Aunt Stella Hunter

1

It was not yet five o'clock and the line already stretched nearly to the road from the big closed double doors of the Grange Hall.

The first-comers would eat at the first table. Those in line after that (the second-floor hall, used for the supper, held eight tables, each seating ten people) would have to wait, hungry and helpless, milling about downstairs. They would feel obligated to buy pot holders and aprons and bedsocks for next year's Christmas gifts from the fancywork tables. They would share the glum realization that the best of the baked beans and brown bread, the crispest cole slaw, the hottest and most savory casseroles would be given to the first seating.

Worst of all, the late-comers also knew that the flakiest pies—the creamiest pumpkins, the airiest lemon meringues, the richest and butteriest apples, the darkest and spiciest mincemeats—would be gone before their turn arrived. There would still be plenty, but the best would be gone.

It was a plain fact of life in Northcutt's Harbor. The contributions of the newest, or least gifted, cooks among the Grange wives were saved for the second table. It was the opinion of the ladies' committee, bustling about pink-cheeked in their matching striped aprons, that the cream of things ought to go to the people who showed their appreciation by getting there early.

Experienced by now in these matters, Mrs. Potter and the members of her party were already in place at midpoint in the queue. She had been invited to join the table of Cole and

Regina Cogswell, friends and her part-time neighbors on the Point—that lovely rockbound tip of the peninsula, perhaps a hundred acres of spectacular rocks and crashing ocean frontage, thrust like a challenging fist into the face of the Atlantic. The peninsula as a whole, above the Point, encompassed the Grange Hall, the white church whose spire she could see down the road, and the entire small Down East Maine fishing village of Northcutt's Harbor.

Cole, as blueberry baron of the town of Cherrybridge, some twenty miles to the north, and also owner of the Northcutt's Harbor lobster pound, was unquestioned squire of the community. His round head shone in the late-day spring sunshine; his round blue eyes gleamed as he smiled at his small party of guests. A gallant elbow, in neat navy flannel blazer, bore the light touch of his wife's fingertips, sharing the support of her fragile body with the light silver-topped cane that she held in her other hand.

"You okay, old girl?" he asked. "Not too long standing here for you? Shall we get a folding chair from inside the hall?"

Regina smiled an easy denial. "Just the old arthritis acting up again, 'Genia," she explained to Mrs. Potter. "Coley's getting to be an awful fusser in his old age." The Cogswells looked at each other, their eyes a complete disavowal of age and infirmities.

"We'll be moving any time now," announced Regina's nephew Herbert, with an air of unassailable superiority. "I can time to the minute when these affairs get started, after all the years Nancy and I have been coming here."

"You two are mere babes when it comes to bean suppers," Regina reminded him. "You only began spending summers here, coming up from Philadelphia right after you were married. And that must be only twenty years ago, so don't put on any airs about being old-timers. Coley and I were *born* in these parts, and a long time further back than you two can remember."

Nancy Wyncote spoke from her husband's side. "Herbert's always right about time, if nothing else," she said, somewhat pettishly. "If you've got the money, honey, he's got the

2

time. And you can underline money.'' Herbert's answering chuckle was hollow.

The Cogswells' party numbered ten. There was their friend and neighbor on the Point, 'Genia, Mrs. B. Lewis Potter, like them a part-time resident of Northcutt's Harbor, living the rest of the year at her cattle ranch in Arizona.

There were the Herbert Wyncotes, Regina's nephew and his wife Nancy, here for an unusually early start on their summer in order to supervise some work on their house on the neighboring and considerably more fashionable peninsula of Millstone. With them was another Philadelphia couple, the Ainsleys, also here for an early opening of their own Millstone house.

There was Carter Ansdale, an on-and-off summer resident, a designer and partner in commercial development of real estate in Atlanta. Carter, a bachelor, held Mrs. Potter's elbow in a firmly possessive grasp, and his gray-flecked brown head stood well above that of the group.

And there were Cole's much younger half sister, Olympia Cutler, and her teenage daughter, Laurie, now glaring at her mother in helpless rage. Mrs. Potter had watched Olympia shrug a cold and positive "no" to what had obviously been Laurie's request to join the party of gangling, noisy teenagers behind them.

The line began to move, not so much a forward motion as a gentle, all-over twitch, a preliminary to possible future progress. An American flag, a giant banner thrust forward on a heavy wooden flagpole, flapped gently overhead between the two upper windows.

Ahead of them Mrs. Potter had already seen and waved to a number of local people. Most of these were husbands and children, since the Northcutt's Harbor wives were already busy upstairs, setting out their generous contributions of good Maine cooking.

Somewhere inside the Grange Hall with them, she knew, was the other, and much beloved, neighbor of hers and the Cogswells on the Point. Harvard Northcutt, patriarch of the village that bore his grandfather's name and past master of the Grange, would be upstairs helping with the final placement of

3

the folding chairs. Or perhaps he was just inside the front door, helping set up the money till with Amanda Wakefield, the town postmaster (both she and the United States Postal Service disdained the term *postmistress*), who was always in charge of selling the supper tickets. The sign had been up in the post office, an L-shaped addition to Amanda's house, for some weeks.

BAKED BEAN AND CASSEROLE SUPPER, it had read, in large handprinted letters. Cut-out magazine pictures of pies and cakes surrounded the lettering. BENEFIT OF NORTH-CUTT'S HARBOR GRANGE. Specifics followed in smaller letters: "Friday, May 21, adults $3, children $1.25."

At the stroke of five the big double doors opened and the line began to move, at first jerkily, then with increasing assurance. Ahead, Mrs. Potter could see one of the first cohesive groups to enter, clearly a party. This was made up of that part of the local population Mrs. Potter privately called the YRPs—the year-round people. Originally summer visitors, staying at nearby motels in Ellsworth or at the slightly flea-bitten Sportmans Lodge in Cherrybridge, they had returned to buy small lots in the two local real estate developments that, gradually and separately, had now come to make up nearly half of the peninsula's population.

She recognized Teedy, T. D. Pettengill, the real estate developer who was responsible for this burgeoning growth, and his wife Eileen, teetering like an egg on impossibly thin legs. She waved to her friends the Weidners, retired school-teachers from Pennsylvania, who were part of the group, and to Colonel and Mrs. Van Dusen, retired army people, standing smartly erect beside them. As newcomers to the community, the Colamarias seemed small and dark beside the command-ing military presence. In the party, Mrs. Potter recognized a newly retired business tycoon and his wife, whom she had only recently met.

"Look, there's Whitehead," she heard Herbert say to his wife. "Big man in real estate investments—someone brought him to the club for lunch not long ago. I want to meet him later, and I suppose I've got to say hello to that little toad,

4

Pettengill. He's doing awfully well around here. Be nice to them both, will you?'' Nancy shrugged.

Most of the rest of the line had merely assembled, singly or by families, and there were really only three distinct parties among them. First, the year-rounders. Then, the Cogswells'. (They would probably be considered by most of the others as ''summer people,'' although—except for the Philadelphians— they were not that at all.) The third group was made up of the town youngsters, boys and girls alike dressed in nearly identical costumes—tight jeans, striped shiny jackets, and garishly decorated running shoes, all somewhat grimy looking in spite of their obvious expensive newness.

It used to be easier to tell the boys from the girls, Mrs. Potter thought, simply by their feet. With the current fashion in fancied-up sneakers it was harder to tell. They all looked equally big and clumsy.

Even their hairstyles seemed alike—tight, uncombed ringlets, newly permed to the roots. Only Shelley Northcutt, Harvard's grandniece, stood out among the girls, her smooth golden cap looking shiny and clean, her long legs smoothly encased in denim, prancing and cavorting like a young filly.

Rodney Pickett, alone among the boys, was likewise unpermed. His light brown English hair, straight and mid-length, his narrow English head, his clear English blue eyes, his posture of elegant nonchalance were a reminder of his heritage as the son of a shipwrecked British sailor. Mrs. Potter thought of a princeling among peasants.

''How's our Lord Beatle today?'' Cole called out loudly and genially, then added to his wife and Mrs. Potter, ''Guess he didn't hear me. Just a little private joke between the boy and me.''

As they moved forward Mrs. Potter noticed young Laurie looking back guardedly at this younger group. Along with Rodney Pickett, whose fair skin seemed suddenly flushed, Mrs. Potter recognized other teenagers—Cooneys and Northcutts and Birdsons. Most of them she had known since their childhood, from a time when she herself had first come, some ten years earlier, to the village.

Now the line was being greeted by the present master of

the Grange, Otis Bewley, dressed in his Sunday suit and wearing a necktie with a pattern of sea gulls.

"You folks go right on up and find your seats anywhere," he told them, "soon's you get your tickets from Amanda here at the card table. Afterwards, while the second seating gets a chance at the groceries, you'll get your turn at the fancywork tables."

With skill born of practice, Dorrie Van Dusen, the military wife, was already marshaling the Pettengill party up the stairs. The Cogswell group followed more slowly, adjusting its pace to Regina's ascent, with the graceful aid of her thin cane and the supporting curve of her husband's elbow.

Harvard Northcutt met them at the top of the stairs. "Get a table on the east side," he admonished them. "Sun's still wicked hot by the windows on the west. Take that one right there, right where you can look out over the flagpole."

Regina Cogswell's fine blue-veined hand was momentarily enveloped in Harvard's big work-hardened brown one, which then fell upon Mrs. Potter's flower-sprigged cotton shoulder in an affectionate thump. "Over there, 'Genia," he told her. "Don't let that Pettengill bunch beat you to it. I told them it was reserved."

When they were seated, Cole directed the conversation from his place at the head of the table. "Seeing that flag out there, I want to know how you all are going to spend Memorial Day. Only a week or so now, isn't it? Speak up, now— we're going to have to wait a bit to be served."

None of the group seemed to have special plans. "You've got to remember, Cole," Carter Ansdale said, "that most of us here at the table came from away. 'Genia's other love is that ranch of hers."

He put a large arm across her shoulders as he spoke. "I know you two, and I guess Olympia too, have your graves to decorate and parades to watch, growing up in Cherrybridge as you three did. But Herbert and Nancy, now, and the Ainsleys—"

"Didn't you know Herbert's a Northcutt, too?" Nancy demanded. "Herbert Northcutt Wyncote. He tells everybody in Chestnut Hill that his family was here in Maine long before

6

mine ever got to Philadelphia, which I may say was *well* before the Revolution."

"I thought you all knew that Regina was a Northcutt," Cole said. "No relation to Harvard. Or maybe, like most of the old families around here, they all stemmed from the same ancestor way back, only they don't admit it today. Only God in his holy heaven knows why."

"To get back to Memorial Day," Regina interrupted easily, "Laurie has been asked to recite the Gettysburg Address this year at the town parade and we're very proud of her."

"Oh, Aunt Regina, it doesn't mean all that much," Laurie said diffidently. Her eyes strayed to the next table, where the local teenagers were pushing and shoving to take their seats, with an occasional noisy crash of an overturned wooden folding chair.

"Of course it does," her mother reminded her stiffly. "I don't know why you're always belittling yourself. You're a Cogswell too, remember, even if you're part Cutler as well. Now please sit up straight and stop twisting around to look at the boys."

Laurie sat red-faced and silent as Olympia continued. "You know I recited it once when I was her age," she told the group, "and I tried to remember the whole thing the other day, starting with 'Four score and seven years ago.' I'm sure *you* wouldn't remember it, Cole," and she looked coldly at her half brother at the head of the table. "Your literary taste seems to run entirely to those atrocious limericks of yours. But I wonder if anyone else here can say it?"

The table erupted in a babble of voices. Everyone was sure he could recite the whole thing, everyone was prompting and filling in and correcting everyone else. Did the sentence beginning, "It is for us, the living," come before or after the one beginning," The world will little note, nor long remember"? Everyone knew most of it, once a line was begun, and the chorus became clamorous.

Only Laurie Cutler was silent, her pale red hair, so like her mother's, falling over one eye as she looked down at slim, twisted fingers in her lap.

The ladies of the Grange, in their matching aprons, advanced at last with the food. "Tell you where you can check that out," Alice Cooney remarked in Mrs. Potter's ear. "Back end of the dictionary. It's there all marked up to show you how to do some kind of punctuation or whatnot."

With that, the bowls and casseroles filled the center of the table. At one end was a big round plate piled with sliced, hot, steamed brown bread, and beside it a plate of butter and a knife. At the other was a great bowl of cole slaw.

There were two baking dishes of beans. One, Mrs. Potter's preference, the small pea beans, was considered here to be a foreign Massachusetts dish, but it was provided at bean suppers to allow for outsiders. These were deep brown with molasses and slow cooking, rich with salt pork, and centered in the pot with a well-browned and tender whole onion, to which Mrs. Potter resolved to serve herself, without apology, along with the beans.

The second bean dish was the favorite of the locality. These were the large yellow-eye beans, also baked long and tender and also rich with salt pork, but sweeter, more golden, and juicier than their Boston cousins.

The steamed brown bread had been made by one of the three local experts—Amanda, the postmaster; Edna, granddaughter-in-law of the original expert; or Tillie Northcutt, widow of Harvard's brother. By whichever hand, it was a credit to the Birdson grandmother—of legendary bad temper but with a sure knowledge of brown bread—who had been their teacher. Each steaming, fragrant slice was almost too meltingly tender to eat with the fingers, and yet uncompromising in the honesty of its stern ingredients—rye meal and cornmeal, whole-wheat flour, buttermilk, and molasses—and an invitation to add a too liberal slathering of butter from the dish that followed it.

For the first time at a public Maine supper, Mrs. Potter made good on her earlier resolve to limit herself to the primary items: beans, brown bread, and cole slaw. Crisp and cold, this was made in the old-fashioned way her own Grandmother Andrews in Iowa had always made it, with a simple dressing of sour cream, sugar, salt, and vinegar.

This was the feast. And this time she was determined not to spoil it with any diversions, however tempting.

The other dishes were passed around and around in their wonderful variety. There was American chop suey, that tomato-beef-macaroni dish that had been known to Mrs. Potter in her Iowa youth as a perennial picnic favorite and had been called there, naturally, Eyetalian Delight. There was a casserole of corn and mushrooms with tiny native Maine shrimp, highly popular. There was a casserole of escalloped potatoes and ham, and another of plain macaroni and cheese, which looked especially tempting with its bubbling golden crust. There was a tuna fish dish, apparently made with noodles and peas.

Ordinarily Mrs. Potter would have done as the others were doing, serving herself a small spoonful of each. The mingling of juices, sauces, and flavors, together with those of the cole slaw and beans, would have resulted in the same rather unsatisfactory muddle she remembered from previous bean suppers and from far too many equally disappointing jumbles she had imposed on herself at buffet tables and smorgasbords.

Pleased with her own restraint, she weakened to the extent of one small spoonful of the yellow-eye beans, just to compare them with her Boston favorites. (Actually very good. A touch of maple syrup in place of the traditional molasses? Maybe she'd been missing something all these years.)

Mrs. Potter's own usual donation to the fund-raising supper was several tins of coffee, and she was pleased to see that it was being poured generously throughout the meal, even though she knew that she herself might pay the penalty of wakefulness later. The ladies in the striped aprons circulated tirelessly with the big aluminum coffee pitchers, inquiring solicitously at each table to see if the diners couldn't use a few more beans, and was there enough butter?

Only the serving dishes were removed when it was time for dessert. "Lick your forks, everybody," Tillie Northcutt told them cheerfully, "and use your same plates for the pie."

The pies were cut in eight slices to the tin, a division ordinarily thought niggardly, to allow for two contingencies: the first, that the diner might be too full for more than a fairly small piece; the second, which proved more likely, that two small pieces, or even three, of different varieties would be needed to fill up the last chinks.

Carter Ansdale beamed at the southern pecan pie, crisply topped with pecan halves suspended in a clear, sweet, brown, praline-tasting jelly. The Wyncotes stuck to chocolate cream. Mrs. Potter was unable to resist something she could not remember having since her growing-up days in Harrington, Iowa—sour cream raisin. She reflected, as she had often done before, on the similarities of Iowa country cooking with that of New England.

Actually, there was nothing so mysterious about it, she remarked to the Ainsleys beside her, since her Middle West forebears had mostly come from New England stock.

The Ainsleys, with their elegantly elongated Philadelphia diphthongs, told her they thought the food was "divoine," although their own ancestral fare had its origin, they thought, in Maryland and Virginia.

Mrs. Potter then noticed that Carter had carefully sliced the firm, jellied point from his slice of pecan pie and had set it to one side.

"I haven't seen anyone do that for a hundred years," Mrs. Potter exclaimed, "only I put mine in back, not alongside, like this."

Laurie watched them both with curiosity, then averted her eyes when she realized they had noticed her regard. "You save the point to eat last, honey," Carter explained, "and then you get to make a wish."

Laurie made a neat triangle of the point of her own pie and set it carefully behind the rim of the crust, as Mrs. Potter had done. Her mother shook her head, with an almost imperceptible frown.

"About time to let the ladies clear away and get ready for their second seating," Cole Cogswell eventually had to remind them. "And now, God help us all, we've got to go down and buy whatever leftover damned junk there is on those fancywork tables."

"Sorry, I'm afraid I'll have to run," Olympia told her half brother stiffly. "I'm a working woman, remember? My day begins too early for any more night life."

Mrs. Potter then recalled that this was the first time she had seen Cole's half sister in anything but working clothes. In worn jeans, a faded red sweatshirt, with a knitted cap pulled down over her pale red hair, she manned (there was no other word for it) the Cogswell lobster-buying operation in Northcutt's Harbor.

Olympia, raised by Cole's young stepmother at the old house in Cherrybridge that was still home for him and Regina, had decided after her married life in New York and her subsequent divorce to return to Maine. She had persuaded her brother to give her a job of managing his lobster pound.

From before dawn every day until after the last lobster boat came in from fishing—any time between noon and dark, depending on the season—Olympia filled gas tanks. She purveyed barrels of high-smelling bait for the lobster traps. She helped to unload and weigh each fisherman's catch on his return. It had been some time since any fisherman in the harbor had complained that this was no job for a woman. Olympia Cutler earned her pay, and no mistake.

However, as Mrs. Potter looked at Olympia now, her fair hair pulled back tight into a single braid down her back, wearing clean white pants and a striped pullover that spoke more of sailing than of lobster fishing, she realized with surprise that Olympia was really a nice-looking woman. And Laurie—what is she, fifteen?—is going to be a beauty, she observed. What a shame they are so stiff and standoffish with Cole and Regina, and, even more a pity, with each other as well.

"Thank you for including us at dinner," Olympia was now saying to Regina, "even if we can't stay now. Laurie was delighted to be one of the party, too, I know." Her eyes, as blue as Cole's, but cool, less open, turned to her daughter in silent admonition.

Laurie's gaze returned quickly from the table at which the teenagers were sitting, and her murmur of thanks to Aunt Regina and Uncle Cole was prompt and proper.

As they prepared to leave the upper room of the Hall, the Cogswell party drifted briefly toward the table of the year-round people—those former summer visitors who had settled comfortably into their small pretty houses in the Pettengill tracts. Mrs. Potter greeted Chuck and Margo Weidner warmly. Her smile included the Pettengills, the military Van Dusens, and the new New York people, the Whiteheads, already engaged in conversation with Herbert and Nancy.

Her greeting to the Colamarias, the other recent newcomers, was a little less brief. "Marvelous food, wasn't it, Tory?" she asked. "I don't suppose you have a recipe for a bean dish—what's the word, *fagioli*?—that's in some way the equivalent of Yankee baked beans?"

"Not exactly, but I do make a . . ." Tory began hesitantly, when her husband interrupted.

"Enough, Victoria. Mrs. Van Dusen is ready to leave."

Mrs. Whitehead put out her cigarette in the last of her coconut cream pie, and moved sideways in her chair. "We all know where little old Carter's from, don't we?" she said in a theatrical southern accent, looking up at the man beside Mrs. Potter, "and what kind of food *he* likes." She raised beringed fingers in a slow touch across his tweedy arm.

Harvard Northcutt made his way from another table in the room. "Edna says to tell you she's baking tomorrow morning," he told Mrs. Potter. "Said come early and you'd have to take it hot from the oven because she's going to Ellsworth as soon as it's done."

Mrs. Potter waved acknowledgment and thanks across the room to Edna Birdson, busy in her pink-striped apron.

Finally the several and quite separate parts of Northcutt's Harbor dispersed, making their way down the wide, worn, wooden stairs. The teenagers clattered down first, their dawdling at the table suddenly halted by Bill Van Dusen's military bark of command. "Finish up now, kids. Let the next batch have this table."

Mrs. Potter noticed that Rodney Pickett was the last of the group to leave. His eyes were fixed upon Laurie, and her response to the intensity of his gaze appeared surprised and questioning.

The local townspeople drifted down slowly, in a comfortable mingling of Down East voices. When speaking to Mrs. Potter, each was clear, totally intelligible. Speaking to each other, they seemed to revert to a completely different language, an unfamiliar rhythm of speech in which she often found herself completely lost. It seemed more singing than talking, an incomprehensible musical cadence covering a great range of sound. Some day she hoped she'd be able to understand every word of it.

Moving at Regina's pace, the Cogswell party was among the last to leave the dining room. The big flag still fluttered in the sun outside the upper windows. Impatient late arrivals in the room below were already beginning to crowd past on their way upstairs. Harvard Northcutt stood in the corner of the landing, saying good-bye, saying hello, his snaggletoothed smile embracing them all, his warm old brown hand reaching out to pat all the ladies, young and old, as they passed.

People do not shake hands here, Mrs. Potter reflected, at any rate not the people of Harvard's home village, even among their own friends. Whenever, early in her village life, she had extended her own hand, it had been accepted only briefly and with a kind of limp surprise.

But one didn't need handshakes to express friendship. Right now it was enough that there was a Harvard among them, with a warmth of affection that seemed to encompass them all, old neighbors and newcomers alike. Even the stiffly erect shoulders of Olympia Cogswell Cutler and the equally stiff young back of Laurie beside her. Even the somewhat dim Philadelphia couple with Herbert and Nancy. Even the young man, Jim or Mark something, with the ponytail, who had done some painting for her at the cottage, and the pretty dark-haired girl in jeans beside him, the two clearly not a part of any local group.

What a man, Mrs. Potter thought, impulsively reaching up to kiss Harvard's wrinkled, firm old cheek as she passed the landing.

2

A narrow pillar of smoke rose straight into the still early-morning air from the crooked cobblestone chimney, then flattened into a precise oval above the small unpainted house before it drifted, retaining its neat but enlarging shape, toward the rocky point to the south. A few purposeful cormorants skimmed the still water of the small cove, then headed out to open sea.

An almost visible aroma of fresh hot bread rose quite as steadily as the smoke column, coming from the open top of a slightly butter-soaked brown paper bag. Mrs. Potter sniffed the moist fragrance happily, trying to keep from squeezing the bread she was carrying so carefully to her neighbor.

"Hi there, Harvard," she called as she approached the small house on the cove. "How about a loaf of Edna's hot bread for your breakfast?"

The door of the house was open to the May morning, but the voice that answered came instead from the ramshackle pier. From behind a stack of wooden lobster traps drying in the sun, the old man appeared. Although as weathered as his house and moving stiffly, his gait and posture suggested the same strength—slightly skewed by work and age—as the sturdy platform of the dock.

"Well, *morning,* 'Genia," he answered. "Breakfast time's a long time back. Scobbledegook. City girl like you wouldn't know."

"Don't be so tarnation smug," she told him. "I'm no city girl, as you very well know, and I know what scobbledegook

14

is. Scrambled eggs with whatever's handy stirred into it—bacon, sausage, fried potatoes, onions, cheese, tomatoes. Well, I was having my fruit and tea just as early. How do you think I got all the way up to Edna's farm and back again with this hot bread for you?''

"Second breakfast then," Harvard said. "That's what we're both ready for. Where's Sindhu?"

Still at the vet's, she told him. They wanted to keep him a day or so to be sure there wouldn't be any infection after they cut out the porcupine quills from his jaw and tongue. "Poor fellow," she said. "I hope he's learned his lesson."

"Some do, some don't," Harvard said. "Had a dog once—Sully I called him for the fellow up in Sullivan who gave him to me—and Sully never did learn. Just got madder'n ever next time he met one. Finally got so he spent most of his time looking for a porcupine just to try to get even all over again."

Together they went up the worn wooden steps and entered the small sunny kitchen. "Kettle's boiling," Harvard said. "One thing you can say for a good wood fire."

He put two tea bags in each clean, heavy mug, and she hastily removed one of these as he lifted the old blue-speckled granite teakettle. "Your tea would tan boot leather back at the ranch," she admonished him.

"Lily-livered stuff *you* drink," he retorted. "Suppose you want milk in yours, too. There's fresh in the icebox—know you don't fancy the canned." As she crossed the room he added, "Get out the butter while you're at it, will you? I'll saw us a little of the bread. We'll see if Edna's lost her touch."

It was reassuring to Mrs. Potter to open the old refrigerator to find it both sweet-smelling and well stocked with food. With the pitcher of milk she found an open plate of fresh butter. She saw a good supply of cheese and eggs, a quart glass jar filled with fresh shucked clams, part of a boiled chicken, an opened can of peaches. No fresh vegetables, she noted, but when a man going on eighty-one was as healthy as Harvard he didn't need any lectures about vitamins and roughage.

Harvard was gently seesawing an old wooden-handled bread knife to cut thick slices of the still hot bread. "Know what this needs?" he asked her. "Sprinkle of maple sugar."

"Mrs. Potter nodded happily. That was the way she and her brother Will used to eat it, she told him, on Saturday mornings when Grandmother Andrews was baking.

With pleasure she watched Harvard's careful, work-thickened hands as he lifted down an old coffee can from an upper shelf and crumbled a chunk of the pale amber sugar over each thickly buttered, melting slice. "Hands are clean," he muttered apologetically. "Just went out to the pier to see the day—no bait bags yet."

He set down the thick blue plate between them on the scrubbed pine of the old table, and pushed it toward her. "Something else tells me you've got an eye on the heel," he said with a grin. "Go on, take it. I'm not the man with crusts I used to be."

They ate in companionable silence, unconcernedly wiping away occasional dribbles of buttery sweetness from their chins with their fingers. Mine show the miles too, Mrs. Potter thought. Lobster fishing in all weather and seasons had given Harvard's hands their character. Gardening and washing dishes and refinishing furniture (and hating rubber gloves) have done as much for mine, even though they've had better care.

"Last night's bean supper was great," she said as she finished the crusty heel. "Never better. And I think I'm beginning to see your point about yellow-eyes."

"Made money for the Grange," Harvard replied, reaching for another slice of bread. "That's the thing. Otis made his brag when we counted up afterward. Think he was trying to show me up. Biggest take ever, he kept saying, now he's master of the Grange. Hell's bells, I don't care long's the hall gets a new roof."

Beaming agreement, Mrs. Potter offered a bit of news. "I'm having guests for Sunday supper," she told him, as she shook her head in a reluctant no to a second piece of bread.

"Heard tell," Harvard said. "Coley was in here yesterday morning after he and Regina got down from Cherrybridge. He said you were having a do."

16

"The two of them, yes, and Regina's nephew and his wife," she said. "It's the law. I can still hear my mother telling me: You have to entertain people's visiting houseguests, unless you're plain flat on your deathbed. I'd have asked Cole and Regina for supper anyway, but their having the Wyncotes there made it absolutely mandatory for Sunday evening before they leave."

Harvard interrupted. "Don't know how she can stand the fellow. Only kin the woman's got—you'd have thought Regina, of all people, could do better."

"Anyway, Herbert and his wife are staying with the Cogswells at the Roost while their own cottage over at Millstone is being opened up. I can't believe summer people are coming this early."

"Used to be *that* bunch was all we had to worry about," Harvard said, sipping his strong tea. "Used to be just *us* here in Northcutt's Harbor, fishing and minding our own business—best way we could, anyhow. Then it got to be summer people around about, hiring all *our* kids to mow lawns and make beds and look after *their* kids. And then came along this batch of doggone hybrids. I don't know what you'd call them. Started out as summer people, but not the fancy kind, ended up hunkering down to stay all year."

"I've got a name for them," Mrs. Potter volunteered. "I call them YRPs, for year-round people. Teedy's made a good thing for himself in his developments, and I hear that both of them are almost sold out."

"Well, whatever, we've got the three separate batches here now," Harvard grumbled. "*Us*, the people who belong here. Northcutts and Cooneys mostly, and a few of the old Birdson tribe, plus an occasional odd one like Addie Pickett, Persy's husband. Then the summer people, like Regina's damn fool nephew and *his* crowd from Philadelphia and who knows where. All of them rich, only come to the village to buy lobsters and to get their places looked after and their boats fixed. And then Teddy Pettengill's crowd, here all the time, God help us, all of them with new pickup trucks they don't need any more than two left feet, all in new houses on their five-acre lots, taking over town meetings and starting something called a planning board, and *doing good*. That's the thing I've most got against them. I don't appreciate being done good to, and neither does anybody else in these parts.''

He now went on more slowly. "You, 'Genia Potter . . . I don't rightly know where to put you. Summer people, I'd have thought, when you and Lew first came here, even though you picked your little house here on the Point instead of a big one over at Millstone with the rest of that bunch. Now, you alone as you are, you seem to come odd times, so to speak. Summer for a while, maybe back for Thanksgiving, here this time in April. Pussy willows and still snow back in the trees when you got here. Some puzzling. You're a hard one to fix.''

Privately, Mrs. Potter felt that this was just the way she liked it, being part of several groups, never too rigidly identified with any of them.

However, from the first she had been at ease with this friendly, curious old man. In fact it had been his easy curiosity that had first endeared him to her. The other local residents of the town had shown no overt interest in the Potters, except for Persy Pickett's possible claim upon them as new customers for the general store.

Gradually, after Lew's death, she had found increasing acceptance and had learned that what she had considered indifference was simply Down East good manners.

"All right, I'll be your maverick," she told Harvard. "It's lots more fun being part of all three parts of Northcutt's Harbor, as you very well know. You manage it even better than I do.''

Harvard swept a last few sugary crumbs from the blue plate into his palm and finished the last of his tea. "Walk you to your car," he offered. "Later on, when you've got time, some day soon, something I want to tell you about. No, no, plenty of time later. Not just exactly sure I want to talk about it yet anyway, and I'd hate to have you think hard of me, which maybe you will when you hear it.''

Mrs. Potter assured him that she could never do that, told him she'd see him Monday with dinner party leftovers if there were any worth bothering with, and started her car's motor,

18

thinking she'd have to stop at Pickett's for a few things for her Sunday supper, then go the post office to pick up her mail. Tomorrow there would be time for the pound, for lobsters for her fish stew.

Harvard's hand remained on the opened car door. "Better tell you now and get it over with," he said. "Nobody's going to live forever, 'Genia, and you know that as well as I do. Might as well save you a shock later on when I join the bunch up on the hill behind the church. Coley's lawyer just made me a will. My boat goes to Tommy, Tris and Sis's boy, no surprise in that. He's a little wild now, and maybe he takes after me in that. I made my mistakes. Anyway he'll make a good lobster fisherman when he settles down."

"That's great," Mrs. Potter agreed. "Nothing in that to cause any hard thoughts of you, and I approve of making wills. At the same time I must say I think you're good for another twenty years. You've told me that all the old Northcutts were still going strong in their nineties and beyond."

"Maybe so," Harvard said, "but what I have to own up to is who gets this place, and why, when I do go. Now there's some who want me to sell the place, and I don't give them the time of day. That little shrimp Teedy, stomping around in his boots, for one. Even had a nudge from that New York hotshot who just got here. Anyway my idea is some different."

Mrs. Potter nodded and waited for him to continue.

"Now, I know you don't much cotton to Persy, up at the store," he began, then paused.

"Well, I don't think anybody very much gets to *know* Persy," Mrs. Potter began doubtfully. "She's certainly a devoted mother to young Rodney." Trying to think of more reasons to like Persy Pickett, she hesitated. "And then, of course, she seems to be kind enough to Winks Cooney, that poor old soul."

"That's the heart of it, 'Genia. Persy does look out for the poor coot, even though he's not what you'd really call right in the head. *Lackin'*, I call it." He shook his head sadly. *"Lackin'."*

Harvard raised his hand from the car door as if to leave, then turned back. "I've let on to Coley and Regina, and I might as well get the thing off my chest to you, since whoever inherits is going to be the next neighbor to your place."

Mrs. Potter waited in silence, her hands suddenly tense on the steering wheel.

"I was pretty wild in my young days, 'Genia, and that's the God's truth of it. Should've married Jessie Cooney, and old man Cooney would've made darned sure that I did, except that Sarbelle Birdson's father had a faster shotgun. Guess I was punished all right. Sarbelle's baby didn't live to be born, and Jessie's boy . . ." Harvard halted, seeming reluctant to continue.

"Doggone it, 'Genia," he said at last, "Jessie's boy turned out to be Winks. Only son I ever had, daughter either. I owe him a place to live, and he's getting on past sixty now.

"Only way I can make it right after all these years is to leave the place here to Persy," he continued slowly. "Never anything between the two of *us*, Persy and me. I just remember her as a fat little girl, back when her father ran the store. They took in Addie Pickett, the British sailor who was shipwrecked—I've told you that yarn a dozen times—and she was still pretty young and Addie was already along in years when Persy married him."

Harvard was silent for a long moment. "Anyway I sold the main part of the point to Regina, some years back, but there's still the house and my land around the cove. Winks wouldn't be able to make a go of it here and alone, but Persy can maybe settle down here when she turns the store over to Roddy, and keep on making a place for poor Winks. I talked it over with her, and she's willing."

Harvard straightened his shoulders. "Now you get along to your party errands. I got it said and it wasn't as bad as I thought. Anyway, you put it right—I don't reckon to go for another ten, fifteen years, way I'm feeling now. Just wanted you to be ready for the word when it comes." He turned abruptly and started back along the narrow sandy lane to his house, not looking back.

3

When she and Lew had first come to Northcutt's Harbor
ten years before, enchanted by the beauty of the harbor and
the countryside, they had been eager to establish themselves
as a part of what seemed an idyllic and uncomplicated fishing
village life.

They had hoped to recapture some sense of their family
roots in New England, after years of shifting worlds of Lew's
ever-increasing business success. Their other fixed headquarters had become a cattle ranch in Arizona where they had
settled part-time to give their then-college-age children a
sense of permanence.

At that time they had been directed to see a Percy Pickett.
Percy would know what was available in the way of oceanfront
property, they had been told. Percy also ran the general store,
the one store in town.

The Mr. Percy Pickett they expected turned out to be an
enormously fat woman in a sleeveless cotton dress—a Bud-
dha figure of a woman, a mountain of flesh, somehow piled
and stacked onto a stool behind the counter in a crowded,
cluttered, unbelievably jam-packed little one-room store.

"I'm Persy," she had told them. "Short for Persis. Suppose
it's natural for outlanders to make a mistake, but now you
know."

Persy was a widow, she informed them. She had a child, a
pale, fair-haired boy named Rodney, who looked to be about
seven, who came in while they were talking, squeezing a
struggling calico kitten.

"Put the cat down!" Persy had shrieked at the child. "Nasty dirty thing! You'll get allergies, just like Mumma's. Here, come here, Roddy boy, let Mumma give her little English prince a nice candy bar."

The child leaned against his mother's knee, eating chocolate, and she and the Potters discussed available waterfront property.

Later, Persy officiated, acting as a surprisingly shrewd and knowledgeable broker, when they bought their beloved cottage on the point of the peninsula. They had quickly learned that their idea of Maine prices had been based on figures from much earlier years. There had been times when those earlier prices had been almost irresistibly seductive, although then they had had neither time nor money to take advantage of the bargains.

In the years since, they had never come to feel that they knew Persy, even though they, and now Mrs. Potter by herself, patronized the store almost daily. She bought milk and butter there, flashlight batteries, dental floss, molasses, postcards. She bought stocking caps, soap, snaps or scissors, her constant supply of lined yellow pads, and fresh-picked crabmeat.

Persy was moderately obliging about securing needed items, but Mrs. Potter always felt that to Persy her customers were interchangeable, without reality or individuality. She appeared to view them all—summer people, tourists, YRPs, and regulars—simply as a succession of animated figures. Each merely represented a special need—a loaf of bread, a box of cornflakes, a pair of fishing gloves—for which she took their money and made their change.

To all her customers Persy issued a relentless stream of personal medical bulletins. Her teeth, her back, her allergies, her current state of digestion were described in stupefying and occasionally rather startling detail. These bulletins were alternated with the local weather forecasts, which she relayed as they came in on the always blaring citizens band radio behind her stool. Persy seldom paused, and she obviously expected little in the way of reply.

"I didn't see you at the bean supper, Persy," Mrs. Potter now remarked. "Wonderful food and a big turnout. I saw

Rodney with the youngsters, of course, but somehow I missed seeing you.''

Persy's disclaimer was prompt. ''Thought you knew I never go out,'' she said. ''Run the store, night and day, every day in the year but Christmas. Thought you knew. That's all I live for, the store and Roddy. I still tell him he's my little English prince. My little blue-blooded Englishman. Of course, he's a pure dreamer, just like Addie was.''

''He certainly is a nice-looking boy,'' Mrs. Potter told his mother. ''Tall. Clear skin. Seems to carry himself well.''

''Pure dreamer,'' Persy repeated, her voice mingling pride and a transparent attempt at feigned scorn. ''Talks all the time about wanting to find out what he calls his *heritage*. Watches all those TV stories, rerun after rerun, about high-class English families. Lord and Lady Dimwits, I call them, counts and no-counts. Fancy houses, like castles. Every time I settle down in the evening with a decent American story—you know, cops and shoot-outs, a couple of good car wrecks—he takes over and makes me sit through another go-round of 'Upstairs, Downstairs.' Or that last one—you remember, about the two little queers at college? 'Visiting Brides' or something like that? Only thing I could say good about that one, there were quite a lot of interesting sicknesses, one kind and another.''

Realizing that Persy was about to compare some observed symptom with one of her own, and one that she had experienced to an even greater degree, Mrs. Potter retreated, consulting the brief list in her jacket pocket.

''Let's see, I need a couple of lemons,'' she said. ''And are there any of those Bake-and-Serve club rolls in the freezer?''

Persy nodded her head, a bouffant mass of hennaed glory, toward the refrigerator and freezer that occupied one side of the small room. Mrs. Potter had already turned in that direction, not expecting that Persy would rise from her stool.

As she peered into the freezer chest in search of the packaged rolls, she saw Winks Cooney in the back of the store. He was eating what appeared to be a large breakfast pastry, from which white frosting and pale yellow filling dripped

onto his chin and the front of his dirty blue sweater. He raised
a sticky finger, by way of good morning , and nodded several
times to emphasize the greeting.

Winks, from one of a number of Cooney families in the
village who, like many of the Northcutts, professed no kin-
ship with others of the same name, was considered to be not
quite bright. Harvard had used the term *"lackin',"* which
seemed a gentler description than that more commonly used.
"He just don't have both oars in the water," was the general
opinion.

Winks lived alone in an untidy shack behind the store, and
he presumably acted as a sort of watchman, perhaps not much
needed since Persy and Rodney lived in an apartment over the
store, reached by an outside stairway. His only clearly de-
fined shift was from two to three each afternoon. At this hour
the sign CLOSED filled the glass-paned door, Persy retreated
upstairs for her lunch break and Winks stood guard outside,
reminding any stray customers that Persy would be down at
three.

For this, or so it was supposed in the village, he was paid
chiefly in pastries, ice cream bars and canned sardines, the
staples of his diet.

In addition, from the time of Rodney's babyhood, Winks
had acted as nanny, baby-sitter, and now personal servant.
"Worships the ground that boy walks on," Persy would say.
"Winks may not be quite right, but I tell Roddy he's just like
having your own English butler."

On the side, Winks mowed several village lawns, charging
briskly for his rather haphazard services.

Fortunately Mrs. Potter had no lawn to mow. The sunny
patches around the cottage supported only her much loved
banks of *Rosa rugosa* and a low-growing carpet of wild
strawberries, blueberry plants, and highland cranberries. Each,
in its season (right now it was nearly strawberry time), provided a small feast for the palate, and each, at all seasons,
provided a changing feast of color for the eye.

Thus, she did not know Winks as one of his mowing
customers, but she did occasionally find him walking through

her woods. If he was simpleminded, she had observed that he was still an instinctively good woodsman. He invariably managed to pick her small crop of wild raspberries just the day before she had intended to do so herself, and she had once in a while come across one of his almost invisible snares, set, she supposed, for an unwary rabbit. When she spotted him, it was only for a second or two. Then, like some wild animal himself, belying his thick, middle-aged body and gray hair, Winks would melt away into the woods or the alder thicket, leaving her to wonder if she had only imagined his presence.

By the time she had found the rolls she sought at the bottom of the freezer, under haphazard piles of frozen popsicles and ice cream cartons, Winks had quietly disappeared, and another, more welcome figure had taken his place.

"Coley!" Mrs. Potter exclaimed with delight, "you're the man on my mind this very minute! Lemons for tomorrow night's bombastics—see?"

"Good Lord, I can't tell you how much Regina and I are looking forward to the evening," Cole Cogswell told her. Looking over his shoulder and lowering his ordinarily assured and highly audible voice, the authoritative voice of the country squire, he spoke in what was, for him, the equivalent of a whisper. "It's a rotten weekend, might as well tell you. That nephew of Regina's and his fool wife are driving us both crazy," he complained. "Brought him along now, supposedly so Frances could get a few odds and ends of groceries she didn't pack up from the house in Cherrybridge, ditched him outside with Curly Gillan for a minute to talk about some electric work he wants done before they move in at Millstone. Oh, great heavenly God above, here he comes now!"

Mrs. Potter made her good-morning greetings to Herbert, the Philadelphia nephew, ostensibly a pleasant and well-mannered man of forty, whom she had known not only through the Cogswells but also at various parties of summer people in seasons back. They spoke of the baked bean supper. She assured him she was looking forward to seeing him and Nancy the following evening; then, clutching her few purchases, she edged her way toward Persy at the cash register.

Maybe, she thought, she'd be able to catch Curly Gillan outside before he left. She wanted to ask him about her electric stove, which seemed to have one faulty burner.

First, however, she and Frances, the Cogswells' elderly cook, greeted each other warmly. They shared years of acquaintance, from Mrs. Potter's frequent appearance as a guest at the Cogswell table, and of mutual respect for their interest in good food.

Frances's whisper was very little more discreet than that of her employer, and not much more subdued in volume.

"You know *she* likes to do the cooking usual times, when she and Mr. Coley come down here for the weekend," Frances confided. "I most always stay home and keep an eye on things at the big house when they're down here at the Roost. But with all this crowd—" (Mrs. Potter could only judge from Frances's glare and nod in the direction of Herbert that "all this crowd" meant the two of them, Herbert and Nancy) "—I reckoned I'd better come along to see to things here this time." Frances sighed. "Hate to think it, but she's slowing down some."

She, of course, was Regina, clearly adored not only by her husband and cook but by a good part of the county as well. Mrs. Potter squeezed Frances's bony arm by way of unspoken understanding and agreement.

As she paid for her few groceries and slid out into the fresh May morning sunshine, away from the small crowded room and the noise of the crackling CB, Cole followed her.

"Can't get away from that damned pest Herbert," he grumbled loudly. "Got him started talking allergies now with Persy and maybe that'll keep him busy for a couple of minutes. I wish he'd tell her about this high-priced retirement center of his that he's making at Nancy's family's old place outside of Philadelphia. He's boring the pants off Regina and me talking about it. Think maybe he hopes to get us to shell out some money for it. Anyway I told him Persy was a great real estate expert around here and he ought to get her opinion."

"Not that she'll listen," Mrs. Potter reminded him. "I'll bet on the allergies."

Cole followed Mrs. Potter to the door of her car and helped

to settle her small bag of groceries on the seat beside her, his bald head shining in the morning sun, his eyes beaming with gallantry.

For a second time that morning, Mrs. Potter's progress was halted by a man's hand on her car door. Small, tanned, blue-veined, well-tended, Cole Cogswell's hand still conveyed an aura of competence and authority, a hand that could hold a fly rod, a tiller, or a book with equal assurance.

"Harvard told me he'd explained to you about his will, 'Genia," he began, "and I had already told him that, while you might be surprised, you wouldn't be shocked by his reasons for leaving his place to Persy. Damned poor idea, both Regina and I think, but you can't help but respect the man's sense of obligation to Winks, poor galoot. Guess it's been weighing on his conscience for years. Not that, from what I remember of Jessie Cooney, it was almighty certain whose son Winks really was."

Mrs. Potter nodded doubtfully. "Let's hope he lives for a long time," he said. "We couldn't have a better neighbor than Harvard. I'm not sure we'll be able to be that crazy about Persy, and I'd certainly hate to have a teenager in our laps, even though Roddy seems to be a quiet one."

"Don't you worry about it," Cole assured her. "I can't get him to change his will at the moment. He's a determined old Yankee. But so am I, and so is Regina. We've decided we're going to sit down with him next week and make him a good offer for his place. Give him lifetime residence and use of the cove. We'll pay the taxes, which are getting pretty steep for him these days, and the maintenance and repairs, plus giving him a good chunk of money he can put in the bank now. Then he can leave that to Persy or whoever he damned pleases later on. He'll see the sense of it."

"That's a marvelous solution, Coley," Mrs. Potter told him. "Just what I'd have expected of the blueberry baron of the world. I should have known you'd know how to handle it."

"Great God above, there's Herbert!" Cole muttered, again remembering to lower his voice, as he had earlier in the store at Herbert's approach. "You better run along. See you tomorrow."

As she neatly backed and turned her small car in the area beside Cole's big station wagon, Mrs. Potter glimpsed a dirty blue sweater and a quick-moving figure sliding away beyond the mud-spattered pickup truck on her other side. That *Winks,* she thought. He'll probably be home to see if my wild strawberries are ripe by the time I get back to the cottage.

Before she pulled out of the small parking lot, she saw Rodney.

Saturday morning, she thought. Like most of the other boys his age in the village, he would be going out in his skiff outboard to haul his lobster traps in the bay. All the boys did so on weekends and after school as a way of earning money and as a preparation for later careers as full-time lobster fishermen, just as their fathers and grandfathers had been.

Rodney's apparel today was, however, an immediate denial of the idea. Instead of worn jeans, a flannel shirt and high rubber boots, the accepted and practical costume for fishing, Rodney was wearing—could it be?—flannel trousers, white flannel trousers, discreetly striped in blue. Perhaps not flannel, but a look-alike version in polyester, less tight than jeans on his long legs. With them he wore a pale blue oxford shirt, sleeves rolled casually at the elbow, and there was a softly tied silk ascot inside the open shirt collar.

Rodney's, "Good morning, Mrs. Potter," was clearly spoken, his gaze direct, his bearing that of the young aristocrat greeting an old friend of the family, out for a morning stroll through the ancestral gardens.

He lifted an imperious hand, and Winks materialized suddenly beside him. "I'll have a Coke, Winks," he said quietly. "Be sure it's a cold one."

She remembered Rodney, at perhaps ten, and Winks proudly beaming when Rodney would say, rather grandly, "Winks, bring me an ice cream bar. And you have one, too."

She remembered Persy's complaints, which were actually rather proud statements, that Rodney was "too much of a

28

somebody" to help much at the store. "He keeps his outboard running like a gnat's eyebrow," Persy would say of young Rodney at fourteen. "He can do push-ups until hell won't have it, but he can't help unload when the bakery truck pulls in, though he runs through spending money slick as a bean."

Once Mrs. Potter recalled coming in upon the two of them when Rodney was perhaps fifteen. "I don't say *Mumma,"* he was saying fiercely. "I say *Mater.*" He had blushed furiously at being overheard by Mrs. Potter and had rushed to the safety of the apartment over the store.

Then there was the time she heard him correcting his mother's grammar. "It's 'you and I,' " he had said, "when we're doing something. But you don't say that Winks brought up stuff from the freezer for 'Rodney and I.' Then it's *me*—for 'Rodney and *me.*' "

Mrs. Potter was never sure that Persy had ever remembered the distinction, although when it came to general intelligence, she felt that Rodney had probably inherited as much from his mother as he had from the long-departed British sailor who had fathered him.

She remembered, too, Persy's wrath at the fancied slight. "Who does that Giselle think she is, anyway?" she demanded of Mrs. Potter once morning. "That Canuck! Nothing too good for that Cathy of hers, of course—piano lessons, braces on her teeth! And then having the gall to ask me if Roddy should be in the school breakfast program! As if I didn't know how to feed my own boy and couldn't afford the best of everything for him!"

There was also Persy's passionate defense when Roddy had been accused of cheating in a school examination. "My Rodney doesn't have to copy from *anybody,*" Mrs. Potter had heard Persy screaming into the telephone, "and if you're his teacher, you know he's too smart to need to!"

Unconcerned at being overheard by Mrs. Potter, Persy had contined her tirade. "All right, flunk him," she shouted. "His grades are good enough, he can fail one lousy little test!"

She slammed down the receiver, muttering meaningless

threats. Mrs. Potter had recognized this merely as Persy's way of blowing off steam, since she subsided almost at once to talk of the weather and chances of rain before morning. And, as far as Mrs. Potter knew, there was no further mention of cheating, and Rodney's class standing, if temporarily lowered, had quickly regained its high place.

Today Mrs. Potter was actually admiring Rodney's picture of himself. The world needs its moments of drama and she was often grateful to the people who presented themselves not only onstage but center front. Still, Mrs. Potter could not repress a faint, quickly restrained smile of amusement as she looked at the white striped flannel trousers.

The boy flushed to the roots of his fair hair, and she had a fearful realization that she might have disturbed the delicate balance of his self-image, which was clearly being rehearsed in this carefully costumed new role.

It's too late to tell him he looks splendid, she decided. Better to behave as if flannels and ascot were customary Saturday morning dress for a young man of Northcutt's Harbor.

"Have you seen Curly?" she asked him from her car window, still hoping she could get the fisherman-electrician that morning.

Rodney's reply was openly contemptuous. "Mr. Wyncote's trying to get him to do some wiring at his house at Millstone," he said. "Curly's a *nothing* when it comes to electricity. Any dummy in our science class at school knows more than he does. He can put in a new fuse, if that's all you want."

Oh dear, what a poisonously superior boy he's becoming, Mrs. Potter thought to herself. Then memories of her own son at sixteen came to mind—the only year she and Lew had ever wanted to disown him. He was so unshakably right about everything and, even worse, so insufferably polite about it all. All young males have to assert themselves. Dressing up and belittling Curly seemed harmless ways of doing so.

Mrs. Potter drove on to her second errand of the morning, to the Northcutt's Harbor post office. On the way she considered briefly what changes Persy's inheritance might make in the lives of the three at the store—Persy, Rodney, and

Winks—as well as to those on the Point. Harvard might indeed live for another twenty years, as she had so blithely assured him this morning, but both she and he knew that half that was a better likelihood. It was a great relief (and a selfish one, she told herself) to know that Cole and Regina had a generous and sensible alternate proposal, one she felt sure Harvard would find acceptable.

4

After leaving Harvard's house earlier that morning, Mrs. Potter had driven slowly north up the narrow peninsula that made up Northcutt's Harbor and its environs. The entire thrust of land, more rock than soil, lay in alternating patches of woods and open rocky fields. It was roughly six miles long, measuring from the tip of the point, the Point, which included her land and Harvard's and that of the Cogswells, to the junction where the peninsula road met Route 1 on its way north to the town of Cherrybridge, or south and west to Ellsworth and Camden and Boston.

At its narrowest point was Harvard's cove, known to him and to the village as First Bite Cove, where his old lobster boat was moored along with the Cogswells' gleaming Fiberglas cruiser. Where First Bite cut its deep, small half-circle into the eastern shore, the peninsula measured less than a mile across.

The next slice above Harvard's land was Mrs. Potter's ten-acre strip, which, like Harvard's smaller acreage, spanned the entire width from the ocean on the east to the bay on the west so that the road, on the bay side, was a privately granted right-of-way through both her and Harvard's property.

There was almost no traffic on this wooded lane. The Cogswells were only occasionally in residence at the house Regina called the Roost, since Cole's chief business centered in his Cherrybridge cannery and in the blueberry barrens to the north.

Harvard drove his rattletrap old truck only within the six-mile strip of the peninsula road, and his goings and comings gave Mrs. Potter no trouble. Unlicensed and unrebuked, he was a somewhat erratic driver, but out of respect and affection the drivers of the village watched for his coming and made allowances for his driving. His route extended to Pickett's, the general store, to the post office and the white church, roughly opposite each other on the road to the north, and to the service station of his nephew, Tristram Northcutt, slightly beyond.

In addition, on Wednesday nights, freshly scrubbed and shaven, Harvard drove to Beano at the Grange Hall. Wearing his blue suit, he played a dozen Beano cards at once, with keen-eyed skill and highly competitive pleasure.

Mrs. Potter had first passed her own driveway, a mere sandy lane going through a small grove of fir trees and hackmatacks, with a few stunted jack pines marking its approach. Her cottage on the oceanfront to the east was just out of sight beyond this miniature forest.

She had then passed the road, also toward the ocean on the right, that led to the low buildings of the lobster pound and the faded sign C.R. COGSWELL & SON, LOBSTER BUYERS.

From this road and extending for a distance of less than a mile toward the north was the village proper, a group of perhaps forty houses more or less clustered about the town's store, her first stop after leaving Harvard's cove.

Now, leaving Pickett's, she continued north to the post office. Most of the houses, like the store, were on the east side, facing the road, oddly, and not the water. Some were white; others were painted in bright colors—mustard yellow, a strong turquoise, cherry red, and a blue that was almost the color of the wild flags that had been flowering at the edge of Harvard's cove. One house was bright pink. Recalling a popular patent medicine of her childhood, a pill prescribed as a mild laxative for children at a time when "regularity" was considered a vital sign of health and of a properly obedient attitude as well, Mrs. Potter could only think of this color as "calalactose pink."

In Northcutt's Harbor, as in much of far Down East Maine,

33

houses often appeared to be too tall. They were too narrow, or ells were too short. Cornices were overpowering and porches often useless. Views were studiously ignored. Sometimes light-absorbing "sun rooms" had been added, in the name of modernization, making dark pockets of the living rooms behind them, and were in themselves too narrow to serve as more than repositories for a few stiff houseplants on an oilcloth-covered table. There were oddly placed windows. And again and again, there were high front doors with no steps to permit entry.

Undistinguished as many of the houses might be, unlovely as the store front had been at Pickett's, with its several rusted signs, its slightly lopsided outdoor telephone booth, and the metal glare of the case for packaged ice, Mrs. Potter came through the built-up section of Northcutt's Harbor with a lift of spirits, as she always did. The small, colorful, close-knit village had become a very dear part of her life.

At the north edge of the central cluster of houses, she reached the Northcutt's Harbor post office. It had not been open when she had gone to fetch the loaves of fresh hot bread. Now, at mid-morning, there were several small cars parked alongside the road in front of the white house that served both as dwelling for its owner, Amanda Wakefield (spinster, sixty-two), and as the post office of the United States of America, Northcutt's Harbor, Amanda Wakefield, postmaster.

Getting the mail was Mrs. Potter's daily prelunch requirement. She found it difficult to sit down to her solitary salad or sandwich without the day's harvest of letters, mail-order catalogs, charitable appeals, and national sweepstakes assurances that even without her knowledge she might already be the winner of a lifetime of unbelievable wealth.

The post office steps were empty, but inside she found Giselle Oublette and Tillie Northcutt. There beside the small block of post office boxes, leaning on their elbows on the counter, the two were in earnest conversation with Amanda.

They parted and stepped back politely to let Mrs. Potter advance to receive her mail, which was handed to her directly over the counter, as was Amanda's courteous custom. Each individual letter box had its own small brass combination lock, but Mrs. Potter could no longer recall which box or combination was supposed to hers.

As she received her mail, Tillie and Giselle, wife of the local shellfish warden, resumed their places at the counter. Mrs. Potter felt it impolite to be leaving with only an initial greeting and a parting good-bye. "It's a gorgeous morning," she said.

As an afterthought she paused at the open door.

"I saw Shelley at the baked bean supper last night, Tillie," she said. "She's getting to be a beauty. Fifteen now, is she? Sixteen? I know she's a special favorite of Harvard's."

"That Shelley," Tillie answered, "that granddaughter of mine! I couldn't have asked for a nicer child around the house to keep me company after Alston went, and I was so proud of her for the basketball victory and all. But lately, I don't know what it is, but seems like she's a different person. Snippety, doesn't pay any mind to anything I say. I'd say it was just her age, but her mother wasn't like that, anyway to my remembrance."

"Our Catherine, she is the same," Giselle stated. " 'Just the age, that's all it is,' Louis says."

"More to it than that," was Amanda's pronouncement. "I'm not going to say another thing, but if you lived where I do, with your bedroom window looking down over the church parking yard, you'd know a thing or two."

She did not say more, and Mrs. Potter noted that neither Shelley's grandmother nor Cathy's mother pressed her further.

To forestall any possible embarrassment, Mrs. Potter returned to the subject of the bean supper. "I never had such good brown bread," she told them. "I know one of you must have baked it—you, Amanda, or Tillie, unless it was Edna Birdson. Do you know whose came to our table?"

"Can't tell us apart," Amanda assured her crisply. "Just the best there is, our brown bread—mine and Edna's and Tillie's. Jake's old grammy taught us all how when we were young. Some cranky, the old lady was, but what she didn't know about brown bread hadn't been writ."

"Some day maybe I could give you the receipt—that's what

Grammy Birdson called a recipe,'' Tillie offered doubtfully. "Naturally we wouldn't favor your showing off with it *here*, but if you promised to make it only out at that place of yours out west. . ."

Mrs. Potter accepted the offer promptly and gratefully, with the assurance that she would never attempt to display this shared knowledge east of the Mississippi. East of the Rockies, she amended hastily. An offer like this was too wonderful to miss.

"Well, I'll call you sometime." Tillie's voice was even more doubtful. Perhaps, Mrs. Potter thought, the three of them, Tillie and Amanda and Edna Birdson, like three Delphic oracles would have to confer and agree.

"I hear you liked the yellow-eye beans this time," Amanda said. "Maybe you'd like my recipe for that, too?''

It was a morning of glorious generosity. "Was it your yellow-eyes at our table, then?" Mrs. Potter asked. "And was there maple syrup in them?"

Amanda nodded briskly.

"My specialty is the *plogues*," Giselle said modestly, giving the word the French-Canadian pronunciation, *ployes*. "My Louis says they deserve three stars."

"I don't know what they are," Mrs. Potter confessed.

"They are not part of the bean supper," Giselle told her. "Little crêpes made of the white buckwheat flour, to fold with butter and eat from the hand. Hot breads, you would say."

"While you're collecting recipes, you better get that one," Tillie said. "Best thing you ever ate, and be sure to finish off with a couple on your plate with molasses for dessert."

"Only don't try to make them with regular buckwheat flour, the gray kind," Amanda advised. "It won't work. Now, the only place I know to get the white is in Aroostook County. I get mine from the I.G.A. store in Madawaska. Five pound bag was two twenty-nine the last time I ordered."

"Fort Kent, Presque Isle, any place in the county," Giselle added. "No labels—the farmers mill their own. The same, some places in Quebec province, too. The flour is the color of pale cream and the batter turns yellow as you stir."

As she left the post office, happy with the prospect of learning these treasured secrets, a man who looked like a great curly Airedale grabbed her shoulders. "I didn't have a minute to ask you last night at the baked bean supper, but just when did you actually get back?"

"In April this year, and still patches of snow in the woods, as Harvard just reminded me. It's been over a month, and it seems like a week. And you—I know you're in Atlanta one day and here the next, all summer. How long are you going to stay this time?"

Carter Ansdale continued to hold her shoulders. "You look wonderful, 'Genia, did I tell you that last night? And do you know how much I've missed you?"

Yes, you told me, she assured him.

"Now I want to cook dinner for you, just the two of us, as soon as I get settled," he continued. "Or how about my taking you to dinner tonight at the Lodge in Cherrybridge, if you can stand the food?"

Not tonight, she told him.

Then, responding to the warmth of his greeting and the flattery of his apparent pleasure in seeing her again, she invited him to her Sunday supper for the Cogswells and their guests.

"Not a party," she told him. "Come in your working clothes if you're still getting settled. Well, maybe not *those,* but anyway don't dress up. I'm going to make something that's a favorite of yours. I think you even named it for me—'Happenstance Bay Fish Stew.' You'll be there? Wonderful! Six o'clock."

For the third time that morning, a man's hand on her car door detained her. Carter's, unlike Harvard's, was untanned, rather thin and bony given the solid bulk of the man himself. Much larger than Cole Cogswell's, it still shared the qualities of the others in its obvious strength and competence—like the rest of him, in fact: the great curly crest of his brown hair lightly touched with gray, the burly torso under the old gray sweatshirt and paint-spatterd khaki pants.

"See you tomorrow, about six at the cottage," she told

him and pulled away, blowing a kiss to ease any possible rudeness in her hasty departure.

All at once, she was overcome with the thought of how much she was missing her dog. I'll go home, she told herself, and call the vet's.

In happy anticipation she entered her own lane. There the quiet, needle-carpeted car tracks ended in a small natural clearing that served as a parking space large enough for several cars.

A path led out of the cool, dark quiet of the little patch of woods into the bright May sunshine. A bank of *Rosa rugosa*, the sturdy wild roses of the coast, grew in an open spot on the north and almost screened the toolshed there, which, like the cottage, was built of cedar siding, weathered by salt air to an indeterminate gray-brown.

Mrs. Potter took the key from its peg under the eaves and opened the single, solid door. This led her directly into the kitchen, a large square room with counters and cupboards of sundarkened natural pine. There were electric appliances—a stove and refrigerator, a washer and dryer—disguised in their efficient modernity by their soft coppery color.

Coral geraniums flourished on the wide windowsill to the south, from which Mrs. Potter could glimpse the flashing blue of the ocean as the coastline made its gentle indentation there, an inward curve scarcely important enough to be called a cove. A pine table and a single chair faced this view.

She entered the main room of the cottage. Its beamed ceiling was slightly darkened by an occasional back-blown puff of smoke when the fire was first lit on a windy day. The chimney breast had been constructed from chunks and pieces of the same rough pink granite that was the only guardian of safety in front of the cottage—the great ledge between the building, with its small patch of rough flowery grass, and the open sea.

This room had windows on two sides only. There were large ones on the east, facing the ocean. On the west were smaller casements facing the small woods, in a wall of bookshelves.

The north end, which might have looked out toward the

alder swamp dividing the property from the lobster pound, was filled by the warm grainy pink of the big fireplace and the stone ledges that flanked it on either side.

There were deep sofas, big tables, a profusion of books both on the shelves and on all available surfaces. A section of cupboard was given over to games—Parcheesi, Scrabble, Monopoly, Backgammon, Old Maid—all popular in their season with visiting grandchildren and with the youngsters of the village in the past—Rodney, Shelley, Tommy, Janine. There was a long trestle table with rush-bottomed chairs around it for eight, and others ranged around the room.

A bathroom occupied the corner of the first floor in front of the kitchen. "The most spectacular bathroom view in the world," was the inevitable comment of Mrs. Potter's guests, since its windows to the east and south looked straight across the Atlantic to Portugal.

A narrow stairway led up through the center of the house to two small bedrooms, and their low dormer windows looked out to the same view, bounded only by the horizon.

That evening, as she stood on the wooden deck of her small house enjoying the last light of the soft blue of the water, Mrs. Potter was cheered by the knowledge that tonight would be her last night alone there. Her big Weimaraner would be ready for release from the animal hospital in the morning.

Ordinarily she was not timid about living alone, either here in Maine or in the rambling ranch house in Arizona. Certainly the thought of poor harmless Winks slipping through her little patch of woods, filching a few berries, did not alarm her. Harvard was a half mile away; the Cogswells and Frances and Herbert and Nancy were in residence at the Roost.

All the same, it was reassuring to know that most people were extremely respectful of the big pale dog with the yellow eyes, and she would be very glad of his good company again.

5

Very early Sunday morning, Mrs. Potter stacked her few breakfast dishes in the sink, in sudden eagerness to get to the animal hospital. Surely no one there would mind her arriving early? She knew that Sindhu, after two days in the place, would be more than ready to come home. She set out his water bowl in his favorite spot beside the stove in the kitchen.

Driving back up the peninsula road, she found several inhabitants of the village already abroad and about their business.

From the first of these, Jumbo Northcutt, heading in his old truck toward the clam beds (or so she thought, since the tide was ebbing), she received a lifted forefinger of greeting. One huge finger raised slightly from the steering wheel in what was, she thought, the equivalent of what in diplomatic circles would be called "correct and courteous" behavior.

When she first came to Northcutt's Harbor, this one-finger wave was as far as the local residents would go in noticing her as she walked or drove about, and they only vouchsafed that gesture after some months. It said *we know who you are and we know where you live.* It did not say *welcome!*

Too late, she realized she should have hailed Jumbo and asked him to bring her a half peck of clams for her Happenstance Bay Fish Stew. She could very well use the chopped canned ones and bottled clam juice she always kept on hand, but still this was an opportunity missed.

The next person abroad, already at work in her flower garden in front of the pink house, was the wife of her

40

caretaker. Lyman Cooney was the town's general handyman and he had been caretaker of the cottage when the Potters bought the place, so that they had inherited his services. Now, this morning, of course he would already be out fishing, for no matter what the secondary occupation of the men of Northcutt's Harbor—carpenter, painter, plumber, electrician (as was Curly Gillan), even the local insurance agent—they were all first and foremost lobster fishermen.

Alice, Lyman's wife, looked up from her flowers, and her wave was of the kind Mrs. Potter had begun to receive, at first guardedly and then with increasing spontaneity, after her first year or two at the cottage. This is what she called a "twinkle." All, or at least three, of the fingers of the slightly uplifted hand were waggled, briefly but definitively. This was certainly *hello*. It might even be *how are you?*

Janine, the Cooney's daughter, her ripe young figure explicitly outlined in skin-tight jeans and purple T-shirt, came out of the house as Mrs. Potter passed. She waved languidly, her ear bent to the small radio she carried, and an incomprehensible burst of sound momentarily filled the early morning.

No one was in evidence as she passed the post office. The white church opposite appeared equally deserted, although she knew that Tillie Northcutt was probably already inside, straightening the hymnbooks, probably arranging a glass jar of newly-opened apple blossoms from some neglected old tree along the roadside, or possibly some lilacs from her own dooryard, making ready for morning worship.

Before she reached the juncture of the peninsula road with Route 1, she passed one of the few small farms there, and at this point she received a gratifying, full-fledged wave of the type she called "number three."

The first of these was Jumbo's lifted forefinger, formal and cool. The second was Alice's waggle, friendly, but with certain reservations. Third was the vigorous open-palm semaphore that she now received from Edna Birdson, already at work in her vegetable garden, an expression of warm and friendly regard. *I'm glad to see you!*

Mrs. Potter and Edna had begun their friendship over the fresh vegetables, eggs, and apples the little farm provided for a passing driver perceptive enough to stop for fresh country provender. When Mrs. Potter learned that Edna baked her own bread—firm, creamy, fragrant, smooth-slicing loaves of white bread made with unbleached flour and her own farm honey—she became an instant and regular customer. In time she became a regular visitor as well, staying for the hospitably offered cup of tea whenever Edna had time to put on the kettle.

Now Edna was setting out brush as support for her early crop of peas. Not pausing, Mrs. Potter continued on her way to Cherrybridge.

An hour later Sindhu was at her side, restored to his natural dignity and his customary air of slightly supercilious, well-bred condescension toward the world outside the car windows. His mouth appeared to be completely healed, with only a few black dots showing where the porcupine quills had been removed. The chief remaining evidence of his encounter was the faint odor of antiseptic still clinging to his sleek gray body.

I hope he'll be wary next time, she thought, remembering the shared anguish when she had begun pulling out the black and white quills with her own bare fingers. The first ones had come out easily. Later ones required stoical cooperation from them both, and she used pliers from the tool shed. The natural action of the barbed needles caused the last quills to imbed themselves more and more deeply. When she came to the last sensitive areas of lips and tongue she had realized that professional help was required.

"All right, you," she had told him as they left the small brick animal hospital and he had jumped, uninvited, onto the front seat to sit beside her. "Back seat tomorrow. Today's a special occasion."

He appeared to have already forgotten that first uninhibited puppylike rush of pure love, that undisguised admission of joy and relief at being rescued from the discomforts and uncertainties of hospital life.

On the return trip there was more activity on the narrow road, more evidence of that second and less apparent community that shared the narrow point of land with the original settlement of Northcutt's Harbor.

The new community made up most of the west side of the peninsula. From the road, it was invisible except for two chaste signs. SHAGS HEAD BY THE SEA, one of these proclaimed, with a cutout in the metal sign indicating what seemed to be a sailboat riding on waves. NORTHCUTTS HARBOR ESTATES—ENTRANCE said the other, in lettering that could only be described as Ye Olde Yankee design.

A new bright yellow pickup emerged from the roadway leading from the first of these designations just as Mrs. Potter approached, and she had to brake abruptly to allow the truck to make its unexpected left turn in front of her. Automatically her right arm reached out to steady the sitting dog beside her, just as she would have reached for an unguarded child. "Back seat, Sindhu," she said firmly, and the obedient sleek body jumped over the seat back to its accustomed position in rear.

"Hey there, 'Genia, *sorry*." The driver, stopping apologetically, was one of the residents of Northcutt's Harbor Estates whom Mrs. Potter had greeted so warmly at the baked bean supper. Chuck Weidner, recently retired professor of chemistry at a small college in western Pennsylvania, was a haphazard driver at best, and he had come late to the world of the pickup. He and his wife, Margo, who had once taught physical education in a Philadelphia junior high school, were among Mrs. Potter's frequent dinner guests at the cottage.

Securing congenial dinner guests, Mrs. Potter had found, was somewhat of a problem in Down East Maine. She loved the country, she loved the people, she loved the cottage. And, wherever she was, she loved having people to dinner.

In Northcutt's Harbor, much as she enjoyed her neighbors, most of these who had always lived here had such different schedules of eating (and drinking) that it had usually been impossible to resolve the differences. Most of them, as Harvard had done, ate dinner shortly before noon, as soon as the lobster boats were in. Supper was about five, to allow for early bedtimes and the next day's early rising. Alcohol was taken only on certain stated festive (or furtive) occasions.

Mrs. Potter had come to Maine being used to lunch as a
minor meal, except on Sundays when lunch really meant
dinner and was preceded by church. Then, it meant drinks
first, followed by a highly sociable meal, and it had its own
special advantages: people went home by three and you still
had a free afternoon ahead of you. You could ask all sorts of
interesting and diverse personalities, even children, in the
name of Christian tolerance, and you usually ended up with a
very good party.

At any rate, most of Northcutt's Harbor ate and drank at
different hours from those Mrs. Potter was used to. Recently
she found she was adjusting her schedule slightly in favor of
the local timing; even so, few of Northcutt's Harbor regulars
invited Mrs. Potter to eat with them, and vice versa.

Therefore, when Chuck Weidner pulled in front of, then
alongside her car, and offered his apologies, Mrs. Potter was
pleased to see him.

"What about coming to supper tonight?" she called out to
him. "The Cogswells are on the Point, too, with some guests,
and I've asked Carter Ansdale."

"Splendid," was the immediate acceptance. (How nice it
is, Mrs. Potter thought, that he needn't rely on that universal
hedge, "but I'll have to see what my wife has planned.")
"Matter of fact, Margo has just invented a new game she
thinks you'll be crazy about, and she's dying to spring it.
We'll be there. Six o'clock about when you want us?"

Stooped, graying, his beard a calico mixture of white,
brown, and cinnamon, Chuck Weidner still retained a boyish-
ness of face and manner. Perhaps it had rubbed off from his
years of teaching. His favorite class was always the freshmen,
he said. His summers had been spent at a summer camp in
Maine where both he and his wife had been counselors.

How very nice, thought Mrs. Potter, pleased at her sudden
inspiration. "Yes, six," she said, "but now I'd better get
some lobsters and get home."

Before she could proceed more than a hundred yards, a
second car caused her to stop. At the next roadway sign on
the right, another resident of the second community was
parked by the roadside. The shiny green pickup bore the same

44

Ye Olde Yankee lettering and the familiar legend: NORTH-CUTT'S HARBOR ESTATES.

T. D. Pettengill, developer of the properties on the west side of the peninsula, was beside his car, walking back and forth with quick, impatient steps.

"You okay, Teedy?" she called, coming to a stop just short of the turnoff. "Car trouble?"

"No need to man the lifeboats," was the reply. "I just dropped anchor to wait a spell."

Mrs. Potter smiled dutifully.

"Actually," he continued, "I'm here waiting on a live one. Got a prospect coming down from Bangor—flew in early this morning from New York and got a rental car at the airport. Said I'd meet him here and show him my last stretch of shore property. Now I'm just luffing my sails, you might say, trying to figure out what to do with him till the tide turns."

Mrs. Potter could sympathize, in a way, although she thought privately that Teedy should not try to sell his subdivision tracts to people who could not appreciate the sights and fragrances of low tide on Shags Head Bay.

"I'm sure you'll keep him entertained, Teedy," she assured the small, nervous, pacing figure. "Why don't you give him a little local color first? You know—go to Persy's and buy postcards with sea gulls on them? Then you can drive by the pound and watch Maine's only woman lobster-buyer in her native habitat. From there you can go to Tris and Sis's for a cup of coffee and a homemade doughnut while you tell him about the place. That might give you enough time for it to put a good shine on the mud, anyway."

Only don't get the idea of coming to my house, she suggested more forcibly but without speaking the words aloud. You may be a fine fellow, Teedy Pettengill, and you have sold your five-acre lots to several people who have proved to be good, even delightful, neighbors. But the truth of the matter is, much as I try to like you and Eileen, I don't very much. And then I make it even worse for myself by talking too much and sounding too cordial, just as I'm doing now.

At least she had at last mastered the art of saying good-bye.

Instead of waiting for a response to her overlong, overeffusive suggestions, she shifted her car and moved slowly forward, even as she continued to talk. "Nice morning for it, anyway," she went on, and pulled out of range for response. Socially I am a dolt in so many ways, she thought, but I do know one useful ploy: Always leave in the middle of your own sentence.

Actually she did not know whom she disliked more—Teedy or his wife, Eileen. Teedy, orginally from Rochester, New York, had become what could only be called a professional Yankee. His accent was a Down East exaggeration. What he perceived with his eyes, he *sore*. Any vagrant thought in that small neat gray skull was an *idear*. All women under twenty and over fifty were addressed as dear, or rather, *deah*. He talked quaint. He *calculated* and he *reckoned*.

Worst of all, he used a great many seafaring expressions, not always with complete accuracy. If he could have managed a peg leg and a single gold earring, he would have done so. He wore red and black checked flannel shirts, and his short quick-striding legs were usually encased in fishermen's boots, whatever the weather. His house had a spinning wheel in front of the picture window.

Teedy's wife, Eileen, was less determinedly Down East, but she had her own shortcoming: She was simply one of the most boring women Mrs. Potter had ever met. Her days were filled with what she called her "needlework." That word, to Mrs. Potter, suggested fine stitchery, perhaps even the Royal Society of Needlewomen, implying honest, perhaps inspired, design and painstaking execution. To Eileen, it meant the steady output of packaged patterns of embroidery, of knitting or crochet, of an easy kind of rug hooking done with a patented device and bright acrylic rug yarns. She turned these out in prodigious quantities and presented them for sale to summer tourists. She had browbeaten the Northcutts, Tris and Sis, into making room for a display in the window of the filling station. She had dragooned Persy into allotting her a crowded corner shelf at the store, for which Persy exacted a percentage commission.

Eileen did not, however, in spite of the vast extent of her production, donate any of these items to the fancywork tables at the Grange Hall suppers, the proceeds of which went to worthy town projects. Mrs. Potter hoped that, after a first stultifying afternoon, she would never again have to view Eileen Pettengill's output of useless and unbelievably banal hand-decorated objects.

The Pettengills had come to Northcutt's Harbor at about the time the Potters bought the cottage on the point. At that time the western side of the peninsula was undeveloped; other than the Grange Hall and the church, it had very few buildings. An early member of the Birdson family had farmed this entire stretch at one time, and there were still foundations showing where houses, barns, and outbuildings had once stood.

This side of the peninsula land had been on the market for some time when the Pettengills arrived. Although parts of it were beautiful, it lacked the drama and excitement that some seekers of Maine coastal property were looking for. It lacked what was called a bold coastline.

This shorefront, unlike that on the Point and on the east, was not outlined by great rocks. Its waterfront was gentle, in places soft mud, in others sandy, in others an edging of coarse gravel. At high tide, Shags Head Bay looked its name—a bay indeed—and one could look out across the narrow band of water to see the next westerly point of land. At low tide, the bay was a mud flat from shore to shore.

While "bay" was a legitimate descriptive term only twice each twenty-four hours, the Shags Head part of the name was totally accurate. On the lowlands of the opposing point, the shags made their nests. Each morning they left, singly or by twos and threes, flying dark against the dawn sky, their long necks extended, their wings seeming to move twice as fast as those of the herring gulls on morning patrol. Serene, purposeful, the steady flapping of their wings almost like those of a mechanical wind bird, they moved in a straight line to their fishing grounds in Happenstance Bay.

"Why, they're *cormorants*!" had been a guest's puzzled exclamation, when asked if she had seen the shags flying over the water at dawn.

Mrs. Potter remembered that this was one of the first things Harvard had taught her. Cormorants were called "shags," just as surely as good garden dirt was called "loom," and as a chunk of firewood was called a "junk." Barren and partly marshy places (some of them rumored to contain traps of quicksand), the kind of areas that back at the ranch would be called *"cienagas,"* were here known as "the heath." Pronounced *hayth*.

"One more stop, and we're home," she promised the dog on the seat behind her. "Lobsters from the pound for my stew, and then we'll go chase sea gulls. And maybe see Harvard."

As she put her hand back to rest briefly on the smooth gray hide, she felt his skin ripple with delight. Sindhu knew the name Harvard.

6

After leaving Teedy at the roadside, waiting for his "live one," Mrs. Potter again passed Pickett's store on her left and the cluster of houses that made up the hub of the village.

Beyond them she could see the lobster fishermen's shacks and the blue of the harbor, almost empty of boats on this fine fair May Sunday. Most of the adult males of the village would be out hauling traps in the deep waters of Happenstance Bay and beyond, just as the teenage boys were doing in nearby shallower waters from their skiff outboards.

The shorefront shacks were where the men built or mended their traps. Here they filled their bait bags with strong-smelling cut-up alewives. Here they kept the skiffs in which they rowed, facing backward, pushing rather than pulling their oars, to their sleek powerboats each clear morning. Here they gathered to talk or to knit bait bags or to play poker on the bad days, the days when fog lay heavy and dangerous over the water.

The bay itself shone blue and white in today's spring sunshine.Encircling this stretch of now-quiet water lay a protective barrier of small islands, sheltering the lobster boats at their moorings, a friendly, immovable breakwater. The pound road led to a series of long, low frame buildings fronted by a large deep-piled pier with a floating dock, its rise and fall built to accommodate the deep tides of the region.

Blocking the way to the pier and filling most of the areaway between the buildings was a huge refrigerator truck. Its driver was unlocking the back gates, preparing to take on a fresh shipment of lobster in heavy, dripping wooden crates for the run to Boston or New York.

"How long do you give these babies before they turn into something '*à la*'?"

The man who greeted her with the question was Alex Whitehead, whom she had seen with his wife Friday evening in Teedy's group at the baked bean supper.

"Oh, hi, Alex," she responded. "Long enough, I expect, to 'g'ant up' a little." Then, remembering that she was speaking to a city man—a retired New York tycoon, as Teedy had respectfully described him—she felt that the statement needed elaboration. "That's what the cowboys say about the ranch calves on the haul to the feed lots. They lose weight. Whatever I mean, we both know that nobody in New York ever gets to taste lobster the way we do here."

"What a place to be!" Alex inhaled the mixed fishy smells, not all of them exactly appealing to Mrs. Potter, who preferred her salt air unmixed with the scent of lobster bait. He expanded his chest in his unbuttoned green velour shirt, hairy beneath the heavy gold chain around his neck.

Mrs. Potter quickly considered asking the Whiteheads to join her supper party. A man so clearly enthusiastic about Maine merited her approval. The Whiteheads were newcomers to the community and she had not yer proffered them any gesture of hospitality. The man was attractive enough, trimly fit, obviously friendly. There was even something engaging about his slightly off-center nose.

At first she decided to postpone any possible invitation. For one thing she found it difficult to speak of Mrs. Whitehead by name. Once she knew that someone spelled her name Bettye, or Bette, she was temporarily reduced to saying "she, her, or you."

At the last moment, the generous impulse overruled.

"Why yes, I expect we'd love to," Alex Whitehead answered, "but I don't know if we're free. Could Bets call you as soon as I get home—a half hour or so?"

Anyway that settles the name thing. *Bets*. And now, how big was her supper party? The Cogswells, Herbert and Nancy, Carter, the Weidners, and now the Whiteheads. Ten, counting herself—her favorite number. Enough to stir each other up. Mostly people who already knew and liked each other. One set of newcomers to add a little variety. She was now delighted at her sudden decision to include Bets (it still seemed difficult to say) and Alex.

A single bark from her parked car reminded her of Sindhu's obedient presence there. *"Stay,"* she told him. "I'll be back in a minute."

Then, relenting, she opened the car door. *"Come."* Not good dog training, maybe, to reverse a command so quickly, but she had a sudden insight into how unsettling it must be for an animal to be left at the vet's. No matter how nice they were to you there, how could you be *sure* you'd ever go home again?

The great obedient gray dog moved quietly beside her. The leash was unnecessary, but she always snapped it in place, remembering that some people mistrusted a yellow-eyed dog.

Circling the large parked truck warily as she waved good-bye to Alex Whitehead, Mrs. Potter reached the upper area of the lobster pound. Here, high above the floating platform where the boats unloaded, she found the man who among her invited guests was her favorite.

"Hi again, Coley," she greeted him with pleasure. "You'll be glad to know I'm patronizing your stand for your supper tonight. Where's Olympia?"

Cole jerked his head in a sharp gesture. "Below, on the dock," he said. "Damn it, I wish that woman would behave like one. Half sister, looks more like a half brother! Felt sorry for her after she discovered that Cutler fellow in New York, gave in to her when she said she could run the lobster business for me—"

"Everybody says she's doing a terrific job, Coley," Mrs. Potter reminded him. "All the fishermen say so. Even the ones like Lyman, my caretaker, who said they'd never give in to a woman lobster-buyer, seem to accept her now."

"Oh, she's doing a hell of a good job," Cole admitted. "Fact is, I don't see how anybody could be doing better. Works like a damned horse, dawn to dark. I guess Regina and I are just bothered that she's so *hellish* independent. She's just crazy determined to make it on her own, not trading on the family name, not owning up to being hired because she's a Cogswell, too. Not even letting us get to know Laurie, who seems like a damned nice little girl, only maybe just as independent as her mother is. . .''

Cole's remarks sputtered off, his voice inaudible above the roar of a rapidly approaching lobster boat. As its motor was cut, she could again hear his complaints. ''There's that buzzardly nephew of Regina's, anyway. Been waiting for him for an hour. He got up determined to go out hauling with Curly Gillan today. God knows why—buttering the man up to get some wiring done at Millstone, I think. Anyway, now I can go on home with him and see if Nancy is up to a set of tennis before Frances calls lunchtime. Man can't call his beastly soul his own around these parts.''

Mrs. Potter knew Cole to be a good man, a devout and generous fellow parishioner at the little church in Cherrybridge they both attended. She knew his profanities were as meaningless as they were automatic, and she felt sure that his sense of family encompassed not only his beloved wife but his aloof and independent half sister as well. Perhaps it even included Herbert, in spite of the older man's grumblings.

Seeing now that his bald head seemed a bit too pink, concerned about a slim blue vein that seemed suddenly prominent above his right temple, she attempted a diversion. ''Thought you two had given up tennis,'' she said. ''Regina told me her arthritis was too bothersome and that your doctor had been laying down the law about your playing—singles, anyway.''

Cole's answer was lost in a brief new burst from the motor below, a roaring finale as Curly Gillan made fast his boat on the dock. Attending the arrival of Curly's boat, Mrs. Potter saw Olympia, worn jeans tucked into dirty rubber boots, frayed red sweatshirt, her wispy hair, as usual, tucked under a knitted cap. She was weighing the catch of an earlier boat at the pier, now unloading.

A nearby wooden bench looked to be a good seat for viewing the continuing performance below, and Mrs. Potter took her place there, Sindhu at her side. Olympia's small, curious dog approached, yapped threateningly once or twice, then retreated to his unchallenged post in a nearby doorway. Sindhu maintained his air of supercilious *noblesse*.

Olympia's helper, a bearded, stout young man dressed much as she was, took each heavy containerful of deep green, writhing, snapping lobsters, wrestling it onto the scales and off again. Then he and Olympia, one on each side of a waist-high center table, picked up and examined and claw-banded each lobster. With incredible speed they tossed the creatures, rendered harmless to each other by the heavy orange rubber band around the large pincer claw, into an open wooden crate on the deck at the end of the table.

As each crate was filled, one of the two would close and secure the heavy slatted wooden lid, seize one of the rope handles at either end, and slide it into an opening in the floating dock. There it would remain submerged and the lobsters would stay alive and safely confined until they were shipped to market.

Suddenly Olympia shot up the long, straight, wooden ladder from the lower dock, her thin body seemingly weightless in spite of the heavy boots. "Lobsters, 'Genia?" she asked. "How many? Pound and a quarters all right? With you in a minute."

With the same speed she descended the long ladder, agile as a monkey, down so quickly it seemed she was dropping rather than climbing the fifteen feet to the floating platform.

While Olympia was fitting six wildly gesticulating lobsters into a bucket, Mrs. Potter seized an opportunity to call a message to the second fishing boat below, now beginning to unload. "Curly!" she shouted. "Curly Gillan!" The boats were silent now but the gasoline pump was whirring and she found herself shrieking to be heard.

"Can you come to the cottage some day soon?" She spoke as slowly and as loudly as she could. "There's something wrong with my stove."

Curly looked up, squinting beneath the bill of his denim cap, his reply deliberate, grudging. "Maybe so. First bad day." He turned then, ignoring her, to give a hand to his passenger, clambering awkwardly over the rails.

Herbert Wyncote's white ducks and his white Irish fisherman's sweater, she could see even from that height, were streaked and grimy. His knees appeared to buckle slightly as Curly solicitously guided him along the floating dock. The morning of lobster fishing clearly had been one of seasickness.

The wind shifted and a strong smell of the half-rotten bait rose from the dock. Sindhu sniffed deeply.

"I know you'd love to roll in that smelly stuff," she told him severely, "but forget it."

Olympia shot up the ladder ahead of Herbert, the heavy bucket of lobsters in one hand. "You know where to pay at the office," she told Mrs. Potter, returning to the dock as she spoke.

There was no point in trying to talk to Curly again. She knew from long experience that it would take at least two more requests and reminders, and more than one foggy morning before Curly put in his grudging appearance, his long upper lip lifted in what could be either a smile or a sneer.

She was about to make her way back around the huge refrigerator truck, still blocking the space between the low buildings, when she almost collided in the narrow passage with a tall man, someone she had not before seen in Northcutt's Harbor. The only way he could let her pass, other than backing up the entire length of the long truck himself, was to come forward a step and then move aside.

With his murmur of apology, something in his "so very sorry" had a pleasant burr about it, a rarity in this *r*-less part of New England.

She paused to smile at her own apologies and take a look at the stranger, noting his well-creased khakis, his soft heather pullover, his well-scrubbed sneakers. She saw slightly graying dark hair, cut short, and a small pepper and salt mustache. Something prompted her to speak.

"Hello, I'm Eugenia Potter," she offered. "If you're looking for Mrs. Cutler, she's down below on the dock."

"Oh yes, Mrs. Potter." The accent seemed definitely of the Highlands. "I'm Deke MacDonald. Our mutual friend—my employer, I should say—Mr. Cogswell, has spoken to me about you. Actually, he's the one I'm here to see, and I was told I might catch him here. But I say, let me carry that for you. That's too heavy for a lady.''

Mrs. Potter relinquished the bucket of lobsters without protest, although she had watched Olympia scale a fifteen foot vertical ladder with it in one hand, and she herself had not felt it any special burden as she had started on her way to the office.

"Have you been with Cogswell & Son very long?" she asked.

"As a matter of fact, only for a fortnight. Mr. Cogswell hired me as general manager for the blueberry part of the operation—the canning plant, freezing, overseeing the field supervisors throughout the county, the crews on the barrens. I'm just beginning to get my teeth into the job.''

"I know the Cogswells both love the blueberry business," she said. "It must be satisfying to work for someone who knows the country and who takes a personal interest in every part of the business.''

"Quite. There seems nothing Mr. Cogswell doesn't know about the entire operation. I've had a bit of experience myself elsewhere in Maine and in Canada, but I never saw an owner like him. Both in the knowing and in the caring.''

"And this is just the start of the busy season, isn't it?'' Mrs. Potter asked. "But I mustn't keep you. Mr. Wyncote just got in—'' she looked at the clean khakis, the soft sweater, and thought ruefully how Herbert was going to dislike being seen in his present state—"and I think you'll find them both on the upper level.''

After her thanks and the stranger's clean handshake and his courteous remark about hoping to see her again, Mrs. Potter, her dog, and her weighed and paid-for lobsters left in the small red station wagon.

As she drove back to the cottage, she wished that she were not resisting a last-minute impulse to turn back to include this new man, Mr. MacDonald, in her supper party that evening.

If I hadn't given in to a halfway decent generosity in asking the Whiteheads, she thought, I could have asked him. However, I feel quite sure that "Bets" is going to call with the Whiteheads' acceptance, and I really should hold the party at ten. That's all I have of the big old heavy soup spoons that came from Lew's family, always so perfect for my fish stew.

Besides, she reflected, I couldn't really very well have invited a new employee of Cole's without first checking the matter with him and Regina. She knew they enjoyed Carter Ansdale's easy southern affability. She knew they both found Chuck and Margo Weidner fun to be with. She was introducing one doubtful new element by including the Whiteheads, and that was enough.

Not that there was anything wrong with the Whiteheads, she told herself. Assured, reportedly rich and successful, retired, even sleekly handsome except for that slightly off-center nose, there seemed no reason *not* to ask Alex Whitehead to dinner. His wife, in well-uplifted middle age, was blond and vivacious and might prove a positive addition to the evening. Cole always had an eye for an attractive woman.

At their earlier meeting, something about Mrs. Whitehead's speech and grammar had not fit Mrs. Potter's picture of the wife of a successful businessman. But, she reflected, New York must be like Washington. Full of successful men—was it Chief Justice Holmes who had said it?—and the women they married in their youth.

Inviting the Whiteheads had been a good idea, she told herself firmly, and, besides, it's been done. Finished business, as Lew used to say.

At the same time there seemed to be a hint of *un*finished business in the air, as she thought of Deke MacDonald.

She drove on briskly, telling herself that the business at hand, at any rate, was to get home with her lobsters and get started on her supper party preparations. First, though, she'd drive on down to Harvard's for a minute, give him and Sindhu a chance to say hello before Harvard's noon dinner.

A sudden inspiration: If Harvard still had those fresh shucked clams, maybe he could spare them and she'd get more for him from Jumbo tomorrow. The canned ones were all right, if a little tough and leathery, but those she had seen the previous morning in Harvard's well-stocked refrigerator would really be much better.

Mrs. Potter smiled to herself as she drove down the sandy

lane. Spring flowers were everywhere, and she enjoyed nothing in the world more than getting ready for a party, particularly for a simple and at least partially impromptu one.

She found herself humming, almost tunelessly, then finding words to an old song. "Oh where and oh where has your Highland laddie gone?" As she laughed aloud at herself, she saw that Sindhu was listening intently. How wonderful to have this loving, undemanding presence. While she was never afraid to be alone, it was an undeniable comfort to have a big, fierce-looking dog around the place. There were times, like last evening, when it was just too quiet without him.

7

If I could just make good French bread, Mrs. Potter told herself, this Sunday supper would be a proper feast.

As it was, crisp, hot, freshly-baked rolls from Persy's freezer case would come out of her oven, well-timed by Cole's second round of cocktails, and they would do very nicely as accompaniment to the combination dish of Maine fish and seafood that Carter—or someone—had christened her Happenstance Bay Fish Stew.

In it, the irresistible flavors of Provence, the blend of wine, saffron, olive oil, sweet green pepper and tomatoes, were a happy complement to the rosy chunks of freshly-cooked lobster, pink shrimp, chopped clams, and firm flakes of haddock.

To enjoy this wonderful amalgam of flavors, Mrs. Potter believed that, while it might be more dramatic and certainly more entertaining (if you were dressed for it), it was not really necessary to pick one's way through a soup plate full of clam and lobster shells submerged in the rich elixir of the broth.

Happenstance Bay Fish Stew was one of her, and her guests', favorite dishes. With good crusty bread or rolls, it was a complete meal, making even a salad seem an unnecessary addition. It was served in a deep soup plate and needed only one of the big old family soup spoons as a utensil, which made for the easiest possible dishwashing later on. It was good either with a simple white wine or a red one, Mrs. Potter had long ago decided, and tonight she had set out (and would ask Carter to open as soon as he arrived) several bottles of a good California *pinot noir*.

The stew used only ingredients that were readily available, except for the saffron, which she ordered from New York and used in carefully meted quantities. The recipe was forgiving— still good made with chopped canned clams when fresh were not at hand; excellent with or without the shrimp. Since she really preferred the big shipped-in frozen ones from the Gulf to the tiny native shrimp of Maine it was easy enough to keep these on hand in the freezer. Scallops, again either frozen or fresh, were a good addition.

Haddock was her favorite and only fish, and she didn't consider it necessary to scout around for different kinds or to make a *court bouillon* with fish heads. It was enough to poach a good piece of haddock, very gently, in water to which she had added a slice of onion, a bay leaf, and a stalk of celery. As soon as it barely flaked with a fork, she set this aside with its strained broth in a covered bowl, rejoicing that she had been hoarding this particular fine thick fillet in her freezer, a special gift from a friend who had brought it down from Campobello.

Lobster was available at all seasons in Northcutt's Harbor, although at widely varying prices according to the catch of the season. The "soft shedders" of late fall were a little less delicious, in her opinion, although there were those who preferred the added whiff of iodine she detected at this time of year.

Today's catch—a half for each guest and an extra for good measure—fresh from the ocean, was hard-shelled, lively, protesting and perfect. She had steamed them immediately on returning to the cottage with Sindhu, bearing with her Harvard's blessings and his quart of fresh clams. When they were cool enough to handle, she had quickly split them, cracked the claws and cut up all the easily reached lobster meat into a large bowl.

Ordinarily, when eating a steamed lobster, she would have enjoyed the leisurely process of picking out each last tiny succulent morsel, of sucking the tiny ribbons of meat from the swimmerets, and of finding the elusive, delicate layers tucked between the spongy devil claws.

Today, in the interest of saving time, she did not permit herself these small delights. When the chunks of body and claw meat were cut up and covered, she took the prodigal bucket of scarlet shells down to a flat rock in front of the cottage, a rock soon to be submerged in the incoming tide.

The gulls were already whirling down to feast before she reached the cottage door. High tide would return the rest of the colorful detritus to the sea, where it would serve to nourish other small creatures of the deep.

As she chopped garlic and onion and green pepper, sautéeing them gently in olive oil, Mrs. Potter continued to reflect upon the advantages of her singular stew. Once put together, it would require no last-minute additions or attention. This was important when one's senior guest was in charge of before-dinner drinks.

She added now a good pinch of saffron threads, the juice from Harvard's glass jar, and a bottle of commercial clam juice. She chopped the clams briskly on the big wooden board beside the sink, discarding the necks and hard parts, then put these back, yet uncooked, in the glass jar in the refrigerator.

To the aromatic mixture now simmering gently on the stove, she put in two cans of whole tomatoes, cut up, and their juice. At this season in Maine, the only fresh tomatoes were shipped in—hard and tasteless. In the fall, with native Maine tomatoes almost as good as those she remembered from her Iowa childhood, she would have preferred six or eight fresh ones, peeled and coarsely chopped.

Again she congratulated herself on the continuing and repeated success of her own adaptation of a classic and traditional recipe. Her original intent had been to reproduce, as best she could, an ambrosial combination of flavors. At the same time she had been determined to do so without splashing every male shirt front and necktie, every female bosom, with later unfortunate reminders of the meal.

She turned off the heat under the stew pot. Before her guests arrived she would add the chopped clams and the big ready-shelled Gulf shrimp. In the short time it took for the pot to reheat and the shrimp to turn pink, the clams too would be cooked.

After that it was simply a matter of adding a good splash of wine—for this quantity her splash would be a good half bottle, and for this she preferred white to red. She would then add the cooked lobster meat and the heavy flakes of haddock with as much of the fish broth as seemed right and put the lid on the pot. It could rest comfortably now to let the flavors blend, the heat turned off, until its final brief reheating just before serving.

There had been time for a romp with Sindhu, time for a catnap, time to shower and dress. Something long and bright and easy, she told herself happily, for an easy evening.

As she put up her long hair, once blond, now lightly graying, an action so automatic that she needed no mirror, then searched through a small jewelry case for gold hoops for her ears, she reminded herself that she must write a note of thanks to the author Peg Bracken for a half-remembered magazine article about last-minute invitations to dinner. She had forgotten many of the details, but the author had highly recommended the practice. In her own case, she realized that she had not had a minute to consider polishing the silver or dusting under the beds. She knew she was going to produce an instant centerpiece for the long table simply by setting out a colorful ceramic figure one of the grandchildren had recently made—a gallant rooster with a beautiful blue-green tail.

She planned to flank this, as she always did, not with candles but with a pair of tall, slim old brass-based kerosene lamps. She found that men liked their added light at the table; that women, including herself, found their soft glow pleasantly uncritical. Lamps did not gutter and drip wax on the table in a vagrant breeze and they never sputtered out to remind guests lingering comfortably at the table over coffee and conversation that the hour was growing late.

One specific part she *could* recall from the article, both truly funny and comfortingly sensible, as that author somehow always managed to be, was the reminder that most people are just as available for last-minute invitations as you are yourself. Very few of us are really booked up with an impressive social calendar.

And then, suddenly, the evening was begun and off to a fine start. The first arrivals were the Cogswells. Herbert and Nancy followed them in through the kitchen, he smart in his dark blazer with prestigious yacht-club buttons, she in something flowered and fashionable, which appeared to end inexplicably below the knee in what looked like knickers.

Cole was in top form. He had composed a new limerick, he announced, and Regina would be the one to recite it as soon as the other guests had arrived. He would give only one little hint: It had to do with renaming *Cog's Wheel*. This, their thirty-foot Fiberglas powerboat, was one of the many delights of their part-time life on the Point. In between its joyous forays into Happenstance Bay and among the outer islands, the *Cog's Wheel* remained at its mooring in First Bite Cove, where Harvard kept it under his benevolent and protective eye.

Herbert, perhaps aware that Mrs. Potter had observed his unsteady and begrimed condition earlier in the morning as he disembarked from Curly Gillan's lobster boat, smiled somewhat sourly. "We're sailing people ourselves," he said. "Nancy's family always sailed on the Chesapeake, naturally, and I practically grew up at Little Egg Harbor on the Jersey shore, before the family started coming to Millstone. I wouldn't think of calling Cole's boat a stinkpot, of course, but Nancy and I can't wait to get our *White Cloud* under sail again when we get settled next week."

"Whose *White Cloud*?" Nancy asked. "You seem to forget, sweetie, that my father gave it to *me*, and he was a man not afraid to say stinkpot."

Carter, after his kiss of greeting, was immediately assigned to his job opening the wine. In spite of all the never-fail openers Mrs. Potter possessed (and she usually did manage a neat job with one or another of these if there was no one else there to take over), she always felt relieved to have a competent man take charge of this operation.

Alex Whitehead, like Herbert and Cole and Carter (who had not taken seriously her invitation to come in working clothes, nor had she really expected him to do so) wore the summer, dark flannel blazer of thin but warm wool that would see a man through Maine summer seasons year after year.

Bettye was wearing something pink and silky, ending in what looked very much like Nancy's flowered knickers, only with less display of bare arms and more of bare bosom. She came in with both arms wide open. "You're *so cute* to include us in your little party," she exclaimed. "We've met so few people here we can really feel at home with, if you know what I mean. *Locals. You know.*"

Regina, in a very kind voice almost imperceptibly altered with the glint of her smile, acknowledged Mrs. Potter's introductions of the newcomers. "You'll just have to get to know us," she said easily. "Nobody's more local around here than Coley and I are, and even Herbert's middle name is Northcutt. Just be patient, and you may even get to like us."

"Anyway you're going to like one of my bombastics," Cole assured them. "Where's my setup, 'Genia? Everything ready for the old master?"

He was already on his way to the long side table, knowing very well that he would find there, ranged alongside the tray of glasses, the items he considered essential to mix his martinis. These, as he always confidently proclaimed, were the world's best.

First, the square bottles of Bombay gin, which had long ago inspired his name of "bombastics." Next, plenty of ice, a small bowl of freshly cut strips of lemon peel, a small bottle of fresh and chilled vermouth.

"Most people use little enough vermouth that a bottle lasts too damn long," he had complained on a previous occasion. "Forget to keep the stuff in the refrigerator, have a hellacious big bottle sitting on the shelf for years, and it tastes like it." From that day, Mrs. Potter had heeded—and learned to agree with—his dictum.

Now, to his surprise and obvious, if slight, disappointment, both Regina's nephew and his wife asked for something else. "Just a glass of white wine on the rocks," Herbert murmured apologetically, "if you've got anything handy. It doesn't have to be anything important, 'Genia. Nancy and I have to watch our figures, you know, at our age.''

Since the Wyncotes were the youngest members of the party and none of the others appeared to be in any way obese, actually perhaps quite as slim as the two of them, the explanation met only rather blank response. Carter disappeared quickly, returning from the kitchen with the filled stemmed glasses. ''I try to be helpful,'' he said in a low aside to his hostess. ''Wish you'd let me prove it.''

Carter was himself overjoyed, as were the Weidners, to be receiving another of Cole's famous bombastics, which he was now making, one at a time, in chunky tumblers of old-fashioned cut glass, treasured bequests from Grandmother Andrews and undoubtedly intended as water glasses for the Sunday table.

First, each glass was filled to the brim with ice. Next, there was a careful one, two, three drops of vermouth dripped over the ice. Just enough to bring out the flavor, Cole assured them. Then came the strip of lemon peel, neatly twisted by those capable, small tanned fingers, the tiny beads of oil rubbed carefully around the rim of each glass, and finally the lemon twist itself inserted into the ice.

When each glass had been filled from the gin bottle with Queen Victoria's picture (incongruous, Mrs. Potter always thought) on the label, there was a last ceremonial flourish. Each one was ritually stirred in five careful clockwise circles with the point of a small pearl-handled fruit knife, ready for its part in the drama beside the bowl of lemon peel.

''There.'' Cole beamed.

His wife, his hostess, Alex Whitehead, the Weidners, each accepted a glass and sniffed the zesty fragrance of gin and lemon with enjoyment.

Mrs. Whitehead shook her head, her smile bright and forgiving. ''I hate to be a nuisance, 'Genia darling,'' she said, ''but I'd be happy with just a glass of Perrier and a slice of lime.''

'Genia darling, when Mrs. Potter had yet to bring herself to say Bets, let alone Betty or Bet? A slice of lime, in Northcutt's Harbor? Perrier, from Pickett's? Again Carter was

quickly, inconspicuously useful. Again he returned from the kitchen with another of Mrs. Potter's best stemmed goblets, filled with ice, a floating slice of lemon, and a clear, bubbling liquid.

This time his whisper was almost inaudible. "Knew you'd have lemon—found a bottle of club soda. She'll never know the difference."

Mrs. Potter whispered soft thanks, adding, "Watch her when she takes a sip."

To avert her own eyes from the meeting of goblet and Bettye Whitehead's pink lips, Mrs. Potter moved to join her senior guest, now mixing the last—his own—perfect bombastic.

"We're all here, Coley," she told him. "First, *cheers*, everybody. And then we're going to insist that you and Regina produce that new limerick, as soon as we've had a chance to sample these bombastics."

"Luckily everyone here is over twenty-one, for I am sure it'll be naughty," Chuck said. "I never knew you to write any other kind."

"That is part of the definition of a true limerick," Cole proclaimed grandly. "Don't take my word for it. Edward Lear was the great limerick fellow, wasn't he? There was Chaucer—you all remember his great one about the young man from Ghent, and all that?"

"Now Cole," his wife put in decisively, "you know very well Chaucer never wrote limericks. Whose college major was English literature around here, anyway? Even if yours *was* a short time back."

Cole continued without a pause. "You never could read Chaucer, as I recall, my dear—admit it. Now take that Ciardi fellow. *All* the experts say so. There is no such thing as a really good *clean* limerick."

"Dear boy, we are ready," Carter Ansdale assured him. "Not a soul in this room is going to sue you for corruption of morals."

Mrs. Whitehead giggled.

Cole continued to hold the floor. "Regina has decided, and I consider it very complimentary indeed to a man of my age, to rechristen the *Cog's Wheel*. Instead of having a public ceremony, which involves wasting a bottle of good champagne—"

"And, as I recall, ruining a perfectly good white silk dress, the first time I did it," his wife interrupted.

"As I was saying, instead of having a public ceremony, Regina is going to read the new ode of dedication to you all here and now."

Cole's blue eyes beamed with deceptive innocence and his round head shone in the firelight.

Regina, fragile and patrician, rose to her feet with the aid of her thin silver-headed cane. "To begin with," she announced, "this is exactly the company I would have chosen for making this very important announcement." She bowed lightly.

"I need not tell you, I think, that Cole Cogswell is a man of parts, a man whose appreciation of feminine charm is, to say the least, enthusiastic. For more years than I care at the moment to number, I have know this, and I may even say that I have found no reason to object, since I have always received more than my share of his attention.

"I must tell you," she went on, "of an incident last weekend that surprised even me, accustomed as I am to his roving eye. He went out by himself in the *Cog's Wheel* for a turn around the bay. When he came back he had a boatload of teenage girls—Janine, Diane, Olympia's darling Laurie, Shelley Northcutt, and two or three more. And he was making his big blue sheep's eyes at all of them—and they were all absolutely adoring it. Can you believe it?"

"Shocking, I must say," put in Margo Weidner. "Sounds like those bevies of coeds who used to tag along after Chuck. Always with the most innocent of reasons, of course." She smiled shyly.

Chuck stroked his tricolored beard. *"Perfectly* innocent," he assured her. "It just happens that there are certain of us who attract pretty young girls. Natural as honey bees around one perfect red rose."

"Let's hear the limerick," Carter put in. "We want to hear the new name of the boat."

Cole passed a slip of paper to his wife, who then read in her clear light voice.

> *"I christen this craft the Old Goat,*
> *Her skipper's quite chipper, you'll note,*
> *A seafaring dandy,*
> *He's racy and randy,*
> *He loves to lure girls to his boat."*

She looked around the room, then continued.

> *"From Kittery to Isle au Haut,"*

Here Regina interrupted herself. "We say *Ile-a-hote* in these parts, but probably the Whiteheads and Weidners say *eel-o-hoe*. Anyway Coley wrote it to rhyme with boat." Mrs. Whitehead nodded blankly and Regina began again.

> *"From Kittery to Isle au Haut,*
> *In his cap and his brass-buttoned coat,*
> *This codger, you'll find,*
> *Has seduction in mind,*
> *The old salt is hot pepper afloat."*

Chuck's roar of laughter led the applause.

"Reputation began when I was canoeing the Allagash," Cole proclaimed, his blue eyes wide. "And now I believe we are all ready for another perfect bombastic?"

The fish stew and crusty rolls were enjoyed and acclaimed. All of the party except Regina, the Wyncotes, and Mrs. Whitehead, whom Mrs. Potter was by now calling "Bets" but not quite easily, returned to the pot on the kitchen stove for second servings.

During dinner, Bets described for everyone the original and classic version of the dish, which she thought they might find interesting to hear about. She and Alex had tried it and found it quite good, she said, on their last trip to Europe, from which they had returned, naturally on the Concorde.

Margo Weidner endeared herself with her comment about

the rolls. "I always think whatever bread you have with stew or soup," she said, in her diffident way, "it should have some *integrity*. I mean, one always tries to drop a bit into the soup plate, accidentally on purpose, of course, and it's not supposed to go *mushy*."

"We'll have coffee by the fire," Mrs. Potter now announced. "Let's see, Herbert and Nancy can help clear away," she told them, believing that newcomers feel more at home when they're immediately pressed into service. "We'll just pile things anyplace in the kitchen and not bother to stack anything. Alex, will you help me with the coffee tray?"

Then, hoping to include her other new guest in the proceedings, she asked, "Bets, will you pass the dessert? All it is is that dish of chocolates you'll find on the little table there. Someone just sent me a box of absolutely sinfully good ones from Belgium, and that's all I'm giving you."

Regina smiled her approval and Herbert bent to peer, at first doubtfully and then with obvious reassurance, at the name of the *chocolatier* stamped on some of the pieces. As the dish made its rounds to Chuck, sitting next to him, he beamed jovially. "Odd you and I haven't met in Philadelphia, old man," he said. " 'Genia tells me you come from there, and I thought I knew most of the Wideners."

"Weidner, not Widener," Chuck corrected him. "My family is in real estate there, although I turned out to be a schoolteacher. Weidner and Goldfeder—maybe that's what you're thinking of."

"Well, I don't think so," Herbert returned, the drawl and the Oxfordian lisp now more slightly pronounced. "No, I'm sure not. Widener you know, old Philadelphia name, that sort of thing. You might have heard of them, possibly not."

"Oh, old families are like the DuPonts from Wilmington," Margo said timidly. "You never know where an odd one will turn up. I'm a shirttail Biddle myself, for whatever that's worth."

Then, bracing her shoulders and turning to face Herbert squarely, she went on with greater purpose. "Cole tells us you're doing a real estate development yourself. Weidner is a very well-respected name in that field, and that is something you should know. Also I think you should know that there were Wideners and Morrises and Hopkinsons and Cadwaladers and Wistars and a few other old Philadelphia names at our wedding, and not a one of them stayed away because the ceremony was Friends Meeting, with Chuck's beloved rabbi there to add his prayers and blessings.''

Herbert was showing mixed emotions. He wanted to deny that his remarks had been intended to demonstrate his own social superiority. He felt obvious new respect for the somewhat awkward yet pretty and fresh-faced woman beside him. And he needed to reassert himself in another light.

''Yes, we *are* trying to start a bit of a good thing,'' he said, both to Margo and to the room at large. ''Nancy's old family house, Whitehall, is something of a white elephant these days.''

He smiled at the Weidners. ''You know how these old places are, Chuck. Hers—we inherited the old place a year or so back—was actually intended to be a copy of the palace at Versailles.''

He continued speaking to Chuck, with hearty camaraderie. ''Now you and I don't have the money to keep up a place like that nowadays, Weidner—taxes, inflation, you know the story as well as I do.''

Chuck again stroked his calico beard and nodded amiably, and Nancy was overheard to say irritably, ''I know the story if you don't.''

''So we're turning the place into a retirement community,'' Herbert said.

Again Mrs. Potter heard Nancy's acid comment, *''You hope.''*

''Only the best-connected people, of course,'' he went on, ''people used to real elegance in their own homes, people used to gracious living and old family servants, that sort of thing.''

''Oh, come off it, Herbert,'' Cole interrupted. ''I haven't heard the words 'gracious living' for forty years, and old family servants went out about the same time, unless you count Frances, and her family tree is every bit as good as mine is. I'm not saying your old folks' home may not be a damned good idea for the place, though, the more I think of it. You may have something there. What do you say, Carter?"

"Oh, my experience with real estate development in Atlanta is something entirely different," Carter protested. "Strictly commercial buildings, that sort of thing. And I don't have anything to do with raising the investment money or showing black numbers on the bottom line, except as it affects my work in design. I'd like to see that Whitehall of yours, anyway, Nancy. It must have been pretty terrific."

Feeling that his object had been achieved and that he was now reinstated in the company's esteem, Herbert tried another tack. "What I've been trying to persuade Aunt Regina to consider," he said with increasing confidence, "is a really top-drawer subdivision here on the Point. Not like those tacky little boxes in Teedy's five-acre lots."

At this point the Whiteheads' backs visibly stiffened and Chuck again stroked his beard.

Herbert continued without noticing. "I'm thinking of a really high-priced, exclusive club community," he went on. "The cove there where old Harvard lives would make a perfect marina. Anybody know who's going to get the place when the old fellow goes? He's sure to any day now—eighty, isn't he?"

The surrounding silence appeared to convince Herbert that his audience was impressed with his business acumen.

"Now, Regina's Roost would do as a clubhouse, at least temporarily," he said, "and there's even room for a couple more tennis courts. I'm trying to get her to think it over."

"Well, you've got another goddamn think coming," Cole began, "and anybody who wants to turn this piece of land into a development is going to have to wait until both of us are dead and gone." His words stopped abruptly as he saw an almost imperceptible twitch of warning, the very faintest shake of his wife's head.

He continued in an only slightly milder tone. "Anyway don't worry about who's going to inherit Harvard's place. For one thing, he's going to outlive you, Herbert."

Bravo, Mrs. Potter said to herself as she got up to bring a fresh pot of her special after-dinner party coffee. Decaffeinated, slightly sweetened, well flavored with rum, it was a wonderful way of dispensing with small coffee spoons, with the occasional apologetic guest who would be so grateful for "just a drop of cream," and most of all with the complications and choices of cordials and liqueur glasses.

Cole was continuing. "And for another thing, Herbert, you might as well know Regina and I are going to see Harvard tomorrow afternoon after we get in from boating, and we're going to work all that out with him."

It was time for a new topic. "I promised you all that after dinner we'd play Margo's new game," Mrs. Potter said brightly. "Let's see, Herbert, would you get that stack of lined yellow pads there on the shelves by the window? And isn't there a little mug full of pencils there, too?"

Margo shook her head, pink-faced, suddenly all shoulders and elbows. "No, no pencils and paper. It's just a silly little thing I thought of yesterday. Are you sure you really want to?"

Mrs. Potter insisted firmly that they did want to.

The point of the game, its author explained, her cheeks now very pink indeed, was that some early member of the year-round former summer people, of which she and Chuck were a part, had, at some disgruntled moment in the past, declared that he had been "picketted."

She was sure they would all understand. It was, in part, a reference to the somewhat higher than supermarket prices that Pickett's store asked for its goods. (Mrs. Potter and some others thought these slightly elevated prices well justified in view of the convenience of not having to drive twenty miles for a pound of coffee.) There were also some, Margo said, who sometimes felt that Persy's addition was not totally dependable in totting up their bills.

At any rate, she went on, among a small group the word had stuck. "I've been *picketted*" had come to mean "I've been *had*, I've been overcharged" or in some other way victimized, as a fleeceable outsider, by shrewd local practice.

"Actually the game is like the old car game for children, remember? Your parents started it to keep you from squabbling in the back seat? Remember the game that begins 'I am thinking of a word beginning with——?' "

She illustrated. "If I said I have been defrauded by a religious character, you're supposed to tell me *how* I've been picketted, always using a word beginning with the letter P."

Regina was quick. *"Piously* picketted, of course."

"And now it's your turn, since you guessed!" Margo, blushing even more deeply, beamed at the acclaim.

Regina produced "gypped by a gentleman," which proved to be "politely picketted." Carter, who made this quick guess, in turn offered "overcharged in rhyme." Nancy pounced on this with a genteel shriek, "Poetically picketted!"

After this, inspiration proliferated. It was possible, it seemed, to be picketted playfully and pathetically, persuasively and punctually, precisely and perfidiously, profusely, perversely, and properly.

Even Herbert got into the spirit of the game, and Alex Whitehead proved quite good at it. His wife slipped away for a moment "to the little girl's room," as she explained, then returned to watch the others with a fixed, bright smile on her newly pink lips.

Before the guests left, well before ten (parties in Northcutt's Harbor, no matter how successful, customarily ended at this hour or even before), Cole drew his hostess aside for a private word.

"About those teenage girls," he said. "I know you wouldn't think I'd be fooling around with any small fry. That part of it was just foolishness, just a reason to make up a party limerick. What I'm trying to do, and I'd like your help on it, is help little Laurie find some friends around here, get to be a part of the crowd. It must be hellish to come into a new place at her age, completely different from New York or that boarding school she went to last year. I fixed up the boat trip with Shelley Northcutt. Damned nice little kid, pretty as a picture. Harvard's grandniece, I think she said. Plays basketball.

"Now you know the kids around here," he told her. "Used to have some of the boys helping here in the yard, Roddy Pickett and the like. See what you can do, will you?"

Mrs. Potter nodded quick assent.

"That Rod seems a nice enough kid. At least he looks you straight in the eye. When I saw him at the store a week or so ago—looked kind of silly in the same kind of striped white pants we used to wear in college, and I told him so—he asked me if I ever knew his father."

"And had you known him?" Mrs. Potter asked.

"Sure, I remember old Addie. Boy seems to have some damnfool idea he was the cast-off son of a titled family. Couldn't help smiling at that. Anybody who remembered the fellow knew he was just a good rough Liverpool lad, but a handsome cuss when he was young. Told the boy so. Thought he'd like that, sort of like the Beatles," Cole said. "He rushed off somewhere then, while I was still telling him about Addie—good enough fellow, I guess, but no Sir Addison. Anyway, the kid might liven things up for Laurie, help to make her feel at home."

As Mrs. Potter was assuring Cole she would do everything she could to help Laurie get acquainted, Regina called the entire party to attention.

"These old lady killers are all alike," she said. "They're forgetful, as well as irresistible. You forgot to invite everyone here to join us tomorrow for a morning spin on the *Cog's Wheel*, now that she's back with her new gas tanks or whatever you had done."

"You are the forgetful one, my lady love. You mean, surely, for a spin on the *Old Goat?*"

It was an invitation everyone most regretfully was forced to decline. Carter had scheduled a visit to a local weaver of homespun yarns. The Weidners had dentist appointments in Machias. The Wyncotes were returning early to their house in Millstone, where they had a date with a stonemason. The Whiteheads were equally committed; they had their architect coming to go over plans for their new "estate" at Shags Head by the Sea. And Mrs. Potter was expecting the arrival of a houseguest from Connecticut.

"We asked a couple of other people, too—those new Colamarias and some others—but they couldn't make it either. Anyway Regina and I are going out, since it will be our last chance for a while," Cole said cheerfully. "The salmon are beginning to run in the Metoosic and for the next couple weeks we'll be up there every day trying our luck.''

"At least Cole will be,'' Regina said. ''These days I mostly just sit in the Jeep and applaud when he makes a particularly fine cast, And, of course, keep the thermos handy with the coffee.''

"And besides that,'' Cole went on, ''the men are putting out hives next week on the barrens, and I like to look things over before the bees take charge. We put them out to pollinate the blossoms—increases the yield, you know.''

"So this will be our last night on the Point for a while,'' added Regina regretfully. ''We'll be salmon fishing for the next couple of weeks, which we both adore, but blueberries are our bread and butter. Coley always walks the barrens with the field men at this time of year, and together we try to inspect all the camps where the migrant Indian families will live when the picking begins later on. Didn't you go with us last year, 'Genia?''

"Not to see the camps,'' Mrs. Potter said, ''but I'll never forget our drive the morning you took me with you to see those miles and miles of barrens north of Cherrybridge.''

"Barrens?'' Alex Whitehead asked. ''Anything grow on a place you'd call 'barrens'?''

"How about meadows?'' Nancy put in unexpectedly. ''Blueberry meadows. That sounds pretty to me.''

"Too pretty,'' Margo said. ''That word is too soft, like dingles and dells. Believe me, blueberry country is *wild* land. Almost scary, even when the plants are in flower.''

No one had noticed that Chuck had turned to the bookshelves. *"Webster's II,"* he said. ''Here's the first meaning: 'a tract of slightly elevated land with shrubs, bush, etc., and sandy soil.' Accurate enough, isn't it, Cole, as far as it goes? But it doesn't say how I'd describe the barrens. Harsh, starkly beautiful. How's that for a description from an old chemistry teacher?''

Then, as if fearing that he had said too much, his tone became lighter. ''Now if you just had someone to run the blueberry business, canning factory and all, as well as Olympia runs the lobster business for you, you two could stay and boat us around all summer long, which would be lovely."

"Yes, yes, of course. Actually we have someone, a damned good fellow I think, but I'll tell you about him another time," Cole said. "Now, 'Genia, give us a ring if you find that your guest isn't coming until later in the day. We're going out about nine, cruise around for a couple of hours, have an early lunch aboard—and you know Frances always sends along enough food for an army. Then we hope to get back around two, pay Harvard a visit, and get back to Cherrybridge by the end of the afternoon. Remember, everybody, we'll be going out anyway, so all you have to do is show up at First Bite by nine."

Mrs. Potter was still thinking of more ways of being *picketted* after her guests had left and she was in bed upstairs, with Sindhu happily settled on his rug at the foot of the stairs. Piddlingly, pointedly, passably, pecuniarily. Presumably and peculiarly. Permanently.

She smiled as she went to sleep, thinking first of Cole's limerick as read in Regina's patrician accent, then of Carter's warm, firm grasp on her hands, the sharp fragrance of his manly cologne as he said good night, and his low-voiced question. Couldn't he stay to help with the dishes? It was amusing to recall his look of surprise at her firm *no thanks*.

8

At a quarter of nine the next morning, Mrs. Potter's telephone rang with the news that the expected houseguest would have to postpone her visit indefinitely. Her sister was ill in Ohio and she was standing by, to go out if she was needed.

Sorry as she was about the sick sister, Mrs. Potter could not help wishing that the change of plans had been announced the night before. Then she reproached herself for such a heartless lack of sympathy. Besides, if she rushed, she still might be able to catch Cole and Regina at First Bite.

Grabbing a sweater (she was already in jeans, shirt, and sneakers), she called Sindhu in from his morning perambulation and hastened by car down the lane toward the cove. She passed Harvard's house. A fine plume of wood smoke rose from his chimney, but his fishing boat was out and she knew he was hauling his few nearby traps on this fair morning.

The lane circled from Harvard's shack to the south of the cove, where the *Cog's Wheel* was regularly kept, just beyond Harvard's sturdy old pier. Before she reached the dock, however, she could see that she was too late to join the morning's outing. The boat was gone, leaving only the skiff floating quietly, attached to the mooring buoy.

Scrambling to the top of a small hummock crested with huge flat boulders, she looked out to sea. There, moving briskly into the calm blue waters of the morning, the boat was already well away from the land, heading toward open ocean, and much too far away for a summoning shout or wave.

Well, it was worth a try, she told herself. And even though

I've missed a morning on the water, the two of them will have a marvelous time together, as they always do. Just as they will later in the week, casting their flies for salmon in the Metoosic. Just as they will tonight, over their usual quick, ferocious game of cribbage before bed, part of a continuing tournament that has gone on through the long years of their marriage.

Mrs. Potter was back at her cottage and outside sweeping the front deck in the sunlight of the warming day when she heard the explosion.

Let's see, who's getting a new phone now, she wondered idly? Possibly they were putting in new poles at the Whiteheads' property in preparation for their future house. In the rocky soil of the peninsula, it was usually necessary to blast a few times, the crews setting off the charges of dynamite under heavy protective steel mats before they were able to dig holes for utility poles.

This blast, however, had seemed to come from the opposite direction. Undoubtedly some trick of acoustics made it sound as if it had come from the southeast, the direction of the open sea.

Shortly afterward, Mrs. Potter walked to the village. The morning ritual to pick up the mail was partly for her own pleasure and partly for Sindhu's entertainment. The big gray dog at her side remained as firmly at heel as if he were chained there. As she had at the pound, however, Mrs. Potter would snap the leash on his collar when they came to the village. Gentle and obedient as he was, many people were afraid of the Weimaraner and she did not want to cause any alarm.

The postmaster of Northcutt's Harbor had the mail ready to distribute at nine-thirty. There was no point in arriving earlier, in spite of the earlier hour stated on the door. In an emergency, Amanda might sell a stamp before that time or make out a money order, but only if she felt that the sender had sufficient excuse for not appearing at the later time she deemed more suitable for such business. Until nine-thirty, Amanda was involved in the sacred rite of sorting the mail. It was suspected, perhaps unfairly, that during this inviolable period she was also skimming the various mail-order catalogs, reading postcards, and speculating about return addresses on out-of-town correspondence.

There was a knot of village women standing on the porch in front of the post office door. Mrs. Potter assumed that they were waiting, and probably willingly enough, since this would provide a valid excuse to prolong the morning's usual post office chat. As she approached the porch, however, she realized that something had happened, something of a catastrophic nature. For one thing, Amanda was part of the group outside, away from her counter.

"A big flash of light, way to the south," Ruth Bewley was announcing.

"We heard the bang clear up to our place," Tillie added.

The words "explosion," "gas tanks," and "big flash" were recurring as the women repeated what one or another lobster-fishing husband had reported to his wife on the CB at the time of the blast.

"Lyman says they're on their way out there now."

"Whoever blew up, must have been about two, three miles out."

"Off the Point, about due south, Doc thought it was."

Giselle Oublette spoke with a voice of authority. "My Louis, he says," she began, and the others fell silent, "my Louis, he says that whoever lobster boat blew up, it isn't from here. Everybody out fishing from Northcutt's Harbor called in or else already they are seen. There is no boat missing from ours."

Mrs. Potter turned quickly, white and silent, and with Sindhu at her side turned back toward the Point.

This time, instead of returning to the cottage, she passed Pickett's, surrounded by cars and a babble of voices, and went alone, quietly, down the road to the lobster pound.

Olympia was in the office. Both the shortwave and marine band radio on her desk and the citizens band radio on the shelf above her head were spluttering with crackling sound and speech.

She motioned for Mrs. Potter to sit, without speaking or moving from her position on the straight-backed chair. Her eyes were blank and unseeing as she listened, motionless, sorting out the reports of the two sets of voices, recognizing individuals from time to time and saying "Doc" or "that's Morton" or "Lyman Cooney" with the apparent purpose of making their identities clear to her visitor.

It was all totally incomprehensible to Mrs. Potter. She was unable to hear either radio receiver clearly for the noise of the other. In any case she had never found it possible to understand the native speech in this medium. The vocabulary of the sea was in itself unfamiliar, and Down East speech, while ordinarily if sometimes imperfectly understandable in face-to-face conversation, became a strange and foreign tongue when spoken by a fisherman out in his boat.

Olympia spoke to her now above the jumble of the two competing radio sets. "There were nine boats fishing in that direction," she reported, "and they are all on their way to where they believe the explosion took place. There should be more word shortly."

She leaned forward again, her back and shoulders narrow under the faded shirt, her head held stiffly, a few strands of pale red hair escaping from the dark cap. Her rubber boots dripped slightly on the scuffed bare wood of the office floor.

Her thin body tensed as a new voice spoke amid the whine and babble of strange noises.

After a minute, she turned again to Mrs. Potter. "There are two boats there now at the scene of the explosion. The sea is calm, they're two miles due south of Grandbury Light, and there's a lot of debris floating over a fairly wide area."

The blue eyes, so unlike her half brother's, were staring past Mrs. Potter's head at the rusty old refrigerator at one side of the room, at the elaborately decorated door of the old-fashioned safe beside it. Her gaze swerved to the window and she directed the same unfocused stare toward the water of the harbor outside in the sparkling sun of the May morning.

"They're covering the area as fast as they can." Olympia

yes, and the Coast Guard has been notified and is on its way.''

The welter of sounds went on and on until the noise became a drone. Mrs. Potter gave up any attempt at deciphering words or meaning. Occasionally Olympia would turn her head stiffly with a report. She gave the latitude and longitude at which the explosion was presumed to have occurred.

She said that Lin Olney was having trouble, probably his carburetor again, and that he was going to have to come in and that one of the Pitkin twins was going to follow him back to the harbor, just to be on the safe side. No point, they said, in having two bustups in one day.

The Coast Guard got there. The Coast Guard had not got there. The Coast Guard was on its way.

Two other boats from the village had joined the search. There was a bunch of stuff floating. Doc Cooney had picked up a life jacket, good as new.

What the searchers of the watery desert were not finding, and what they were so passionately seeking, was the floating human being, somehow miraculously alive after that great fiery explosion, after all this time in bone-chilling Maine waters.

Sindhu nudged Mrs. Potter's knee, and she looked up at the old round clock on the office wall. The search had gone on for more than two hours now, and the blast had taken place, as she reckoned the time, at least a half hour before that. Two and a half hours, in forty-degree water. She thought of Regina's thin, frail body and of Coley's bad heart.

Finally she sighed and rose to her feet. "We're going to my house now, Olympia," she announced, "and we're going to have some coffee and a sandwich. The boy down on the pier can come up and listen for you and telephone us the minute there is any more news."

Olympia did not at first appear to hear the words, and when she understood the suggestion she shook her head with unmistakable finality.

and Regina are gone, just as well as you do, but this is where I belong, on the job.''

As she went to the door of the office, Mrs. Potter paused. ''This is going to be hard on Laurie, I'm afraid. Would you like to have me go to the high school to get her, or meet her when she gets off the school bus? I'm afraid she'll have heard the news, and . . .'' she hesitated, ''. . . and if you're going to stay here? . . .''

''Thank you, 'Genia, but she'll walk from the bus as she always does. Her job is to go home, do her homework and cook our dinner. She'll do her job and I'll do mine, and I'll see her, as usual, at our house after work.''

Silenced, Mrs. Potter left the pound.

It was not until several hours later that a tired fisherman, eyes red-rimmed from the continuing, searching patrol, picked up the bit of flotsam that answered all questions beyond further doubt. Part of a thin, broken walking stick floated among the bits of boat cushions, shredded insulation, pieces of shattered and unidentifiable objects. Everyone knew, once they saw it, that its graceful silver head, along with that of its owner, and along with the round genial bald head of her true love, was at rest in deep waters off Happenstance Bay.

9

At two in the afternoon, Mrs. Potter walked to Harvard's shack on the cove. His boat was in and Harvard was already coming down the path to meet her.

Tears she was no longer able to hold back brimmed in her eyes as the old man took her, like a child, in his arms. With their warmth around her shoulders, she found herself giving way to hard sobs against the fish-smelling comfort of the flannel shirt front.

As the two stood there sharing their wordless grief, Sindhu performed a strange ritual of his own. Rising on his hind feet, he gently balanced himself with a paw on each shoulder—on Harvard's, firm and sturdy, and on her own, still shaken with sobs.

All three stood together, locked in a tableau, an almost mythological communion of man and beast.

Mrs. Potter straightened, blew her nose; Sindhu dropped to all fours; Harvard led the way to his own front doorstep.

"I knew," he was saying, "as soon as I heard the explosion. I knew there was something wrong all along, only I didn't follow my hunch like I should have."

He, too, now blew his nose, then went on. "Last night I dreamed there was somebody out there fooling around on that boat. Old men have crazy dreams, 'Genia. Just don't talk about them much.

10

Dawn next morning was clear and quiet and the lobster boats had already begun their quick, orderly procession out the channel in front of the cottage. Disaster at sea was a fact of life in Northcutt's Harbor, a fact to be mourned, to be accepted, to be woven into the pattern of the years. There would be no pause in the daily job of hauling traps.

Mrs. Potter felt sure that Olympia was already at the pound and that Laurie would be on the yellow school bus later, bound for her day of geometry and tenth-grade English.

From the foot of the stairway, Sindhu cleared his throat and Mrs. Potter put on a cotton robe to greet the day. Together they left the front deck of the cottage and walked into the cold dew of the May morning. Then, leaving the dog to his customary morning patrol of the little patch of woods, Mrs. Potter returned to the warmth of slippers for her wet bare feet and to the comfort of a morning pot of tea.

Everything told her this was to be a joyless day. First she started an unnecessary load of washing just for something to do, then sat down, feeling leaden, for a dull stint at her desk.

Later she'd go to see Harvard, of course. Right now she hoped that his was among the boats on their way to haul. She had not liked the tired slump of his shoulders as they had sat together on the steps to his house, or his sudden talk of being a useless old man, prone to bad dreams and premonitions.

She looked from her desk out across the water. It was going to be a beautiful day, but that in no way lessened her knowledge that it would be a cheerless one.

The first thing she must do, of course, was to write notes of condolence—to Olympia and Laurie, to Herbert and Nancy, and to Frances.

To postpone even thinking of it, she found a few bills to pay, then jotted a reminder to herself on one of her ever-present yellow pads to have the quarterly Maine car inspection done next week. She began a letter to a local congressman, deploring the current state-highway spraying program. Before completing it, she tore it to pieces, realizing that she did not know enough about spruce budworms to be giving advice.

What was foremost in her mind, throughout these futile attempts to put it off, was a letter to Olympia. Once she had begun, it had been simple enough to write her note of shared sorrow to Herbert and Nancy at their Millstone address. More difficult, but still now completed, had been the note to Frances at the Cherrybridge house, in which she promised to come to see her soon. Frances's life had centered on Cole and Regina for so long that it was hard to think of her in any other setting.

However, even a second draft of a letter to Olympia, scribbled on another of the ubiquitous yellow pads, was torn up, just as the first had been. She would have to do better than that before copying it on her best heavy white notepaper, the writing paper she reserved for letters of sympathy and for replies to wedding invitations—the only formal correspondence of her present life. The second draft had sounded just as false and overdone as the first when she tried to see it through Olympia's cool blue gaze.

For one thing, Olympia and her half brother had never seemed close, and Mrs. Potter knew her more in the context of her job at the pound than she did through her own friendship with the Cogswells. It was difficult to know what to say or write to such a seemingly contained, remote person. Almost everything she wanted to say about Cole and Regina sounded effusive, an intrusion upon Olympia's dignity and well-preserved privacy.

At this point, having had only her early tea as the lobster boats went out at first light, she decided to heat a cup of soup as a kind of late breakfast before she left to get the morning mail.

Inadvertently, she touched the top of the stove with a metal spoon and again, as she had done before, she felt the tingle of a small shock through her fingers and hand. I think it's just whenever that small back unit is turned to medium heat, she thought. It must not be properly grounded. She felt sure that the necessary repairs were undoubtedly just a matter of checking simple wiring patterns, scarcely a problem warranting the expense of a service call from the appliance shop in Ellsworth.

She had earlier considered the local possibilities.

Lyman Cooney, her caretaker, was terrified of anything electrical. His specialties were small carpentry jobs and painting.

Otis Bewley provided the town with various minor plumbing services. He was the able fellow you called in for a dripping faucet, a frozen water line, or a toilet that would not stop running. (Mrs. Potter reminded herself that she was in Maine and should say "flush," which was the polite word for toilet here, just as "commode" was considered more refined in ranch country, back home in Arizona.) Above all, Otis was a genius at clogged drains.

When it came to minor electrical matters—rewiring connections, diagnosing blown circuits and fuses, even putting in a new light outlet in cellar or attic—the man you called was Curly Gillan, and she had already begun her appeals to him.

On the yellow pad on her desk, Mrs. Potter added a note to call Curly again, perhaps this evening after his supper and before hers, which meant about six, right before the news. With the help of the manual that came with the electric range, fortunately still at hand in a pile with others in a kitchen drawer, they should be able to figure out why she kept getting that small shock, and he could get it fixed.

After the soup, the question of Olympia and of her own need to express her sympathy and concern continued to press upon her. Still another note, again drafted on the lined yellow pad, seemed wrong—stilted, unfeeling.

No other way, she finally decided, than simply to go see the woman and tell her how sorry you are about the accident. Skip trying to write about your grief over losing two delightful friends, and about the loss to both Northcutt's Harbor and Cherrybridge. Skip the part about whatever you can do for her or for Laurie. There will be *nothing* you can do now, perhaps ever. But you've got to tell her you're sorry, no matter how you say it.

This is simply part of living in a small town, she thought to herself as she and Sindhu began their walk, slowly, through the little patch of woods and toward the pound. And you have chosen this way of life voluntarily, my dear Eugenia.

Trouble is, she told herself, you will never be anything but a small-town person. You're content with books and records instead of concerts and theater, and you know, no matter how shameful it is to admit this, that you can't stand (or understand) grand opera. You seldom enjoy shopping and you prefer to do it by mail or telephone whenever you can. You have eaten too many overpriced and overrated restaurant meals, and perhaps even enough really good ones. Except for city walking—and there are fewer places all the time where this is possible or pleasant—you don't enjoy any part of city life anymore.

What you like, what you want and need is people—people close enough and few enough that you get to know them, what they do and what they like, what they eat and what they say. How their children grow up, who they look like, and how they behave. Briefly she thought of what kind of man Addison Pickett, the shipwrecked British sailor, might have been. From what ancestry had Rodney inherited his undeniable presence, his innate attitude of superiority?

She continued the litany of her small-town concerns. She wanted to know who's getting married and who's sleeping where and who goes away and who comes back. Most of all, *why*.

She wanted to know who is putting up new wallpaper on her kitchen walls, who is buying new galvanized lobster traps to replace his old wooden ones, and how much they cost.

Who is born and who is dying.

And although you sometimes find yourself feeling critical and superior, as you did recently, my good woman, just because your taste and Eileen Pettengill's do not coincide on decorative arts; just because the wife of a perfectly nice retired businessman seems to you a little pretentious, a little stupid; just because Persy Pickett bores you out of your skin when she starts on her allergies, you still choose to be right there, a part of Northcutt's Harbor and even of Northcutt's Harbor Estates and Shags Head by the Sea.

At this point she remembered gratefully the get-well cards, the offers of doing shopping errands, the casseroles and fresh bread, the flowers brought them when Lew had been ill a few years ago. She thought of the amusing and newsy Northcutt's Harbor bulletins that arrived in occasional letters to her at the ranch during the time of the year she was not at the cottage.

Part of all this, she concluded her monologue (later unsure whether any of it had been spoken aloud or only in her own head), part of it is having to go to speak some word now, whatever it is, of shared sorrow, and if possible of comfort, to Olympia Cogswell Cutler. She is the half sister of a man who, with his wife, were your very dear friends, and with whom, but for the grace of God, you too would have been blown up and drowned in that boat explosion yesterday morning.

This last thought had not occurred to her until this moment.

The same thing applied to all her dinner guests Sunday night, of course. And Cole had mentioned—or had it been Regina—that they had earlier invited several other people who also could not join them for that last cruise and picnic. Who else, she wondered, might be coming to this same chilling realization?

At least not Olympia, she thought, as she approached the wooden buildings of the lobster pound. There had been no mention of the Cogswells including her in that last invitation.

Sindhu now on leash at her side, Mrs. Potter was, as she had been on Sunday, on the upper level, again watching Olympia's thin figure on the deck below, long wisps of hair blowing free from the cap on her head. Again she watched as Olympia came straight up the long wooden ladder. "With you in a minute," she said as she disappeared toward the office.

When Olympia returned and stood beside the wooden bench,

Mrs. Potter began quickly. "I've come by to tell you how sorry I am," she said.

Before she could continue, a lobster boat swished to its sudden halt at the dock below.

"Yes. I know. Thanks." The small figure sped down the long drop to the floating platform.

Clearly, her mission was accomplished. There was nothing more to be said.

As she turned to leave, again she met Deke MacDonald, the man who had momentarily blocked her way past the big truck in the passageway on Sunday morning.

"Mrs. Potter," he said, "I was thinking of you. May I tell you how very sorry I am? Such a loss this is going to be for you. It fair breaks my heart to think of their going—partly for you, partly for all their friends. And then because Mr. Cogswell had been looking forward—like a boy he sounded—to fishing the Metoosic this very week, with the salmon just starting to run there."

"There's sorrow for Olympia, too," she told him. "She seems so aloof, and yet I'm sure she's grieving deeply inside."

"At least she has her job to keep her busy," he said, "and, from what the lawyer at the company told me this morning, she doesn't have to worry about the losing of it. The whole business, blueberries, lobsters, and all, are hers now. The house in Cherrybridge, everything. All but that bit of land down there past you on the Point, past Mr. Harvard's. That was special to Mrs. Cogswell, the lawyer said, and their wills say it goes on to her people. Forgive me if I go on too much about all this, but the sorrow and the shock of it has put everything else out of my mind."

Mrs. Potter was grateful for his concern for her, for his very special recognition that the loss was hers, too. What an exceptional person this Deacon MacDonald seems to be, she thought. I hope Olympia keeps him on to manage the blueberry end of the business, but I have a feeling it will be more like her to decide she can run the whole thing herself.

Her brief stop at Pickett's was next. As she walked into the small parking lot, she was surprised to see a familiar figure coming down the open outside stairway at the side, the stairway to Persy's apartment.

"Afternoon, Curly," she greeted him, noting that his descent had seemed both furtive and at the same time oddly at home, the air and tread of a man who knew those steps very well.

Curly attempted to back out of sight, then, realizing he had been seen and recognized, he sauntered toward her. "Just doing a little fixing for Persy," he said. "Woman alone needs things done some times, electrical, that is."

Reminding him that she, too, was a woman alone and had a small but specific electrical problem, she again secured his promise to come by the cottage to look at her stove. First day they gave fog on the weather, he assured her.

It neither shocked nor surprised Mrs. Potter to consider that Curly might be a frequent visitor above Persy's store at the closing hour between two and three. Persy's husband had died when Rodney was a baby. Curly and his wife had been divorced several years ago. There would seem no reason, she felt sure, either to them or the rest of the village, that they needed to marry in order to have a more than casual relationship.

The thought of Persy and Curly as lovers actually was not too incongruous. Fat women seemed more prevalent in Maine than anywhere else she knew, and their pounds did not appear to lessen their attractiveness there.

At any rate, it was none of her business, although she couldn't help speculating about Rodney's reaction if he knew. Roddy had been the apple of his mother's eye, indulged, cosseted, adored. It seemed unlikely that he would accept his mother's lover, if that's what Curly was, with good grace.

It was at the post office that Mrs. Potter received the official village acceptance of Cole and Regina's death at sea.

"And them with everything to live for," Tillie was saying wistfully. "All that money, the pound and all. I suppose Olympia stands to inherit?"

"I will find out from Louis and tell you," Giselle assured her and Amanda behind the counter.

"Tris Northcutt is telling everyone the boat repairs weren't

93

the cause of it,'' Amanda announced positively. "Must say I believe the man. Honest worker, and so is Sis in her line. Anyway, a body isn't likely ever to find out, one way or the other. Boat just blew up sky high, so they think now, not enough left for anyone to know what caused it. And in that deep water. . .''

Amanda paused, as they were clearly all thinking the same thoughts.

"What better grave is there, anyway?'' she demanded of them. "Clean, peaceful. Seems right as any for the two of them. Their people all came from around the sea, as far back as there's been anybody in these parts.''

"And they both loved it,'' Mrs. Potter added, hoping to cheer herself as well as the others.

As they spoke, Amanda had handed her her mail. A neat, rounded backhand, standard boarding school script, with a Millstone imprint on the flap, indicated that Nancy had indeed been prompt with her thanks for the Sunday supper party, which now seemed so long ago. A proper Philadelphian, she had undoubtedly written it the minute she and Herbert returned to their own house the previous morning and had mailed it before the news of the boat explosion had reached them.

Mrs. Potter was about to leave to walk back to the cottage when a lank figure, wearing grease-stained shirt and work pants, entered the little office.

"Went down to check on Uncle Harvard,'' he said slowly. "Sis was looking for him up to breakfast. He told her yesterday he didn't think he'd go out to haul today—too cut up about the Cogswells, he said he was.''

Tris folded his height, like a jointed ruler, into the one stout wooden post office chair, next to the window filled with Amanda's leafy jungle of plants.

"Guess it was too much for him,'' he told them heavily. "Found him there in his chamber, quiet and peaceful as a baby. Died in his sleep.''

"Have you called the doctor? Have you called Clarence?'' Amanda wanted to know, and Tris nodded dumb assent.

Amanda turned away from the counter, her back to the

others for a long moment. When she turned back, her long New England nose was pink and her eyes were wet.

Still, with what seemed to Mrs. Potter to be typical New England courage and stoicism, she managed a final remark, clearly intended to be spoken tartly, although her voice cracked a little before she got it all said.

"Seems like you're running out of neighbors, 'Genia, down there at the Point."

11

The harbor was full of sleek, powerful fishing boats at their moorings, all facing into the light southwest breeze. Mrs. Potter did not pause to count them as she drove up the peninsula road to the white church on the hill ahead of her. It appeared that the entire lobster fleet of Northcutt's Harbor had come in early this bright afternoon, the last Friday in May, to be on hand for the funeral.

The small parking area in the churchyard had been paved by nature, its surface the face of a huge flat granite boulder lying partly exposed in the skimpy soil. This area was already filled and she had to drive on for a hundred yards or more before she could find a place to park.

All of Northcutt's Harbor, it was clear, was coming to Harvard Northcutt's funeral.

From the gleaming new trucks of the prosperous lobster fishermen; from the big cars—red, blue, and gold—of their wives and womenfolk; from the small, foreign, gas-saving cars and shiny pickups of the summer people; from the commercial trucks and vans lettered with the names of builders and business firms and well drillers and septic tank cleaners (CALL THE HONEY WAGON) or suppliers of home insulation (WE'RE FOAMING FOR YOU); from a few battered jalopies filled with thin hairy young men and tired-looking young women with infants at their breasts; from several elegant motor homes with out-of-state plates; from at least one black limousine exhibiting impressive Augusta credentials; from an unmarked station wagon recognized by Mrs. Potter

96

as holding the chancellor of the state university; from Jeeps and vans and vehicles of all sorts, people were pouring into one small church, into one very small Down East village, to pay their last respects to one old fisherman.

I suppose we all have different reasons for being here, she thought. The village people knew him as one of their own, and he had been a part of life here for longer than most of them could remember. He was the town's respected and acknowledged senior, although far from being its oldest resident, until three days before.

But how did all the rest—the painter's truck she recognized from Cherrybridge, the young back-to-nature couples with their ponytails and work-roughened hands, the retired colonel, the vacationing designer from Atlanta, the important personage from the state capital—how did we *all* come to enjoy, to admire, this one old man, and why have we gathered now in these numbers and variety to mourn his death?

Mrs. Potter found herself, as she approached the church, greeting neighbors and tradespeople, a local sculptor of some renown, a best-selling author whose presence in the area was ordinarily a well-kept secret.

As she neared the door of the small white church, she did not at once recognize the dignified and imposing black-clad presence meeting her there with a deferential outstretched hand.

"Hello, Clarence," would have been her usual greeting, once she had known who it was, and what she certainly would have said a day or two earlier when she had gone to Osgood's furniture store in Cherrybridge. There, Clarence was the respected proprietor, a nice man. She knew him fairly well, well enough to call him by his first name at any rate, at the store. There he was simply a tall, thin, middle-aged and quiet man, somewhat stooped, wearing a misbuttoned gray cardigan.

That Clarence was a lesser being, a pale echo of the august impresario, manager, and distinguished interpreter of events that he was today.

"Mr. Osgood," was the name for today, as she bowed rather formally to the impressive personage at the doorway.

I had forgotten he was an undertaker as well, she told herself. And he is absolutely perfect. I must remember to include his name in those delightful plans for my own last rites. I'll put it down along with my favorite hymns, my alternate provisions for dying in Arizona or Maine, along with who gets Grandmother Andrew's ironstone dishes—all of those enjoyably envisioned arrangements, which so far she had not got around to writing down. She knew she would only be able to contemplate them with this much pleasure if she knew for certain that she'd be on hand to approve and applaud every nicely planned detail.

Mr. Osgood was at least six inches taller than she had remembered from last week at the store. His bearing was noble, his face a perfect blend of dignity, sympathy, and reassurance. He led Mrs. Potter to a pew, exactly where she would have chosen to sit, about two-thirds back from the altar and in the middle section of the church.

Across the aisle Mrs. Potter saw Carter Ansdale duck his head briefly, as she had done, fearing that any active obeisance, bowing, or kneeling would appear to be Episcopalian airs, even papish behavior, to the regular congregation of Northcutt's Harbor Community Church. He apparently had quickly compromised, as she had done, by folding his hands and looking at his knees.

Clarence Osgood was moving with quick grace and precision, ushering in each new arrival. On Mrs. Potter's other side, he seated Olympia, her pale hair twisted high, her navy blue dress, beautifully cut, not new, obviously expensive, smelling slightly of fish.

On the outside of the pew, next to Olympia, Clarence seated Amanda Wakefield. Amanda lifted a single white-gloved finger—in this case a rather formal gesture—toward the others in the row. Amanda was wearing a hat, a dark straw with a flowered wreath, as well as her white cotton gloves, so far the only hat and gloves to be seen. (Mrs. Potter herself had only recently overcome her ingrained resistance to going to church hatless. Her smooth head was bare today, as were those of most of the women she could see.)

The side pews, it appeared, were mostly filled with women

of the village, alternating, according to Clarence's fastidious and instant decisions, with couples from the Pettengill developments and people from the summer colony at Millstone.

The Ainsleys, Herbert and Nancy's friends, were placed on her other side in the same pew, thus filling it to capacity. They and she exchanged polite smiles, by this slight turn of lip acknowledging each other's presence, and Mrs. Potter noticed that Mrs. Ainsley, as a proper Philadelphian, was dressed in perfect and proper costume for the occasion: a decorous silk in a muted print of gray and white.

Late-comers, including the Whiteheads, Clarence now crammed into the back pews, and from the sound in the rear of the church it was already clear that many of the congregation were going to stand for the service.

Perhaps the tall man with the pepper and salt mustache was there, Mrs. Potter thought, but she kept herself from turning to look. But no, he could scarcely have known Harvard in the short time he had been in these parts, and he certainly must be busy with his job in Cherrybridge, if Olympia was keeping him on.

In the pew directly in front of her, Clarence had placed, with a deference that contained no hint of obsequiousness, the august one from Augusta.

Next seated, the chancellor turned and smiled his greeting, giving Mrs. Potter a chance to whisper an invitation to come by the cottage later, thinking that he and Wendy, his wife, might welcome a sandwich and a drink before their drive back to Orono. The invitation was obviously relayed, and Wendy turned her head to nod their thanks and acceptance.

In the front pews of the church Clarence now ceremoniously seated three rows of Northcutts, most of them villagers and regular members of the congregation. There were Tris and Sis—Tristram Northcutt, Harvard's nephew, and his wife, who ran Northcutt's Harbor's small gas station, garage, and restaurant, providing fresh-cooked boiled lobsters to eat on the spot or to take out. Their handsome son, Tommy, a high school senior, was beside them.

There was Matilda—Tillie—widow of Harvard's younger brother Alston, who had been drowned when his lobster boat had crashed on the rocks of the Point in the fog. With her was her granddaughter Shelley, who had come to live with her after his death.

There was Virgil, Tristram's brother, the Cogswells' caretaker, also a lobsterman, with his wife Margaret. There was Jumbo (whose real first name Mrs. Potter had never heard), the clam digger and wormer, and with him were several elderly women Mrs. Potter did not recognize.

In addition there were the relatives from New Jersey, both the smoothly groomed ones from Summit, and the ones who looked like early western pioneers, the ones from the pine barrens down near Cape May.

And with the family were Herbert and Nancy, claiming their Northcutt heritage—which came as something of a surprise, it seemed, to the others. Nancy's dark green linen made every other woman in the church, Mrs. Potter thought, look as if she had dressed from a yard sale.

Behind the Northcutt family, but in front of the row of state house and university dignitaries, there were three remaining rows of pews Clarence had not yet filled. In the meantime, more and more people entered the church and squeezed into those side pews not already jampacked. Mrs. Potter's row now held yet another person, and Olympia moved closer to her on one side and the Ainsleys on the other. The little church was growing warm as the May sunshine streamed through the colored windows.

To restrain her impulse to look around, Mrs. Potter concentrated on the coffin below the altar and the mass of flowers behind and around it. This was the season when everything blossomed at once in coastal Maine. Other places might have apple blossom time or tulip time or the separate glory of summer peonies. Here in Northcutt's Harbor everything came on at once. Every garden in the village had produced its special display to the glory of God and the memory of Harvard.

There were florists' pieces as well, including an imposing one of red and white carnations with a silver ribbon from the Grange. Mrs. Potter, having no flower garden of her own at the cottage, had sent one of these, a sheaf of yellow roses.

Her more honest tribute, however, was a small low bowl at one side, which she had brought to the church earlier in the day—an arrangement of purple flags, the wild iris that grew in a low place on the north of Harvard's cove, the sight of which they had enjoyed together the morning of Edna's hot bread.

Suddenly from the back of the church there was the sound of purposeful feet, and coming down both aisles were the chief representatives of the village. These marchers, these mourners, were Harvard's lodge brothers and his fellow fishermen.

Most of them (although she knew them by first name, knew who was married to whom and who their children were), Mrs. Potter had never before seen except in their daily work clothes. She knew them in baggy jackets, often greasy from the engine repairs that were an important part of their jobs. She knew them in billed and knitted caps, in high rubber boots, and often in oilskins.

Now, the men of Northcutt's Harbor, looking sorrowful, looking both dignified and sanctified, were in unfamiliar dark suits, in Sunday shirts and neckties. They looked like biblical patriarchs, larger than life.

Around each dark middle there was tied a small white apron. Mrs. Potter had not seen one of these for many years, but now she remembered her own father's white lodge apron. Somewhere, she knew, she still had it, carefully put away—a square of thick, white, soft kidskin, with a V-shaped overlay at the top and heavy ties of thick white twill tape, now yellowing. As she had thought in the past, but had never got around to doing anything about it, it occurred to her again that it would be nice to give it to some young man going into the Masonry, if such a gift would be welcome and acceptable.

Then, as the plump young minister mounted to the pulpit, she forgot everything except the words of the service and her prayers for Harvard, who had really been too young, too healthy and vital, to die at not yet eighty-one.

12

The service ended. Olympia's thin reddened fingers, in a touch as light as a feather from an eider duck in the Bay, rested briefly, surprisingly, on Mrs. Potter's tanned and larger hand as they heard the last words, although their eyes did not meet.

Then, soundlessly, Clarence performed his final small miracle of perfect drama. Pew by pew he directed the congregation, starting from the back of the church, down the right-hand aisle and back on the left. In quiet procession, his actors, his supporting cast—for so he must have viewed them—came to see the star of his production. With a final nod of farewell they passed the open coffin. Some, like Amanda, said goodbye with a final, barely lifted forefinger and a tiny rueful smile.

As Mrs. Potter bade her old friend good-bye she tried to see only the tanned and ruddy face, the glowing skin, the bright eyes, the contagious sudden grin of her last happy memories of him, the morning they had shared a second breakfast. She remembered the comfort of his strong old arms around her after the Cogswells' death, the reassurance of his sturdy presence at the cove beyond the cottage. She tried not to think of his slumping shoulders when he told her he should have trusted his inner warning, that he should have kept Cole and Regina from going out that morning, when he called himself a useless old man.

Now, with the briefest look compatible with courtesy—certainly one could not close one's eyes to these once dear mortal remains—Mrs. Potter saw instead only the undertaker's handiwork. At the fringe of the thick white hair she saw a line of blue pallor that Clarence's cosmetic art had not quite covered. In the same quick, compassionate glance she noticed Harvard's preternaturally scrubbed and manicured hands, an incongruous coating of shiny clear polish covering each ridged and horny fingernail. A pink-beige gloss of lipstick on the quiet mouth was equally startling, the more so because the lips appeared oddly roughened and chafed.

There was no time for further prayers or farewells. Mrs. Potter moved quietly with the slow procession past the coffin, then back and out into the soft May sunshine.

The last to leave the church were the Northcutt family and the lodge brothers, and only these would proceed to the little cemetery in the clearing in the woods behind the church. Burial would be a separate and private ceremony. In respectful silence, the village waited in the churchyard for their departure.

Then small groups began to gather here and there on the huge flat rock and around the cars in front of the church. Conversation began as a quiet hum, then became a more solid orchestration. There was comfort to be found, at times of death, in ordinary human talk.

"Family's going to the Grange afterward," Amanda said. "Nobody had a house big enough. Everybody's sent food of course, plenty for an army. Tillie baked the Northcutt Reunion Rocks, the full ten dozen. Too bad Harvard didn't leave a widow; she'd have enough to eat for a month."

"You know, I approve of a good get-together after a funeral," the famous author said. "It's a good time to speak out, have a drink or two, say things you never got around to before or were too embarrassed to say. All of it too late, maybe, but it still seems to me a good thing."

Olympia entered the conversation. Her eyes, as blue as Cole's had been but less open, less innocent, narrowed against the afternoon sun.

"None of that for me," she said crisply. "Cremation, no fuss, no carrying on afterward. You all can have your emotional orgies if you want to, but spare me if you will when my time comes.''

No one replied.

''I've got to get out of these clothes and back to work,'' she continued. ''You all have *time* for this kind of talk, grief therapy, whatever you call it.''

Her thin, taut body was outlined sharply as the wind blew against the soft, dark silk dress, and she moved quickly away, high heels in a light staccato across the bare gray rock.

To Mrs. Potter, a sharing of grief seemed a healthy custom. Words of condolence could be spoken then, in the freshness of mourning, which might be held back out of fear of mawkishness on a later, more inhibited occasion. Words of praise, of remembrance, of affection for the dead could be spoken more freely than they might ever be again. There could be the joy of a funny recollection, or the vital reminder of continuity noted in the family resemblance of a child to the one who had with one departing breath turned into an ancestor.

''Not many of us live where we can get together with family like this anymore,'' Carter Ansdale said. His strong tanned face in the sunlight created a disturbing contrast to the tiny line of blue pallor Mrs. Potter had seen in that last brief glimpse as she passed the open coffin.

''I went to a sort of funeral reception in Portland last month,'' said the well-known sculptor, ''only it was more like a regular cocktail party than anything else. Mostly just a lot of business acquaintances. I suppose I was one of those myself, since the man who died had been the owner of the gallery that shows my stuff there. I really didn't know him all that well as a friend.''

''For whatever reason, we all need to feel close to someone after a funeral,'' the chancellor put in unexpectedly, ''and for this we thank you, 'Genia. Wendy and I will join you at the cottage as soon as we get unparked and turned around. We're up the road a half mile or so.''

As far as Mrs. Potter could see, before she made her way toward her own car, all of Northcutt's Harbor was out in full force except for the children, other than those of the immediate family, who had not yet returned from school.

One village personage whom she did not see, however, and it would have been impossible to miss her, was Persy Pickett.

Amanda Wakefield gave voice to her question. "A body'd think Persy could have closed up for an hour," she remarked, the flowered wreath on her hat quivering with disapproval. "Think it's queer she couldn't make an exception for Harvard, since it's common knowledge that he left his place to her to make a home for Winks."

Mrs. Potter was, as usual, speechless at the speed at which news travels in a small town.

"Curly Gillan never showed up either," Amanda continued. "Of course everybody knows what's going on with the two of them every day when the CLOSED sign goes up."

As Amanda walked away toward her own house, across the road from the church, she added a last brisk comment. "Can't imagine why Clarence thought nail polish was the thing. And *lipstick*. Mouth looked funny."

Moments later, Mrs. Potter waited in her car for an opportunity to pull out and turn back down the peninsula road. Before she could find an opening, the familiar big yellow school bus came down from the north, on the opposite side. It halted, its lights flashing, almost directly across from where she was parked.

Several teenagers spilled out, shoving and jumping, dropping papers. Of these and also among the faces still remaining behind the bus windows, Mrs. Potter recognized eight or ten whom she had known since they were small children, including several who had been at the baked bean supper the previous week. Near the front of the bus she saw the ruddy face and tightly curled hair of Skip Cooney, and she waved.

To her surprise, the only response—and it seemed the same on each young face—was a flat, almost insolent stare. Surely they must recognize her? And teenagers were always so knowing about automobiles that they must recognize her small red car, if not the driver, since it was the only one of its make in the village.

She waved lightly again, before the bus ceased its flashing signals and lumbered on down the narrow road through the breakup of the traffic around the church. The only apparent response had been the lifted forefinger of the driver, a perfunctory courtesy.

As the bus pulled away, there was another blank, unseeing face in the back window, that of Rodney Pickett, a face turning quickly away.

This was surprising. These were all children she *knew*, children who had come to the cottage to play Parcheesi on rainy afternoons, children who had devoured her "Angels on Horseback" until she had to send to Pickett's for yet more boxes of graham crackers, more bags of marshmallows to toast, more milk chocolate bars to break into squares.

As they had grown older, some of them had worked for her there at the cottage, helping to clear brush, to stack wood, or to clear away storm-tossed debris and rocks in the spring—all probably overpaid and all apparently pleased to have the occasional job, well-fortified with Potter colas and homemade cookies.

Granted, she saw very little of most of them now that they were past Parcheesi age and at this season away for the day at the high school at Cherrybridge. Still, she could not imagine what had provoked the expressionless, almost challenging stares.

Attempting to shake off the small hurt that she felt, Mrs. Potter remembered her invitation to the chancellor and his wife. They knew their way to the cottage without guidance, but she wanted to be there to welcome them.

Halting frequently, making her way slowly through the unwinding skein of cars leaving the funeral, Mrs. Potter drove slowly south down the narrow peninsula.

What was it Amanda had said? "Mouth looks funny." And what had she said earlier? "Looks like you're running out of neighbors down there on the Point." Pay attention to the road, she told herself, and get yourself home.

On her left, below the church, Mrs. Potter passed the gas station and lunch counter owned by Tris and Sis, who would still be at the final burial rites on the hill behind the church.

Later, still moving slowly down the road in the traffic, she saw that Rodney had already been delivered home to the store by the school bus. Automatically she waved a friendly hand. Rodney, again it seemed, did not notice her passing, or perhaps, like the other youngsters on the bus, he was preoccupied with some greater concern, perhaps plans for year's end school festivities.

She was relieved to see that Curly's pickup truck was not in the small parking area. If what Amanda had said was "common knowledge" was true, and Amanda was rarely mistaken, she hoped that at least it was not known to Persy's son.

He just didn't see me, she told herself again, and besides, Winks had been bringing him a bottled soft drink, waiting on him happily, as he always had.

Mrs. Potter continued down the road toward home. She passed the roadway that led to the left, to the pound, and thought again with surprise of Olympia's quick, light touch upon her hand at the end of the service.

The funeral traffic was behind her now as she entered the small lane leading only to her house, then Harvard's, then Regina's Roost.

Lambkill, the wild azalea, was a shock of magenta between the birches. The edge of the roadside, wherever there was sufficient sunlight, was bright with that same prodigal flowering that had overtaken the cultivated gardens of the village. It had been scarcely a month since there had been patches of slow-melting snow in the woods alongside the lane, and the pussy willows of which Harvard had reminded her had only just disappeared, vanishing overnight into gold dust and green leaf.

Now there was color and a profusion of wildflowers whose varieties were too many to count from a car window, and whose beauty deserved more deliberate homage. For this brief moment she determined to focus her entire attention upon it, trying to obliterate the sorrows of the past week. She thought she had identified nineteen different flowering plants along one sunny stretch, although she was not sure about a couple of possible duplications. Perhaps, she thought, the chancellor and Wendy would have time for a walk before they had to drive home. It was something they'd both enjoy.

Now she must proceed, to be there ahead of them. The little road at this point bisected her own land, her ten-acre crosswise slice of the peninsula. On the west was the bordering water of Shags Head Bay—narrow, sheltered and shallow. Twice a day, at low tide, its waters drained back into the ocean and its surface was a glistening quicksilver of mud, in continuing harvest by the diggers of clams and of fishing worms.

As her own drive turned sharply to the left toward the ocean, she rejoiced, as always, in the majesty of the trees overhead. The quiet and the fragrance of this small stand of forest always came as a surprise and a joy after the cleared ground, the open sunlight, and the huge flat rocks of the village area to the north. Pine needles carpeted the drive and small woods flowers appeared here and there between the tall trees. Mrs. Potter and Lew had enjoyed clearing the underbrush to make the woods floor clean and to highlight the occasional patches of sunlight. The sporadic labors of her teenage assistants had kept the small woods as beautiful as a cathedral.

What *can* have come over the children? Mrs. Potter again felt mildly puzzled over the encounters at the school bus and at the store.

Once at home, her preparations for her guests were quickly accomplished: a peek to be sure there were both white wine and beer in the refrigerator; a slab of prime Vermont cheese to be set out so that its fine flavor could be enhanced. She took a loaf of homemade bread from the freezer to thaw in its foil wrappings in a warm oven. This was a twin of the loaf she had taken to Harvard, and it seemed fitting to share it with friends today.

"Anybody home?" came Wendy's lilting voice from the woods outside. "Aren't you *nice* to ask us to come by!"

Mrs. Potter's guests were considerably younger than she

but quite at home in the cottage, where they were frequent visitors.

"Could we sit outside, do you think?" they asked. And, yes, they were *starving* and had not eaten since leaving Bangor, and the chancellor hoped he'd be allowed to put all that good food on a big tray and bring it out to the deck.

Beer for him, thank you, and wine for Wendy. Mrs. Potter had another idea, which they both promptly acclaimed, changing their own choices.

"I'm going to have Nova Scotia rum," she announced. "It was Harvard's favorite drink, for one thing, and I'm going to have a tot in his memory. For another, most funerals are sad, but the thought of not having Harvard around makes me sadder than losing a lot of other people I can think of.

"What was it," she continued, "that made so many people really love that man? Why were there so many people like you, from away—as well as people from here in the village—at his funeral?"

Wendy's hand slipped into her husband's.

"Why *do* we feel so upset?" she asked him. "I don't understand it, but both of us feel as if we'd lost something sure and safe in our lives."

"Why do all of us feel this way?" Mrs. Potter repeated. "Why does Harvard's death come as such a shock to us? After all, he had what would be considered a good long life, at least any place outside of Down East Maine."

The chancellor lit his pipe. "Eighty good years—almost eighty-one. None of us can ask for much more," he said slowly, "but for Harvard it seemed just the shank of the evening."

"He was so open and friendly," Wendy said. "Before we came to Orono I'd heard about hard-bitten, taciturn old Yankees, and I've even met quite a few of them up our way since. But Harvard *liked* people, and he wasn't afraid to show it."

"He had wonderful stories to tell, of course," said the chancellor, "a regular history of this part of the world for almost a century. I've been recording some of his yarns, as you both know, and maybe next year when I'm due for sabbatical I can put them together in some kind of book. Only I had expected he'd be around to check things over and to enjoy it with me."

"Remember how he'd say, 'dear, d'*dear, dear,*' almost like a birdcall, and shake his head, and laugh?" Mrs. Potter asked.

"His smuggling stories were my favorites," Wendy continued, "about when he and his brother Alston, the one who was drowned later on, used to smuggle rum by the boatload during Prohibition."

"Speaking of rum, *cheers,* Harvard," said the chancellor as he poured the three small glasses and they raised them together.

Not only did he have great stories to tell, the chancellor said, but he told them without undue fancification and without undue urging. There were stories about what it was like to grow up in the little coastal village of his ancestors, about school there before the days of the big yellow bus. There were tales of lobster fishing and of great storms at sea. There were the adventures of smuggling illegal liquor, which in the eyes of the village at the time was considered no more than a harmless and profitable sideline.

There was the story of how he and Alston gave up smuggling, but not from fear of the law. That was the night the bootlegger arrived in his darkened roadster and joined the two of them on the little pier at First Bite Cove to await the arrival of the truck that was expected to pick up the shipment. Alston and Harvard never knew what underground warning had prompted the gangster's grim all-night vigil. The brothers only watched, with growing apprehension, as the man in the dark fedora pulled up an upturned fish keg beside the wooden crates of contraband and sat there, the long night through, with a sawed-off shotgun across his knees.

The truck, when it arrived just before dawn, proved to be the right one, the safe one, the one belonging to the man with the shotgun. It was not that, for which the brothers gave silent thanks, of the rival who had been rumored to be on his way to hijack the cargo.

After that night, the Northcutt brothers gave up rum-running. Figured it might be fatal, Alston used to say.

Most of the other men in the village, those who had been old enough in the twenties and early thirties, had continued to run liquor. That was when lobsters were so cheap that thrifty housewives used them to make mincemeat, with plenty of suet and spices and raisins, and so plentiful that poor fishermen's children used to peer hopefully into their school lunch pails, hoping for peanut butter or bologna instead of lobster salad in their sandwiches.

"Do you think that's why so few local people seem to eat much lobster now?" Wendy asked. "Did they just get too much when they were young?"

"But they *do*," Mrs. Potter protested. "When they have a lobster feed, a real feast, they each eat two or three!"

"It's just a matter of economics, I think," the chancellor said thoughtfully. "When the price off the boat is up to nearly three dollars a pound, it makes a pretty expensive meal to bring any home for family supper. You don't keep any back except for a very special occasion. And then when it's low—what's the boat price now, 'Genia?—you need to sell all you bring in just to pay for the gas and the engine overhaul every so often, or the payments on the new pickup."

"The interesting thing to me is that people around here don't consider melted butter and lemon a natural accompaniment," Mrs. Potter said. "I think my Northcutt's Harbor friends steam lobsters in a little seawater, just as I do, but then they think a drop or two of vinegar is all that's needed to bring out the flavor."

"I learned to make lobster stew from Harvard," Wendy said, "and that's our favorite. He showed me how to sauté cooked chunks of lobster in butter until they turn bright red—as red as if you'd added paprika—and then to pour in some hot milk and let the whole thing cool for at least several hours. Then you heat it up, not quite to boiling—"

"And as he'd say, that is *some* nice eating," the chancellor declared.

"Has either of you ever heard of lobster gravy?" Mrs.

Potter asked. "No? People around here seem a little embarrassed to mention it. It's popular—I'm sure of it—but maybe thought a little too plebeian to discuss with outlanders."

"Tell us about it," Wendy begged. "We're plebeian."

"It's simply chunks of cooked lobster in a plain white sauce," Mrs. Potter said, "and you serve it hot over mashed potatoes. Myself, I love it over a split hot baked potato. Some people make it with salt pork bits instead of butter, use cornstarch instead of flour, water instead of milk, all of which to my taste buds has a sort of Chinese flavor. Anyway, either way, it makes a good meal for a person living alone, if you have, say, a half cold lobster left from the day before."

"What I want to learn to make is lobster pie," Wendy said, and Mrs. Potter promised to tell her if she ever found a recipe for it. To her knowledge lobster pie was not a local Northcutt's Harbor dish.

"To get back to the smuggling stories," the chancellor said, "did Harvard ever tell you the story of the smuggler's shipwreck on Bessie Island?"

"I adore that one," Mrs. Potter said, "and I don't think there's a family in the village that doesn't claim they salvaged at least a bottle of Scotch that night, if not a full case. If you ever want any more details to add to Harvard's story of that night, for your book that is, you might see if you can get anything out of Persy, at the store."

"Oh, Persy Pickett, of course. Hard to tell how old she is, being that fat, but I wouldn't have thought she was around to have been in on that one. I only know all the town turned out in skiffs, chasing crates and bottles on the rocks in the dark, everybody half-drunk. Harvard said there were some women there, all right, even some of the proper older ladies we all saw at church today, I expect. But I wouldn't have thought that Persy was among them."

"She wasn't, as I've heard the story," Mrs. Potter said, "but her husband was the one survivor of the wreck. Not her husband then, of course. I mean he was the one British sailor who was rescued when the rum-running vessel went aground. He was brought in by Persy's father, along with whatever share of the whisky the old man had been able to salvage. And later on, although he was quite a lot older, he and Persy were married and continued to run her father's store.''

"You know, the last time I saw Harvard—when was it, Wendy, a couple of weeks ago, when we sneaked out for an hour of rock-hopping and ran into him down at the cove?—he said young Rodney Pickett was pestering him to hear the story again, trying to get him to say Pickett had been the owner of the ship, or at least the captain. Of course the man was undoubtedly just a little limey punk making extra money running contraband, but Harvard said Rodney was determined to hear another story.''

"I'm sure he was tactful with the boy," Wendy said. "He wouldn't have said anything to hurt the boy's image of his father.''

"Oh, Harvard could hand it out straight, if he chose to,'' the chancellor reminded her. "I expect he simply laughed the boy out of it.''

With a second tot of rum in Harvard's memory, accompanied by most of the loaf of freshly warmed bread, the cheese, and a bowl of fruit, the three sat on the deck of the cottage, edging forward toward the warmth of the sunlight and out of the shadow, moving closer and closer to the sea as the afternoon sun lowered into the tall trees behind them. Finally they left their chairs by the railing and went down the steps to the wide, rugged pink ledges of rock where the sunlight still remained.

The warmth was illusory here, as they all had known it would be. The tide was going out, and a cold, kelpy breeze came in over the slowly uncovering rocks, a reminder that the afternoon was over and that there was a two-hour drive between Northcutt's Harbor and the Orono campus.

"We'll be back soon," Wendy promised, "and certainly again late summer to harvest your crop of rose hips from the *Rosa rugosa* bushes.''

"Be sure I get another little jar of that wonderful rose conserve of yours," Mrs. Potter said, "and I'll help with the gathering if I'm here then, although I don't expect to be.''

She was shivering as she stood under the big trees at the other side of the house, saying good-bye. The shelter of the woods and the soft sound of the late breeze through the fir trees and hackmatacks, ordinarily so welcoming, seemed chilly and damp. I've run out of neighbors, she thought.

13

Bone tired, feeling the weight of the day and her years, whose number, in fact, almost never occurred to her, Mrs. Potter had gone to bed before the late May sky was entirely dark the evening after Harvard's funeral. The rushing sound of the wind through the trees at the back of the house mingled with the soft, continuing crash of the light surf below her dormer window, a combination of sounds at once overpowering and soothing, punctuated only by the sound of the bell at the entrance to the harbor.

East, beyond the islands, Grandbury Light flashed its arc of light across the sky each seven seconds, a reassuring sentinel of safety and order, and at last she slept.

She awoke very early, before daylight, with the same feeling of unease that had held her the evening before. She thought of Harvard, looking so scrubbed and cosmetically altered in his coffin, and of the summer scents of lilac and peony and of the red cascade of old-fashioned bleeding hearts in the big vase above his head. These must have come from Amanda's garden in front of the post office, she thought. Those bushes had flowered with particular vigor in the last few days.

Was it that she was feeling guilty that the old man had died alone? Had he needed help? Had he tried to get from his narrow iron bed in the dark little ''chamber,'' as he called his bedroom, to get to the telephone, to the CB radio in the kitchen, to summon aid?

Finally a first line of rose appeared above the violet streak of the horizon, and the sun was about to come up behind Bessie Island.

Mrs. Potter had already, in the back of her mind, been counting the lobster boats as they came out from the harbor, moving in quick single file out the channel in front of the cottage. After they passed Harvard's cove they would disperse, a few of them continuing south to round the tip of the peninsula. There they would haul their traps off the great rocks circling the Cogswells' place.

Most of them, however, would head east to tend their traps in other and more remote sections of Happenstance Bay and even beyond the islands, farther away, farther from home.

It was a prudent and caring group. They kept close track of one another by radio, since most of them fished alone. Only the largest boats held a second, or stern, man. A disabled boat would be quickly shepherded back into the harbor by one or two nearby comrades. They watched for sudden squalls, or, more dangerous, sudden fog that could transform what was ordinarily a hard but free and exhilarating job into one of real hazard and challenge.

Mrs. Potter felt a chill in the early dawn as she went downstairs. Finding part of a carton of light cream in the refrigerator, she decided to make oatmeal as a special treat to herself. Oatmeal, so namby-pamby with the skim milk that her larder usually provided, so rich and comforting with the occasional windfall of cream.

Had the cream turned sour? Had she overcooked the oatmeal, which she always purposely tried to keep *al dente*?

Or was it just, all at once, too *damned* lonesome around here (she spoke to herself in Coley's voice) without the Cogswells and Harvard?

At least she had her dog. Wearily, she debated dumping the oatmeal from her bowl into his feeding dish, then consigned it instead to the garbage disposal in the sink. Much better to stay with his regular schedule, and she certainly didn't want him ever to get in the habit of expecting food from the table.

At least she could go for the mail, find some human companionship there at the post office or along the way.

Saturday morning and boys out in their outboards, she noted, as she caught a glimpse of the inner bay beyond the lobster pound. The morning was cool and bright, and she and the dog beside her were walking briskly, as she tried to lighten her troubled mood.

Before heading for the village, however, she and Sindhu made a brief farewell visit to First Bite Cove. For the first time she could remember, there was no friendly drift of wood smoke from the cobblestone chimney. The worn old door of the house was closed and it bore a new padlock, perhaps put there by the family after the funeral. Probably the first lock it ever had, she thought. Through the clean, uncurtained window she could see the old wood stove, the clean bare pine table, Harvard's worn, tweed-cushioned rocker alongside.

There had not been time to say good-bye. Not to Harvard, not to Coley and Regina.

Squaring her shoulders, purposely lengthening her stride, she turned in the direction of the post office. When she and Sindhu arrived, Amanda, alone for the moment, surprised her with a question. "Harvard look okay to you that last day you saw him 'Genia? Heard you were there that day after the Cogswells were lost, him standing with his arms around you there in the lane."

Marveling at Amanda's sources of intelligence and also realizing that she had never known her to be wrong, Mrs. Potter tried to respond honestly. Harvard had looked tired, yes, and he was upset, she said, as everybody was, about the explosion on the boat and the loss of his two old friends.

"That man never saw a doctor in his life, including when he was born," Amanda said. "That's why his going so sudden came as such a surprise. First time the new young doctor from the clinic laid eyes on him, Tris told me, was that morning, Tuesday, when he was already dead. Gone, right there in his chamber."

"I suppose they would have had to call him, the doctor, that is," Mrs. Potter said, "for a death certificate. It must have been hard for Tris to be the one. He and Harvard were good friends as well as relatives."

"Not always the same thing around here," Amanda replied.

"Anyway the new man said natural enough for a man Harvard's age, just passing away peaceful in his sleep. Said sometimes they go that way, old people living alone. Just stop wanting to live."

Mrs. Potter's eyebrows raised slightly. Too bad the new doctor hadn't known Harvard. He might have revised his thirty-year-old's opinions about when one stopped wanting to live.

"Ordinarily we don't even take heed of birthdays in the Northcutt tribe until they get to ninety," Amanda said, shaking her head ruefully. "Anyway Tris said everything was neat and tidy, the way Harvard always kept things. A mercy to know he didn't suffer, wasn't thrashing around in his bedcovers trying to get help."

Mrs. Potter felt a slight sense of relief easing her muscles.

"But did you take notice of how funny his mouth looked?" Amanda went on, "even under Clarence's paint and lipstick? Looked some unnatural to me. Are you sure he hadn't taken up heavy drinking, 'Genia? You saw him oftener than most folks."

Mrs. Potter disclaimed any such idea, while admitting, her muscles again tense, that Harvard's face had looked unnatural to her, too.

"Well, never saw a corpse that didn't." Amanda was finally, and almost cheerfully, willing to change the subject. "Remember I promised to tell you about the teenagers in the churchyard at night?"

Mrs. Potter could remember no such promise, but she nodded her head dutifully.

"Well, *as I was saying*, if you could see out my bedroom window at night you'd know what's going on around here. I wouldn't for the world say it in front of Tillie and Giselle, but what those high school kids are up to is no good, I can tell you that."

Amanda was determined, and her description of the evening scene in the church parking lot was graphic. "Sometimes one car, sometimes two of them," she said. "No lights on, and I don't know for sure which of them's in there, except I know Roddy Pickett is one of the crowd. They all play

118

follow-the-leader with Roddy, even though he acts so high and mighty superior. None of the local girls good enough for him, of course—never had a girl friend."

Amanda paused, and Mrs. Potter nodded yet again, this time in agreement.

"Whole town knows, of course, that Harvard left his place to Persy, and that'll make Roddy kingpin of the bunch for sure," Amanda added. "Anyway, about the cars. First you see a little glow here, and then there. Then from one to the other in the back seat. They're passing around those pot cigarettes, that's what they're doing."

"Amanda, they're probably just experimenting with regular cigarettes, the way we all did when we were that age."

"Now, 'Genia, you know better than that. Every one of them has been smoking *tobacco* cigarettes since they were twelve or maybe before. Some of them already *quit*, they've been smoking so long. Some of the girls, especially, still smoke tobacco cigarettes and in front of their folks at that, which we never did. You just watch that bunch waiting for the school bus some morning and you'll see about *regular* smoking. This night rigmarole is something else. I tell you, they're smoking *joints*, and that's what's making them so crazy these days.

"And another thing," Amanda added as Mrs. Potter prepared to leave, "I have it on the best authority that out of the twelve couples going steady at Cherrybridge high school, ten of them are on the pill. And there's one more couple, right here in town, that should have been. *Now* what do you think the world is coming to?"

As she left, dismayed by both bits of gossip, Giselle Oublette and Tillie Northcutt met her on the post office porch.

This was the time, Mrs. Potter thought, to try to match Northcutt's Harbor's special kind of courage. "It's a beautiful morning," she said, "and Amanda's bleeding heart bush never was prettier. Her bouquet at the funeral was lovely."

That wasn't much, but perhaps in time she would learn to hold up her end of things, too.

Then, as she walked back toward Persy's store, her second errand of the morning, she had time to reflect that gossip was perhaps all that Amanda's remarks might be this time. She was glad she didn't have to decide about the pill, balanced against the problem of a young high school mother. Or father.

As to marijuana being the cause of any local teenage upheaval (she wondered briefly about the blank stares of the previous day), she wasn't so sure about that. From what her own grown children had told her, its effect might be simply that of indifference, lethargy, a lack of ambition. If they're acting—what had Tillie and Giselle said? uppity, difficult? —that doesn't seem to make sense. It's a fad, she thought, and they'll get over it.

She reflected, as she had before, that if marijuana had been the fad at Harrington High, in her long-ago Iowa school days, she might well have been experimenting with the rest. In those days we were protected in another way, she thought. We simply didn't have that kind of spending money. Northcutt's Harbor teenagers, on the other hand, had plenty of ready cash. It came in part from their own fishing, for the boys, perhaps from baby sitting, for the girls, and from great parental generosity in the way of allowances, some of which seemed quite unbelievable to her.

When she reached the store, she found her entrance blocked. Persy's bulk, for once removed from her stool behind the counter, filled the doorway, and there with her in conversation was Alex Whitehead.

"I'll think about it," Persy was saying. "Roddy'll have a say about it, too, don't forget."

As Alex was leaving, Mrs. Potter tried to be cordial. "Say hello to Bets for me," was the best she could manage. "How's she coming with the new architect?"

The Whiteheads, Teedy had told her, were at the moment temporarily established in an enormous and ornate trailer, an arrangement condoned by the restrictive articles of the development only while they chose a building site on their lot and decided on house plans.

"Same old problem," Alex now replied. "She's set on bringing up the furniture from our former place on Long Island. Most of it is simply too big for the new house plans, he keeps telling her."

Once he had left, the scene at Pickett's was much as usual, enlivened only by what were obviously vacationing tourists arriving to spend the Memorial Day weekend somewhere nearby.

Outside the store, there was a large motor home with Wisconsin plates, and beside it two pale, thin men in bright-billed caps, a company name emblazed upon them, and plaid knit slacks.

Inside, two plump middle-aged women with blue hair and red pantsuits were buying postcards. Persy was describing to them her latest back symptoms. The postcard ladies were attempting, in turn and unsuccessfully, to top her with symptoms of their own. Winks was in the back of the store eating something chocolate with a sticky white filling. The CB was crackling.

Over the conversation of the postcard ladies, Mrs. Potter could hear incomprehensible snatches of sound coming from the shelf behind Persy's stool. Occasionally Persy would turn and touch a button on the set, giving a long number and saying, "This is Persy. Come in."

All at once Mrs. Potter caught an intelligible phrase. Someone was saying, "Ask Alice does she want any wrinkles?"

She suddenly knew this was the voice of Lyman, her caretaker. She felt inordinately pleased with herself, just as she had the first time she understood an overheard remark in Spanish in Nogales. Here, as at the ranch, it was a small triumph in learning a new language.

Crackling incoherence again followed the exchange with Lyman in which he had asked Persy to telephone his wife.

Mrs. Potter considered, then rejected, telling Persy to have him bring some wrinkles for her too. These small whelks, known as periwinkles or winkles in other regions, often came up in the lobster traps, and were prized by many in the village as a TV snack, simply boiled, chilled, and marinated in vinegar.

Mrs. Potter herself felt that wrinkles were about on a par with the conchs of Key West. That is to say, rubbery, flavorless, undoubtedly high in protein and low in calories, and as such excellent if you were dieting. To be edible, they were dependent on a really good and savory sauce, along the lines of that of her Happenstance Bay Fish Stew.

As she slid around the blue-haired ladies, who were now pausing over the display of Eileen's craftwork on the corner shelf, Mrs. Potter heard another clear, brief message on the CB behind Persy's vast bulk.

"There! I understood another one! It sounded like Curly. Is there some kind of fisherman lingo, like the truckers and their Smokey Bears?"

Persy had swiveled on her stool and was speaking into the radio. "Ten six, ten twelve," she said quickly. "Ten six, ten twelve."

Then turning laboriously back to face Mrs. Potter, she answered, "Doesn't mean a thing, 'Genia. People use this thing for personal messages all the time. I don't pay it a bit of mind."

"Then I suppose you were just giving your own call letters then, or something of the sort?" Mrs. Potter persisted, out of some curiosity to know how these communications were managed.

"Yes, that's the way you do it," Persy told her. "Sometimes this personal stuff is a terrible bore, but I have to keep the set on all the time and acknowledge the messages. It's part of running the store, to have a place where the men can keep in touch, especially now when so many of the wives are working over to the sardine factory daytimes and aren't home to keep their base stations turned on."

The next speaker had something to say about spark plugs, apparently directing his remarks to another boat, and again Mrs. Potter felt vaguely pleased to be catching a word or two. As she was paying for her purchases, she mentioned this small satisfaction.

"Takes a while, I guess," Persy admitted. "Some days I don't hear anything at all unless I keep it turned up high. You get that way after bad ear trouble, you know—one day deaf as a post, next day you can hear a pin drop. Now my allergies are just terrible today, wouldn't you know? Everything in town is giving off pollen like crazy. Next thing will be the black flies, and even *one* bites me, I swell up like a balloon, have a terrible sore that won't go down for a week. And then the hornets, and then the ants. One sting right after another all summer long from now on. Sometimes I get hives and my throat swells up, it's so bad."

She paused delicately. "The doctor says it's the *hymenoptera* that gives me the worst of it. Some kind of female trouble, sounds like. With that starched-up nurse in the office, 'twasn't seemly to *ask*." She laughed mirthlessly. "Anyway, I keep going. Can't keep a good woman down." She laughed again, as if she had repeated a familiar, but unfailingly amusing, joke.

Mrs. Potter debated, then rejected, the idea of explaining the meaning of the word Persy had found both puzzling and slightly embarrassing. No matter, she decided. Persy knows what she's allergic to, and my defining hymenoptera is only going to sound like putting on airs.

"Roddy's the same way," Persy went on, as she unlocked the register to make change. "We always used to keep a cat or two to be sure there wasn't mice in the store at night, and he loved to devil them until the doctor said they were what was giving him the asthma. Had to have the needle for it once, until we finally called it quits with cats. For all he looks so strong, Roddy's delicate, like all those blue bloods. I finally let him give up weekend hauling, even though I have to keep up his spending money now out of the till."

"I suppose the fishermen are still worrying and wondering about the explosion," Mrs. Potter said, to change the subject. "It must be unsettling, to say the least, to think of being out there at sea with a possible time bomb underneath you."

"Whoever said such a thing as a *bomb*, I'd like to know?" Persy demanded.

"I didn't mean bomb. I'm sorry, Persy, I was just using it as an expression, thinking of all that gasoline and the chance of an explosion any time, for any of them."

Persy, as usual, quickly lost interest in two-sided conversation. "Something Tris did wrong and doesn't want to own up to, that's all it was, most of them think. Or that Coley Cogswell made some kind of fool mistake aboard. Nobody's talking about a *bomb*, 'Genia. Use your head."

123

Rebuked, Mrs. Potter left the store. The Wisconsin tourists, the men in the plaid trousers, tried to engage her in conversation, beginning, "What's it like to live around here, anyway?"

"Nice," was the simple answer, which obviously surprised them, but before they could continue, the two blue-haired wives emerged from the store, and she smiled brightly and left.

Sindhu, who had been glued to her side, sitting with bored patience at every pause in her shopping, now asked to step out a little more briskly.

Of course we don't want to go home yet, she told him, and these few small packages are light and small enough to slip into the carrying bag with the mail.

They headed up the main road, and at the sign saying SHAGS HEAD BY THE SEA they turned down the road to the developments on the west side of the peninsula.

The narrow road was flanked with small woods at first, and then larger trees and a deeper, denser green. Every few hundred yards a bright orange plastic ribbon was tied to a bush or sapling. Lot markers, she judged these to be, of future home sites Teedy had not yet sold or upon which new owners had not yet begun to build. She remembered his saying that he had only one lot left on the waterfront, but possibly there were more still available here in the wooded part.

As if in answer to her thought, a bright small pickup with Teedy at the wheel pulled up beside her and came to a halt.

"Ahoy there, 'Genia. Just the person I'm out looking for. I've been down to your home port. Eileen is having all the gang in for coffee this morning, and when we couldn't raise your sail on the phone she said for me to go down and look around, cast out a lifeline, so to speak, in case you were out with the dog on the beach."

Mrs. Potter managed to raise several weak reasons why she was unable to join "the gang" (which she assumed meant the current residents of Shags Head by the Sea and Northcutt's Harbor Estates) at the Pettengills' for coffee. None of these sounded convincing, even to her, so she brought up the impossibility of coming to a party with Sindhu.

"Nobody's going to mind the pooch. If he doesn't behave, we'll string him to the yardarm."

With this, Teedy looked more closely at the dog sitting courteous and bored at Mrs. Potter's left side.

"You've got a leash for him, I reckon? I see he's running free before the wind, so to speak, and we wouldn't want him to get into any of Eileen's fancywork, of course."

Before she could further marshall her defenses, Mrs. Potter found herself, with the dog, on the car seat beside Teedy, and a few minutes later at the house with the spinning wheel in the picture window.

A quaintly lettered sign in the front yard proclaimed "T. D. PETTENGILL, REAL ESTATE." Beside it was a smaller one, decorated with what appeared to be the silhouette of a deer, flanked by two black and white striped skunks, one larger and one smaller, the script below saying, "Eileen, Teedy, and Ted."

Several cars were in the driveway, among them the Whiteheads' new pickup and the Weidners' slightly battered yellow one. The latter, Mrs. Potter noticed, had its two right wheels on what looked to be freshly graded and seeded lawn.

The Pettengill living room was filled with people sitting in armchairs with embroidered headrests or on the two matching, facing sofas, each covered with a crocheted afghan, or on curved-back mahogany chairs brought in from the dining room. Mrs. Potter had been asked to admire the seats of these chairs before. Each was centered with a machine-worked nautical motif—a sailboat, a sea gull, or an anchor—and Eileen had filled in the needlepoint backgrounds in a rose color.

A long table at one side of the room was covered with a cloth of ecru cotton worked in a heavy cross-stitch pattern with bright blue windmills and tulips. At one end of the table was a large blue and white coffeepot, again with a windmill design, ringed with matching coffee mugs. At the other end was a platter of fancy doughnuts—chocolate, coconut, pink-frosted, orange-frosted, and some covered with pale chopped nuts of indeterminate origin.

Mrs. Potter knew at once that the coffee would be instant,

neither very hot nor very strong, that there would be non-dairy creamer for those taking it "regular," and that the doughnuts—not fresh-made by Sis at the station, not even from yesterday's market at Cherrybridge—had most certainly been bought last week in Bangor, when, as she recalled, Teedy told her they had taken their son Ted to buy a suit for his high school graduation in June.

Remembering this, she spoke to her host. "Your Ted's graduating soon?" she said. "I expect he's made a lot of friends here by now."

Teedy replied with pride. "Part of the regular gang, that boy," he said. "They come here to play pool evenings, or used to before all this homework seems to keep them in at night. Glad to say he's found a good mate in Rodney Pickett. Fine lad, Rodney. Even Herbert Wyncote was telling me the other day what a well-mannered boy Rodney is, for a local, that is."

Mrs. Potter had no opportunity to learn where and why Teedy and Herbert Wyncote had been speaking of Rodney Pickett. It seemed an unlikely meeting and an unlikely topic.

Instead, averting her eyes quickly from the table and keeping Sindhu firmly at her side, she detached herself from Teedy and made the rounds of the room greeting the various guests, all of whom she already knew.

The first couple was the Whiteheads. Alex rose to his feet with heavy grace, and, to her surprise, bowed and kissed her hand. As he bent forward, she felt Sindhu stiffen at her side and she heard him sniff furiously. Either he doesn't like Alex's cologne or he disapproves of hand-kissing, she thought. She tightened her grip on the leash by an almost imperceptible degree, and Sindhu relaxed.

Bettye Whitehead peered suspiciously at Sindhu before she, too, rose uncertainly to her feet and offered a cheek for a glancing embrace. "We're sorry to hear about your neighbors," she said rather loudly, turning to include all the company in her statement. "It always seemed so nice for all you older people to be down there on the Point together. I suppose you'll want to move out now. You could build you a nice new modern house up here, near Alex and I, you know. Teedy still has some good lots.''

No response seemed possible, and Mrs. Potter proceeded around the room, at this point greeted by her hostess as she entered from the kitchen with a second coffeepot. As always, Eileen walked unsteadily, an egg supported on toothpick legs and very high heels.

Mrs. Potter managed a careful, gingerly sort of handshake, fearful that she might upset an uncertain balance and, with it, the pot of coffee.

"Don't bother about me," she implored her hostess. "I'm sure I know everyone here, and Sindhu and I will just make our rounds and say hello. Incidentally, I'm sorry about the dog, but Teedy insisted, and he was afraid he might damage the new seeding if I left him outside."

"Quite all right," Eileen assured her nervously. "I suppose he's completely housebroken?"

This proved another remark Mrs. Potter could not bring herself to answer, other than with a strained smile and a nod. *Housebroken!* Sindhu von Warzenberg, winner of every obedience trial he'd ever entered, schooled for her and with her by one of the best handlers in the country! And besides that, a natural gentleman of impeccable manners. Housebroken, indeed.

She went on to the next couple. Apparently people had been seated as they arrived, two by two, and they remained in those positions instead of moving about. Couples talked across at other couples over intervening small tables and stands covered with painted china bric-a-brac; with crocheted dolls holding folded paper napkins in their pocketed Bo-Peep skirts; with decorated clamshell ashtrays; and with a great many turtles, owls, cats, and rabbits made from glued-together polished beach pebbles and stones in varying sizes.

She was pleased to see her new friends, the Colamarias. Like the Whiteheads, they were temporarily established in a large trailer while they were waiting for their house to be built. It will go up in no time at all, they kept assuring their neighbors, since it was to be one of the new modular structures, partly prefabricated, recently popular in the area. They were

127

awaiting delivery of their chosen split-level model, the Alhambra.

The Whiteheads, Teedy had said, were conferring daily with their Bangor architect about house plans. It was clear he was not going to rush them into speedy compliance with the development covenants about trailer occupancy as only a brief and temporary measure. The Whiteheads were very important people, Teedy had told them all privately. Alex had been a big shot with a big real estate investment firm, with offices in New York.

Al Colamaria, on the other hand, might not receive any special concessions. Fine, worthy people, Teedy had assured the other residents of the community. Well fixed, paid cash for their lot, *quiet*. Why, you scarcely saw Mrs. Colamaria— Victoria, Tory, that is—out of the trailer from one week to the next. A lot of wop relations came up on the weekends from New Jersey or Long Island or someplace, but they were quiet too. Quiet dressers, no commotion. The men played *bocce* ball, or whatever they called it, in a spot they leveled off there beside the trailer, and the women and children stayed pretty much off by themselves.

Fine people, Teedy had repeated, salt of the earth, and I want everybody to be friendly to them and nobody using words like wop or dago.

Mrs. Potter greeted them. "Did I see you digging clams the other day, Tory?" she asked. "And are you two as crazy about steamers as I am?"

Both of the Colamarias seemed younger, smaller, darker than the other residents of the community, and Tory appeared shy. "I do ours steamed home-style," she said, "you know, *Vongoli Siciliana*. I don't know if you'd like that, but Al does."

"My dear, I'm going to get back to you on that," Mrs. Potter told her. "I'm sure it's marvelous, whatever it is."

"Just like your steamers, only add a little garlic, a little oil, some parsley in the bottom of the pot, under the clams," Tory said. "Not worth writing a recipe for, but I'll tell you how I do it, any time you say. The children like it."

"Twenty-one grandchildren now, did I tell you?" Al said

proudly. Tory, plump and richly colored as a summer rose, smiled and started to speak again. "Enough now, Victoria," he admonished her, "Mrs. Potter has other friends to speak with."

Beyond the Colamarias was the pair that a sociologist—one who might have called Rodney the "dominant juvenile male" of the younger community—would have termed the "dominant couple" of this group, at least until the recent arrival of the Whiteheads.

William West Van Dusen, Colonel, retired, U. S. Army, and his wife, Dorrie, herself the daughter of an elderly retired army officer, lived in Maine to be near the old general, now in a retirement home in Cherrybridge. Bill Van Dusen was a physical fitness buff and a jogger, and Mrs. Potter and Sindhu had first made his acquaintance on the peninsula roads and lanes as he trotted past them.

Adaptable, indomitable, as all good army people seemed to be, they had quickly fitted into the life of both communities, both that of the development colony and of the separate, original Northcutt's Harbor social structure as well. They were active in the church. Dorrie was on the school board and Bill was chairman of the town planning board. They assumed, and were accepted in, a natural position of leadership wherever they went.

Several other couples lined the seats around the room, and Mrs. Potter greeted them in turn, with only one fudge on first names she could not remember. She hoped it was the first time she had exclaimed, "How nice to see the Larsons! How *are* you both?"

Among the group were two elderly sisters Teedy called his "early settlers," since theirs was the first house in the development. These two, whom Mrs. Potter privately termed the "pot ladies," raised houseplants and did macramé, presumably for the single purpose of providing support for the hanging plants that filled their windows and a great deal of the living area of their house. Walking from one room to another presented the challenge of an obstacle course. They were extremely generous in pressing small plants and macramé slings upon their friends and in donating these in quantity to every charity bazaar and church rummage sale, where they were always a best-selling item.

There were Herbie and Jean Allgood, who had owned and run a chain of small bakeries in western Maine and New Hampshire before they came to Northcutt's Harbor Estates to retire. Mrs. Potter repeated a mental note to herself to discuss French bread with Herbie sometime soon. There must be a trick to the art known only (or *possible* only) to commercial bakers, she thought, since her years of research with home breadmakers had never produced what she thought of as really *good* French bread.

After Bettye's public statement, there had been no further mention of Harvard's funeral and the Cogswells' death at sea. Most of this group had but slight acquaintance with them. And, Mrs. Potter thought, the constraint was part of an unspoken agreement. This group of retirees may have decided that by coming to Maine they could also retire from the knowledge of human mortality, including their own.

Carter Ansdale was not among the gathering, she noted. Perhaps he was questing for more local weavers. He always seemed to be on the move, buying antiques or modern work of local artisans, rushing about in his van or else flying off to Atlanta with crates of newly acquired treasures.

At the end of her tour, Margo and Chuck Weidner rose to give her an affectionate embrace, and their eyes met in shared sorrow with the unspoken recollection of their last evening with the Cogswells. Gratefully she accepted a seat on the sofa beside them, and, less gratefully, a cup of the warm, weak coffee, pleading, as the doughnuts were passed, an unfortunate inability to eat another thing after an enormous late breakfast (dismissing her recollection of the uneaten oatmeal).

Sindhu settled with a sigh at her feet, assuming what was often described as his pharaoh position: on his belly, back haunches tucked neatly beneath him, head erect, and his front forepaws crossed in a posture of quiet elegance. *Housebroken!*

As she sat, alternately in conversation with the Weidners on her left and the Allgoods on her right, she found that Alex Whitehead was pulling up a footstool to make himself part of their small group. Before he sat she had a glimpse of the upholstered stool seat, a hooked pattern depicting a large owl on a small branch, black and brown on sulphur yellow.

"I know what you're begging for, with your paws crossed like that," Alex told Sindhu. "Sit up and say *please*, now, that's a good boy!"

Sindhu stiffened. He looked up at Mrs. Potter, who put her hand firmly on his head. He sniffed again, then gazed straight ahead into space.

A chunk of frosted doughnut was dangled before him. "Sit, boy, sit, and get your goody." The man's voice began as a command and ended an entreaty.

"What's the matter with him?" he queried somewhat testily. "I thought these dogs were trained to obey. Or doesn't he know what a doughnut is?"

"I'm sorry, Alex, you were nice to offer him a treat," Mrs. Potter said apologetically, "but he's been trained never to eat away from home, in his own spot and from his own dish. We even have a hard time with him at the vet's. It was part of his schooling before he came to me. It's actually a wonderful protection for a dog, you see, against dog thieves or the occasional crank who decides to poison every dog in the neighborhood if his garbage can is knocked over. I assure you Sindhu doesn't mean to be bad-mannered, and I'm sure he'd like me to say thanks just the same."

Alex looked only slightly mollified. "Why does he cross his paws like that, anyway? Makes him look like some kind of a statue."

"If that pose bothers you, Alex," Chuck Weidner put in, "you ought to see the one Margo calls 'chairman of the board.' He sits in his own special chair at 'Genia's, the only one he's allowed on, and he sits straight up, with his back well braced. Then he crosses his paws over his chest and looks straight ahead, very dignified, very important, very rich."

"Exactly like you used to look when you were chairman of Landinvest International, darling." Bettye had joined them, and she ran her coral fingertips through her husband's thick, dark, well-cut hair. "We've got to be going now, sorry to remind you, Alex. *'Bye,* everybody. Don't you forget now,

'Genia, have Teedy show you that last shorefront lot of his and then you can move up here where you'll have some of we younger people around to look after you.''

Mrs. Potter was again speechless. She considered the White-heads her contemporaries in age, and she knew with fair certainty that this was true of the other development residents, either her age or older. The possible exception might be the slightly younger Colamarias.

At any rate, the Whiteheads' departure seemed a chance to rise, too, to make her own farewells.

The Van Dusens, at the other end of the room, hurriedly approached their hostess with the apparent aim of being the first to leave, as was their due according to rank. They won over the Whiteheads by a hair.

Refusing with thanks Teedy's repeated insistence that he wanted to drive her back home, Mrs. Potter found it difficult to separate her hand from the plump fingers of her host. ''I want to talk to you, 'Genia. Stick around for a minute while everybody leaves, and at least let me walk you down the gangplank, won't you?''

In spite of the unintended implication of Teedy's question, Mrs. Potter found herself being walked halfway back to the cottage. Teedy's short legs stumped alongside her, and his best sales technique poured into her ears. The gist of it all was this:

One, 'Genia wouldn't want just any cheap developer to get hold of the Point. Might be a trailer park, and you know when that happens you've lost the ball game. At best maybe house lots, four to an acre, all those kids in school and taxes going up, crime, more police, more garbage collection.

Two, 'Genia knew what a high-class operation, what a tight ship, so to speak, he, Teedy Pettengill, could run. Couldn't she just see from that gang at the house this morning—friends of hers, all of them—that these were the kind of folks who ought to be coming to the peninsula? That's the reason he had asked Eileen to get everybody together with her there today, so she'd realize this.

Three, her help could be mighty big in persuading Persy

and Herbert Wyncote to sell him their property, and he might even be able to make it worth her while if she did.

Mrs. Potter interrupted. How did he know about the new owners? she asked. Public information, he assured her hastily.

Four, and *important*, he wanted 'Genia to know he had plenty of horsepower backing him on this, plenty of wind in his sails. Alex might even bankroll the whole project.

Did 'Genia know what a big shot Alex really was? It wasn't out yet and she wasn't to breathe a word, but he, Teedy, knew for a fact that Alex might buy control of the Cherrybridge Savings Bank.

Now that's the kind of muscle he, Teedy, had behind him in this. It wasn't going to be any fly-by-night operation. And if they needed any more of the old *do-re-mi*, he'd just found out from talking to good old Al Colamaria this morning that *he* had an uncle who was a big man in the real estate business. Had a hand in opening up Atlantic City to the casinos, big-time stuff. Anyway, maybe Al could lay hands on a nice piece of change for that land. Said he'd like to have it, cash on the barrel head. Either way, there was plenty of money.

And last, and it wasn't, he added, any of his business (tired of the little man's importunings and shocked by this discussion less than a week after Cole and Regina's death and the day after Harvard's funeral, Mrs. Potter very nearly stated her complete agreement to this), he, Teedy, couldn't help but think Bets had put it pretty well: Down there on the Point was no place for a woman alone, now was it? Especially with Harvard and the Cogswells gone, old as they were.

How he'd like to sum it up was like this: Why didn't she sell him her little strip, then pull oars together with him getting Persy's piece and Herbert's? No problem about that little formality of her deed restriction—he'd iron that out in a minute.

She'd come out ahead on the deal, and he knew where she could rent a nice trailer, just like the Whiteheads', in fact. That way she could live right on her new lot in Shags Head by the Sea while she put up a spiffy new modern house. It made sense, didn't it?

It made sense like a hole in the head.

That was the only retort that occurred to her, and Mrs. Potter kept repeating it to herself, from time to time, in silent outrage after her return to the cottage.

She fed Sindhu in his place by the stove, and as always gave thanks for the training that kept him safe from poisoners and from frosted doughnuts and from bad-mannered begging at the table.

She searched for activity, in part to try to contain her fury.

How could Teedy Pettengill have dragooned her into coming to that dreadful coffee party, then have had the gall to admit that he had arranged it all in order to talk her into some kind of real estate shenanigan?

And not a word of sorrow about Harvard's death, not a word about the loss of the Cogswells to the community in which he, Teedy, had been making a good living for himself now for some years.

The utter *presumption* of the little man!

A walk along the rocks above the water helped, as it always did. She wrote to the friend with the ailing sister. She began a double-crostic saved from the previous Sunday's *New York Times,* but it seemed to lack Thomas Middleton's usual wit and precision. She read a few pages of a new Dick Francis mystery novel, then turned to an old favorite instead. Was Lord Peter Wimsey one of Rodney's heroes, she wondered, or was he too young to have heard of Dorothy Sayers? She turned on the six-thirty news and poured her usual before-dinner-drink—this time another tot of Harvard's favorite rum.

Could rum go flat? This small glassful was tasteless.

Finally, she set out her supper, finding nothing more inspiring than a dish of cold canned pears, a glass of milk, and a few limp graham crackers.

And finally it was again morning, and Memorial Day.

Shortly after dawn she drove to the little cemetery behind the church. Trowel in hand, she carried the three bright coral geraniums from her kitchen windowsill in a carton to Harvard's grave. She had just finished setting them into the raw earth when Tillie arrived with a flat of purple petunias. They worked together quietly, and then stood back and agreed that the combination made a good show. Tillie gathered up the wilted funeral floral pieces and put them in her own small car. There seemed nothing more to be said, so they left as separately and quietly as they had come.

14

That was a miserable kind of breakfast, Mrs. Potter told herself two days later, at least three hours after she had prepared and eaten, with great lack of interest, a badly poached egg on toast. She knew that when the bottom of the yolk breaks just as you're trying to lift it out of the simmering water, you really should throw it out and start again. Except that by then the bottom of the pan is slightly roughened with cooked egg white from the first one, and the water is full of what the Chinese would call egg drops from the broken yolk, and it is just too much trouble to empty the pan, wash it out, and start heating water all over again. Easier to eat a depressing egg with a sunken center and forget the whole thing.

Now, much later, she was suddenly hungry, and she realized she was no more likely to starve to death with sorrow over Harvard and Coley and Regina than over any of the few earlier sorrows and bereavements of her life. She would eat a proper meal and then she would do some honest work.

She even knew what needed to be done. She would cut down that swath of alder thicket that blurred her view to the north. Cutting alder was a never-ending task, for its wily roots were everywhere. The only herbicides she knew to be effective seemed rife with ominous hints of—what was that place in Italy that had the disastrous spill?—and of headlines screaming ARIZONA WOMAN POISONS MAINE VILLAGE.

At least when you cut alder back sharply to the ground (and it cut very easily with a good pair of loppers, besides which the cuttings were light and unprickly and easy to pile and

136

stack for a later removal), it took four or five years to resume the height at which it again spoiled the view.

Food and work. Just what she needed. Summoning Sindhu (why hadn't she given *him* the treat of that badly poached egg in his dinner?) she took off in her small red car for Tris and Sis's, up the peninsula road and past the post office.

Several cars and trucks were parked at the side of the building, well out of the way of the gas pumps and the garage area on the left. Seeing the sign OFFICIAL INSPECTION STATION reminded her of her memo to herself and she pulled up before the open garage door.

"Have you time to do me now, Tris, while I have a cup of coffee?" she asked the man in the battered aluminum deck chair.

Slowly unfolding his considerable height, Harvard's nephew rose to his feet. "Glad to, 'Genia. Whatever it is I'm doing, I haven't got started yet. Registration in the glove compartment?"

He took her place in the driver's seat. "Everything all right with you down there on the Point? Teedy's been at us trying to find out who has the say about disputing Harvard's will, and I have a feeling he's been hammering on you some, too."

"He has some ridiculous idea about my selling out and moving, but I'm sure you know I wouldn't think of it. And I certainly wouldn't think of trying to influence you and Sis, if you do have any thoughts about what happens to Harvard's house and land on the Bite."

"Wouldn't do any good if you did. So many Northcutts to inherit, they'd never get together on what to do, and anyway we all understand right enough what he was trying to do when he left the place to Persy. No way we're going to argue against what Uncle Harvard wanted. Of course, I sort of wish he'd left it to the Maine Heritage, myself. But he knew his mind, and Teedy Pettengill can go jump in the bay as far as I'm concerned."

"The Heritage would have been a wonderful idea, Tris. I think Harvard would have wanted that if he hadn't thought he had another obligation. I wonder if he ever talked with that lawyer from Augusta. You know, the one who's on the board of the foundation, or whatever it is? The two of them were good friends. They used to go duck hunting together."

With this, Mrs. Potter went into the smaller building attached to the garage, under a large sign proclaiming LOBSTERS LIVE AND BOILED and a smaller one saying COFFEE—LUNCH—WE MAKE OUR OWN DOUGHNUTS.

The room inside was clean and bare except for four square pine tables, each with four straight old-fashioned chairs, and a long counter with stools along one side. The stool seats were of red plastic and most of these had been patched with strips of gray plastic tape. Behind the counter a plump middle-aged woman in a pink two-piece pantsuit was filling a coffee maker, and over her head hung a display of hand-lettered signs showing the specials of the day.

"Too early for lunch, 'Genia," Sis announced without turning her head, a neat cap of close-cut gray. "Saw you drive in. The chicken pie isn't out yet, and I'm a little late getting the potatoes cooked for the fish chowder—that's the other special. Want a hamburger?"

"What I need is a decent breakfast, Sis. What I started out with was a disaster, and I've just decided I'm hungry, *really* hungry. It seems to me I haven't had anything you'd put in front of a dog for a couple of days, at least."

"Well now, that's easy. I've got a nice little slice of ham and Tris brought eggs fresh from Edna this morning. You just leave it to me. Unless you feel like some blueberry pancakes? I've got the frozen."

"Ham and eggs sounds wonderful, thanks. And while you're fixing it, a cup of that coffee would save my life."

As she sipped the fragrant, freshly made coffee, Mrs. Potter surveyed the other occupants of the counter stools. Nearest her was the blue-jeaned young couple she had seen at the baked bean supper, and she smiled hello.

The young man, new to the village, she knew as Jim Markham. James Russell Markham III, she had learned from the day she had written a check to him in payment for some painting he had done at the cottage. Jim was tall, blond, and his long hair was held back by a rubber band in a ponytail—to keep it out of his eyes and, she presumed, also out of the paint. With him was the pretty dark-haired girl she had seen with him before but whom she had not yet met.

"Mrs. Potter, I'd like to have you meet my lady, Anne-Marie. Anne-Marie Loeb."

"Jim told me about you, Mrs. Potter, and your making coffee for the boys when they were there painting. It's nice to meet you. And if you need any more painting done, I'm getting pretty good at it, too, although I'm not as fast as Jim."

A few minutes' conversation as Jim and Anne-Marie finished their coffee revealed several interesting facts. Anne-Marie had gone to the same college as Mrs. Potter's older daughter, although more recently. Going out for coffee and one of Sis's blueberry muffins was a special treat because they were saving their money for a hi-fi. They had met the previous summer as volunteers at a camp for underprivileged children and had fallen in love with Maine (and, clearly, with each other) there. They were both mad about cooking and they took turns on a weekly basis. Right now they were concentrating on regional Down East dishes and cooking their way straight through all the old cookbooks they could find.

"Then maybe you can tell me about lobster pie!" Mrs. Potter exclaimed. "A friend of mine asked about it recently and I didn't know a thing to tell her."

"I wish we could help," Anne-Marie said, "but mostly we're sticking to dishes like beans and cornbread, good cheap Yankee food. Lobster isn't in our budget very often."

"If we manage a splurge, we'll let you know," Jim said. "I'm the pastry expert."

As they left, two newcomers entered and, with emphatic and friendly greetings, took their places beside Mrs. Potter.

"Dill, Dorrie, how nice to see you again!" she told them, albeit with still-rankling memories of the Pettengill coffee party the previous Saturday. "You'll forgive me, I know, if I begin to eat at once, now that Sis has brought this wonderful food. I am starving."

The rosy slice of ham, its edges just sufficiently charred, was flanked with two plump-yolked eggs, sunny side up. There was a hot crisp mound of hashed brown potatoes, creamy on the inside and well laced with onion, and hot buttered whole-wheat toast. There was a separate little saucer of homemade plum jelly. None of those little paper squares here at Sis's, with their infuriating plastic covers and their tasteless contents. Sis spooned out a scoop of her own preserves or jelly, whatever kind happened to be open. If you didn't eat it all, she scooped it back into another jar of mixed fruits and juices she saved as moistening for her mincemeat, as a proper Maine housewife should.

Mrs. Potter ate hungrily. She had just enough room for another cup of coffee, she decided, but not for the sugary homemade doughnut she had earlier promised herself when she saw the stack on the wooden spindle under the glass cover behind the counter.

While she drank the coffee, the Van Dusens extracted her promise to come to see them some day soon—the kind of invitation and acceptance, with no date set, that counts as a pleasant and meaningless assurance of mutual goodwill.

She reached the post office a few minutes later, in her newly inspected car, to find Alex Whitehead coming down the steps. Seeing him was another uncomfortable reminder of Teedy and Eileen's coffee party.

"Carter Ansdale has been trying to call you," he told her. "Got me on the CB finally and asked me to relay a message. He had to make a quick trip to Atlanta and expects to be back at the Bangor airport tonight—said he'd call you from there if it wasn't too late, otherwise tomorrow."

Mrs. Potter thanked Alex, briefly reflecting on what seemed to her the casual speed with which Carter commuted to Atlanta and back; she then went in to collect her mail.

"We no more than got the church cleaned up after Harvard on Friday," Tillie was saying, "then regular morning worship on Sunday. Good thing they're having it up to their own church in Cherrybridge."

"Memorial service for the Cogswells tomorrow," Amanda explained. "Olympia has been trying to call you about it."

"My Louis, he still thinks there is something crazy about that boat blow-up," Giselle said. "He says Tris Northcutt does good work, but who knows?"

"Well, no help to either of them now to find out," Amanda told them. "They're gone. So's Harvard. He left his boat to Tommy, you know. Not all he left, either. Tommy's going to be an early daddy himself, come fall. You invited to the showers yet, 'Genia? You're going to be. Combination bridal and stork. Both mothers giving one—Sis and Alice."

"Well, that's all *right*," Tillie said defensively. "All the girls threw themselves at Harvard, and you ought to remember that well, Amanda. He just happened to end up with Sarbelle Birdson, and we all know all of their women turned mean after they were thirty, so maybe a good thing she died early. Remember old Grammy, taught us all how to make brown bread? Edna's always quick to say she's just a Birdson by marriage."

"Who's to say Janine won't make Tommy a good wife, if that's what we're talking about?" Mrs. Potter asked. "He's going to be a good lobster fisherman, anyway, so Harvard told me, or otherwise he wouldn't have left him his boat."

"Good start for a young man," Amanda said in summation. "He'll do fine, and if prices keep up and he has a few good seasons, he can probably save enough for a new Fiberglas one from the boat yard in a couple of years."

From the post office, Mrs. Potter continued her morning errands with a stop at the store.

An improbable trio lifted their heads as she entered. Persy was, as usual, overflowing on her stool behind the counter. Beside her stood Teedy Pettengill, in checked flannel shirt and high rubber boots, looking too hot on this fair summer morning. Bending over the counter between them, papers spread out beneath his hands, was Herbert Wyncote.

Herbert was the first to speak. "Good to see you, Eugenia. Nancy wrote to thank you for your dinner, I think? And we both appreciated your note about Aunt Regina and Cole."

Before she could reply, he spoke quickly, gathering up his papers. "Now I just came over this morning to see Virgil about continuing as caretaker for the Roost, and I wanted to get Persy's and Teedy's advice about a site for a new septic tank, which the place may need," he said. "Of course we may not move to the Point, since all our friends are at

Millstone, but if we do we'll need more room. And in the meantime, of course, the house shouldn't be exposed to vandals.''

Mrs. Potter sent her greetings to Nancy, remembered to inquire about the progress of the house alterations at Millstone, said hello to Persy, and offered Teedy only a slight lift of the chin—the barest acknowledgment of his presence consistent with common courtesy.

She turned toward the refrigerator case, noticing as she did the incongruous appearance of the two men as they left the store. Teedy in his boots was rolling along in his version of a sailor's swagger, and she stifled a smile as she remembered would-be cowboys at the ranch in their attempts to walk bowlegged. He was dwarfed by the tall, bronzed good looks and long legs of Regina's nephew in white tennis shorts, an open-necked shirt with the obligatory emblem, and striped sneakers.

In the refrigerator case, she did not see the fresh crabmeat she had stopped to buy. Several of the village women provided fresh-picked crabmeat in round half-pound plastic containers, decorating the tops with a pinwheel of pink crab claw meat that looked very pretty through the clear plastic lids.

Instructed by a veteran of the art, a friend who assured her it was as easy as shelling peanuts, she had herself tried at one time to learn to pick out the meat of the fresh-cooked crabs herself. An hour later, surveying her small bowl of crabmeat and her own sore, lacerated fingers, she had decided that this was a skill she did not want to pursue. She was delighted that Persy maintained a dependable supply from the village.

"I don't see any crabmeat today, Persy," she called across the store.

"Be in later, 'Genia," was the answer. "I've got a promise of a fresh batch from Ruth Bewley by three-four o'clock."

"Save me one, then, will you? I'll be back later." Heartened by Sis's good breakfast, Mrs. Potter had found her normal good appetite was back. Cold fresh crabmeat with mayonnaise for her own dinner was suddenly appealing.

Then, remembering Cole's last request to her, she tried to

engage Persy in conversation, difficult as it was now proving to be over the continuing noise of the radio.

"How's Rodney these days?" she began. "With school almost out, I expect he'll be lobstering?"

"Now 'Genia, you know Roddy is not too strong, healthy as he may look to you. Takes after me in that, and you'd never guess what *I've* been through this week."

Interrupting quickly, Mrs. Potter tried to keep the subject on track. "So I expect he'll be helping you around the store and then, like all the young people, having some vacation fun with the rest of their crowd? You know young Laurie Cutler, don't you?"

Before she could advance the cause of Laurie's acceptance into the local group, which had been her uncle's benevolent concern, Persy spoke out sharply. "That young whipstitch! In here most afternoons after school to get something or other, since she says she gets the supper for the two of them, her and Olympia. 'Good afternoon, Mrs. Pickett,' she'll say. Some high-hat, I call it."

Baffled, Mrs. Potter persisted. "She seems a nice child to me, and I just thought you might want to know that Cole was concerned about her. He thought she might be lonely here, coming as an outsider. And I expect she was brought up to say 'good afternoon' to older people, instead of 'hi, Persy,' or nothing at all."

"Be that as it may, she acts uppity, and I'm not all that old," Persy said. "I just say she's part of what's wrong with Roddy these days and I keep on telling him she's not good enough for him."

Uncomprehending, Mrs. Potter continued to probe. "You mean you think his ancestry is better than Laurie's?" she asked incredulously.

Persy sighed, pink and white cheeks rippling behind the counter. "Addie always said he was what he called 'of noble birth.' Maybe so, maybe not," she admitted. "Addie was always one for a good story if it suited his purpose. Anyway, anybody with an eye in his head can see Roddy's got blue blood in him. Right now he's at me for money for a magazine ad he wants to answer, a place where they look you up. I told him he didn't have to bother with that stuff. Who needs it?''

"Well, you can't blame the boy for being interested in that side of his family," Mrs. Potter began, again to be cut off by Persy's continuing complaint.

"All I can say is that he's off his feed these days, *spleeny*. Mooning around about that Laurie Cutler, skinny little witch just like her mother, talking about all that English hootenanny. Won't eat, even when I fix him a good supper like last night. Bologna, frozen french fries, the special de luxe pizza from the freezer I baked for him with my own hands. He wouldn't touch a thing except the ice cream and chocolate sauce."

Persy, for the first time Mrs. Potter remembered, was talking about something other than the weather and her own ailments, talking with what seemed a very human need to communicate. She went on. "Then they pile on all this homework on the kids, up at the high school. Every night he has to go out and study with some of the kids, Skip Cooney or whoever, and he's just plain done in by the time he gets home."

Again, Persy sighed heavily. "It's always been only the two of us," she said, "so maybe I do give in to him too much. Right now it's new clothes, a fancy tennis racket, hair styled and blow-dried in Ellsworth. All so he can get in with that Millstone crowd. Regina's nephew Herbert is putting fancy ideas in his head. Tennis club! Sailboats! Rich summer kids!''

In spite of her scornful tone, Persy was clearly gloating at the thought of her son's joining the world of the privileged young of Millstone. "He just has a natural taste for that society stuff," she explained.

She then returned to the subject of Laurie. "Roddy never was one for girls, though, for which I've been thankful. It kills me to think what he'll learn from that stuck-up little hussy."

Mrs. Potter tried to be sympathetic. "At least you needn't worry too much if he has a teenage crush," she said. "That's one thing they're pretty sure to get over. And it's natural enough for a good-looking youngster to take a sudden interest in clothes.''

As if to indicate the end of the conversation Persy swiveled on her stool and pointedly turned up the volume of the CB.

"I'll be back later for the crabmeat, then," Mrs. Potter said, and left the store.

Cutting alder was hot work, satisfying, therapeutic. Sindhu sat nearby, in his favorite sunny spot near the patch of *Rosa rugosa,* and alternately slept and considered the gulls in the blue sky overhead.

It was after three before Mrs. Potter remembered her earlier request for crabmeat. If she did not appear after she had asked Persy to save a carton for her she might as well forget about getting any the next time. Persy would clearly consider this order a special favor, to be duly appreciated.

She had been working too hard to realize how warm the afternoon had become. First day of June, she suddenly realized. Tossing aside the thin jacket she had worn for the alder cutting (she'd shower and change out of old jeans and T-shirt when she got back), she picked up Sindhu's leash and her stout carrying bag and left on foot for the store.

Before they reached the lane which turned off to the right toward the lobster pound, Mrs. Potter could see up ahead on the main road ahead of her three figures, and two of the big wide-tired, three-wheeled motorbikes—ATVs, she thought they were called. Two of the figures wore white helmets. She assumed they must be boys heading for their after-school jobs at the lobster pound, where they would cut up bait and fill bait bags for those fishermen who elected to buy their bait ready-packaged instead of filling their own string bags.

Remembering vaguely which boys owned three-wheelers, she guessed that the helmeted figures might be Orrin Bewley, son of the master of the Grange, and Skip Cooney, Doc's son.

Clearly the other with them, she now saw, was Rodney Pickett. There was no mistaking his added height, or the deferential bearing with which the two helmeted boys appeared to be facing him.

As she passed the pound road, she heard the roar of the two motorbikes as they started up, coming toward her, leaving the tall boy behind.

With one hand already raised to wave, Mrs. Potter saw that the speed of the bikes was increasing. As they drew almost abreast of the spot where she and Sindhu were standing, both bikes swerved sharply on the broken and pock-marked black surface of the road. In a burst of speed, both riders, their adolescent faces intent and unsmiling beneath their white crash helmets, aimed their enormous front wheels directly at her and at the dog by her side.

Startled, then terrified, she jerked Sindhu with her in a stumbling, lurching sidestep into the bramble-filled ditch at the side of the road.

The roaring bikes went on. As they turned down the narrow road toward the pound, the air was full of a raucous, jeering sound, audible above the roar of the motors. "Yaa-aaaah!"

Sindhu pulled his leash free from her scratched and bleeding hand. Lips raised, teeth bared, he growled a low and certain preface to attack. As he started after the motorbikes, his muscles tensed for the chase.

Mrs. Potter's command was instant, emphatic. "Sindhu, *come!*"

Quivering, the low menace in his throat continuing, the Weimaraner returned to her side.

"Good dog," she praised him. Then, trembling herself, she stroked the sleek gray coat, as much to calm her own turmoil as that of her dog.

At last, sucking a bloody scratch on one bare forearm, she stepped up out of the weeds and the bramble of the wild rose bush in which she had taken her sudden refuge.

She went on to the store. Sindhu, although obedient as always, was watchful at her side. His wary sidelong glances and his occasional nervous tug at the leash showed that his agitation had not abated.

With a piece of spit-moistened tissue she wiped at a dried bloody scratch newly discovered on the other bare, tanned elbow.

She still intended to pick up that crabmeat from Persy.

Later, on her way home, the carrying bag seeming uncommonly heavy with the weight of the single small carton, it was a relief to pass the lobster pound road and to enter her own special lane, a right-of-way that no longer led to any habitation but her own safe and beloved cottage.

There were more wildflowers in blossom in the sunny, open stretches along the road before she turned into her small patch of woods, and she tried to concentrate on counting them, as she had not had time to do the afternoon of her return from Harvard's funeral.

There was pink clover, and both pink and blue lupine, with a great many intershadings between. Hawkweed, which she called Indian paintbrush in the west, was both yellow and red-orange. Wild daylilies. The near-magenta lambkill she had remarked on the other day. Daisies, just beginning now. Apple blossoms on wild trees, relics of forgotten orchards or grown from seeds dropped by the birds. Buttercups. The pink bells of a few blueberry blossoms. Wild columbine in three colors—the deep purple her favorite. Wild flags, more deep blue than purple, like those she had picked as a last tribute of love for Harvard.

She stopped counting, her eyes now blurring with tears, stopped even looking or seeing, and Sindhu led her the last stretch of the way, over the last steps of the small lane soft with pine needles to the door of the cottage.

15

Olympia had telephoned the evening before. Mrs. Potter in turn, at Olympia's request, had telephoned Carter Ansdale. Thank you, she had told him, I'm glad you're back and I knew you would want to be at the church too, tomorrow, but I'll drive myself. I have errands to do afterward.

It was Wednesday, the second day in June. The memorial service would be at the small brown church in Cherrybridge, its building newer and less impressive than either the Congregational or the Baptist churches, since the Episcopalians had a late start in New England.

The event itself put a stamp of finality and authenticity upon Coley and Regina's death at sea. After examining the floating wreckage, the Coast Guard, so Lyman Cooney had told Mrs. Potter, had found only that an explosion had occurred. In view of the apparent violence of the blast, the two occupants of the boat had undoubtedly been killed instantly.

The *Cog's Wheel* had gone down in deep water, too deep to bring the motor or tanks to the surface for examination. It was thought by some that there had been faulty work on the recent installation of new gas tanks, but Tristram Northcutt, at the garage, insisted that he had done the work himself and that it had been done right. The bodies had not been found, and it was likely, at that depth and after this length of time, that they would have a permanent grave in the Atlantic.

These official findings, and now the service at the church, made the accident a part of Cherrybridge history. It was an event that would have profound consequences on the life of the town.

The Cogswell enterprises, known as C. R. Cogswell & Son, of which Cole had been "Son," were the biggest single employer in the community that thought of Cherrybridge as its "shire town." This phrase had such an archaic, old-English sound that, when Mrs. Potter first heard it, she could not believe how commonly the ancient term was still used in present-day Maine. Later she came to realize that Cherrybridge was shire town not only as a center of stores, services, medical care, and entertainment (two small restaurants and a larger one and one movie theater) but also as the seat of the town government.

There was a small, rather down-at-the-heels inn called the Sportsmans Lodge, which had been popular in the earlier days when the Metoosic ran clear and unpolluted and was considered one of the great Atlantic salmon streams of the coast. In the past few years, as the town had learned more about water pollution in a drive sparked by Cole's own expensive changes at his blueberry canning and freezing plants, the salmon were returning. Each year more and more came back to the Metoosic to spawn.

Each year, too, a few more impassioned salmon fishermen came to the Sportsmans Lodge, enough, finally, to tempt a new young owner to take over from the rather dispirited former management.

Both of the Cogswells would be deeply missed in Cherrybridge. Regina had been the quiet force behind the excellence of the town library. Cole was known to be a just and fair employer.

In addition, the Cogswell gardens made Cherrybridge a place of arresting beauty and color. Passing tourists on Route 1 found themselves slowing to admire each season's new display. Sometimes they were rewarded as well by the sight of Regina, always in white, leaning on her silver-headed cane and directing the changes that kept two experienced old gardeners busy throughout the year.

In a more personal way, a few, a special few, were going to miss the Cogswell evenings of bridge, following a good dinner by Frances in the big old-fashioned formal dining room, and the chance of hearing a new limerick composed for the occasion by their host.

It was not surprising, therefore, that the small church was overflowing for the memorial service. Rustic in its architecture and appointments, the structure appeared to reflect more of the deep woods and wilderness of the surrounding country than it did the clean, white, clapboarded look of Cherrybridge itself.

Mrs. Potter found herself squeezed between people she did not know and had not even seen before. Clarence had given up on any attempt to determine the seating. His problem, instead, was how many people would have to hear the words of the service through the open doors, flung wide to the sunny, fragrant early-summer afternoon.

The words were solemn and final. "And we commit their bodies to the deep."

Mrs. Potter promised herself to look up one psalm and read it again when she got home. The verses began, "If I take the wings of the morning, and remain in the uttermost parts of the sea."

She had seen Olympia and Laurie's straight narrow backs, sitting unmoving and untouching in the center of the front pew below the rough-hewn altar. At one far end of the family pew were Herbert and Nancy, their heads bowed. At the other end, stiff and erect in black, was Frances.

In the back of the church and across from her she saw Carter Ansdale, his big curly gray-brown head towering over his smaller neighbors.

At the end of the service, Mrs. Potter stood with the rest outside as the five who had been seated in the front pew departed. Olympia and Laurie appeared oblivious of the respectful crowd in the little churchyard and left abruptly in the small battered truck with C. R. COGSWELL & SON, LOBSTER BUYERS painted on the side. The Wyncotes, it was clear to see, only at the last minute remembered Frances, and Herbert turned back to ask her—or so it appeared—if she wanted a ride home. Her brisk refusal was equally obvious, as she got into the car of a young man Mrs. Potter thought was probably her nephew.

Carter was waving to Mrs. Potter above the crowd across the churchyard, and she could see the Whiteheads, Alex grave in a dark suit, Bets in a pantsuit of rich churchly purple. Before any of them could reach her, there appeared at her side the tall man with the pepper and salt mustache.

"May I give you a cup of tea?" he asked.

The idea was welcome. She accepted gratefully, at the same time with certain curiosity as to where the newcomer had found a place to live, in a town devoid of apartment buildings and lacking many likely quarters for bachelor occupancy, if indeed a bachelor he was.

"I'm at the Sportsmans Lodge," he told her in his pleasant burr. "Will you meet me there after we each retrieve our cars from amongst this jam?"

A half hour later they were sitting at a table in the deserted dining room of the Lodge, overlooking a placid stretch of the Metoosic. "I didn't know they even *had* a teapot," Mrs. Potter was telling him. "However did you manage to wangle more than a cup of tepid water with a tea bag on the side? That's all I've ever been able to get here."

He smiled without answering, and their angular, middle-aged waitress brought in a plate of toasted, split, blueberry muffins.

"How do you do it?" Mrs. Potter asked again. "Whenever I eat here, and I must admit that's not very often, no one in the place has ever heard of a blueberry. Or a muffin. Or a decent cup of tea. Didn't you know one comes to the Lodge in spite of the food, never because of it?"

"It may be I'm giving them a bit of a push when it comes to the blueberries, although, of course, these are frozen ones until the harvest. I'm making them cook my own catch of salmon properly, to be sure. That's one thing I'll be doing for the public good in Cherrybridge, no matter how short my stay on the job at the plant."

"You mean you'll be leaving?" She felt an irrational disappointment.

"That depends on Mrs. Cutler, to be sure. I'd like to stay.

I like the job and it's one I know and can do well. And the salmon fishing is the best I've had short of Scotland. But she is the one to decide, and, to be honest, we don't get on. She couldn't be rid of me fast enough when first I went to the pound."

"Olympia's manner does put one off a bit," Mrs. Potter admitted, "but she's a good businesswoman, and I should think that, even if there is some kind of personal feeling, she wouldn't let it stand in the way of keeping a good manager. Particularly at the season when the business most needs one."

"Quite. We'll see, of course. More tea, Mrs. Potter?"

"It's 'Genia, please," she told him. "Eugenia really, but no one seems to use it but me when I'm talking to myself. And you are Deacon?"

"Deke it is, if you please then, 'Genia," he said. "I'm Deacon only to my mother in Toronto, the only family I have now.

"And may I say, 'Genia, that the color of your frock is remarkably becoming?"

Mrs. Potter's "frock" was a simply cut pale gray-blue suit with a soft, matching ruffled blouse. She was inordinately pleased that the man—Deke, what a nice name—had noticed it.

"And now if you'll forgive the rush of it, I must see to the cannery," Deke was saying. "The employees were given the afternoon off for the service, of course, but I asked the foreman to meet me there at four to go over some matters. May I hope to see you again soon?"

She smiled her answer.

Later, leaving the Lodge, Mrs. Potter spoke to Dwight Henderson, the new proprietor, and complimented him on having bought a teapot and adding blueberry muffins to the repertory of the kitchen. Dwight looked rather flustered and said something about there being more call for that sort of thing now that the fishermen were beginning to arrive.

"We've spruced up the rooms a *s'koshi* bit, too," he told her. "Couldn't do much this year except new mattresses and new carpets, but I've found a young couple to help with the painting and some of the rooms look pretty good now."

"At last I can find out about that word *scoshi,* however you spell it!" Mrs. Potter pounced on this. "It must be Japanese. At least the people I hear using it all seem to have had army or navy duty in Japan, or to have lived there for a time."

"Navy for me." Dwight straightened his shoulders. "You know the word means about the same thing as a *dite* around here. It's spelled *sukoshi,* but the Japanese skimp that first syllable. Same with the dish *sukiyaki.* We pronounce it with four full syllables, but in Japan it's *s'kiyaki,* just three. Incidentally, that's a specialty of mine—hope you'll let me make it for you some day."

When she had found out, to her satisfaction, that the young painting couple were Jim Markham and his lady, Anne-Marie, Mrs. Potter took her leave and did a round of quick errands before returning to the cottage.

At the supermarket she bought some cheeses that Persy's small refrigerator case did not stock, plus olive oil, such fresh vegetables as looked to be worth carrying home, and a few packages of lamb chops, small steaks, and stewing beef to put in the freezer. She added several flats of petunias for a planting box at the end of the sunny deck at the front of the cottage, and some new flowering geraniums for the kitchen windowsill.

She went to the state liquor store to replenish her stock of Nova Scotia rum and of gin, and there ran into Carter Ansdale. On his recommendation she bought a bottle of a particular sherry he favored.

"So sad and final, the service for Coley and Regina," she said, remembering that Carter had been with them that last happy evening at the cottage.

"A terrible loss to us all," he agreed. He'd call her later in the evening, and maybe she'd let him cook that dinner for her at his place soon? And was she going to insist on staying there all alone at the Point, without any neighbors? He shook his head ruefully.

His brown van moved out from the curb and she noticed that its back springs seemed to sag under unwonted weight. Perhaps this was a load of odd-shaped pottery turned on the wheels of all those tired-looking young women with all those new babies.

She stopped at the furniture store to pick up new slatted blinds she had ordered for the downstairs bathroom. The old lined chintz curtains had not stood up to the sun and salt breezes. If she could get the blinds to the cottage, she knew that Lyman, albeit after several calls and reminders, would eventually come to put them up.

There at the store she found Clarence, like Cinderella after midnight, bereft of his earlier glory. He was back in the misbuttoned gray cardigan, and his shoulders had resumed their gentle, apologetic stoop.

This seemed a little sad until she reflected that he did, after all, have his moments of supreme importance, which not everybody gets in this life—his moments of elegance in black suit and tie and shiny black shoes.

She complimented him gently on the two services, Harvard's last week and today's memorial for the Cogswells, meanwhile wondering if this was somehow an improper allocation of praise. No matter, it apparently pleased Clarence to hear the words.

Suddenly she found herself voicing a question she had not before realized was troubling her.

"Clarence, was there anything that seemed unusual to you about Harvard's face after his death?"

Clarence took his time. "You mean, did anything about the departed look queer?" he asked.

"Exactly. His lips were so chafed-looking. I hadn't noticed that the day before. Amanda spoke to me about it, too."

"*Well.*" Clarence paused lengthily. "Well, I did have a little trouble with the subject's mouth. The departed lacked a few teeth here and there"—(he looked at her intently)—"and I suppose that's why he'd snagged himself a few places on the tongue. Black and blue, like. Never saw that before, but who's to say? All I can tell you is that I had a real job on that mouth to make it look like anything."

Mrs. Potter considered how to phrase her next question. She was, after all, only feeling a vague and uneasy awareness that

Harvard's dying might not have been the quiet slipping away that Northcutt's Harbor appeared to believe.

"I only thought his lips didn't look *natural*," was all she could think of.

Clarence was affronted. "If you're suggesting he didn't receive the best of my professional care and personal attention . . ." he began.

Hurriedly Mrs. Potter tried to reassure him. She was suggesting nothing of the sort. Undoubtedly just a trick of her imagination or the lighting in the church. Such a quick glimpse of the coffin, after all, in that crowd in the procession. . . . Such a beautiful funeral. Then, suddenly remembering, she told him how nice Harvard's hands had looked, so nicely manicured.

Clarence, slightly mollified, interrupted. "Thought that part of the job was pretty good, if I do say so myself. My manicures are pretty well admired."

Mrs. Potter continued her compliments, remembering the flowers and reciting the names of the most prestigious mourners in attendance. At last Clarence relaxed into his usual amiable, gray-sweatered self.

Before she left Cherrybridge, she drove up one side of the Metoosic as far as the dam and fish weirs, then back on the other, enjoying the sparkle of the clear water dancing over the stones, dividing to flow smoothly around tiny wooded islands, rushing under the bridge that joined the two narrow roads, one on either side of the river.

South of the bridge, the Sportsmans Lodge, the drugstore, and the clinic were on the west bank, while across from them on the east bank were most of the other commercial establishments of the town, including the Cogswell offices. North of the bridge, the two roads, one on either bank, served as the main residential streets.

The stream itself, every hundred yards or less, was lined with fishermen in waders, casting their fly rods with what appeared to be delicacy and precision. Although she looked for him—would he have had time to change after his appointment with the foreman?—she did not see the tall man with the short-cropped hair and the pepper and salt mustache.

I really must learn to fish, she told herself. It's silly to live near one of the world's great salmon streams and not know how to cast a fly.

What I am going to do tonight, tomorrow at the latest, she suddenly decided, is to call Olympia and Laurie and ask them to Sunday lunch—this coming first Sunday of the season, when there will be no lobster fishing. And if they can come, I'll ask Deke MacDonald too. Perhaps this might give him a chance to persuade Olympia that he is needed in Cherrybridge to manage the blueberry operation.

Amused at herself for such a transparent ruse for seeing the tall Scotsman again, Mrs. Potter continued toward home.

16

It is absolute nonsense, my dear woman, to think you can't sleep after a small cup of coffee, Mrs. Potter told herself severely. Besides, that was several hours ago, with Dorrie's stupendous cheesecake. Since then you have had some of Bill Van Dusen's very nice brandy, and, as everyone knows, brandy is a therapeutic drink and very possibly sleep-inducing.

The earlier daytime breeze had slacked so that the trees were quiet in the dark behind the house, but the tide was high and the splash and murmur of the water on the rocks beneath her bedroom window was a gentle invitation to drowsiness.

She put down the book, which had held her attention only briefly, and turned out the light. Teedy made a pest of himself at the Van Dusens' tonight, she thought, but Bill handled firmly Teedy's suggestion that the Van Dusens buy liquor for the Pettengills, as well as themselves, at the nearby post exchange.

"Us taxpayers shell out for your retirement, Colonel," was Teedy's untactful approach, which he obviously considered a witty remark, "so how's about picking up a few bottles for the poor folks next time you're at the PX? Good stuff, don't mind if I have a little more."

The first time Bill had ignored the question, answering only with a short, barking laugh.

The second time, his response was quick and curt. "No. Against the law. You ought to know that."

To Mrs. Potter's vast surprise, Dorrie Van Dusen had telephoned her that Thursday morning, the day after the

Cogswells' memorial service, with a specific invitation, not at all the "do come to see us sometime" variety.

"We all need a bit of cheering up," Dorrie had told her firmly. "I can't manage dinner on such short notice, and besides I want to include quite a few people—dear Olympia among them, naturally. So I am simply going to make what Bill calls 'Dorrie's Absolutely Stupendously Divine Cheesecake' and ask people to come by about eight for dessert and coffee."

Accepting, sharing the feeling that Northcutt's Harbor needed all the cheer it could muster these days, Mrs. Potter was still puzzled by the Van Dusens' intention to include "dear Olympia," and, to add to that, "naturally." Except for business dealings connected with the buying or selling of lobster at the pound, Olympia had never been a part of any of the various social divisions of the town. Only rarely, as at the baked bean supper, had she taken any part in Cole and Regina's diverse and active social life.

"Of course we're asking dear Nancy and Herbert, too," Dorrie had continued. "It's so important for them to take their place in our little community now, don't you agree, with the Cogswells gone?"

Were the Van Dusens moving up into summer people, or were the Wyncotes branching out a bit from their small rather separate Millstone enclave?

Mrs. Potter remembered seeing Herbert with Teedy and Persy at the store recently, seeking their advice about a septic tank and a caretaker. This was a decided point in Herbert's favor. Perhaps there was enough of the Northcutt heritage, through Regina's side of the family, to redeem the man from what seemed inborn myopia of spirit.

The evening at the Van Dusens' had been decidedly interesting. To begin with, the obvious focus of the party was the announcement, early in the evening, that Alex Whitehead had become the new owner of the Cherrybridge Savings Bank. There had been appropriate toasts, first with the coffee, which was served with Dorrie's indisputably superb cheesecake, then with Bill's brandy as the evening progressed.

Mrs. Potter had sighed with delight at the dessert, her glances and upraised eyes intended—and received—as a compliment to its sublimity. "Nothing to it," Dorrie had said, clearly pleased with the praise in spite of her disclaimer. "I think I clipped the recipe from *McCall's*, years ago, and it's in their cookbook. Bill says he's going to have to be out jogging doubletime tomorrow to work it off, though."

The most heartening news of the evening was that while Herbert and Nancy were going to look after the Roost and the inherited property on the Point, they planned to remain in their house at Millstone, where their children could be with their friends.

And I suppose, Mrs. Potter told herself, as she continued to lie awake in bed, I suppose there could be worse neighbors if they did decide to move to the Point.

The disquieting part of the earlier evening had to do with Olympia. "We were so disappointed that she wasn't free," Dorrie had confided. "Alex particularly wanted to get acquainted with her, you know, in view of his purchase of the bank."

Overhearing this, Mrs. Whitehead (whom Mrs. Potter was learning to call "Bets" with greater ease) entered the conversation. "You know that we plan to go ahead with our plans for building *here*," she said, "but I think we'll begin to think of it as just a little playhouse, a cozy hideaway for us now that Alex is going to be so busy again. Since Olympia has her own little home here in the village—and heaven knows she and Laurie wouldn't know what to *do* with that big house in Cherrybridge, let alone having proper furniture for it—we're thinking of making an offer for it."

"You know her better than we do," Alex interjected. "Think she'd go for a good cash offer?"

"You're forgetting that Olympia grew up in that house," Mrs. Potter said doubtfully, "and that she grew up with the beautiful furniture that's in it." Internally she was writhing at the thought of Bets Whitehead in Regina's gardens, and Alex at the head of Cole's table.

And still later in the evening, Teedy, undismayed by Bill's rebuke and emboldened by brandy, had resumed his campaign to persuade Mrs. Potter to sell him her cottage and land. As they returned from a tour to view the new Van

Dusen wood-burning auxiliary furnace, he managed to corner her briefly for a confidential aside. "Remember, Alex is behind me in this, all the way. He and Bets are serious about moving into the Cogswell house up in Cherrybridge, you know, after they've spruced it up a little, of course. And if *he* doesn't go in with me, the Colamarias are a cinch. Al is serious, and he's got the right connections."

Mrs. Potter was pleased that she had been able to sound as definite as Bill Van Dusen, although her voice lacked his military tone of command. "No, Teedy, not a chance of it, and I really wish you would not speak about it again."

It was after the encounter with Teedy that she and Herbert had found themselves together. "Great chap, this Whitehead," Herbert was saying. "Real business head on his shoulders, don't you agree?"

"You know, Herbert, I'm delighted to see you and Nancy start to become more a part of things here," she told him, "and since you're interested in real estate now, I think your idea for converting Nancy's Whitehall into what sounds like a wonderful place for one's old age. . . ."

Her voice faltered, but Herbert did not notice. For her, Whitehall, no matter how nicely converted for communal living for the affluent elderly, would never be her own willing choice. Perhaps a nursing home, yes, if she were incapacitated, but in that case she would still opt for a nurse, if she could, and for living at home.

Herbert nodded sagely into his brandy snifter. "Just the place for you," he said. "I know I wouldn't want *Maman* living there alone on the Point. Have you thought about selling? Let me know if you have, and we'll talk."

To change the subject, irritated at Herbert's being yet another to urge the sale of her property and resenting being classed with his doddering old *maman*, whom she met at too many dull and identical summer cocktail parties at Millstone, she continued in another vein.

"I've been thinking of the waterfront development on Nantucket," she said. "Lew and I had a summer house there while our children were growing up, just as you and Nancy have here at Millstone."

"Oh yes, Nantucket," Herbert said approvingly. "Good friends of ours there. Thoroughly nice yacht club. Sailed in there more times than you can shake a stick at."

Realizing that Herbert might have had one more brandy than the rest of them, Mrs. Potter continued what had apparently become a somewhat one-sided conversation.

"It's this idea of mine, Herbert," she went on, and then, as Alex Whitehead joined the two of them, she included him in what was purely a party-talk suggestion.

"All of those little fishermen's shacks on the water here are right on the harbor," she said, "each one heated by its own little stove, each one with its own little wooden pier, all of them occupying the most beautiful waterfront of the village. What do you think might happen if they could all get together, have one good cooperative working headquarters? One good shared pier, and maybe even a clubhouse for poker on bad mornings? What do you think?"

Herbert seemed fuddled, but Alex was quick to follow her reasoning and to give it instant reality in a way she had not quite intended. "Absolutely. Harbor-front marina and a complex of shops. Simple little rentable apartments. Have to be expensive, of course. . . ."

Bets entered the conversation. "I'm with you, Alex darling. *Terribly* chic, all the roofs and angles a little out of joint, just to make it look really quaint and old. Artists' shops, a few really good boutiques, some super little restaurants."

Alex warmed to the subject. "I can see this as a sort of shared-time vacation condominium," he announced grandly. "Herbert, old boy, you've got another inspiration there."

Brandy is speaking, Mrs. Potter reassured herself. The day a boutique sign goes up in Northcutt's Harbor is the day I'll take to the woods.

Pleased with her firmness with Teedy earlier, she had been equally pleased with her firmness in saying good night to Carter Ansdale as they left the party. "I have my own car," she reminded him. "Thanks so much, but it's just a five-minute drive, I'm used to seeing myself home, and we've had our nightcap here with Bill and Dorrie."

As she finally drifted off to sleep, she thought again of

Carter. Ordinarily, she was both amused and mildly flattered by what seemed his rather ardent importunings, although she certainly knew herself to be less than *totally* irresistible. If Carter's design was to sweep her off her feet, he could certainly find a prettier, younger, more responsive partner.

But consider Carter as the masculine version of an old-fashioned southern belle. Instead of feminine coquetry, instead of the "oh, you great big wonderful man" approach—charming, but often meaningless—Carter was using the same time-tested technique in his own way. And the purpose was undoubtedly the same: simply a basic old-fashioned wish to be *polite*.

Relieved by the thought that Carter neither expected nor wanted to be taken up on his amorous-sounding advances, Mrs. Potter slept at last.

She wakened suddenly from a deep sleep, and a dream of hiding in a French farmhouse while mortar shells exploded above a thatched roof. She heard Sindhu growling low in his throat at the foot of the stairs.

Then she heard the click of his toenails on the floor of the little hall outside her bedroom.

She was about to call to him to be quiet and to go back down to his rug when the cannonading sound came again to her now wide-awake ears. In irregular bursts, something was being fired at the roof of the cottage. This was not the sharp sound of gunshot, but the varying thuds of impact were nonetheless alarming.

Hard thumping, clattering objects were being pitched at the roof of the cottage on the side of the peak facing the woods.

Mrs. Potter lay very still, trying to think, unwilling to move. What could explain this terrifying, erratic bombardment? She could think of nothing at all. It was not thunder, it was not hail.

Were people outside throwing hand grenades at her roof, not that she would know what a hand grenade sounded like?

She tensed, waiting for the explosion she was sure would follow each thud.

Suddenly there was the unmistakable crash and tinkle of

broken glass and she knew that a pane in one of the small west windows of the living room downstairs had been shattered.

She reached for the telephone beside her bed. Lyman, her caretaker, was also her closest neighbor now, living up the peninsula road beyond the road to the pound. She tried to think of his number and dial it in the dark. She certainly did not intend to risk a light with someone outside breaking the windows of her house.

The line was dead. It seemed impossible, at the moment when she most needed the phone. Another pane crashed in the living room below, and Sindhu's low growl became a deadly threat.

With this reminder of protection at hand, Mrs. Potter forced herself to leave her bed. She found her slippers and robe in the dark, opened the hall door and put Sindhu on leash. Only once before, the day of the three-wheeler attack, had she heard that low menace in his throat.

Together they descended the narrow stairway and picked their way cautiously in the dark through the living room, trying to keep to the ocean side, away from the broken panes. The cannonading on the roof continued above them and she felt Sindhu's body a tightly coiled spring of bone and muscle at her side. His low growl deepened.

They entered the kitchen and faced the solid, heavy door to the outside.

This was the moment of decision. Could she confront an unknown threat, even with the protection of a trained dog at her side? Or would she cower there in her own kitchen and wait for what might be coming next?

As she debated, she heard a hoarse giggle, sounding close to the broken panes of the adjoining room. She acted.

Opening the door wide, Mrs. Potter spoke loudly, hoping she sounded controlled and authoritative. "I know who you are out there, you boys, and I've had quite enough of this nonsense. Every one of you go home *right now*. I'm going to count to five and then I'm going to give Sindhu the command to *attack*."

There was a sound of scrambling from the roof of the shed,

then the soft sounds of running feet departing through the trees.

"Two, three, four. . . ." she shouted, trying to keep her voice steady.

And then with Sindhu still straining on his leash, she closed the kitchen door, sat heavily on the straight kitchen chair, her body suddenly weak and shaking uncontrollably in the dark. Sindhu put his head upon her lap, and the two of them sat in that position until the first light in the eastern sky.

17

Fortunately, Mrs. Potter thought to try the telephone again on Friday morning. She had showered and dressed, swept up the broken glass in the living room, and was sitting at her desk with her morning tea, shortly after dawn, trying to think what to do next.

The dial tone was clear. Had she not waited long enough last night (there were sometimes unexplained delays on the local lines) or had there been a temporary lapse of service, now corrected? Possibly the cause had been only her own panicked sense of isolation in the darkness, with the sound of the pelting rocks on the roof overhead.

Her first call was to Lyman, her neighbor and caretaker. Could he come at once?

The unexpected early morning summons brought him to the cottage with a squeal of brakes as his new pickup stopped in the clearing.

"What's all this? What's going on here?" Lyman was shaken out of his usual lethargy by the sight of the stones on the roof, the two broken windowpanes, the bait bucket beside the shed, still half full of beach stones and rocks ranging from the size of eggs to baseballs.

"Hasn't done those shingles any good, I should say," was his comment. "Think I better order more of the same gray asbestos and do over that side of the roof?"

Mrs. Potter told him that she would think about that later. Now, the important thing was to replace the windowpanes.

"Well, can't say as I could do it today," was Lyman's

165

answer. "Weekend coming up and I mayn't be able to get that glass cut in Cherrybridge. Think I'm out of putty and points too, come to think. Guess it'll have to wait until next week. I'll rig you up something till I get to it."

The brown cardboard will keep out the birds and mosquitoes until the permanent replacements can be installed, she thought. "But first thing next week, please, if you will," she implored him, knowing how easily Lyman might delay any second step after coping with an original emergency.

"There's something else I want to discuss with you, Lyman," she told him as he put the bait bucket in the back of his truck, dumping the stones at the base of a tree, where, she realized, she would have to pick them up later. "It's about who was here doing this mischief last night, and about what's going on with the high school crowd in the village."

Whatever it was, Lyman did not want to hear about it. Their Janine was no part of it, whatever was going on. Prettiest girl in her class. Popular, too. Don't talk to *him* about things going on. Too much gossip around here, anyway, and besides Janine and Tommy were going to get married right after graduation, big church wedding and all. Tris was going to give Harvard's old boat a good going over and Tommy could go right to lobstering, and they were going to live in the trailer behind the garage.

Lyman's fulminations trailed off as he backed up and turned out of the small clearing.

Wearily, Mrs. Potter went to the shed for another bucket, picked up the stones by the tree and as many as she could around the base of the house, and took them to the shorefront to dump them out. Later she realized that she probably should have left them where they were for an insurance adjuster to see, and that she should have kept the bucket Lyman had carried away. Wasn't there something in the homeowner's policy about "malicious mischief"? Well, it was too late now and, anyway, whatever damage there was would undoubtedly, as was usually the case, prove to be the one contingency the policy did not cover.

She was suddenly overwhelmed with the memory of Harvard. She tried not to think of that unexpectedly raddled face, once so dear and lively, now quiet and cold as she had last seen it, surrounded by the heavy scents and summer colors of the flowers around his coffin. What would he have made of this?

The living room was desolate and dark with the tacked-up brown cardboard. The kitchen would be equally depressing after the long hours she and Sindhu had sat, first rigid with fear and rage, then finally in a kind of cold paralysis of will, until the coming of the summer dawn.

Rousing herself, she passed by an old mirror above the pine chest where she kept sheets and towels, and caught sight of her pale, lined face.

No excuse to look *that* bad, she told herself. At the ranch someone would have told her, "You look like you've been rode hard and put away wet." That was pretty much the way she felt.

Now, as she looked out to sea, she saw that the morning sun was bright and warm.

She acted quickly. She would spend the morning on the rocks in front of the cottage. She'd put on an old bathing suit and get some sun, let the soft wind blow the whole blasted mess out of her mind.

18

A bare toe tested a small tidal pool in the pink granite rocks and was withdrawn hastily. This shallow basin, its water clear as rain, was lined with pebbles and small rocks variously stained with bright colors of microscopic growth—burnt sienna, viridian green, cadmium yellow, even specks of Prussian blue and vermilion.

Althought the tiny pool was warming with the morning, Mrs. Potter drew back, knowing that the water beyond the rocks was much too cold for swimming this early June day, as Maine water would be, for her, any other day in the year.

The sun-warmed rocks were rough against her back. Had she been sleeping? She squirmed to a smoother backrest.

She knew that offshore on Seal Rock and Old Nic, under water at high tide but now showing as dark ledges on the horizon, the seals were also basking in the sun. Without field glasses it was too far to see them, but knowing they were there seemed companionable. It was also comforting, after her sleepless night, to feel the sleek warmth of the big gray dog at her side. He stared with total absorption into the tidal pool, apparently seeing something she could not.

Here in the clear soft light of a day filled with early summer sweetness, here on the edge of a blue and placid ocean, in front of her own secluded small house on a quiet and almost uninhabited point of land below a tiny, tidy Down East fishing village, here, away from city crime and international violence, here on a day when her world would appear utterly serene, Mrs. Potter was uneasy and troubled.

Without thinking, she tried the big toe of the other foot and as quickly brought it back out of the water into the sunlight.

I don't like this, she told herself. Northcutt's Harbor is a place where I have always felt safe. What's happening now, disturbing my peace of mind, overturning the traditional patterns of this little town?

Part of her sense of things gone wrong had been summed up in that dry statement from Amanda. "Looks like you're running out of neighbors, down there at the Point." She was, in fact, alone there now, after the accident at sea and the death, the next day, of an old man.

Another cause for her unease was the mystery of the teenagers. Why was she suddenly afraid (she hated to admit the word, and now spoke it to herself for the first time— afraid!) of fifteen- and sixteen-year-olds she had known and liked, most of them, from the time they first started school?

The tide was turning and the breeze had shifted from the southwest, now coming in cool and salty from over the water, losing its land-based warmth and grassy fragrance.

Mrs. Potter pulled a faded sweatshirt over the bathing suit she had put on for sunning—certainly not for swimming—slid her bare feet into a pair of tieless sneakers, and went up to the cottage to think.

As she went up the steps to the salt-bleached wooden deck, the question repeated itself: What in the name of all that is holy, she asked, is going on around here? Am I just imagining things?

At any rate she knew she had not imagined the rocks she saw scattered about the place or the broken panes in the windows. She would, as usual, try to sort out her thinking by making notes for herself on one of the lined yellow pads at hand in each room of the house. She settled herself resolutely on the deck with one of these.

The boat explosion was her first entry. Cole and Regina had perished in what was apparently considered by the entire village, and by the Coast Guard as well, to be a dreadful accident. But was such an accident *likely*, with an experienced old skipper, with a fine boat whose constant and careful maintenance had always been in the hands of an expert mechanic who was also an old and trusted friend?

Harvard's death, she wrote next. Something was wrong there. She knew it, although what it was she could not name.

The teenagers, Mrs. Potter then noted, sighing deeply, causing the dog at her feet to look up in quick attention.

Perhaps, she thought, she was magnifying her own personal discomfiture and embarrassment and her hurt feelings. Remembering Amanda's words about the pot-smoking behind the church, she did feel concern about the young people. Still, their behavior did not seem of sufficient importance to share the same page with her first two entries.

The faded cushions of the old chaise longue were soft and warm after the slight chill she had begun to feel on the rocks. Sindhu yawned and stretched on the warm planking of the deck.

Just as they were again beginning to doze, there was a brisk knock at the kitchen door, on the other side of the cottage.

Nerves and muscles snapped to a quick alert. Sindhu's growl was only a murmur, but a reminder of the threat it had held the night before. Mrs. Potter snatched up a fallen sneaker. Together, her hand on the hard, sleek gray head, they went through to the kitchen to answer.

There on the flat granite slab that served as a doorstep was the tall man with the clean khaki trousers, the short dark hair, the pepper and salt mustache.

"My dear Mrs. Potter. *'Genia,'*" he began quite formally. "I hope you will forgive an unannounced call at this hour?"

It was a very good hour indeed, she assured him. "I've been out getting some sun, as you can see, and if you don't mind my missionary barrel getup" (she looked down at the tieless sneakers and the faded sweatshirt) "and if you can overlook a few cardboard front windows in the house, this couldn't be a better time."

He had been exploring the Point, he told her, and marveling at the beauty of the rocks around the tip of the peninsula. He had to own that he had even walked up and around the

170

Roost, thinking that he had never seen a place where he himself would like more to live.

"As a matter of fact," he said, "I'm simply cooling my heels. Mrs. Cutler bade me to a morning appointment at the lobster pound, then discovered she would be occupied for a bit. I'm to report to her again at two, and I decided I'd best stay nearby and not waste the day in a drive to Cherrybridge and back."

Then, he said, as he drove back toward the village he chanced to look down her drive. Again, and he asked her forgiveness, he had taken the liberty of coming by for a moment to wish her good morning and to hope she was all right after the bereavements of the past days.

"Please come in," she said, "or better yet, come around outside with me to the deck. The house is much too dreary as it is now, on such a lovely morning."

"I say, the place seems littered with stones," he remarked as they circled the cottage. "There's not been a blow to do all this, surely?"

It was a tremendous relief to tell someone—this strong, handsome Scotsman—about the stoning of her house the night before.

He listened in silence, his hazel-flecked eyes watching her intently. "The house" (to her ear it sounded more like *hoos*) "was not actually entered by the lads?" he asked. "You personally were not attacked?"

It was a further relief to recount the whole misadventure a second time, this time including mention of the earlier surprising rudeness of the teenagers, and what had seemed a deliberate attack upon her by the three-wheelers.

Finally the entire story of all her worries spilled out, begging to be told to a quiet and responsive listener.

As she spoke, she realized that, apart from the minor insults to her person and last night's not very serious assault upon her house, there was very little to report after all. Her terror had arisen chiefly because she did not at first know the nature of the bombardment and what it might be leading to. The teenagers were behaving badly, yes, but some teenagers do so, and most of them get over it.

"And I don't imagine it's serious," she went on, finding it more and more easy to confide in this new friend, "but what do you know about marijuana, Deke?"

It appeared that he knew a great deal. "Mayhap the problem is not quite so widespread in the other provinces," he told her, "but it most assuredly is in Toronto. And I'm not the one to take it lightly. I've read too much about what it can lead to. Not just the lethargy and the lack of ambition but the possibility of real brain damage."

She sighed. Then, finding herself increasingly relaxed, strangely secure in feeling that here was a person she could talk to freely and in confidence, she went on.

"I've got two other worries, not related ones," she said, "which are much more vague and obscure but much, much more serious if they're not just vapors in my head. I might as well tell you what I've been writing down, here on my yellow notepad."

Again Deke listened in silence. "You're wondering, then," he said at last, "whether there has been something amiss in our understanding of what happened to Mr. and Mrs. Cogswell and, the next night, to Mr. Northcutt."

"Yes," she agreed, "and even, crazy as it might seem, if there might be some connection between them."

"I see three jottings of yours on the notepad," Deke said. "The boat explosion, then Harvard's death, then the teenagers. A connection, you think, among them all?"

"Oh, no," she said. "The teenage thing is something else. But the three deaths, and if there's a reason behind them . . . that's something I've been afraid to even let myself thing about."

"I'm not so sure," he said. "If there is indeed a reason, the whole thing may be a parcel. I wish I knew this place and these people better." He looked out to sea, again in silence.

At length he stood up. "We must get to the bottom of this, and I want to help. But right now, and please forgive the boldness of it, could I bring you a wee bit of something in the way of spirits from your kitchen? You look done in, for fair. And may I take a quick look at the toolshed?"

Mrs. Potter gratefully accepted both suggestions. The tall

man vaulted over the deck railing, first to inspect the shed, and then, following her directions to cupboard and glasses, to bring them both a whisky and water from the kitchen.

It had been a help and a relief to have someone to talk to, particularly after Lyman's half-contemptuous dismissal of her story earlier in the morning. It was nice now to share a smoky dram of whisky with a new friend. Further easing her stress, Deke talked briefly now of other matters—of blueberries and lobsters and the weather, and finally of salmon fishing.

"Cole and Regina adored it, as you knew, of course," she said. "I wish I'd learned how years ago, when we first came here."

"I say, would you really like to learn?" he asked. "There's nothing I'd like better than to teach you, at least whilst I'm still kept on here at my job by Mrs. Cutler."

It was diverting to think of something new. She'd have to borrow some waders, they agreed. He'd manage the other gear.

But no, he would not stay for a pick-up lunch. And was she sure she still wanted luncheon guests Sunday? Reassured that she did, he thanked her for the drink; he told her again that no great damage had been done either to the cottage roof or the toolshed; then, without their setting a time for a possible fishing lesson, he said good-bye.

Mrs. Potter had another shower, took a nap, felt better, and after her quiet supper she worked a satisfyingly fiendish crossword puzzle from the previous week's Sunday *Times*.

As she went to sleep, she even found herself able to laugh at an admission of her own vanity. She caught herself hoping she wouldn't look *fat* in borrowed waders. But then, she reminded herself comfortably, she could never look worse than she had this morning.

Her last question, before completely falling asleep, had been this: Was Deke MacDonald old enough to have heard of a missionary barrel?

19

The next morning Mrs. Potter telephoned the Van Dusens to thank Dorrie for her evening coffee party on Thursday and to compliment her again on that absolutely superb cheesecake, worthy of all the adjectives Bill had claimed for it.

It was Bill who answered, and he was sorry Dorrie couldn't come to the phone but she was busy packing. Anyway he'd deliver her message, and she was good to call.

"Packing?" she had asked. "You're taking off for somewhere, just as the weather is so perfect?"

"We just decided to go, 'Genia," Bill said, "and we were lucky enough to get a last-minute space on an economy group charter flight out of Bangor. Our daughter and her husband are on duty in West Germany—I'm sure you know that. And the old general seems to be doing well up in Cherrybridge at the moment, so this just seemed a good time to take off."

He paused. "I think I just heard Teedy honk out front. He's going to drive us to the airport and I see that he's five minutes early."

As she wished the Van Dusens a happy trip, Mrs. Potter was glad she had restrained a momentary impulse to mention the stoning of her house and to ask Bill's advice as to what, if anything, to do about it. His army experience with marijuana-related behavior would undoubtedly have been helpful, but this was not the time, with Teedy's impatient horn sounding at the front gate, to begin such a discussion.

"See you when we get back," Bill was continuing. "One thing almost as bad as being late for report is being early.

Dorrie hates to be rushed and she had this planned exactly to the minute.''

"Have a great trip," Mrs. Potter repeated quickly. "See you soon to hear all about it." Given the army precision of the Van Dusen organization, she was not going to be blamed for an ill-timed phone call. No more did she think Teedy should be criticized for being a few minutes ahead of time if he was being good enough to drive them the hour trip to the airport.

At least I have some news for Amanda, she thought later, as she and Sindhu went up the post office steps. I can tell her about the Van Dusens' trip to Germany.

"Leaving on the 10 AM plane for Frankfurt," Amanda was telling Tillie and Giselle at the counter as Mrs. Potter entered. "Haven't seen their daughter for over a year, and if the old general keeps well they're going to stay for little William's second birthday on the Fourth of July."

"How nicely planned for an army general's greatgrandson," was all Mrs. Potter could say, realizing that she could never hope to top Amanda as the town's quickest newsgatherer.

"Teedy drove them up," Amanda continued, "and you know, I suppose, that he's got Persy convinced that Harvard's little bit of land there around the cove is going to make her rich. The whole town's heard about it, including where the boat harbor will be. The *marina* is what they're going to call it. Just for summer boats. They're talking about a yacht club where Harvard's old shack is."

"I think that's pure guesswork on somebody's part," Mrs. Potter said. "You told me last week young Roddy was lording it over the other kids because his mother had inherited the property, and now you say she's going to sell the place."

"No contradiction there, far's I can see," Amanda sniffed, "just means he'll come into his own a little faster. You can't imagine Roddy Pickett wanting to live in a shack like that, now, can you? The one thing I haven't got figured out yet is whether the money will keep him here if she sells. Maybe Persy won't be able to let him go. Maybe he won't really be able to leave Persy, for that matter. No matter which, don't you imagine for a minute they'll lose out on getting rich on the place.''

"Speaking of news, Amanda was just saying you'd been seeing quite a lot of that Deacon MacDonald, the one Cole hired to run his blueberry business," Tillie offered. "Down at your place yesterday morning, wasn't he? Before that, Wednesday last week you went to the Sportsmans Lodge with him after the memorial service in Cherrybridge, had tea with him in the dining room, stopped and said hello to Dwight Henderson afterward?"

"Well, what else is new?" Mrs. Potter asked with resignation. She not only marveled at Amanda's sources of information but at the fact that they were so often accurate.

"Teedy sold one of his lots back from the road," Giselle informed her, "but still not the last one on the bay, Louis says."

"Alex Whitehead went down to New York on business yesterday," Tillie added. "She didn't go, the Mrs. Left his car at the airport overnight so no one had to drive him up, and he's already back this morning."

"Naturally you'd know about the bank," Amanda told her, "but if that man thinks Olympia Cogswell Cutler would sell that house of Cole and Regina's to the likes of *them*, he's got another think coming."

Remembering Cole's identical phrase concerning the sale, not of his ancestral home but of the more recently built Roost, Regina's property, Mrs. Potter was afraid to say more. She reminded herself that the Point seemed to be in protective hands now that Herbert had taken charge.

Tillie had more. "Carter Ansdale sent off a big load of weaving, decided to use United Parcel instead of the mail, though the boxes would have come under the limits either way."

"And that's about all," Amanda said, concluding the conversation, "except I expect you know Al Colamaria's rich uncle came up from Newark for a three-day visit and Teedy decided to give the Colamarias a little more grace on living in the trailer. Strike at the prefab factory, Al says, and a slow-down in getting the Alhambra model."

176

What a rich and interesting life we live, Mrs. Potter reflected as she and Sindhu walked back through the morning sunshine to the cottage. I'm going to forget that yellow pad business and simply devote myself to living in the here and now of Northcutt's Harbor.

Telephoning Edna at the farm to ask about fresh strawberries and asparagus, then Persy at the store to order crabmeat, she was assured of all three of these for her Sunday lunch party. She told them both that she would be around shortly after three to take delivery.

She ate a good lunch, read the preceding day's *Wall Street Journal*, with particular attention to the "Real Estate Corner," as usual having not the slightest intention of buying or selling a house but simply for her weekly entertainment, like doing Sunday's crosswords.

And then she took a nap. At your age, my dear Eugenia, she told herself, you need more than one night's sleep to make up for what you went through night before last. It shows on the face, whether you like it or not.

Thus it was, rested, freshly showered, in the car, and with Sindhu in his usual seat in back, that she began her afternoon errands. These proved to be interlaced, as her morning had been, with town news, plus a few unexpected confrontations, both real and imaginary.

Edna was picking the last of a heaping quart of strawberries as she arrived. "They keep better when they're picked dry," she explained, "after the morning dew dries off. I cut the asparagus the minute you called though and put it right in the refrigerator. Earlier in the day, the better for asparagus."

As they made their way back to the house from the strawberry beds, Mrs. Potter thought to ask about bread. "Did you bake again this week?" she asked. "I had friends come by after Harvard's funeral and that cleaned me out. I took the other loaf to Harvard, you'll be glad to know, right from your house the morning after the baked bean supper."

"Hope he had a chance to enjoy a couple of slices," Edna said somberly, "although I always wondered if he didn't like store-bought better. The main thing is, and I might as well ask you straight out, was he okay the last time you saw him?''

"He never looked better than the morning we had your fresh bread,'' Mrs. Potter assured her. ''After the Cogswells' accident, of course, and that was two days later, he looked pretty old and tired, but I only thought of it as being a temporary thing, something he'd throw off the next day. His death still comes as a shock.''

"Shock to all of us,'' Edna said. ''Jake was one of his lodge brothers. He said maybe the old man had been coming down with something, the way his mouth looked there at the funeral.''

From the farm Mrs. Potter drove back down the peninsula road toward the store, encountering Curly Gillan in his truck headed in the opposite direction. Hailing him to a stop, and somewhat surprised that he had heeded her outstretched hand signal, she called loudly across the road between them.

"Curly, I really need to have a ground wire fixed on my stove,'' she reminded him. ''I'm sure that's all it is. It shouldn't take but a few minutes, and it really disturbs me to be getting a little tingle every time I touch the stove. Could you come back with me now and take a look at it?''

She persisted. "Well then, what about tomorrow? No, no, I'm having lunch guests tomorrow,'' she said. ''What about Monday?''

Curly's long upper lip lifted and he pushed at the bill of his cap. "First bad day, just like I told you,'' he said with obvious reluctance. ''It hasn't slipped my remembrance.''

Several teenage boys were lounging against the ice machine when Mrs. Potter reached the store, all of them except Rodney obviously just in from Saturday hauling of their traps, all of them melting away behind the store at her approach. With fresh amusement she saw that Rodney was wearing white tennis shorts and a short-sleeved knitted shirt with an alligator emblem, a young lord surrounded by courtiers in rubber boots and greasy jeans.

Alex Whitehead greeted her as she got out of the car. "Nice bunch of kids, aren't they, 'Genia?'' he asked, not noticing that they had all slipped away as soon as they saw her. "Herbert and I both think young Rod Pickett is a real winner, head and shoulders above the rest of the local pack. I'm going to take him down to Regina's old place and give him a tennis lesson a little later. Herbert said to go ahead and use the court there, and he has it fixed up with Virgil to open the gate for us."

Mrs. Potter had not known that the gates were barred, but she found this news strangely comforting. She refrained from any comments about the "nice bunch of kids."

Inside the store, she found the two cartons of crabmeat that Persy (or Ruth Bewley, more likely) had set aside in the refrigerator case with her name taped to the lids.

There were no other customers in the store, and Mrs. Potter decided she was going to bring up the matter of the vandalism at the cottage while she could confront Rodney's mother alone.

"I'm sorry to tell you this, Persy," she said carefully, "but I was scared out of my wits Thursday night by a bunch of kids throwing rocks at my roof. The only real damage was a couple of broken windowpanes, and maybe some shingles to be replaced on the roof, but it seemed such a mean sort of crazy thing to do. Do you think Rodney would know anything about it?"

"Seems to me you're pretty free with your accusations, 'Genia Potter," Persy told her with sudden ferocity. "First of all claiming you were run off the road by a couple of boys on their bikes"—(Mrs. Potter could not remember mentioning this to anyone except Deke MacDonald)—"and now accusing our children of stoning your house. You'll be looking for communists under your bed next thing, I shouldn't wonder."

Mrs. Potter was suddenly furious. "I am not inventing any mysteries," she told Persy sharply. "Some of the young people, and it's possible that your son may have been among them, have behaved in a very rude and uncalled-for way toward me, and I cannot imagine what the provocation may be. I intend to get to the bottom of this, and I will be grateful for your cooperation."

The pink-cheeked mountain on the stool seemed to grow

slightly smaller. "Well now, I didn't mean to get you riled up, 'Genia. Let's not be hasty, dear."

Winks, who had drawn near to the counter to listen, blinked and nodded.

"I'll tell you what," Persy continued. "I'll see what I can find out about all this from Roddy when he gets home from his tennis lesson. Just take it easy now."

Retreating with dignity, Mrs. Potter went out again into the parking lot. The area was deserted except for Giselle's husband, the much quoted "my Louis says" Louis Oublette, the shell-fish warden.

Louis wore a uniform, very becoming to his dark, broad-shouldered good looks, and he carried a gun in a holster on his hip. He drove a big blue station wagon with the official state seal in gold on its side. His job was the enforcement of state regulations dealing with clam digging and lobster fishing. For all she knew, this also included the taking of shrimp and mussels and even wrinkles.

Now, while Mrs. Potter had never heard of his actually having arrested a poaching clam digger or a lobster boat with an unlicensed stern man aboard, she felt sure that whatever came up, Louis could handle the situation.

"Louis, what do you know about why some of the town young people are behaving so oddly?" she asked him. "I know your Cathy probably doesn't have a thing to do with it, but maybe you've heard something."

Louis wanted to know specifics. It seemed ridiculous to tell him that the teenagers were snubbing her, and she was not going to be drawn into anything like an argument about the boys on the motorbikes. That might so easily turn into a "you did so" and "I never did any such thing" sort of argument.

Instead she simply described to him, briefly, the stoning of her house roof.

"Just horseplay, sounds like to me," he told her. "I can't think why they'd pick your house, except maybe knowing you were there, a woman alone, and that they could throw you a scare. I think I'd just forget it, if I were you—the less said the better. Unless you really want me to call the consta-ble for you and prefer charges."

Hastily assuring him that she could not, after all, identify the assailants, Mrs. Potter thanked the warden and left for home.

It was not until later that she realized she had not learned from him the name of the town constable. The only police she had encountered in Maine had been the highway patrol, who had stopped her on the way to Ellsworth one day because her turn signal light was still flashing long after her turnoff onto Route 1.

Anyway she did know two of the town selectmen, and they could supply her with the constable's name if she decided she needed to talk with him. Unfortunately, both of them had boys who might have figured in her harassment—Skip Cooney, Doc's son, and Orrin Bewley, son of the Otis who was also master of the Grange.

Louis Oublette's advice seemed sound, at least for the moment, and she decided that "my Louis says," the preface of so many of Giselle's announcements, might be based on something more than the warden's almost Hollywood good looks.

As she drove home, she mentally rehearsed possible conversations with the two selectmen fathers.

To start with, confronting them with her questions would be embarrassing and painful. She reassured herself, however, with the recollection of an old French saying: Better to endure the brief discomfort—*le mauvais quart d'heure*—than extended possible later suffering. Or however it went.

She imagined the bad quarter hour of telephoning the Bewley house. Ruth would answer the phone, and assume that she was calling about the crabmeat. Hadn't 'Genia found the two cartons Ruth had left for her at the store? she'd be asked. Then, learning that Mrs. Potter wanted to speak with Otis, her voice (as Mrs. Potter continued to imagine the conversation) would become doubtful. Otis was watching the Sox on the TV right now, she'd be told. Ruth wouldn't like to disturb him unless it was town business and something that couldn't wait. Well, maybe for a quick minute, unless Yaz was up, in which case, *no way*.

Otis used the same two words, once he was on the line

with her in the imaginary phone call. *No way* his Orrin would have tried to run her down with his three-wheeler. Likely just skidded on the old paving. *No way* it was anything but a harmless prank if a few of the other kids (*not his Orrin*) chocked a few pebbles at her roof some night.

In her mind Mrs. Potter heard sudden loud cheering and the clearly spoken initials ''RBI'' on the television in the background. She knew Otis was going to rush back to his plastic recliner, shouting into the phone as he left, ''Thanks for calling, nothing to worry about.''

As she sat in the car, at last back in her small parking spot in the woods by the cottage, Mrs. Potter rehearsed an equally imaginary, perhaps even less satisfactory, telephone conversation with Doc Cooney, the other selectman she knew.

Doc, red-faced and stocky, as choleric as Skip would be in another twenty years, was meeting her question with one of his own. Why did people from *away*—now he meant no offense, present company excepted of course—always think they understood local town business? If some people didn't like living in a good, clean, quiet place like Northcutt's Harbor, he was asking, what were they doing traipsing all across the country to come live here? Easy enough to criticize when people aren't even registered voters, he was reminding her. She was (barely) restraining herself from reminding him that she was, at least, a registered taxpayer, and that even as a property owner she was not allowed to vote, not even a protest to the ever-increasing tax rate when it came up at Town Meeting each March.

This was going to get her nowhere.

She did allow Doc, in her imagination, to soften his counterattack. What was he saying now? This time his answer, clearly heard in her mind, was to an unspoken question, one of those two she had earlier decided to put out of her mind.

''About the boat explosion,'' Doc was saying, ''there's no reflection on Tris, of course, even though he didn't do such a hot job on *Fernette II* last time I had her in. What you should know is—can't recall who told me—it's been said Coley was fixing to change the name of his boat.''

Doc's voice continued, unheard except in her own head,

and she nodded dumb assent. Everybody knew what that meant, he said. Bad luck for sure. He knew a fellow down to Jonesport who did that when he got divorced and married again. Changed the *Mary B.* to *Carleen,* ended up last place in the lobster boat races that year on the Fourth, broke both legs right after that in a car wreck.

The imaginary conversation ended, and Mrs. Potter wondered where in the world she had heard, or why she had been able to imagine, the part about the fellow in Jonesport.

She was losing her marbles.

As she got out of the car and went into the cottage with her berries and asparagus, with her cartons of crabmeat for tomorrow's lunch, she caught sight of Winks disappearing silently among the trees with the limp body of a rabbit hanging from a cord on his wrist.

20

Sunday morning Mrs. Potter was up early. Ruth Bewley's crabmeat was ready in the refrigerator. Other guests she might have given cold lobster with mayonnaise and lemon, but she remembered a visiting nephew who said he was "lobstered out," and she thought Olympia must feel the same way. She picked a great bunch of field daisies for the table.

She felt happy now and busy, preparing for her luncheon guests. Only a few reminders from the previous week intruded on her thoughts.

The immediate one was the still dismal look of the house with the brown cardboard panes, now slightly curling and stained. She solved this problem by pulling the heavy linen curtains across that wall of the room. Their soft gold, yellow, and cream pattern was sunnier than dark cardboard.

For her lunch preparations, she filled big, plate-size scallop shells with a mixture of sherry-laced cheese sauce and fresh crabmeat, sprinkling each with buttered bread crumbs. These she quickly covered and put in the refrigerator to await a later quick baking.

She scrubbed and tied bundles of the crisp young asparagus from Edna's garden, ready to steam and serve hot with fresh lemon butter.

If it had only been earlier in the season, she thought, she would have picked and served wild fiddlehead ferns, a great deal of trouble to wash and clean and yet worth it for what she considered the world's very best green vegetable.

She hulled, but did not yet wash, Edna's heaping basket of

Maine strawberries and let them stay on the kitchen table so that no chill would dim their native sweetness.

She mixed, rolled, and cut out rounds of rich biscuit dough to chill and then later bake for shortcakes with the berries and a pitcher of heavy cream. A man eating his meals at the Sportsmans Lodge deserved a decent lunch.

Even with getting ready for her guests, even with occasional recurring distractions in her mind, there was time for a short walk along the rocky beach with Sindhu. There was time to shower and put on clean white silk pants and a favorite old red and white silk shirt, which she hoped would deflect attention from the still undeniable circles under her eyes.

Sindhu was nervous as Deke's small car came into the lane, followed closely by Olympia and Laurie in the mud-spattered pickup that belonged to the pound. When the guests were settled in the sunshine on the front deck, the dog also settled, falling immediately into a noisy sleep with his nose touching the tip of Mrs. Potter's white sandal.

"It seems it's white pants day," she said, hoping to break the social chill she felt as her three guests sat upright, looking first at her and then at the sea but not at each other. "Aren't we all handsome, though?"

Deke was wearing white ducks and a gray-striped white seersucker jacket. Laurie's crisp white jeans were taut against her slim young body, topped with a classic pink cotton shirt, open at the neck.

Olympia's white trousers, perfectly fitted, certainly not new, were of heavy raw silk. A loose ivory silk blouse floated lightly over her thin body, even slimmer than her daughter's. Like Laurie's, her shirt collar was unbuttoned, and a fine gold chain circled her throat, almost invisible except as she moved. The whiteness of her bared skin was in surprising contrast to her face and her work-roughened hands, darkened and freckled by the weather. Olympia's long pale red hair was pulled back into a tortoise clasp, a few wispy strands escaping into the light summer breeze. And Olympia, today, did not smell of fish.

"So why don't we all have a drink since we're so beautiful?"

Mrs. Potter continued, still with the feeling that, in spite of festive Sunday dress, this party was off to a very cold start. "Deke, could you possibly? You remember where things are? And a Coke for you, Laurie?"

While her obliging guest was in the kitchen, she realized that the drawn curtains and broken panes, which they must have seen when they drove in, made it impossible to avoid the subject of the previous week's attack on the cottage. Mrs. Potter told the story to Olympia and Laurie as simply as possible, without conjecture about reasons, only adding the fact that some of the young people seemed to be behaving rather rudely, which surprised her.

She watched Laurie's impassive young face for possible reactions. Something of the fright she had felt then must have returned to her voice as she recounted the happenings, and Sindhu, sensitive to the sound of her voice even in his dozing, awoke and looked at her closely.

Olympia and Laurie had listened in silence, while Deke returned quietly with a tray filled with glasses, a pitcher of water, a bottle of whisky, one of gin, and one of Coca-Cola. He poured drinks for them all—the gin untouched—then sat quietly on the broad steps of the deck, looking out to sea.

"This seems crazy," Olympia said finally. "What do you know about it, Laurie? Could it have been some of the boys from school, and, if so, why would they have done it?"

Laurie's answer was brief, almost sullen. "Don't ask me. I don't know anything about it. You wouldn't even let me sit with them at the Grange supper and I'm not allowed out of the house at night."

Mrs. Potter decided to ask her own question of Laurie, without any great hope of a helpful answer. "Laurie," she asked, "is there much of a problem at the high school these days with drinking, drugs, things like that? One reads such dreadful stories."

The candor of Laurie's blue eyes, so like Cole Cogswell's, seemed genuine. "Maybe a little," she admitted. "Everybody has to try smoking pot at least once. I mean, even Mother knows that." She shook her head lightly and the pale straight hair fell across one eye.

"I'm beginning to think that letting you come here to high school was a total mistake," Olympia told her icily. "I should have insisted that you continue at Farmington as we had originally decided."

"You know we couldn't afford that any longer after you walked out on my father," Laurie replied with equal coldness. "I know, *I know*—not in front of people." She hunched over her Coke and did not look up.

"My apologies, 'Genia. Our private business is, of course, of no concern to you. However, I can usually vouch for my daughter's honesty, if not always her manners."

"Let's forget the whole thing now," Mrs. Potter said brightly. "I'm sure you'll have a little more whisky, Deke, and pour a splash for Olympia as well? And if you all will excuse me I'll check on lunch and this crazy mixed-up stove of mine in the kitchen."

As if as an afterthought, she called back from the doorway. "I wonder if you'd give me a hand, Laurie dear? I'd welcome a bit of help."

She continued chatting as she moved about smoothly, setting the long pine table for four. "Now if you'd put these field daisies I picked this morning into this pottery jug," she requested. "That's right, the bunch sitting in the jar of water in the sink. I completely forgot to arrange them once I brought them in.

"Oh, that's nice," she told the girl, "perfect. I always just jam them in by the handful, but you really have made a lovely arrangement. Now, if you'd put these berries in the sieve beside the sink and rinse them under the faucet?"

Not expecting answers, but guessing that Laurie would much prefer being kept busy indoors to sitting silent and raging inwardly beside her mother on the deck, Mrs. Potter continued with the cooking of asparagus, the squeezing of lemon, the melting of butter.

"Careful, Laurie, please don't get close enough to brush against the stove," she warned her. "I'm being very, very careful here, as you can see. Nothing dangerous, but it gives you a little tingling shock when you touch it just right. I'm hoping Curly Gillan will be here to fix it soon.

"Now tell me, how are things at Miss Porter's?" she asked.

And yes, Laurie replied to a second question, yes she liked it very much here at Cherrybridge High as well. Her field was marine biology, she said, a statement gaining Mrs. Potter's instant respect.

They moved about the kitchen together easily, continuing the preparations for lunch. Mrs. Potter had quite purposely planned this delayed schedule, hoping that over drinks on the deck Olympia and Deke might establish, if not any degree of cordiality, at least the mutual respect necessary for a continuing business arrangement. Surely Olympia must realize she needed this competent man to run the blueberry part of the business?

"What about new friends here?" she asked Laurie.

Oh yes, Shelley Northcutt was terrific. *Totally*. "She's going to be captain of the girls' basketball team next year and they almost won the regional last year," Laurie said. "So next year should be, I mean, really super."

"And do you play?" Mrs. Potter asked.

"The only thing I really worked on at Farmington was field hockey, and they don't play that here. But Shelley says she'll give me some special coaching this summer whenever she can," she went on eagerly. "She thinks I might even make the team by the time the season really starts." Laurie's voice became happier, more animated. "And *she* doesn't know how to play tennis, so I can help her with that. I wish mother would ask old Herbert to let us use that court of Aunt Regina's. It's just sitting there."

Mrs. Potter continued her casual questions. What about the boys in town? What about Ted Pettengill?

"He's a nerd, and anyway he's too old. He graduates next week." Laurie was becoming more outspoken as their talk went on. "And I suppose you're asking about Skip Cooney and Orrin Bewley too?"

Mrs. Potter nodded, busy with melting butter.

"Let's face it," Laurie said. "I mean Skip is just too loud and silly, and Orrin is at that terrible stage when he can't decide whether to shave every day or not. Now he says he's going to grow a beard this summer, and I bet him he'd never make it."

Mrs. Potter was draining the asparagus at the sink and arranging it on four separate plates so that the lemon butter would not run down under the scallop shells on their larger plates. "What about Rodney Pickett?" she asked.

Laurie's earlier rush of comments slowed. "Well, that's kind of exciting. He's the best-looking boy in school, and he's really smart, the science teacher says. Not my kind of natural science, but physics, computer stuff, things like that."

"And he probably has the best manners," Mrs. Potter added, with a silent mental change of the word "has" to "had."

"I guess so. Anyway, all the girls think he's really neat, and they say I'm the first girl he's ever, well, fallen for."

"That sounds nice," Mrs. Potter said.

"I suppose it's just because I'm new, and, you know, sort of different," Laurie said. "Anyway he wrote me a poem and called me his Lady Laurie. I never had anybody write a poem about me before. And did you know he's really the son of an English lord, and that Uncle Cole and Aunt Regina could have *proved* he was, if they hadn't died?"

Mrs. Potter's eyebrows raised, but she did not offer a contradiction.

"Anyway, Mother says he can't call me on the phone every night and she says I'm too young to be going out on dates," Laurie said.

After a pause she continued. "It's going to be hard on Rod if he finds out about his mother and Mr. Gillan. That's a tough one to handle, and I know, only it was my father who was playing around."

She sighed. "It *is* kind of great to have someone say I'm beautiful and his dream princess and things like that. I never went to school with boys before."

Mrs. Potter found that lunch was ready to take in. As they began, she realized that she herself had something to say.

"Laurie," she began, "you don't know how much I admire your mother. It must have been miserable for her coming here after the divorce, and hard for her to ask your Uncle

Cole to give her this job. It must be very difficult and lonely for her sometimes. She has earned everybody's respect, you know, and she's making a success of a very demanding job. She must be so tired every night she can't see."

Handing Laurie two plates of asparagus to carry to the table, Mrs. Potter went on. "And I want to tell you I admire you just as much. You do your share at home. You're making a few new good friends and I know you'll find more."

As she set out the carafe of chilled white wine in front of Deke's place for him to pour, she wanted to add more, hesitated, then finally plunged ahead. "One thing you've got, Laurie, which your mother doesn't have, is the ability to open up and talk to people. Why don't you just admit to her that you're dying for a basketball practice hoop and for time to practice evenings with Shelley and Cathy—I'm told she's pretty good too—and why don't you ask her if you can go to a school dance with Rodney or something of the sort?"

Without waiting for an answer she called Olympia and Deke in from the deck to the cool and shady living room, where lunch was now waiting.

Shortly thereafter, Mrs. Potter mentioned the subject of Laurie's interest in marine biology to Deke, hoping to find a mutually agreeable topic. It seemed clear that he and Olympia had not progressed beyond chilly formalities in the time she had left them alone together with their drinks in the sun.

Marine life, to her relief, proved to be a subject of interest to all of them.

Engaging Laurie's rapt attention and her own growing interest, Deke talked about the life cycle of the Atlantic salmon, and specifically about the return of the salmon to their spawning grounds in the headwaters of the Metoosic at this time of year.

"You fish, do you, Laurie?" he asked her. "No? Would you like to learn? I've already promised our hostess a lesson."

Laurie's ordinarily rather inexpressive young face lighted with a tentative sparkle. Mrs. Potter herself felt a small rush of excitement, a definite change of spirits from the somber mood of the past week.

"What will we need in the way of equipment?" she thought

to wonder aloud, remembering the booted fishermen along the riverbanks, their creels, broad-brimmed hats, and long springy fly rods.

To her surprise Olympia provided an answer. "It takes a lot of gear," she said, "and I should know. I used to have it all. I haven't fished for years now, though, and I'm afraid I simply left mine all in New York when I walked out on Laurie's father, as she now chooses to put it. Anyway I can fit you both out with Coley and Regina's stuff—I'm sure they'd have wanted you to use it. Then if you decide to take it up seriously later on, 'Genia, you can see about getting exactly what you want."

Regina's waders, she said, would be all right for Laurie, and Coley's, those of a shortish man, perhaps right for Mrs. Potter. There should be a good choice of fly rods at the Cherrybridge house, as well as boxes of flies, everything they'd need.

"Except later on a license for 'Genia," Deke put in. "I'll check the law on this, but I don't think Laurie will require one if she's under sixteen. But of course you may be? . . ."

Laurie blushed with pleasure.

"I hate to presume, Mrs. Cutler," Deke spoke more formally now, "but do you think it would be possible for me just to see those rods and flies of your half brother's, maybe even later this afternoon? I'll leave to you the choice of whatever my pupils are to use, of course. But Mr. Cogswell had promised to let me see his gear, and there are some things I'd just like to touch and examine—the kind of stuff one doesn't often get to see. Could I drive you there later on and ask you to show them to me?"

Olympia's manner was again cool. "Yes, that might be possible, Mr. MacDonald, since this is my free day. Sunday is the only day I'm not buying lobsters now."

Mrs. Potter, feeling that it was Olympia's turn to talk, led her to explain about Sunday fishing.

Most people thought Sunday restrictions were a conservation measure, she said, just to restrict the quantity of the catch, intended to reduce overfishing.

"Actually," she continued, "the fishermen put through

this piece of legislation themselves, just to make it harder for outsiders to break into the business. The cost of a license is high enough that it's scarcely worth while for a summer resident to get one if he can only fish on Saturdays. If his fishing weekend covered both Saturday and Sundays, it might be a different matter.''

After Labor Day, this amateur threat to their livelihood safely back home in the city, lobster fishermen could again operate legally seven days a week, with the only limitations on fishing days being those of the weather.

"Tell me, is it true that some of the chaps cut loose a man's traps from the marker buoys, so they can't be found, if they want to keep him out of their fishing grounds?'' Deke's question was serious.

"I'm told that it's been done,'' was all that Olympia would say.

Mrs. Potter listened for the bell that told her the biscuits should be done for the shortcakes, and, as she left for the kitchen, Laurie rose without being asked and began to clear the table very quietly and neatly.

Maybe it will work, after all, Mrs. Potter thought with satisfaction as she split and buttered the flaky biscuits. Deke and Olympia had obviously taken some sort of dislike to each other from the beginning, but at least now they're *talking*. She must plan to get them together again soon.

Laurie carried plates and silver to the sink, where she rinsed them quickly and put them into the dishwasher without comment. Then, as Mrs. Potter was heaping the slightly sugared berries between and on top of the biscuit layers, she spoke, somewhat diffidently.

"About what you asked me, Mrs. Potter,'' she began, "you know, Cherrybridge High probably isn't much different from any place else. I mean there's somebody coming in smashed once in a while, and I suppose most of the Northcutt's Harbor kids smoke pot, or at least they've tried it. I mean, it's easy enough to get it. I just don't happen to do drugs myself, although I must say I did enjoy that little glass of wine Mr. MacDonald poured for me at lunch. He looked at Mother first with his eyebrows up, you know? And she didn't bat an eye, except she poured a little water into my glass before I drank it.''

The shortcake was ready. Two still rather stiffly formal guests awaited them at the long trestle table, and talk returned to the subject of fishing.

Mrs. Potter's guests left shortly after three. Meantime Laurie's excitement over learning to fly-cast had taken root. Olympia had given permission for the lessons to begin the following week some day after school. Deke would meet the two of them, Mrs. Potter and Laurie, at the Cogswell house in Cherrybridge, where he and Olympia and Laurie were going now to look over the fabled collection of rods and flies.

After her guests' departure, she had intended to stretch out on the deck in the sun, but after she found her book and her glasses and prepared to settle herself there, Mrs. Potter saw, advancing from the east, a thick gray layer of fog above the ocean. As she watched, it came closer. The breeze had died, the air was still warm, but she shivered slightly as the fog, thick and inexorable, rolled in upon Northcutt's Harbor.

"They're maybe giving fog for tomorrow," Lyman Cooney admitted doubtfully when she called him, at a time when she thought the Cooneys would have finished supper. "Well, yes, maybe if I can't get out to haul in the morning I'll try to get at those windows. Can't promise, now."

Curly's answer was much the same. He agreed that the forecast was for more fog in the morning. He agreed, as nearly as it was possible for him to give an unqualified agreement or assurance, that he might, he just might be able to come to the cottage tomorrow to take a look at the stove.

Not wanting to give him the slightest excuse for further postponement, Mrs. Potter pressed her advantage. "Now you remember where the key is, if I should be at the post office or should be out with the dog when you get here, don't you, Curly? That's right, on the nail under the eaves. And I'll leave the range installation manual on the counter, right where you'll see it.''

Then, never quite trusting Curly's qualifications, she told him as tactfully as she knew how to remember to throw the main switch. You need to cut off all the power before you begin to look for the trouble, she reminded him. And the fuse box was right there in the kitchen, on the wall next to the outside door. She considered telling him that *up* was OFF on the switch box handle, but decided that he might (and rightly) take any more instructions as an insult.

Finally, knowing that she had come as close as she was likely to in getting a definite commitment from either Lyman or Curly, Mrs. Potter called it a day.

She bade Sindhu *stay,* and he obediently composed himself on the rug at the foot of the stairway. Suddenly weary, she started up the narrow steps.

Then, as she thought of fishing lessons, her spirits lifted and her step was lighter. She thought about the Metoosic sparkling in the sun, about the great shining dark shapes gliding through the clear water, and about a tall Scotsman teaching her how to cast a fly rod.

21

Monday morning "they" were still, indeed, "giving fog." Mrs. Potter had learned the forecast with the radio news that accompanied her early tea, but a glance out the window would have sufficed.

Schools in the area were closed, the genial voice of the announcer told her from his microphone in Ellsworth. This did not seem too important, she thought, since, as everybody knew, nothing much got taught or learned in the last week or two of school anyway.

The Monday morning of the Puffs and Pants exercise class was canceled. The garden tour for the benefit of the community center in Millstone was postponed until Wednesday. The town planning board of East Downington would meet one week from today at the home of Mrs. Ira Guptil.

The long list that followed made Mrs. Potter realize anew what a tremendous round of activity was going on all about her every day of the week. Summer people, village people, year-rounders, they were all unbelievably busy. She caught only a sampling of all this from time to time when she learned what events the fog or snow, in its season, had caused to be canceled or postponed.

Here at the cottage, the ocean to the east and the tall trees to the west were invisible in the thick gray-white cloud. The hooter, the foghorn off the end of Bessie Island, sounded regularly, sorrowfully.

Sindhu returned from his morning inspection of the premises, and she toweled his feet, back, and head while he stood motionless and dignified in the kitchen doorway. "We'll have a good walk later," she promised, "when the fog lifts enough that we can find the road."

No sign yet of either Lyman or Curly. Should she risk offending them by yet another telephone call? No, that might be considered *too* pushy. She decided to wait until after she came back from the post office and then give them another nudge if she had to.

The fog was no less dense when Mrs. Potter—outfitted for the day in yellow slicker, sou'wester, and high boots to keep the legs of her jeans from being drenched by the heavy, leaning, dew-beaded grasses along the path—set off with Sindhu on her usual walk for the morning mail. Fog condensed and dripped from the brim of the stiff yellow hat, and her bare hands were wet. It was like walking through water instead of air, she thought, like being a two-legged fish. The road, what she could see of it, seemed totally unfamiliar, with all landmarks lost to view.

As they neared the post office, she heard a liquid tenor, perhaps magnified by the fog, singing in Italian, *"O Sole Mio."*

"Al, that's lovely," she said as she recognized the small raincoated figure on the post office porch. "The sort of mournful, swooping sound of that is just right for this day."

As he greeted her, Al Colamaria patted Sindhu's wet head. "Hi there, *paisano*."

He'd been wondering, he said, he and Amanda, if she would be out in this weather.

"We love it," she told him. "It's hard to see, but it's beautiful."

"Will you let me drive you back, to be safe? I have the pickup here and the fog lights are good. And if you'd stop on the way at the trailer, I'll have Victoria make coffee."

Mrs. Potter begged the excuse of the expected handyman and electrician at the cottage. "Thanks, Al, but we need the walk. I'm going to stop for a few things at Pickett's, and then I have to go right back home. Say hello to Tory."

The linoleum-covered floor of the post office was slippery from wet boots and dripping slickers. Mrs. Potter unfolded the square of plastic she kept in her carrying bag and wrapped her newspaper and letters snugly.

When she came back out to the porch, Al had left, but the sound of his singing seemed to hang in the fog.

At the store, Persy was busy with an account book, her huge bare arms spread out over the counter. The CB blared, faded, then rose again in volume, crowding the small store with noise in the heavy stillness of the foggy morning. Winks lounged against the freezer case, methodically intent on a box of marshmallow-topped cookies.

"That crabmeat was wonderful yesterday, Persy," Mrs. Potter told her, deciding that she no longer intended to speak further to Persy, or to anyone else, about the rock throwing. "I had guests for lunch and they loved it."

Persy seemed disinclined to talk, and Mrs. Potter went quickly about her rounds of the crowded room. A spool of heavy thread to sew on some loose blazer buttons, a job she'd been postponing for an indoor day. A couple of rolls of thick paper towels—the other indispensable staple of her household, she realized, in addition to lined legal pads. That should be about all she could wrap and keep dry with the mail in her satchel on the foggy return to the cottage.

The CB made strange loud noises, then cleared for an instant.

"Why is anybody on the CB?" Mrs. Potter asked. "I thought all the boats would be in today for sure."

Teedy stamped into the store, his boots and his sou'wester dripping, just in time to hear her question. "Ahoy there, mate," he said. "We don't use these things just for going to sea, you know." She tried to think where it could have been that Teedy Pettengill had gone to sea in Rochester, New York.

Looking up somewhat crossly from her ledger, Persy entered the conversation. "Thought I told you, 'Genia, but I guess at your age you forget things. Most everybody's got a CB in their houses. Almost everybody's got one in their trucks too, just like Teedy."

"You really ought to get one yourself, 'Genia," Teedy told her, tilting his head back to see from under the dripping point of his hat brim. "Great safety feature for a woman alone like you. You might have a flat tire driving by yourself at night, the way you do. I certainly wish you'd listen to me about living down there all alone. I've got a good prospect for that last waterfront lot, but no earnest money, so it's still yours if you want it."

Persy's voice became conciliatory. "Teedy's right, 'Genia," she said. "You got scared to death the other night, you said so yourself, thinking that someone was throwing pebbles at your roof. I was some worried about you after you left the store Saturday."

"What's this? What's this?" Teedy spluttered. "Things aren't shipshape down there at the cottage?"

Mrs. Potter had not intended to confront another unbelieving parent, but she was forced to explain. "I did have a little problem late last Thursday night. In fact, there *was* a small amount of damage done at the cottage."

Teedy was quick to respond. "Thursday? Wasn't that the night we went to the Van Dusens' party? Matter of fact, 'Genia, the kids were at our house that evening." (Mrs. Potter had no recollection of any mention to Teedy of the age of the possible assailants.) "They were playing pool, the way they used to before they all got so busy evenings with homework. Ted was reading in bed by the time we got home, and he said they all went home early. After all, school isn't out yet, you know, and that was a school night."

Mrs. Potter turned to leave, realizing that she'd never know the truth behind what she was beginning in her mind to call "the night of the bombardiers." This time she really would forget it.

As she came out into the parking lot, the fog seemed even thicker, almost like walking into, then through, a white wall, only to find the same white wall still around you on all sides.

It was only by a nudge from Sindhu against her knee that she realized she was about to collide with an approaching figure.

"Alex!" she exclaimed, as she recognized the outline. "Isn't this fog something?"

She was, it seemed, just the person Alex Whitehead had

hoped to see. He'd been thinking about her since that night last week at the Van Dusens'. He'd been worrying about her, he and Bets had, living all alone down there by herself on the Point, with all her neighbors gone.

"Thanks, but everything's fine," she assured him. "Sindhu and I manage very nicely, and, in fact, we both find it rather fun to feel our way down the road in the fog."

"I know, but are you sure there hasn't been any little thing bothering you?" he asked solicitously. "Somebody said, I can't remember who, that there was trouble at your house last week."

Mrs. Potter hesitated. Was she going to tell this silly little story again? As she considered the matter, she saw faint fog lights on the road, apparently headed in either the direction of the pound or her own cottage.

"You can tell me about it," Alex urged gently, his face close to hers. She was aware of the interest in the surprisingly soft brown eyes and of the drop of water condensing on the tip of the slightly off-center nose.

Well, maybe here was someone really willing to listen, someone who'd have an idea whether she should take the rock throwing seriously. Alex would have an outsider's approach, perhaps objective enough to advise her whether she, and the rest of the village, really should be doing something about the odd behavior of the village teenagers.

Again, as she had to Olympia and Laurie, she told, briefly and without emotion, the story of the Thursday-night stoning of her house. Additionally she decided to mention, but again as unemotionally and as fairly as possible, the fact that the teenagers were pretending they did not know her. Finally she even told him of the other occurrence—still possibly only a childish prank—when she was forced into the ditch by the swerving motorbikes.

She had intended to be dispassionate, but when she came to her fright and dismay at the charge by the giant three-wheelers, she realized that her voice was mounting in pitch and that her hands were trembling when she shifted the bag holding mail and groceries.

Standing there, wet and dripping in the warm fog, encouraged by a sympathetic ear, she found herself repeating the offenses, describing the teenagers as they had been before this recent, incomprehensible change in their behavior, even re-counting the indifference of the parents she had questioned.

"I'm repeating myself!" she apologized to the tall, some-what fog-blurred figure standing beside her in earnest attention. His obvious concern led her to continue. "Alex," she said, "please, have *you* any idea about what might be wrong with these kids? Would they be acting like this from smoking marijuana? I really know so little about it."

A patient and understanding listener, Alex answered gently, the two of them in a quiet cocoon of white fog. "You are certainly right to wonder about it," he said. "How about letting me talk with the right agency for this in Washington? My lawyers will know, and we can get straight input on the subject from people who know what they're talking about."

For the first time, someone was taking her seriously. Per-haps Deke MacDonald had done so, but he had only listened without offering any helpful suggestions.

Alex's hand on her wet shoulder was firm yet reassuring. "But the first order of business is this," he said. "Are you sure you still want to keep on living alone down there? I just wonder if your place is the right one for you now.

"You love the area," he continued, "so what about doing what we're doing? Build another house just like the one you've got, only on Teedy's shorefront lot. It would be right next to ours, which is really going to be quite handsome even though, as Bets says, we may just use it for a hideaway on weekends. I expect to take over a great deal of the actual management of the bank very soon now, as well as setting general policy, and I must say it will feel good to be back in harness. I've had enough of this retirement life."

Another set of yellow fog lights went by slowly, this time coming from the south and heading up the peninsula road.

Mrs. Potter was suddenly impatient to be home and out of wet clothes and she had heard quite enough about Teedy's last waterfront lot, the lot on the bay which twice every twenty-four hours held water. This as an alternative to her own pink-granite boulders and crashing surf?

"Thanks," she said. "You were good to listen, Alex, but I've got to go now. I'm hoping for two people to come this morning to do a little work at the cottage. Probably neither one will show up, but I just saw a truck go up and down the road."

She wondered vaguely what errands might have brought Teedy and Alex out on such a morning. Possibly they just found it exciting to walk in the fog, as she did.

She moved slowly through the fog down the familiar lane to the cottage, guided more by Sindhu than her own disoriented senses. Her thoughts returned to Lyman and Curly. Maybe I'll be lucky, she thought, and one or both of the jobs will be done by the time I get there.

Droplets of fog condensed on her brows and eyelashes, and Sindhu's coat was frosted, each hair thick and wet, his great gray body seemingly surrounded by a misty, watery nimbus of light.

It was apparent as she reached the cottage that whoever had come had not been Lyman to replace the windowpanes. She stepped close to the living room wall of the house to make sure. The cardboard replacements, dark brown now, sodden and wet, remained in place.

Well, maybe the stove will be fixed, she encouraged herself. The key was on its accustomed nail, but she was cheered by dark prints of heavy boots on the wet stone doorstep. Someone had been here.

The room was dark as she opened the kitchen door. She switched on the light as she entered, stopping inside the entrance to shed her wet slicker and hat and to hang them on pegs by the doorway.

Sindhu brushed past her, not waiting for his ritual toweling, thirsty for the bowl of fresh water he knew he would find by the stove.

There was one brief, incredulous, agonizing yelp, a howl of pain cut suddenly, mercifully short.

The overhead light went out.

A flash like a bolt of lightning crossed the end of the room and Mrs. Potter felt a powerful blow that sent her reeling back against the hanging wet slicker. She reached for the handle of the fuse box beside her spinning head and pushed it upward, convulsively.

There was a smell in the quiet room like that which follows a summer thunderbolt. It was only then that Mrs. Potter knew she was also smelling burnt hair and flesh.

22

Dwight Henderson was solicitous. His neat red beard quivered with concern.

Was the room all right? Would she be coming to the dining room for dinner or could he have Agnes bring over a little tray? Would she like another window open?

Mrs. Potter could not remember what her answers had been when the young innkeeper finally left and she was alone in the small motel cabin, one of a row of twelve in the rear of the Sportsmans Lodge. Her mind seemed to be saying "yes, thank you," so presumably that had been her response to all his questions. However Dwight chose to interpret that in relation to her dinner, it was of no importance.

She hoped she had thanked him for having this room available and making it ready for her with such dispatch in answer to Deke MacDonald's telephoned request. Jim and his lady, Anne-Marie, it seemed, had rushed to do the painting, and Barbie, the chambermaid, had helped with the job in order to have the room ready for her that late afternoon, although it had not been scheduled for occupancy until later in the week.

There was still a smell of drying latex in the air, but the clean beige walls were dry to the touch. The bathroom was clean and bare except for a stack of thin towels. The twin beds were made up with clean, worn, white seersucker bedspreads. The windows were covered with green roller shades overlaid with faded net curtains with crossbars of pink and green. The bare floor was uncarpeted, with only a cotton rag rug between the beds and another in front of the painted white table that served both as desk and as a stand for a small television set. There was a wicker armchair with cretonne-covered cushions of indeterminate color.

The room was not only all right, it was perfect. A haven, a den, a clean cave in which to retreat from a world in which a stupid, careless mistake by a stupid, uncaring workman could cause the death of a noble and loving friend.

The wicker chair creaked beneath her, and she looked at the unopened overnight case at her feet. Time enough to find out what she had packed. At least her hairbrush and toothbrush, she hoped, and something to wear tomorrow besides her now-dry rumpled jeans and dark jersey. Time later to find out.

Snatches of the afternoon passed through her mind.

Deke MacDonald's small car had raced down the lane and braked with a little spin of wheels on the pine needles in the clearing.

"Are you all right? What happened?" He ran toward her through shreds and wisps of mist, now lifting and lightening as the late-morning sun burned through the fog.

"Have you been hurt? Why are you sitting like that on the doorstep? Can you move?"

Wordlessly, Mrs. Potter barred the way to the kitchen door. "I'm all right," she managed, "but how did you know?"

"The power is out at the transformer, the one that serves both the pound and this whole end of the point. When we couldn't find anything that had gone wrong there, I realized that there had to have been a problem, maybe an accident, here at your house."

He had, it seemed, been in the office at the pound with Olympia. Suddenly all the lights had gone out, the power had stopped for the gasoline pump and the whirring old refrigerator beside the painted safe.

"Mrs. Cutler checked and we could find nothing amiss in the buildings there. I determined by ringing up Pickett's that everyone on the peninsula, above the transformer that is, still had electricity. That's why I thought I'd better check down here."

Was it immediately thereafter that Alex Whitehead's pickup swerved into the clearing?

"What's going on here? What's the trouble? 'Genia, are you hurt?" Alex dropped to her side on the wide flat stone and put an arm around her shoulders. It felt good to be held.

It had taken such a long time to explain to them—the little shocks she had been receiving when she touched the stove, the diagram of the ground wires she had studied in the onwer's manual. The decision to have Curly fix what seemed a simple matter instead of calling the appliance service man from Ellsworth. The phone calls and reminders to Curly. Even the heavy boot prints on the shining, fog-wet stone of the doorstep on her return from the store.

It seemed so very complicated to tell, and it took such an effort to make herself understood. Deke interrupted her once with a question about the key to the back door. When she pointed to the nail above her head, he reached up, removed it, and slipped it into the pocket of her shirt front.

Alex asked about the footprints. Dried and gone now, unfortunately, he averred, half rising to inspect the stone where he was sitting at her side.

"I'm going to call the doctor," Deke told her. "It looks as if you're all right, except for the mental shock of it, but we'll have to make sure."

She put her hand on the doorknob behind her and shook her head without speaking.

"No," she said. "No. Not yet."

The next coherent memory must have been after Deke finally insisted on entering the cottage, and Alex suggested that, in addition to calling the doctor, he should call the veterinarian in Cherrybridge as well.

She remembered her own vehement protest. "*No*. Absolutely *no*."

"Would you like him to be buried here on the place, then?" Deke alone seemed to understand her refusal. "If you'll just tell me where you keep the linens of the house. . . ."

He went back into the cottage and she heard thumping sounds from the kitchen behind her. The fog was burning away and she sat in the fast-breaking sunlight of midday on the step, Alex still beside her, with his protective arm about her shoulders.

Deke returned. "And now for a spade? The toolshed, of course. Where would you like him to be buried, do you think?"

For the first time, she was able to stand and move.

Without speaking, but with utter certainty, she went to a patch of open, sunny ground beside the bank of flowering *Rosa rugosa*. Sindhu had liked to lie here and look out at the gulls.

Pulling off his soft sweater, Deke outlined an area with the spade and began to dig. Mrs. Potter watched him. She was quiet, back on the doorstep, half asleep now in the sun. Alex began to tense and move restlessly on the stone beside her.

"This looks like a straight case of criminal negligence," he announced. "The best thing to do, in my opinion, is to get some good legal advice in the matter. I'm going home to call my lawyers in New York, 'Genia, if you have no objection to my acting for you in this."

She had nodded, as she now remembered, and Alex went back into the kitchen to assess the damage.

Sometime after Alex's truck had left the lane, Teedy drove in and stayed briefly. He viewed the kitchen and left saying he would bring Eileen back if she could be of help. Mrs. Potter said she would be fine and she'd rather not see anyone now.

Then two other equally new and shiny pickups, similar except for color, pulled into the space in the clearing. Deke took charge firmly.

"Lyman, you get busy cleaning things up in the kitchen," he told him, "and have you the new panes of glass with you? No? Well, be sure that you get them and take care of those replacements the first thing in the morning without fail.

"Curly, you take a turn now on this digging. Put your back into it now, man."

And then somehow it was later.

It must have been early afternoon when Laurie had come racing down the lane on her bicycle. "Mother told me," she said. "I just got home from Shelley's. She said she couldn't

206

leave the pound now but that I could come over. Oh, poor Sindhu."

Laurie had said she would pick some flowers, she remembered.

Were they field daisies, like the ones for their lunch party yesterday? Or purple flags? No, the flags had been for Harvard's funeral.

It had been Laurie, she thought, who mentioned seeing Winks in the woods. "Quiet as an Indian," Laurie (or someone) had said. "First you see him and then he's gone, sliding between the trees."

"I know," Mrs. Potter had said. Hadn't she seen him earlier in swirls of the fog? She could not remember.

Deke took over again from Curly with the shovel, and Curly went into the kitchen to survey the scene of his presumable negligence.

There was a big rectangular hole and a big pile of gravel and earth beside it. Deke took off his shirt in the hot June afternoon. His shoulders and back were white. He dug steadily and his muscles rippled under the untanned fair skin, turning pink in the sun.

One of her last clear pictures was of Deke, back in his shirt, carrying a heavy body, wrapped firmly in a clean white sheet, to the newly dug grave.

"Take off your cap, man," she heard him tell Curly. "We're burying a gentleman worth two of you."

There was Curly, bareheaded, as she had never seen him before. The sandy, curly hair proved to be only a thick round fringe around a high, bony, bald dome. I would never have guessed he was bald, Mrs. Potter told herself, still unable to focus on more than one thought at a time.

There were Laurie's flowers (they had been daisies, she now remembered) strewn over the mound of raw gravel, and the clear, young voice, cool and sure as her mother's, repeating the words of the memorial service for Coley and Regina: "And we commend to the Almighty God our brother Sindhu, and we commit his body to its resting place."

The rest of the afternoon was a blur, even though her mind by now seemed increasingly able to comprehend the day's happenings. The young doctor came and proclaimed her to be unhurt, although he wanted to check her over again at the clinic tomorrow. The Colamarias stopped for a short time, just long enough to tell her they were sorry and for Al to inspect the scene in the kitchen.

"Mama mia!" she clearly remembered hearing him say as he came out.

Rodney Pickett arrived in the Pettengills' truck with young Ted. As soon as he, like the others, had gone in to view the scene of the disaster, Laurie slipped away quickly on her bicycle, saying that her mother would be down later to help if she could.

Alex returned to accost Curly and tell him that he had been in touch with his lawyers, who demanded to know all the details.

Curly, his back propped up by the toolshed, protested his innocence and lack of responsibility for the accident.

"She knows I'm not a licensed electrician," he repeated, his long bare skull covered again with the denim cap. "I never claimed to be a real electrician. I was just going to do her a favor. I just told her I'd come to help her out if I could. You can't blame a man for trying to be a good neighbor. But who says I was here this morning? Who saw *me* here anyway?"

Mrs. Potter had been unable to make out whether Curly was admitting that he had come and had made some faulty connection that had caused the short circuit, or whether he was attempting to make the case for complete noninvolvement.

Again, no matter. Alex would sort it out and with his high-powered lawyers, would know what should be done about Curly. It was a matter of very little consequence.

Deke had gone in again to telephone, and came back to tell her that he had engaged a room for her at the Sportsmans Lodge. They were completely booked now with salmon fishermen, it seemed, but Dwight had one last cabin not yet renovated for the season's occupancy. He had promised to have it at least clean and habitable for her by the end of the day.

Olympia arrived in the Cogswell truck, and it was with her

help that Mrs. Potter was able to enter the house, by going around to the front door and coming in from the deck.

Maybe Olympia packed this case for me, she thought. I know she looked all over for my reading glasses and apparently found them undamaged on the kitchen table.

No, she did not drive her own car to the Lodge, for she remembered distinctly sitting beside Deke as he brought her here, after his insisting that she lock the cottage and return the key to her own pocket where he had placed it earlier.

She remembered that Olympia had followed them with Mrs. Potter's own small car. That way she'd have it there in the morning if she wanted it, one of them had told her.

Now there was a knock at the cabin door. "It's Agnes, with your supper," she heard, and the tall, bony waitress let herself in. "Here you are, on this little table right in front of your chair, and I'll turn on the TV so's you can hear the local news while you eat."

Supper was stewed chicken, mashed potato, creamed carrots. The news was equally predictable. Governor promises state austerity program. Questions of drug smuggling continue to plague Maine coast. New winners in state lottery. Red tide threatens Florida shellfish. Local schools to finish season. Mr. Somebody-or-other, Lewiston convict, excapes and is caught an hour later by state police. The escapee, as always in Maine broadcasts, was given the dignity of being called mister, and the report also mentioned the fact that Mr. Whatever was in jail for setting fire to the trailer of his common law wife, incinerating her and their three children.

Mrs. Potter finally rose, set the tray on the doorstep, locked her door, and went to bed knowing, at long last, that whatever had begun with the explosion at sea and Harvard's death, it was not yet finished.

23

Just as Mrs. Potter took her responsibilities seriously as a member of the small community, so also did most of the other residents of Northcutt's Harbor.

There was no telephone in her small cabin at the Sportsmans Lodge, so Dwight, Agnes, and Barbie, the chambermaid, were kept busy throughout the next morning relaying messages.

"Mr. Teedy Pettengill called and he wants you to know how sorry he is about your pooch, said to remind you what he said about moving out. Should he locate a good rental trailer for you?"

"Amanda Wakefield called, from the post office. Says she's sorry about the accident, and what should she do with your mail?"

"Mrs. Bettye Whitehead" (I wrote it down just the way she spelled it, Barbie told her) "wants to know how you are feeling, and please call her back."

"Lyman Cooney says he's taken out the stove and it doesn't look much good. Should he take it to the dump or try to have it fixed up?"

And there had been a Mr. and Mrs. Weidner who said they'd be in Cherrybridge this morning and that they'd stop by about noon in case she felt like having lunch with them.

There was a long note from Carter, written in a firm, clear half-printed hand, along with a basket of flowers from the Ellsworth florist. He had not got the news until after she had left the cottage, he wrote, and he had immediately gone over and got Lyman to let him in so that he could see what had happened.

Curly ought to be hung by his toes, his note said. Herbert Wyncote came by earlier, Lyman said, and he agreed.

The important thing was knowing that she was unhurt. He hated to leave just when she'd had this awful loss and he understood how brokenhearted she must be about Sindhu. However, he'd had a problem come up with an important client, something about a new bank building he was doing in Atlanta, and he had to fly off at once, leaving this note with the florist as he went by on his way to the airport in Bangor. He sent his love and told her he'd be back as soon as he could, a few days at most. He told her to take care.

And there was a single spray of apple blossoms, its woody stem carefully peeled and crushed, in a tall, clear jar of water, with a small attached note. "Everybody's so sorry," it said, signed *Deke*.

The overnight case had provided for the morning's needs—toiletries, a fresh cotton dress, shoes, and underthings. Mrs. Potter showered and dressed, telling herself it was irrational to consider her world at an end because of the death of a pet dog, no matter how intelligent and responsive, no matter how much she had loved him.

You're behaving as if this was of greater importance than Harvard's death, she told herself severely, more important than Coley and Regina's tragic accident at sea.

It is to me, an inner voice admitted guiltily. *It is to me.*

No matter how you feel about it, my good woman, it happened. Sindhu is dead and his beautiful, obedient, sleek gray body is buried beside the bank of wild roses.

Alone in the small, clean, bare room, the morning sun blazing through the pink and green net at the window, she wept in sorrow and undefined fear.

Now, Eugenia.

Now, listen to me, my good woman. Get up off this bed, blow your nose, and wash your face. The first thing you must do this bright June morning is to go see Clarence at the furniture store and order a new electric range for the cottage.

The second is to come back here and have lunch with your

good friends Chuck and Margo, who are being kind enough to drive to Cherrybridge, hoping to be of some comfort to you. Your part of the friendship is to let them do just that, to accept the gift of their sympathy and their companionship.

And this afternoon, of course, you must remember that the doctor asked you to stop for a check at the clinic.

Clarence had already heard the news of the accident. He was deeply sorry. He extended his heartfelt sympathy. He wished he might be of help to her in her hour of grief. Mrs. Potter knew that his professions of sorrow were unfeigned, for she had seen his hand reach to touch the head of the black Labrador whose footsteps paced his own as he moved through the store. On impulse, she told him of Laurie's words when Sindhu was buried.

"Nothing wrong with that," he assured her. Clarence was speaking now as a funeral director and his shoulders straightened.

"That's the way I felt about it, too," Mrs. Potter admitted. "But now I've got to accept the fact that my dog is dead and try to get on with the business of living myself. And that means getting a new stove so that I can move back to the cottage."

Clarence was sorry, he explained, as his gray-sweater-clad shoulders sank to their everyday apologetic stoop. Not a range in stock after his May sale. But he'd be glad to order one. Would she take a look at the spec sheets?

It only took a few minutes to find the model that most closely resembled the old one in color and size. It had several new features—a self-cleaning oven and a removable griddle top—which she eyed favorably. The price, of course, was twice what she remembered the former stove had cost.

"This will take about ten days, I'm afraid," Clarence told her. "I just phoned the distributor in Portland, and that's the best he can do for me. I'll give him a prod every few days and see if we can hurry it up. That all right with you?"

It would have to be all right. Mrs. Potter preferred to buy through Clarence, a local and trusted merchant, and she certainly didn't want to have to drive to Bangor to shop around, probably to end up with the same delay facing her.

"That's fine, Clarence," she told him wearily, "Call me at the Lodge as soon as you have a definite date for delivery."

At least this gave her some kind of answer to a question she vaguely remembered Dwight Henderson's asking her the evening before, along with his solicitous inquiries about her comfort and her room.

"I think you asked me how long I'd be staying," she said, when she found him at his desk in the lobby upon her return.

"I don't mean to rush you with your plans, Mrs. Potter," he assured her earnestly. "I did have a reservation for that cabin and we intended to have it all fixed up, new carpet and all, by the end of the week. But I can juggle things around and there may be somebody who'll cancel out. I just wish we could be booked up like this the rest of the year, after salmon fishing season is over."

He peered at the open ledger before him, rubbed his beard, and frowned. "Anyway, you let me know what word Clarence gets on the stove, and I'll figure it out some way so's you can stay right here in number eight until your own place is ready again."

Margo and Chuck came into the small lobby as the conversation ended. "Will you be staying for lunch?" Dwight asked them, "I don't usually open the bar until later, but if you want a drink. . . ."

Chuck raised a questioning eyebrow, but Mrs. Potter said no, not for her thanks, and Margo agreed.

"Although if you could manage a glass of white wine while we're ordering lunch?" Chuck suggested, and the two women nodded.

Both Chuck and Margo held her hands as they walked into the dining room. "We just can't begin to tell you how sorry we are," Chuck said.

"Curly is a dolt, and his mistake was unforgivable, whatever he did." Margo's eyes were wet as she whispered, "What will we do without the 'chairman of the board'?"

When they were seated in the nearly empty dining room and as they surveyed the limp, slightly smeared menu Dwight had brought them with the wine, Chuck tried to sound matter-of-fact. "If this place doesn't change the bill of fare from one year to the next, I'll be darned if I see how they get any business at all. Hamburgers, french fries, tuna salad sandwiches. Western omelets. Chicken salad. Minute steak. All of them lousy. I've got it memorized. What'll you have, ladies?"

"I had some hopes for the place the other day," Mrs. Potter told them woodenly, trying to sound cheerful. "Deke MacDonald—he's the new manager of the blueberry business for Cogswell & Son, that is if he stays on now that Cole is gone—asked me here for tea the other day after the memorial service. And they actually had *tea*. In a *pot*, real tea. And toasted blueberry muffins. I couldn't believe it."

Chuck ordered a second glass of wine. "I should have got a bottle of something better in the first place," he grumbled. The talk continued, with proposed recommendations for improving the food at the Lodge.

"I expect the place is full at night and for breakfast, when the salmon fishermen are in," Margo said, in her tentative, questioning way. "But they pretty much have to take what they get, or else go out for even worse food at the Rope Walk. You know, Dwight could have this place filled all the time if he'd hire a decent cook and make a specialty of really good regional dishes—lobster stew, fresh crabmeat, chicken pot pie, good hot breads."

"Baked beans, of course," Chuck put in, enthusiastically. "Lobsters every which way. Hot gingerbread. Blueberries in everything—anyway blueberry muffins and blueberry pancakes on the menu all the time, and blueberry pie, no matter what else. The place could be a ten strike, if the poor bastard only knew it."

"Blueberry fool, blueberry grunt, blueberry buckle, blueberry cobbler." The litany was continued by the pretty dark-haired girl who appeared, neatly aproned over jeans and a white T-shirt, as their waitress.

"Anne-Marie Loeb! What a nice surprise!" Mrs. Potter, brightening, introduced her to the Weidners. "You both remember Jim Markham—he's done some painting for me at the cottage. Yesterday he and Anne-Marie must have knocked themselves out getting my cabin ready. I do thank you, my dear, and Jim, too."

"It was the only thing we could do to help," Anne-Marie said resolutely. "We were both so sad about Sindhu. Jim adored him when he worked for you that week in April. But I shouldn't be talking with customers, should I? I do know how to serve, of course, but it seems I haven't learned not to join in the conversation at the table."

"Don't be silly," Mrs. Potter told her. "Where's Jim? What are you doing playing waitress?"

Anne-Marie, it seemed, was not playing. This gave her a chance to make some extra money, and tips were supposed to be good during the fishing season. Looking at Chuck, she flushed slightly. Anyway Jim had a job on a house-remodeling crew for a bit and while they didn't need *her*, it was too good a chance for him to pass up—good pay and a chance to learn about refinishing floors.

And part of the good luck for them was that Agnes—did they remember the old waitress? They did—Agnes had to go home for a week or two to nurse her grandmother. That's right, *her grandmother*. And guess why? She had tripped over the pail while milking her goat and had broken her arm; so, while she didn't need nursing herself, she did need somebody to milk the goat.

"Only in Maine," Chuck murmured. "But now I suppose we'd better let Anne-Marie earn her tips" (his smile removed any possible reproach in his words) "and order us some lunch."

As she was leaving with their order, Anne-Marie volunteered another comment. "I heard what you said about serving lobster, too," she said. "Dwight has it listed on the menu at night, but actually it isn't always available and the cook is usually pushing the special, anyway. What he ought to try is lobster pie. Remember Jim told you, Mrs. Potter, he was going to learn to make it? Well, he did and it's terrific. Something like that could just make this place, or his mother's blueberry fool as a special dessert."

She returned with pallid plates of chicken salad. Its sole garnish was a small and lonely sweet pickle slice on a single limp leaf of lettuce. The cold, damp rolls had a small plastic-encased square of butter beside them. The coffee was almost as bland as the chicken and had cooled to something less than hot by the time the filled cups arrived from the faraway kitchen.

"I know it looks awful," Anne-Marie said sympathetically, "but at least I know the chicken is fresh. I saw the cook boil it this morning. I just wish I could have made the salad myself, with my own homemade mayonnaise and a pinch of tarragon, and have given you some pretty garnishes. There are nice cantaloupes and honeydew melons, both, out there, and a slice of each would have been so good and so easy to do."

"What's the matter with Dwight, anyway?" Chuck asked. "Is he trying to go out of business?"

"He told me he made his own sukiyaki," Mrs. Potter said. "That must mean he knows something about food. Or is he only interested in Japanese cooking?"

"Frankly, he only *talks* about sukiyaki," Anne-Marie said confidentially, speaking the word, as Mrs. Potter had, with its four good American syllables. "Nobody knows that he's actually ever made it. The fact is, Jim and I agree that Dwight has all the qualities of a good inn-keeper, except one. He cares about his guests, he's making the place much nicer and more comfortable, he likes the business, and he really thinks he can make it succeed now that the fishing is getting so good again in the river. But—well, you know people who are tone deaf? Dwight just has a tin ear when it comes to food. He kept the old cook who was here when he bought the place, and the same old menus, and he just doesn't seem to notice how dreadful it all is."

"Well, we three are going to have to face him with this some day soon," Mrs. Potter asserted, without much determination. "This may not be the day, but we'll get to it."

Chuck then urged dessert, and Margo said, "Might as well have some ice cream, 'Genia, it comes on the lunch anyway."

"Hey, why don't we have some of that melon?" Chuck asked Anne-Marie.

"I've already asked," Anne-Marie said resignedly. "The cook said no. Melon is only on the breakfast menu."

They all dutifully spooned up their brick-hard orange sherbet, bright as a hunter's orange jacket. And just about as tasty, Chuck pronounced in final judgment. "Sorry we couldn't give you a better lunch, 'Genia, but at least it's good to be with you. When are you coming home?"

"You two are wonderful," Mrs. Potter told them. "Not only are you very dear to come and be with me today, but you're wonderful for making all this talk about food, which I know you're doing to try to divert me."

She wished she could keep them a little longer, to speak of her deeper fears. Maybe tomorrow, when she felt a little less wobbly, she could ask for their help.

Deke MacDonald was the only person in whom she had confided, and then only fleetingly. Here at the Lodge this evening she would talk with him again. She had to face the realization that Sindhu's death might have been her own. Deke had offered to help that morning after the stone throwing, and this was something he should know. They could talk the whole thing out together.

Reassured by the thought that she would see him tonight, she could now force herself to report at the clinic.

Most of the rest of the afternoon was spent in the waiting room of the Charles Robbinsford Cogswell Clinic, the small community emergency-first-aid facility and general health center Cole had founded some years back as a memorial for his father.

A young dentist and young doctor maintained office hours here daily, and a succession of invariably pretty young women from the town worked as receptionists and nurses.

"Quite a line ahead of you," the blond girl at the desk said, "but I know the doctor wants to see you again, quite specially, to check you after the electrical shock you got yesterday. If no emergencies come in, things ought to move along pretty fast."

Mrs. Potter had time to glance through a magazine on jogging, a subject she found less than fascinating, and one called *Free Flight*, or something of the sort, about gliders and recent changes in hang-flight techniques. There was another about skiing, which occupied her only briefly, and then one devoted to fashions for the young woman in business. Finally there was one about toilet training and sibling rivalries. The interests of the staff were represented, she noted. Proving that you really *are* getting old, my dear Eugenia.

It was not hard to let her thoughts return to the previous day, and a relief when she heard her name called. The examination was brief but reassuring, and she was able to tell the doctor that the headache she had felt all of yesterday, following the electrical shock, had gone away during the night.

It was not until she was leaving, making her way through the still crowded waiting room, that she remembered the question she had intended to ask. What could cause what Clarence had told her was unusual about Harvard's body after his death? Was there significance in the black and blue marks on his tongue and the pronounced chafing of his lips that both she and Amanda had remarked?

It would have been hard to ask without affronting professional dignity. The questions themselves implied some sort of oversight or negligence at the time the death certificate had been signed.

It was not going to be easy to ask, and her head began to ache again. Looking at the long line of patients now ahead of her before she could return to the doctor's small office, she decided to postpone her question a little longer.

There were more messages at the desk of the Lodge when she walked back the short distance from the clinic. Mrs. Sis Northcutt. Mr. Alberto Enrico Colamaria and Mrs. Victoria, offering their condolences. Mrs. Edna Birdson, saying she had a new puppy for her. Mrs. Cutler, calling from the lobster pound, saying she was coming to Cherrybridge after dinner and would telephone again then if it wasn't too late.

Dwight had written down every word of this in his careful backhand. There was no message from Mr. MacDonald. Inquiring casually, Mrs. Potter learned that his cabin was number three.

However, as she turned to leave the office, Dwight called

218

her back to the telephone. It was Deke. He was terribly sorry he hadn't been able to see her today, but he was completely tied up going over business matters with Olympia, and he knew she would understand. He no doubt would be unable to get back until after dinner, possibly too late to look in on her. Was she all right? Good show! He'd see her tomorrow then, or as soon as he could.

Later, her head again ached slightly and it was an effort to persuade herself to leave the cabin for dinner. She refused to think that this was the time when she should be calling Sindhu in from his patrol of the rocks and the bayberry patch near the cove, the time for him to settle himself with his head on her knees while she watched the news and sipped her evening drink.

The overnight case provided no second change of clothes, but she forced herself to shower and repin her long hair in a freshly twisted knot. At least she (or Olympia?) had packed her gray eye shadow and a favorite cologne. She moved purposefully, determined that her thoughts focus on the present moment only.

The bar at the Lodge was not a separate room, but part of the main dining room. You could sit at the bar end of the barnlike, bare room, at a regular square table, looking into space as you sipped your before-dinner drink, or you could carry it back with you to an identical square table at the other end of the room and drink it there as you were ordering dinner.

Tonight Mrs. Potter chose the former procedure.

Dwight, his red beard twitching with his eagerness to please, came from behind the bar to take her order. "We're so happy you feel up to coming to the dining room tonight, Mrs. Potter," he said. "Not that Anne-Marie—nice kid, isn't she?—wouldn't be glad to bring dinner to you, you know that. I'm just glad to see you out, that's all. What can I bring you?"

He returned with her order. "Just a glass of the regular house white wine," she told him, "the same thing we had with our lunch today." As he brought it, two large, roughly dressed men seated themselves at the table next to hers, carrying their filled glasses from the bar.

Their shoulders were massive. Their dark hair was shaggy, and one had an untrimmed black beard. Even their big hands were covered with black hair, she noticed. They both wore laced boots, open-necked khaki shirts, and hunting pants.

Their voices were surprisingly soft. "Evening, ma'am," one of them said politely. "Been a nice June day, hasn't it?"

A country inn, like a house party, serves as its own introduction. The weather was duly praised. "You here for the fishing, ma'am?" one of them asked her.

"Well, yes," seemed a possible answer, in view of the promised fly-casting lessons from Deke. "And you two are here for it, too?"

This she had asked somewhat doubtfully. The bar end of the dining room was now filling up, and the rest of the company appeared to be much smaller people than her present companions. The men were wearing jackets and ties, all of them, as far as she could see. The few who appeared to be accompanied by wives were mostly middle-aged, and the women were wearing flowered prints or pastel pantsuits; wherever they appeared there was a flash of bracelets and earrings. An occasional bright madras jacket stood out among the dark blazers of the men.

"Us, *no!* It's hard enough to get a reservation this time of year with all those fishing dudes around, but this is the time *we* go bear hunting," her hairy, gentle companions told her. "Don't you know about bear hunting?" They seemed incredulous.

At times, Mrs. Potter felt that all her life had been conditioned to saying, "No, do tell me more." In this case, it was easy to plead complete ignorance. She sipped her wine and glanced occasionally at the doorway, looking for a tall, neat, dark head and a nicely trimmed mustache.

As usual, she ended up hearing what was at first more than she wanted to know, and then finding that the subject was actually fascinating. Hunting bears in Maine, they told her, was legal from the first of May to late November. You could take one bear, either sex. Dogs were allowed as long as you didn't hunt with more than four, and then not in deer season. They didn't use dogs themselves any time of the year.

The word *dog* was a quick stab, which Mrs. Potter resolutely ignored.

In late spring or early summer, they told her, the owners of the blueberry barrens brought in hives of honeybees.

Yes, Mrs. Potter had assured them, she'd been told of this. Cole had said that the bees served him by pollinating the pink cups of the blueberry blossoms, thus raising his production enormously over that of the fields whose fertilization was solely dependent on wild bees.

What she didn't know was the role of her hairy friends.

Bear hunters, they explained, filled a dual need in the balance of man and nature. They described the white, boxlike hives, stacked in long rows on the barrens. They told her that the honey the bees so assiduously gathered and stored there each day attracted wild black bears from the surrounding woods.

Since the depredations of the bears were a threat to the bee colonies—one swipe of a rough black paw, one night of ursine feasting, could wipe out an expensively maintained bank of hives—the blueberry-field owners welcomed the hunters.

Bees make honey, they said. Honey attracts bears; bears attract hunters. Their sport protected the hives and, in turn, the blueberry harvests of Maine.

Another thing, they asked her, had she noticed the new state highway signs? WARNING, BEES, CLOSE CAR WINDOWS. These had been put out on the barrens north of town, they told her, and that, of course, was where they'd be hunting.

"I will never know where to stand in a matter like this," Mrs. Potter told the two as she left for the other end of the big room and for her dinner. "I don't know if I should be on the side of the bees, the bears, or the berries, or if they're all one cause. Anyway, this has been interesting. Thanks, and I may see you another time."

The hunters rose and bowed with large sweeping gestures.

Do all hunters look like the creatures they hunt? she wondered.

Do the rest of these smooth, rather elliptical people in their neat clothing look like salmon? Do the men have slightly jutting jaws, developing a nasty hook as the male salmon do, growing these pugnacious features in time for the spawning season?

Still hoping that Deke would appear, she said good night to the large, gentle bears and went on to a just-edible dinner. The fish, billed as haddock, turned out to be a previously shredded and shaped triangular piece of anonymous fish life from unidentified waters. The cole slaw was thick and soggy; the rolls were, as at lunch, damp and cold. Only the french fried potatoes were passable, and even those were not up to ordinary "fast food" standards, Mrs. Potter thought. She ate quickly, had a spoonful of a wet custardy dish full of soggy brown nuggest ("The Grapenuts pudding is the best bet tonight, at least better than that pie with the canned apple filling," Anne-Marie had advised), and left for her cabin.

Barbie, it seemed, was at the desk at this time of the evening, while Anne-Marie was busy waiting table in the dining room, and Dwight was still occupied at the bar. She came to Mrs. Potter's door, bustling with importance. "Mrs. Cutler's on the phone, but she said not to bring you back to talk with her. Said she and Mr. MacDonald were going over the fishing tackle at the house again and that they'd have you outfitted for a first lesson tomorrow afternoon. You're *not* to be disturbed to come back over to the phone, just to let me know and I'll tell her. Shall I tell her okay? And isn't that Mr. MacDonald the best-looking thing that's hit Cherrybridge for a while? Wouldn't it be *wonderful* if he and Mrs. Cutler made a match of it?"

The idea was startling. Mrs. Potter almost forgot to give Barbie the message, a hesitant reply that, yes, she would be ready for her first fishing lesson tomorrow.

Several times that night Mrs. Potter awoke. Once she lifted an edge of the cracked roller shade and looked at the green glare of the sodium vapor light on the pole far overhead, making the small courtyard almost as light as day. The door lock was secure and the sliding bolt above it seemed solid. The only sound was that of fitful snoring in the next-door cabin.

24

One cotton dress and one stiff, wrinkled pair of jeans was not a wardrobe for an extended stay anywhere, even at a hostelry as undemanding as the Sportsmans Lodge. It would be necessary to go back to the cottage. And, with or without Deke's help, she had questions to pursue.

The peninsula was fragrant and flowering on the early June morning. Pink clover perfumed the field at the farm, and she paused for a few minutes with Edna, who was in the huge vegetable garden placing more brushy supports for long rows of early peas.

"There's asparagus today, and new rhubarb," Edna told her, "and I just baked. Need any bread? That is, if you're moving back to the cottage?"

Mrs. Potter walked along the edge of the garden, sniffing the air gratefully. "Edna, you wouldn't believe it, but at the Lodge they believe there are only three vegetables in the world—canned beets, canned carrots, and canned peas. They think that if the bread and rolls are bad enough they may be able to cure their customers of a wasteful habit. The first meal I have when I get back to the cottage again is going to be just this: green peas from your garden, a bowl of fresh rhubarb sauce, and about half a loaf of your homemade bread. Just thinking about it is going to give me strength to live through the next ten days in Cherrybridge, because I'm going to stay there until the new stove comes."

Edna insisted there was time for tea and that she had just made a pan of blueberry buckle for Jake's dinner at the same time she had baked her bread. That was just what they needed now with a cup of tea. They sat on the sunny, breezy back porch of the farmhouse while the farm dog paraded her puppies below.

"No, thank you, Enda, it's awfully good of you to suggest it, but I'm not going to have a dog again." The little dogs and their mother retired to the large carton under the open back steps and Mrs. Potter tried not to remember the big feet and soft ears of Sindhu's puppyhood.

At Tris and Sis's, she paused again.

"If you want anything done to the car, Tris'll be back around noon," Sis assured her. "He's down to his dock now, working on a boat. Lucky the men around here don't take heed of the idea that Tris fixed the Cogswells' boat wrong, though there's some that don't know him so well who are saying that. Makes me mad, especially since he dropped everything to get it done for them on time; then they changed their minds and let it sit here at our dock for two days before they had Virgil pick it up. But no point in trying to tell people that. Most folks know Tris does good work and keeps his word on when he'll get jobs finished."

Mrs. Potter reassured Sis that anyone who knew Tris, both as a man and as a mechanic, would not be likely to think that his work had caused the sinking of the *Cog's Wheel*. "After all, no one knows what caused the explosion, do they?"

Sis shook her neatly trimmed round, gray head doubtfully. "Coast Guard never said. Explosion was too big and the boat too far out for any real inquiry. I only know that some folks—like that nephew of Regina's, Herbert something, the one who came into her property—are saying things about Tris,, but the fishermen hereabouts have stayed with him."

Sis's coffee was a bracing change from the pale brew of the Lodge. A crisp brown homemade doughnut (unsugared, to ease her conscience) was a comfortable sequel to Edna's cinnamon-fragrant blueberry cake.

As she ate, she pondered. The *Cog's Wheel* at the dock for two days?

Her mind raced ahead. The timing of an explosive device— she knew there must be such a thing—would have been easy

to determine. Cole and Regina had been most specific about
the hour they planned to go out in the boat that last morning.
They had mentioned inviting several other people as well as
those at Sunday supper at her house the night before. Any of
them, or probably anyone else in Northcutt's Harbor, could
have known just when the boat was going out and could have
computed what time the cruiser would be well out to sea.

With an effort, Mrs. Potter wrenched her thoughts back to
her conversation with Sis. Yes, she would certainly like to
come to a shower for Janine next week. What would she and
Tommy like? This was a good time to find out, by inquiring
directly from the hostess, the mother of the groom.

Anything at all for the trailer, it seemed, or anything in the
way of baby things. They hadn't really got anything much yet
of either kind.

Mrs. Potter remembered a wicker changing-table she had
seen the previous day at Clarence's store. She'd stop on her
way back and have him set it aside for her. It could make a
fine and generous plant stand or even a small sideboard in the
trailer, she thought, and then serve its original and avowed
purpose when the time came.

A combination wedding shower and baby shower, she
thought, given by the mother of the new husband-to-be—how
solidly practical and how comfortable in its acceptance of
facts.

She then realized that there certainly would be more than
one such shower, and decided that some kind of small electrical appliance would be suitable as a second gift. After all, the
father of the bride was Mrs. Potter's caretaker, and some
tangible appreciation of his position, on her part, would be in
order.

An electric wok, she decided. Clarence had one of those,
too. It would seem a more up-to-date gift than a percolator or
toaster; it could be displayed on the wicker tray table in the
dinette in that phase of its use; possibly it could be used to
warm baby food as well as to stir-fry. In this case, it would
be the show that would count, not necessarily the utility of
the gift.

As she continued down the peninsula road, she continued

to think of Tommy and Janine. They're not too young to be married, by earlier standards of Northcutt's Harbor, and the world has always had its beautiful, pregnant young brides. I just hope this works out for these two as well as it has for many of their forebears.

She paused at Pickett's, then decided to go first to the cottage, down the narrowing lane to the Point, her spirits dwindling with the road, sinking bleakly as she pulled to a halt in the needle-carpeted pine clearing.

Using the key Deke had removed from its peg and placed in her pocket the day of the accident, Mrs. Potter forced herself through the still oppressive, scorched smell of the kitchen. Lyman had taken out the old stove, she noted, and the narrow oak floorboards where it had stood were stained and darkened. Without pausing, she decided that the kitchen floor should be sanded bare, then refinished with several coats of clear polyurethane to obviate future waxing.

The living room was hot in the early June sun and several large black flies were buzzing against the windowpanes. Lyman had replaced the two broken panes on the west side, she noticed, and the outer edges of these were smeared and fingerprinted with putty.

With the toe of her shoe she pushed aside the faded hooked rug at the foot of the stairway. Time enough to deal with that later, and with the leather chewing toys and with the several leashes hung near the kitchen door. It was not the same as it had been to dispose of Lew's pipes, his favorite boots and closetful of city and travel clothes, as well as his ranch jeans and beloved old, soft L.L. Bean flannel shirts, and yet it was going to be painful to clear the house of Sindhu's presence.

Whatever would be needed for the next week or so was quickly packed into a large suitcase, retrieved from its storage place in a low cupboard under the eaves. Clothes, shoes, the spare pair of reading spectacles. She found room to include a few recent magazines yet unread from a table in the living room and several books to be returned to the Cherrybridge library. She added a double deck of playing cards for her solitaire game of Spider on possible future wakeful nights in cabin eight.

She was leaving the cottage, knees slightly bent as she carried the heavy suitcase, when a familiar big gray and yellow truck pulled into the clearing.

MAIN COAST POWER & LIGHT, its door sign told her, was on the job.

"You the lady here?" A quick look at the clipboard in his hand refreshed the driver's memory. "You Mrs. Potter?

"Your man Cooney let me in here yesterday and while we were in the place I helped him carry the old range out to his truck," the uniformed man told her. "He said nobody's been in the place since the short circuit Monday afternoon. That right?"

"As far as I know," Mrs. Potter told him. "Lyman Cooney, the caretaker, had the only key except the one I have here with me, and anyone who had reason to come in would have had to find him to have the house opened. I guess one or two friends did come in with him to inspect the damage after I left. Everyone else in town was here earlier in the day, before that."

"We've got a kind of mystery about this accident," the utility workman continued. "My name's George, incidentally, George Gibbs, from over to Schoodic. Now I don't know how much you know about electricity. . . ." He paused doubtfully. "Anyway, let me try to explain what happened the other day when your dog got killed. The range ground wires came completely loose, see, and besides that the hot wires leading to one of the surface units apparently came into contact with the frame of the range. Don't ask me how, but that's what happened."

"So anyone who had wet feet or was standing in a puddle of water would have got the full force of the current?" Mrs. Potter asked. "The full 220 volts?"

Reassured by this apparent familiarity with electrical terms, George went on. "A lot more than that. There would have been a short circuit all right, when the current made contact with the wet dog, but something else had to happen, too. The main fuse had to have been out of the circuit. There wasn't any fuse to *blow*, that's the only explanation of it. The stove and the dog got the full force of the main line current from

228

the transformer. That made the electrical shock here in the room like a big bolt of lightning. That's what blew the transformer up the road. The power went off at the lobster pound, too, when it happened.''

"I threw the main switch here, you know," Mrs. Potter continued weakly. "I turned off the power to the house."

"Actually, ma'am, by the time you pushed that switch, the power was already out. What I'm trying to figure out is how it could have happened. The main fuses and the ones for the range seemed to be perfectly okay when I looked at the box. Only thing I can figure out, and it sure sounds crazy, is that something got stuck in that main panel, like some kind of heavy copper slug. Even a heavy copper wire would have done it. Do you follow what I'm saying?''

Mrs. Potter, after her years of experience as a householder, understood enough to know what George was telling her. To start with, there had been a faulty rearrangement of wiring, either accidental or contrived, in the stove itself.

The true fury of the lightning bolt, however, had resulted from a bypass of some sort in the main kitchen fuse box, allowing the full force of Maine Coast Power & Light, unimpeded by the normal cutoff of a household fuse, to hurl its deadly charge.

"Can you show me where the main box was bypassed?" Mrs. Potter asked carefully. "It's very important to me to know how it was done, and we've got to find out how it happened.''

"Can't find a sign of anything," George told her cheerfully. "Everything looks fine. I'm just telling you how it *had* to be for the transformer to blow like that. There *had* to be a bypass of some kind, or the short circuit here in the kitchen would just have blown out your own range fuses and that would have been the end of it. Might of killed the dog just the same. Maybe so, maybe not. 'Twould have given a body more than a tickle, however he touched it.''

Mrs. Potter felt an inward shudder.

Then another thought came to her. "The stove—I suppose that it would show if the wiring was in any way, well, *out of place*?" She chose not to say *tampered with*.

"Expect it would," George told her. "Your man will know about that most likely. He was carting it off when I left him. Said he didn't think it was worth fixing. What I'd kind of like to know is if anybody was here after the accident who'd know about that main panel. Simple enough thing—mybe just a couple of heavy copper wires. You could put 'em on or take 'em off in a minute if you knew what you were doing. Only thing is I can't figure out why anybody would do such a darn fool thing. Anybody who knew *come* from *sic-em* about electricity'd know better than to do a thing like that, I should think."

As she drove to the Cooneys' house, Mrs. Potter tried to remember, out of the daze of the afternoon following Sindhu's electrocution, who might have been in the kitchen alone, with opportunity to remove the slugs or wires or whatever had been there. Deke, of course. She remembered, too, his later insistence that Lyman go in and clean up the kitchen while he was digging the grave. Didn't Curly go into the kitchen alone, maybe first, after he and Lyman arrived? Alex? Olympia? Teedy? The Colamarias? Even Laurie? This was getting to be *insane.*

Lyman hadn't yet come in from fishing, Alice Cooney told her, but maybe she'd meet him on the road. Or would she want to leave a message for him? Meanwhile Alice wanted to tell her about the little neighborhood shower they were giving for the young people—you know, Janine and Tommy—and hoped that she would be back for it.

Mrs. Potter asked if maybe an electric wok would be a nice idea, and Alice agreed with enthusiasm. A wok was one thing Janine knew for sure she wanted. Not that she was much of a cook, but she'd learn.

Lyman's truck pulled into the drive as she prepared to leave. "About the electric range, Lyman," she said, "I've ordered a new one from Osgood's, since you said that the old one was damaged beyond fixing—is that right?"

"Yep, I know you like things cleared up quick and proper, and that MacDonald fellow said to clean up," Lyman told her. "Curly said the same thing—'twasn't worth saving. So I hauled her right to the town dump."

"Curly went over the stove with you too, then? Did he check out the main entrance panel too?"

"Yep, at least he went over the stove, best he could. Said it must have been defective all along, finally just went bad on you, being such a wet day and all. And now what did you have in mind for that kitchen floor? I could put down some of those tile squares pretty fast, if you say the word."

It took a little persuading to convince Lyman that the beauty and utility of properly refinished oak floors would be worth the trouble of renting a sander and doing the initial hard work. Finally she was able to secure his grudging agreement to do what she wanted, and, as near as she could achieve it, his promise to do this job within the week.

"Remember, I want to move back to the cottage the day Clarence gets the new stove," she reminded him, "and the wood floor will have to be sanded perfectly clean and smooth, right down to where the wood looks like new. Then you'll need at least a day for each of the three coats of finish to dry after that. You'd really better start it tomorrow afternoon after fishing, Lyman, so the stove can be moved in the minute it comes."

Not completely reassured as to his intent, Mrs. Potter drove on to the lobster pound, her mind reeling with thoughts of woks and sanders and crazy electrical circuits and connections.

"She's not in the office," Alma warbled sweetly. "First boats are already coming in. You'll find her down on the dock. Unless there's something I can do for you? Norwood and I were so darned sorry to hear about your dog. That Curly!"

Above her head the two radio receivers, now turned low, droned their inexhaustible outpouring of weather reports, personal messages, and snatches of sporadic conversation.

"I don't see how you can work with that going on," Mrs. Potter said. "Doesn't it bother you?"

"Actually I don't hear a word of it unless I happen to hear my own husband's voice," the bookkeeper told her. "That's him now, Norwood." She cocked her head attentively. "Wants me to pick up a new car battery from Tris on my way home before dinner."

"It sounds like a foreign language to me, most of it," Mrs. Potter admitted.

"I hope you don't mind my saying so," Alma told her, "but maybe it's because, well, you do have kind of an accent. That's probably why."

It came as no surprise to Mrs. Potter that she, as an outlander, was thought by some to have a strange and difficult accent. She remembered a relayed comment Amanda had told her a year or two after her arrival in Northcutt's Harbor: "That Mrs. Potter means well, like enough, but I can't understand a word she says."

She accepted Alma's words meekly, and went on down to the front of the building above the dock, where she expected to find Olympia.

Again she found the narrow passageway between the various sheds blocked by a large refrigerator truck. Apparently the driver had just backed in and was unlocking the ponderous back doors of the van. Mrs. Potter peered into the dim, empty interior, thinking what a large and valuable cargo it would haul, and of the obviously needful precaution to lock it up against possible lobster hijackers, if there were such, along the route.

Her mind flashed to the memory of Harvard and his brother Alston and the night of the bootlegger. How she missed that man. It would be immeasurable help today to be able to talk with him.

A straight, slight figure in a frayed cotton shirt, jeans, and rubber boots shot up the ladder from the platform below. Clearly in a hurry, Olympia merely repeated the gist of the previous evening's telephoned message.

Deke would meet her at the house in Cherrybridge at five for the fly-casting lesson. Laurie would come there after school to meet them. There would be the necessary fishing gear, which she and Deke had picked out last night.

She was calling him Deke. On the strength of that, Mrs. Potter ventured a question about the continuing managership of the blueberry operations.

"Yes, I've decided to keep him on for the rest of this season," Olympia told her rather stiffly. "Cole thought he was well qualified, and I don't yet know enough about that end of the business myself. By another year I hope to be able to manage the whole thing myself, both blueberries and lobsters. I don't intend to be dependent on another man, ever, 'Genia, any longer than I have to be.

"Are you all right at the Lodge?" she continued. "Did I pack the right stuff for you?"

"Exactly right," Mrs. Potter told her, "and I do thank you. But I'm going to have to stay on there for a week or so, so I came back for a few more things today."

"It must have been awful to go to the cottage," Olympia said, repeating what Alma had said earlier. "That Curly!"

At that moment, Mrs. Potter's head began to ache again and she realized that she could not exactly remember why she had come to see Olympia. To confirm the fishing engagement? Her mind was a jumble after the talk with the utility repairman. She left quickly, saying she knew this was a very busy time of day at the pound.

At Pickett's shortly thereafter, Winks was languidly unpacking several cartons of canned vegetables, picking them up and studying each can as if he expected to find some surprising new picture on its label, some message of infinite importance revealed in the red tomato or the yellow kernels of corn.

Persy, as usual, was spilling over on her stool behind the counter. Today's sleeveless dress was a green and white check with pink daisies outlined in alternate white squares. There were a great many daisies to be counted from one side to the other as she turned her back to adjust the CB.

She squared herself again on the stool and her small eyes were sharp and questioning. "Hear you had quite a time of it down to the cottage. Suppose you'll be closing up the place, won't you? Folks wouldn't blame you a bit was you to sell out now, I can tell you."

"As a matter of fact, I'm moving back in just as fast as I can, Persy. Just as soon as Clarence can get a new stove for me and Lyman gets the floor refinished."

Persy again gazed at her sharply. "Hope you get a good stove this time for a change. Downright criminal if Clarence sold you the last one. Anyway I wish I could clear out of this place as easy as you could if you took a mind to," she said, now in tones of complaint.

Mrs. Potter recognized the beginning of a health bulletin that would cover details of the continuing list of afflictions Persy had endured since Mrs. Potter's last visit to the store.

The allergies were worse, Persy said, and even the new doctor up to the clinic was puzzled what to do next. Then there was the new plate that didn't hold, and it had got so a person couldn't relish a square meal anymore. Her feet were giving out, and some nights it was all she could do to get up the stairs to the apartment. With a sideways gesture of her big head, made even bigger by the mane of teased, sprayed, dark red hair, she indicated the open outside stairway at the side of the building, leading to her living quarters above the store.

She went on. Rodney, it seemed, was ailing too these days. It would be a mercy when they were out for the summer, they worked him so hard up there at the high school. He was just plain done in when he got off the bus these days, too tired to help with the stock orders. It was all he could do to drink a Coke or two and crawl up those stairs, even with Winks to help him. Still, other days he'd be wild to go off taking tennis lessons from Mr. Whitehead, or racing around with young Ted Pettengill in Teedy's pickup.

At least he was a good boy, Persy continued. Even Mr. Ansdale said so.

Mrs. Potter had heard enough of the Picketts, mother and son, and she left, speaking only briefly to Herbert and Teedy, who were arriving in Teedy's pickup.

"Nancy and I are terribly sorry about the accident," Herbert told her. "Beautiful dog, that Sindhu. She was such a lady."

Oh well, some people don't notice dogs much, she told herself, and she was too tired to attempt a correction.

"Miserable sort of accident," Herbert repeated. "I've turned over all the work at Millstone to a proper electrician. Don't know why I thought I ought to patronize the local talent, but thank heaven he hadn't got around to our house yet."

"This will be the last wiring job for Curly in these parts," Teedy prophesied. "We'll see to that. And I'd like to see Tris

Northcutt out of business, too, after that boat explosion. We've got to have some standards around here.''

Mrs. Potter had started her car as Teedy was speaking. Her head now felt as if it had been stuffed with cotton wool. What was it that the Maine Coast Power man had been trying to tell her? She had better look at that stove.

The town dump was off on a narrow road to her left as she drove up the peninsula, about a mile north of the Grange Hall. A sawhorse barred the narrow entrance road, and against it a wooden sign was propped. *No Dumping Today* it said, in fading, hand-drawn letters. *Town Burning Crew at Work.*

A light pall of smoke hung above the dumping ground beyond the sign, and Mrs. Potter could see an old truck on the hill and a pair of lounging figures leaning against it.

She paused and studied the sky. A cloud of herring gulls was circling overhead, and as she watched she saw these begin to descend to the ground, first one brave leader, then the less adventurous followers. Obviously the fire must be nearly out if the hardy scavengers were returning.

She would be no less venturesome herself. Leaving her car at the roadblock, Mrs. Potter advanced on foot down the little road between the odd bits of paper and plastic, bottles and cans, that marked the path of those trash dumpers who had not quite made it all the way to the official site with their loads intact.

"Hey there, lady, keep out!" one of the lounging figures called to her hoarsely across the few rising swirls of smoke from the pit. "Can't you read? This is burning day."

Mrs. Potter continued until she could look into the unlovely hollow between them. At first she could not see it, a crushed and blackened box in the center of the burned-over dump. When she did spot the remains of her old kitchen range, she realized there was no point in trying to have someone retrieve it. The bulldozer had done its work first, it was plain to see, and after that the blaze of the morning's fire.

It would be futile to try to explain her errand, and apologies would be wasted. "My mistake," she called as she turned and left.

And what had she expected to find, if the stove had not

been reduced to crushed and blackened anonymity there in the smoldering ashes? Only what she knew quite well already— that Curly Gillan had botched up the wiring when he came to fix that shorted wire?

That Curly might have arranged the deadly bypass in the kitchen fuse box was impossible. Yet if the service man was right, someone had removed the incriminating evidence of this, the copper wire or whatever it was, that very afternoon while she sat there, dazed and shocked in the sunshine, watching the burial of her dog beside the bank of wild roses.

Curly Gillan was a procrastinator, a somewhat sullen workman, but he certainly had no reason to do her any harm. Why did *anyone* have reason to do her harm?

She needed to talk with Deke. He'd know what to do. She could talk with him after the fishing lesson later on, although at the moment her anxiety and her returning headache made the lesson itself seem less appealing than when it was first planned at lunch last Sunday.

At least she'd go back to her cabin at the Lodge and rest until—when was it Olympia had said? After school? Oh yes, she was to meet Deke and Laurie at the Cherrybridge house at five.

25

"Aye, lass, you're getting it!"

Laurie flushed with pleasure at Deke's praising as the casting lesson went on. The three of them were on the level back lawn of the big old Cogswell house in Cherrybridge, not on the banks of the Metoosic as Mrs. Potter had envisioned. They were each holding a long, limber fly rod, the reels smoothly wound with line but lacking the leader and fly that Deke assured them would come with future lessons.

"Remember 'Genia, throw the line *up*, not back. Now watch that line out on the lawn in front of you. You've got about fifteen feet of it out there, girl, plus that extra ten feet you're holding in your left hand."

This seemed impossible. She continued to try, and Deke's words went on.

"That's it, Laurie. Flip it *up* and *out*. Watch Laurie, 'Genia, she's getting it."

Laurie was beaming, as Deke continued.

"When it straightens out, flip it forward again. Keep playing with this length of line now, lassies. I want you to be able to flip it back and forth without touching the grass in front of you."

Mrs. Potter watched Laurie's increasing skill.

Today may have been a nightmare, she thought, but I am too weak-willed to have canceled a promised engagement. Later on I have *got* to think this thing through and let Deke help me.

The late afternoon sun was hot on the lawn behind the

237

Virginia Rich

barn. There was a dry wind from the west, which not only made it harder to flip the line back and forth without its wobbling, but which also brought biting flies. Deke and Laurie appeared impervious to them, and they both looked cool.

"Be back in a minute," she told them. "Frances is in the kitchen, I think, and I'm going to stop and have a glass of water." The two nodded happily and continued with the practice.

Once inside the cool, high-ceilinged old house, she decided to take a slight breather. Frances, the Cogswells' former cook and her old friend, had taken upon herself the prerogatives of hostess now that she was presently remaining there alone in charge of the house.

"You look tuckered," she told Mrs. Potter kindly. "Now just let me pour you a glass of fresh lemonade, and while I'm at it I'll fix it up the way Mr. Coley liked it."

The clink of ice cubes, the crisp aroma of fresh mint, and the fragrant jigger of gin (Coley's touch, of course, Mrs. Potter realized) were restorative.

"Best lemonade I ever had," she told Frances. "Maybe this will give me strength for some more of this fly-casting. I simply can't get the feel of it so far."

"Some can, some can't." Frances's tone was not particularly encouraging. "I've been watching you out there. That Scotchman is a natural, I can see that, and Laurie is going to be just like her mother. Everybody always said Olympia had the lightest hand and the best eye on the river. But I'm wondering, if you don't mind my saying so, why you really want to fish, at your age and all."

Mrs. Potter leaned forward in the kitchen rocker, not quite sure what her reasons really were after all.

Frances, misinterpreting her movement, went on quickly. "Now don't be so tarnation touchy," she said. "I didn't say you were *old*. After all, I've got a good ten years on you myself, that's certain, and I'm still going strong."

"I know what you meant," Mrs. Potter assured her, "and I've just about come to the same conclusion myself. Laurie can learn something in an afternoon that is going to take me all summer. I've just decided one thing: If I'm going to learn this kind of fishing I'm going to that Orvis school up in Vermont and stay there until I get the hang of it.''

"Will you have a dite more gin in that glass?" Frances asked. "Let me add another ice cube, too, while I'm at it.''

"What's a dite?" Mrs. Potter asked suddenly. "Yes, I know it's the same as a *mite*, but why do you say one and I say the other?''

"Now that's interesting," Frances said. "It was Amanda's gentleman friend who looked that up for us a long time ago.''

"I didn't know she ever had one," Mrs. Potter said, relaxing, cooler, relieved to be in out of the hot wind and biting flies.

"I suppose you always thought of Amanda as a spinster," Frances began. "Not to say she was exactly married. He was more of a boarder to start with, I guess you'd say.

"Came here to write a book about Maine," Frances went on. "Never got it done, far's I know. Just stayed on at Amanda's, and really nice for both of them, I always thought, until one day he up and left, quick as he came. She never mentions him, so don't you bring it up.''

Anyway, it seemed that once he had told her and Amanda where the word *dite* came from. They both knew what it meant, right enough, but nobody ever guessed it came from an old Dutch word called *"doit,"* which was a little Dutch coin—old-time money. Worth about a quarter of a penny in the old times, he told them, when occasional coins from Dutch traders still circulated in these parts.

How nice to have a friend equally interested in the human news that Amanda Wakefield's chaste white house had once harbored a lover, and in more academic questions of word origin as well. Frances was a rare human being, and she could not keep from worrying about what she would do, at seventy, if this house were to be closed up or sold. Being Frances, she told herself, she'll think of something.

When, refreshed yet not really eager to go out again into the sun, she rejoined the two on the broad green lawn, she was relieved that Deke declared the day's lesson to be over. "We'll take up again tomorrow," he told them. "And now

I'd best be taking wee Laurie home to her mother to report on what a good pupil she is showing herself to be.''

Laurie blushed. ''I hope I got a wee bit of it today. I mean, *aye*, you're a wonderful teacher.''

Deke spoke again as they turned to leave. ''Is Dwight taking good care of you? Are you all right there at the Lodge, 'Genia? Anything at all I can do?''

Mrs. Potter was about to say yes, you can come back and take me to dinner. You can let me tell you I'm afraid. You can be my sword and shield against danger.

The late sun and the west wind made her feel blown and frowsy. Pique and wounded vanity had their momentary triumph.

She handed him the fly rod. ''Not a thing, thanks, Deke. Not a thing.''

26

Her dinner at the Lodge that evening was as predictably bad as the two previous ones. The first, as she remembered, had been a pale, oddly cut piece of stewed chicken under a coating of colorless, pasty gravy. The second had been the unnameable reconstituted fish, or whatever creature it originally had been. Tonight she elected beef stew in the hopeful belief that there was very little anyone could do to completely ruin beef stew. In this she was very nearly mistaken.

It is criminal, she told herself, to take any kind of stewing beef, potatoes, onions, and carrots and turn them into this kind of unholy gray mess. She didn't feel up to a discussion tonight, but someday she'd sit down for a talk with Dwight Henderson. A young man who had spoken with pride of making sukiyaki, even if he never made it, must have some feeling for food, in spite of Anne-Marie's insistence that he was tone deaf and color blind about it.

"He's not paying attention to the one most important thing he can do to bring life to the old Lodge," Mrs. Potter said to Anne-Marie as she brought the canned fruit cup that was dessert.

"I wish I could bring you some of the blueberry fool I made for Jim yesterday from his mother's recipe," Anne-Marie said. "Using frozen berries, of course, but I can't wait for the new harvest to make it again then, along with my special unbaked blueberry pie. That really *is* a winner."

"Tell me about it," Mrs. Potter said, trying to sound

interested. Blueberry pie was a better thing to consider than
the fear she was trying to ignore.

"Well, you know how rich and wonderful cooked sweetened blueberries taste, but sort of mushy, and how irresistibly
crunchy uncooked berries are when you bite into them?"
Anne-Marie asked. "My pie puts them both together in a nice
crisp pie shell Jim bakes for me, and then we pile it with
whipped cream."

Mrs. Potter said that sounded wonderful. They again agreed
that paint and carpets are fine, but if Dwight would only
support a decent kitchen, he could have his place filled the
year round, not just for the few weeks of business from the
fishermen now and the deer and bird hunters in the fall.

Anne-Marie's position was emphatic. "We're working on
him, Jim and I," she said. "He says we're just a couple of
rich kids who don't understand business. I wish my father
could hear that, and Jim's too. We were both brought up
knowing how to read a balance sheet and a shareholder's
report—how to *really* read one, I mean, and to know what
was being said underneath all of the platitudes."

The dining room area was nearly deserted at this early
hour, since the salmon-fishing people were still congregating
at the bar end of the room. Anne-Marie had time to continue.

"Neither Jim nor I choose to live the way our parents do,"
she said, "but they're awfully understanding and supportive.
I mean, mine like Jim and his like me, and they're saying
how we live is up to us. But we can't talk to Dwight. He sees
us as a couple of irresponsible back-to-nature freaks, and
we're really quite sensible people."

Finally alone in the clean, spare, faded little room, Mrs.
Potter had to acknowledge the canker, painful and insistent,
that she had been trying to force to the back of her mind.
Throughout the frustration of the fishing lesson she had denied its presence, with the hope of talking it over with Deke
later on.

She had used the excuse of going to dinner, and there she
had dawdled with idle talk of meddling with the management
of the Lodge.

It could not be put off any longer.

As she always did in perplexing matters, Mrs. Potter reached for a yellow pad, one of those she had put in the larger and newly packed suitcase earlier in the day.

Sitting at the small white table that served as a desk, Mrs. Potter stared into space, then began to sketch a quick map.

A large rough oval, open at the top like the letter U, was its outline. She added crosswise lines that divided it into three slices: a smaller one at the top, a middle one with an irregular indentation on the right side, a larger one making up the oval's bottom half. To keep herself straight, she put an arrow at the side of the page, with an N at the top.

Inside the left-hand edge of the oval she drew a slightly winding line, which she labeled *"road."* The indentation on the right was identified as *"cove."* Three quickly drawn small rectangles were entered: *"Cottage," "Harvard,"* and *"Roost."*

Below the map, Mrs. Potter did a bit of arithmetic: 5,280 feet in a mile? This much she could remember from school in Harrington, Iowa. She knew from her many walks, as well as her recollection of peninsula maps, that the border, the shoreline of her oval, was roughly three and a half miles. Say 18,000 front feet, just to make it easy, she told herself. Was one hundred and fifty dollars a foot still the going price for good Maine ocean frontage? Let's see. Add two zeroes—no, three zeroes. Two million seven hundred thousand dollars. She multiplied again to be sure.

Hastily she extended the winding line of the road so that it no longer ended at the spot labeled *"Roost,"* its present dead end, but instead made a loop that now continued up the right side of the oval, skirting the inner edge of the cove.

From this line, she drew small wedge-shaped divisions to the line representing the shore. To her surprise she found that by encircling the cove she was going to have even more of these wedge shapes than she had originally estimated. In addition to sixty wedges with 300 feet on the ocean, she was going to be able to add at least a dozen more smaller wedges around the shores of the cove. Perhaps for boat owners these would be even more desirable. She made these divisions even a little smaller to create twenty wedge-shaped lots fronting the cove. And there was still a nice wooded central area enclosed by the road in the center of the map. Well, she wouldn't count that. Clubhouse and tennis courts, maybe, she thought, remembering Herbert's earlier suggestions, the proposal rejected so vehemently by Cole at her supper party on the night before the last fateful excursion of the *Cog's Wheel.*

To dispel the memory, she did more brisk multiplication. Eighty lots? It sounded a great many, but the figures seemed correct. Three-hundred-foot lots would be a minimum requirement for an expensive and exclusive development, she thought, and each of these, as well as those around what now must be labeled *"marina,"* instead of *"cove,"* might easily bring fifty thousand dollars from affluent and eager buyers seeking just such beautiful sites.

Eighty lots at fifty thousand dollars. She counted all the zeroes again carefully. Four million dollars. *Impossible.*

Mrs. Potter stared at her map and her figures. Of course she had not taken into account the cost of surveys and of the new road, or of underground utilities and tests for soil percolation and environmentally approved septic systems. There would be sales commissions, taxes, advertising.

The small room was still hot from the afternoon's sun. She decided to take another shower in the small rusty cubicle and undress for bed.

Shaking slightly as she sat in bed in her thin nightdress, the yellow pad now propped on her knees, she flipped the map page and began a fresh sheet.

Who stood to profit from this enormous potential? It was easy to list the names. Herbert and Persy, the inheritors, had to be at the top of the list. Teedy would grow fat on commissions. Someone had to finance the enterprise, not only the costs she had thought of and more, but also the purchase of her own strip of land. So Alex Whitehead must go on the list.

Her own strip of land. Suddenly she had the key.

Teedy had mentioned a "small legal matter" in speaking of her title. Her own sketch, as she flicked back to the first page, showed just what this might be. The entire plan depended on access over her own slice of the Point.

Pulling the thin blanket up around her shoulders, she tried to remember the terms of the deed by which she and Lew had bought the cottage.

Yes. There was a ninety-nine-year deed restriction, which allowed access to Harvard's property and from that to the land he had sold to Regina.

It permitted, she now recalled more clearly, that any of the three properties might be subdivided, but not until the end of the ninety-nine years, unless all three owners approved such division.

Legal language was always confusing, but she was sure of the agreement that had become part of each deed. No owner on the Point could divide his holding into smaller parcels without the consent of all parties, or her ninety-nine-year right-of-way (it must have about eighty more years to run, she calculated) would no longer be valid.

And that, of course, was why every one of the four— Herbert, Persy, Teedy, and Alex—had been trying to get her to sell out.

Even Carter had been urging her to move. Could he . . . could Carter be a part of this too?

She paused, not adding his name to her list. Of course not Carter. How would he share in such a scheme? As an exchange for his special skills and knowledge in Atlanta developments? She shrugged this off as pure foolishness.

Then a second flash of revelation told her that the right-of-way completely explained the behavior of the teenagers: If other appeals for her to sell out and move failed, as they had, harassment was intended to do the trick.

Rodney was the obvious place for someone to begin. It could not have been hard to persuade him that his interests lay in getting her out of the picture. His influence over the other teenagers would ensure their aid. She had been completely off the mark in her concern about pot-smoking behind the church, except perhaps as one of Rodney's ways of exercising his leadership.

She was shivering now, as a cool breeze lifted the cracked roller shade. Quickly she rose, closed and locked the window, and peered out to be reassured again by the brilliant green clarity of the empty courtyard. She listened again for comforting snores from the next cabin. By now Deke is nearby and asleep in cabin three, she told herself, and Dwight is in his rooms in the main building. She wished that her room had a telephone.

Climbing back into bed, the room now too hot with the window closed, she knew it would be impossible to sleep. She had the *why* of the whole thing, and now she might as well think about the *how*.

She went back to her list of the four who stood to profit. Just how could any of them have arranged for the three deaths, which, now for the first time, she was admitting to herself might have been murders?

A timed explosion on the Cogswells' boat, as she had earlier realized, would have been possible. Anyone with a bit of specialized information (she thought of a world of not too bright-looking terrorists) should be able to rig up something of the kind. The boat had been unguarded for several days at the dock where Tris had done the repairs. Someone could have gone aboard as she swung at her mooring in Harvard's cove the night of her Sunday supper party, after the Cogswells had gone home and Harvard was asleep. His bad dream might have been all too real.

She still rebelled at the thought of Harvard's own death being murder. If it was murder, it must be somehow related to the bruises inside his mouth and his chafed lips. However it was done, she saw no reason to cross anyone off her list.

Persy's name had at first received a question mark in the *how* column. Store-bound Persy, nearly immobilized in her obesity— could she have managed three murders? *"With Curly's help,"* her entry read. Curly, bound to Persy in ties either of shared greed or of fleshly delights, however unlikely that seemed, could have executed any of her commands.

All four—Persy, Herbert, Teedy, and Alex—were capable of inciting the annoying attacks upon her by the teenagers. Teedy could have appealed to Rodney's desire to be a rich and important local landowner. Herbert and Alex might have pandered to his dreams of social advancement. She tried to suppress the vagrant thought that Carter, too, may have encouraged the boy's romantic aspirations.

Anyone on her list might be guilty.

She again checked the door lock, the bolt, the locked window, the green light showing as a queer pinpoint on the old window shade. Eventually she slept, and the yellow pad slipped to the floor.

First dawn was a faint pinkness in the sky above the Metoosic when she awakened with sudden awareness of the fallacy in part of her reasoning. Everything made sense up to the point of the electrocution of her dog. Persuading her to sell out was a logical step in the real estate scheme she had imagined, whether this was the work of one person or of a cabal. Killing her was not.

Since Sindhu's death now seemed a planned assassination, one that was more likely intended to be her own, any one of her chosen four—or was it five?—should have been smart enough to know this was the wrong thing to do. Certainly they'd have had to realize that her heirs might prove even more recalcitrant than she about selling her land and its all-important right-of-way. For the plan to work, she had to be alive.

Anyway, she told herself, cheered by the dawn, people don't kill for real estate. Money, power, revenge, sexual conquest—none of these seemed to her more than secondary reasons for killing. One person destroys another only if he is threatening the essential *me* that one's whole life is dedicated to preserving.

She slept again, a brief but restorative half hour.

27

After her brief morning nap, Mrs. Potter reviewed the conclusions of the night and some of the last uncertain jottings on the yellow pad, now on the floor beside her bed. Clearly she had no real proof of any of her theories. She would have to decide today what steps to take next to test them.

Barbie, in the office to answer calls before beginning her chambermaid rounds, said that Mr. MacDonald had already left for the barrens.

It was too early to go to the courthouse to study the filed copy of the deed to the cottage. She hoped they could find it without knowing page and volume—information she had somewhere, but certainly not with her now.

It was too early to decide who to talk with about timed explosives. Too early to call the young doctor about Harvard's mouth and lips. For the moment there seemed to be nothing she could do.

Poor Persy, she thought again. Caught up in eagerness to please her son, to advance his dreams, and to win his approval, perhaps she as well as Roddy and his friends was being used by other people—Teedy and Herbert being the most obvious suspects.

The day was bringing the hot west wind again, beginning early. Everything that stings is going to bite me today, she realized unhappily.

The lodge provided an indifferent breakfast. There was a tiny glass of canned fruit juice and a poached egg that resembled her own last disastrous one at the cottage. At least she had by now established her morning right to the newly acquired teapot, and Agnes, back as waitress, had remembered this morning to warm the pot first and to see that the water was boiling to make the tea.

Outside, the Metoosic was already mirror-bright in the morning sun. The banks of the river were lined, upstream, with early fishermen in waders. Their motions seemed effortless, slow motion, easier to watch than worry about theories of greed and murder. She told herself again that there was nothing else she could do at the moment. There had been a certain catharsis in her yellow pad scribbling of the night, and her fears abated slightly as she continued to watch the fishermen.

Maybe you've been too quick in giving up on fly-casting, she thought. You've always loved lake fishing, casting for bass with a spinning rod, trolling from your own boat, and, best of all, simply dangling a line from a sunny wooden dock and watching the bluegills nibble your bait in the cool shadows below.

This new kind of fishing looks like wonderful fun, once you know how to do it. Guessing where those great, dark, almost invisible shapes may be, placing that little fly—exactly the *right* little fly—in the most tempting spot. Where to cast, when to ease, when to play your line.

Right now she might as well spend a few minutes driving upstream. She'd park near a series of fishing pools, rocks, and rapids in a good vantage spot below the dam. She'd watch the fishermen there a while and maybe she'd be a better pupil when she and Laurie met Deke again late today for a second lesson.

One absolutely necessary preliminary, she reminded herself, was to go to the drugstore for a can of good bug repellent. The black flies would be out along the river at this season, and she remembered that everything stings more fiercely in a hot, dry west wind.

Returning to her cabin, she put on a long-sleeved shirt and sturdy jeans. She covered her head snugly with a knotted bandanna. She sprayed herself thoroughly and conscientiously with repellent and put the can in the glove compartment of her car for a later application if it was needed.

As she drove out of the parking lot, a small pickup truck was crossing the main bridge of Cherrybridge, the bridge linking the two roads that followed the banks of the Metoosic on either side toward the north.

With jolting surprise, Mrs. Potter recognized the figure on her side of the pickup's front seat. There was no mistaking the big pink and white checks, the bushel basket of teased, henna-red hair, the huge bare arm, resting like a great, pink ham on the open window beside her.

The small truck went across the river from her, heading north along the east bank. Persy was on the far side from her now, and the driver was a blur in the bright hot sun. All colors were hard to distinguish in the glare from the river, even those of the truck and of the pink and white checks she had seen so clearly a moment before.

But Persy never goes anywhere, Mrs. Potter reflected. Persy never closes the store except for Christmas Day. What in heaven's name is she doing driving through Cherrybridge on a brassy, hot June morning, and who was that with her?

If she only paid more attention to makes and models and colors of cars, Mrs. Potter felt she should have been able to guess. They all looked alike to her, these bright new pickups.

Slowly she drove north. The truck across the river outdistanced her, disappearing on the main road north of town. Her own road, on the west bank, curved back around and over the river to the fishing pools.

She stopped her car at the head of the river, below the dam. She watched the neat cast of a man with thick dark red hair and a bushy beard to match.

At that moment, she felt her first fly bite of the day. A black fly made its attack, finding a spot on the back of her neck just at the hairline where the repellent apparently had not reached.

All at once her mind screamed *Persy!*

Persy, and bug bites, and *bees!* Persy and the allergies, which were nonetheless real for all her constant talk about them.

Bees and blueberries and bears.

And Persy, headed on an unimaginable journey north out of Cherrybridge, passenger in a little pickup truck whose driver was crowded by that great henna-haired pink-checked body beside him.

She knew at the moment, beyond all doubt, that another tragic Northcutt's Harbor accident was in the making.

What road went past the blueberry barrens? she asked herself as she raced out the highway to the north. She remembered an earlier drive with Cole and Regina and turned off with a screeching complaint from her car tires as she left the hard-surfaced highway for the gravel.

She whirled through a patch of heavy woods, with a moment's thought of black bears and hairy hunters, then came out into a wide clearing.

Thatched with low bushes, their flowering apparent more as a pink haze than as a real show of color, the clearing stretched out like a western prairie to the edge of the dark woods beyond.

And several hundred yards back from the road was a straight line of white boxes.

The bees.

Ahead was a narrow wooden bridge for which she slowed slightly to allow for the jolt she rightly felt it would deal to her speeding car.

The real jolt, which brought her to a tire-screaming halt, was the sight of the pink-checked hulk by the roadway, lying facedown in the ditch just a few yards from the small stream ahead. There was an angry hum in the air, a furious yellow cloud of bees in a dive-bomb attack upon the huge pink body on the ground.

Heedless, ignoring her own opened car windows and her own vulnerability, Mrs. Potter jumped from her car and ran to the prone figure below the road bank. She felt a first stab on her face, another on the back of her hand, but the main army was intent on its venomous assault on the motionless bulk below.

There was no way she could lift that great, groaning, sobbing, screaming weight. Instead, she ran back to her car for the can of repellent. Its hissing spray at first only seemed to further enrage the angry bees. She was stung several more times as she tried to aim at Persy's exposed flesh, the huge bare arms and legs already swollen and flaming.

She felt one of her own eyes closing. She looked down to see crawling angry insects on her clothing, felt the horror of a first bee sting inside her shirt, another under her trouser leg.

The truck approached before she was aware of it. *"What's this? What in the world?"*

It was Deke, and with him there was a man whose features looked as if they had been chiseled from stone.

As the two, somehow transformed into dark monsters in netted head coverings and gloves, struggled to lift the great bee-covered body to the back of their open truck, Persy's screams continued.

One red-rimmed and swollen eye opened a small slit and then closed. "Curly!" she was screaming. "Curly said Roddy was down in the ditch! Find Roddy, 'Genia. He's been hurt. *Find Roddy!*"

The sounds became a wordless roar of pain and outrage; then Persy's voice again was clear. "It was Curly," she shrieked wildly. "Curly did everything! Everything! Harvard, the boat, the stove, it was Curly!" The screeching words ended in an animal howl of pain and torment and then in merciful silence.

And then there was a blur of being driven back to Cherrybridge.

Persis Pickett. Persy. Palely picketted. Pinkly picketted. Poisonously picketted.

"What is it you've given me?" Mrs. Potter was asking the doctor weakly. "I can't hold my head up."

The small examining room in the Cherrybridge clinic had expanding walls and a ceiling that rose and fell. Mrs. Potter tried to hold onto the sides of the narrow, paper-covered table upon which she found herself.

Whatever had been the answer, she'd have to ask again later.

"Where's Persy?" she asked suddenly. "Is she here too?"

The clinic ceiling unexpectedly began to lower again, bringing with it an odd pattern of beige acoustic tiles.

When she awakened, it was to learn that epinephrine had been too late for Persy. Even a few bee stings might have been fatal for Persy, with her massive allergies. The tremendous amount of bee venom that her defenseless fat body had absorbed had ensured her death—from shock, from choking, from asphyxia—even though she still had been clinging to life and consciousness when Mrs. Potter had entered the field of the furious attacking bees.

Deke was at her bedside. No, Roddy had not been found along the roadway, he told her.

Curly Gillan, however, was in custody in the Ellsworth jail and was being questioned there. Louis Oublette had received Deke's CB call as they raced back with Persy and Mrs. Potter to the clinic. Persy's screaming statement that Curly had brought her to the barrens had alerted a sudden rush of police action.

No, Roddy had not been found along the roadside, but he turned up just where he was expected to be on a Thursday morning, in class at the high school, where the principal was now trying to tell him of his mother's death.

Curly was going to have to answer some tough questions about how and why he lured Persy to that particular spot, Deke was saying, and then why he abandoned her there.

"He's going to have to answer more questions than that," Mrs. Potter tried to say, but the words were slow in forming.

Later, still lying on the narrow examining table at the clinic, Mrs. Potter roused herself again. To think that people who visit us at the ranch worry so much about rattlesnakes, she thought, as she gathered her wits. Bee stings kill more people than snake bites, and snakes are a lot easier to avoid if you know what you're doing.

Now *what* was it she'd been trying to say about being picketted? Publicly, painfully, *permanently* picketted? And what was she trying to remember about Curly?

Only Curly would have been able to persuade Persy to drive with him to the barrens. And the only possible reason she would have gone would have been the thought of Roddy's lying injured somewhere, needing her help. Persy's dying accusations had to be true. For whatever reason, Curly was the one behind all of the terrible things that had happened since the night of the baked bean supper.

28

I am certainly old enough not to require anyone's permission to drive out in my car, she thought defiantly.

Mrs. Potter nevertheless left her cabin at the Sportsmans Lodge rather quietly the morning after Persy's death. She had already appeared at breakfast in the dining room, and Agnes seemed reassured about how well she looked after yesterday's ordeal. It was still too early for Barbie to arrive on her morning round of the cabins.

Mrs. Potter slipped out of the parking lot without attracting notice. Deke had brought her back to the Lodge yesterday in her own car. It was he, and the man with the face on the buffalo nickel, who had hoisted Persy's body into the truck, and that same helper who had followed Deke and her in her car to the clinic.

If anyone *had* insisted that she spend this day quietly in bed, she was not quite willing to remember who had said it.

And she was in no danger now from anyone. Curly was in jail. If any others had been conspiring with Persy to get the valuable land on the Point, their schemes were certainly silenced by now, perhaps as permanently as Persy had been silenced in death. She had no difficulty seeing or driving, despite one swollen eyelid and a number of still slightly warm spots on her hands and ankles. The antihistamine injection had done its work for her very nicely.

When she stopped at Pickett's the little store was closed, for the first time in her recollection. However, the person she had come to see was at home in the small shack in the back.

"Hi there, Winks," she greeted him. "I brought you a box of frosted things from Cherrybridge. How are you doing?"

Winks reached for the box and patted Mrs. Potter with one grimy paw on her forearm by way of thanks.

"Persy isn't coming back, you know, Winks," she told him gently. "Did you know? Do you know what you're going to do?"

Winks answered with dignity, even as he began the first soft pastry. "Coming for me today, they are," he told her, "Norwood and Alma. They're going to take me up to Aunt Melly's, up on Toddy Pond. I can be a lot of help to Aunt Melly, Norwood says, and she's got a nice little house for me there in the woods."

Mrs. Potter continued her questioning. "You were a lot of help to Persy and Roddy, too, I know that. But how did you let her go off like that in that truck to Cherrybridge?"

"Couldn't stop her." Winks's reply was flat. "They called on the CB about the accident. Said Rod needed her. Nobody could've stopped her."

"Of course. I can believe that. Did she tell you who called?"

"Police. State police, maybe. I didn't rightly hear."

"And Curly drove her up to find Rod?" she continued. "Did he hear the CB report too?"

"Yup. He said he heard it in his truck just as he was driving in. Didn't haul yesterday."

"And Persy heard it in the store?"

"Yup."

"And they left right away?"

"Yup, and left me in charge after she locked up," Winks said proudly. "Rod drove to school with Teddy and she didn't like that. Awful worried."

"I didn't know Teddy drove to school."

"Oh, sure. Teedy lets him drive any time he wants if he don't need the truck. Persy worried."

Mrs. Potter continued her gentle questions.

"Winks, there are several things I really need to know, and you're the only person who can help me. First one is, did Persy know Mr. Cogswell wanted to buy Harvard's land?

256

That is, before he had the boat accident and before Harvard died?''

"Sure. I heard him say so and I told her, all right all right. That land was Persy's by right. Harvard already promised it to her.''

"Of course. And the next thing—did Curly ever do, well, special jobs for Persy?''

"Yup. Persy called the tune for Curly.''

"And now another one, Winks. I know how good you are in the woods—quiet, careful, just like a shadow in the trees.''

"That's me. Just like a shadow. Indian blood way back, folks say.''

"Then tell me, Winks, did you watch the Pier at First Bite for Persy? Did you come and tell her when the Cogswells' boat came in?''

Winks nodded, as he slowly finished the second sweet bun. "But I wasn't the one who fixed the boat, and I didn't hurt Harvard, and don't let anybody tell you different.''

A car horn sounded explosively from in front of the store. "There they come, Norwood and Alma,'' he said. "Said they'd be here, and I'm all packed.''

"Oh please, just one more thing, Winks. Did you go to my cottage too?''

"Yup. As soon as the lights blew out all I had to do was slip in and take out those little shiny wires, like he told me. After that he said everything would be fine.''

"Curly explained to you how to do this?''

The horn sounded again and Winks lifted the rope-tied suitcase. "No matter what they ask me, I didn't hurt Harvard and I never went onto Mr. Cogswell's boat, and all I did at your house was to get those wires out before you woke up good. No matter what they ask me, I can't remember. I don't care if they kill me, that's all I'm going to say about it.''

As he left, Winks turned back. "Besides, I'm not all there. Nobody'll believe me whatever I say.''

At the post office, Amanda was bursting with news. To begin with, Teedy and Eileen were going to take Roddy, at least for the time being. Persy hadn't any kinfolk in these parts anymore, and heaven knew it would be an uphill job to find any relation of Addie Pickett's, coming from England all those years ago. So Roddy was going to move in with young Ted. Pretty good neighbors, those Pettengills, in spite of all his silly sailor talk, wouldn't she say?

Mrs. Potter agreed.

And had she heard about what might happen to the store? It was too early to say, but folks were telling her that the Colamarias might be planning to take it over. Seems *their* folks, grandparents most likely, had run a little mom and pop grocery store, way back in the twenties, some place in New Jersey.

Now she wouldn't want 'Genia to repeat it, but their folks ended up rich, back in the bootlegging days, sort of like gangsters. Anyway the point of the story was that somebody in the family used to have a little store, and now maybe Al and Tory would buy this one.

Mrs. Potter agreed that this was an interesting idea, and that it would be good for the village to keep Pickett's open and operating.

Preliminaries out of the way, Amanda introduced the main topic of the day. "Now I'm sure you know everything about Curly, up at the jail," she said.

At this moment Giselle and Tillie arrived, both wearing shorts and sleeveless tops over matronly and grandmatronly curves, ready to begin an early summer tan.

"My Louis, he stopped him with his pistol," Giselle said quickly, clearly feeling that this part of the news was hers to tell. "Louis caught Curly coming back to town in his truck, his face all covered with stings of the bee so he could hardly see."

"Notice you have a few yourself," Tillie observed. "Sure you're okay?"

Giselle had not finished. "Curly said he drove Persy up to the barrens, yes. He said they heard on the CB Roddy was hurt, there by the first bridge."

"When they got out to look for him," Amanda said, "that's when the bees got stirred up. He couldn't lift her, Curly says, and they were stinging him so bad he couldn't think, so he was driving back for help."

"He says," Tillie added.

"My Louis drove the barrens road later, looking for Roddy, but he was right in the school all the time. All Louis found was a BEES—WARNING sign thrown back in the bushes."

"Clear case of premeditated murder," Amanda announced firmly. "Now comes the part you won't believe. Curly isn't admitting anything"—(*where* does Amanda get her information? Mrs. Potter wondered, as she so often had)—"but the story seems clear enough to me. Curly killed Harvard some way, who knows how, just so Persy could get her hands on that property of his."

"Which meant he had to get rid of the Cogswells first, before they had a chance to buy Harvard out," Tillie continued, "so Persy got Curly to rig their boat to blow up."

"Everybody thought it was a plain dumb accident of Curly's when he wired your stove wrong," Amanda said, "but by then he and Persy were getting greedy and maybe they thought they'd give you a scare into selling out."

"Yes. My Louis thinks that's what it was," Giselle pronounced with certainty.

"Persy and Regina's nephew, that Herbert, have been thick as thieves ever since they both inherited," Amanda went on. "Teedy Pettengill, too. Shouldn't wonder at all if the three of them planned to go together on the whole Point— your place, Harvard's, and Regina's—and make a real pile of money out of it."

"With Curly in there pitching for his share," Tillie said.

"We think he dumped her there by the bees because she wasn't cutting him in," Amanda asserted positively. "He says he was crazy about her, even wanted to tie the knot, but she wasn't sure how Roddy would take it."

"Some old fur flying, if he ever found out," Tillie added.

"And did he know? And how is he taking it now, her death, that is?"

"Can't say to the first, not so good the second," Amanda said. "Anyway Curly's story now is that she backed out. He won't have it that he was going to marry for money."

Mrs. Potter was silent, trying to sort this all out in her mind, and Amanda was free to go on to less dramatic matters.

"See you all at Persy's service," she told them cheerily, as Mrs. Potter was leaving. "Cremation, of course. Clarence just couldn't manage any other way."

One more errand: to check at the cottage to see that everything was all right and that Lyman had begun the refinishing of the floor.

The answer was disappointing. Things were just as she had last seen them. The putty smudges remained on the new panes in the front windows and the oak boards of the kitchen were stained, untouched, now dusty.

Tucked under the back door, however, was Lyman's current bill. Glass cut to measure, points, putty, labor, and she noted that he had for the second time raised his own hourly rate of pay without discussing it with her. Well, all right, she decided grudgingly.

Under the bill was another folded sheet, this one written in a decisive hand.

"Call us the minute you get back," it said. "Hope you're all right. Important news for you." The note was signed "Alex and Bettye."

While she was debating whether to call the Whiteheads from the cottage or to wait until she got back to the Lodge, the telephone sounded commandingly from the closed and empty living room.

"Amanda told me you were on the Point," Alex told her. "Look, I've talked with my lawyers about your stove. Bets isn't here right now, but let me come over and tell you what they think."

Mrs. Potter waited for him on the open deck at the front of the cottage. The air was bracing and her slight giddy feeling abated.

"What you're telling me is beside the point now," she told him fiercely, a few minutes later. "Liability in an electrical accident isn't the important thing. Don't you know Persy's been killed? Don't you know that Harvard and the Cogswells were killed too? And that Curly did all of this?"

The sun of late morning seemed intensified, and Mrs. Potter saw that the red spots on her wrists and her ankles were more noticeable.

She sipped the icy martini and nibbled on a hot cheese puff. Imagine having someone make hot cheese puffs, she thought, just for one person!

She lay back lazily and admired the delicate tracery, just visible beneath years of ivory paint, of the pressed tin of the ceiling.

When it got cooler, Frances said, she'd be back with a little tray of dinner. She just happened to have a little mold of jellied veal with a sauce of celery and almonds and sour cream (*just happened!* Mrs. Potter decided to stay all summer and eat whatever Frances *just happened* to have on hand). She thought she might find some nice little garden peas to go with it. She was going out now to see if any of the first ones were ready to pick, and maybe watch that Scotchman teaching Laurie to handle a line. That girl was a some different person since she started getting those lessons.

Comfortable, relaxed, noting with satisfaction that a second bombastic was awaiting in the chilled crystal carafe on the tray, Mrs. Potter settled herself again on the cushions of the chaise longue. Nothing disagreeable, nothing frightening could find her here.

Curly was in jail. And she had been ridiculous in her suspicions of Alex and Herbert at the cottage. The bee stings and the medication had gone to her head, in more ways than one.

The telephone on the small table beside her, where she had earlier talked with Olympia, offered further reassurance. As an extra safety measure, she would inform the law—as she knew it, in the person of Louis Oublette—of her whereabouts, in the impossible event of Curly's escape.

"My Louis will be so glad for your word," Giselle was saying. "But naturally, he was the one to apprehend Curly."

Louis would be in very soon, Giselle said, and she would give him Mrs. Potter's special message of thanks. Yes, Louis had in truth worked hard searching for Rodney. Moreover, he was very astute in learning that Rodney was safely in the school, where he belonged, in class with their Cathy in the American history. Whoever told Persy that he was in an accident had made up the big lie.

The second martini was, as always, better than the first. Frances's dinner on the silver tray was even better than that.

Best of all was the big soft four-poster bed and the cool summer dusk, the feeling of being a good and well-loved child, as Frances bade her good night. She slept.

But there was no air.

She could not breathe.

She felt strong legs astride her knees; sharp hard elbows bearing down upon her shoulders. Her body was immobilized except for the falling of her pinioned hands and forearms against the remorseless weight that was holding her prisoner.

The only protest she could make—feeble, futile—was the working of her mouth, greedy for air, against the soft silk of the pillow that was suffocating her.

She was falling.

Harvard's lips had been chafed, just as hers were being, and the cushion pressed down upon his face had been rough and tweedy.

A voice spoke, sounding far away at the top of the funnel into which she was descending, a slow downward spiral.

"I'll teach you to laugh at me. Old Harvard learned his lesson. So did Mr. Cogswell. Nobody makes fun of *me*."

There was no air.

The dark was pressing down, only it wasn't dark at all, it was red. It was a bursting, blazing *white*.

There was no air.

Even without hearing that last, soft, hoarse giggle, the same sound she had heard the night of the stone-throwing, Mrs. Potter knew who was pressing down that relentless downy pillow.

In her last conscious thought, she knew whose *me* it was that had been threatened.

And then, unbelievable, the intolerable pressure lifted and her head and frantic arms were free. With a convulsive burst of strength, an almost impossible effort of will, Mrs. Potter pushed aside the murderous pillow as the room sprang into light.

Blinded, gasping for the air her lungs had been so cruelly denied, she could not see who was in the room.

She could hear a voice, and it was unmistakably that of Frances.

"Put 'em up," Frances was saying. "Put 'em up, you rowdy, or I'll shoot."

There was a tremendous bang and a gaping hole appeared in the delicate tracery of the patterned ceiling.

Frances had made good her threat, while a scrambling figure hurtled through the tall open window on the north. There was the sound of a racing motor and a screech of tires.

30

The sun was streaming through the tall windows to the east, the soft, pale, silk curtains stirring in the morning breeze. Mrs. Potter looked apprehensively at the windows on the north. They were, she noted, firmly shut and the long, slatted interior blinds were closed and bolted.

"Now you're going to stay right here for a time, my girl," Deke was saying. "Frances will look after you and I'll be living in the house as well, until we decide you're ready to move. Frances's nephew will be on hand daytimes. He's out of a job now and glad to have a little extra guard duty."

Mrs. Potter looked from Deke to Olympia and Laurie beside him, then to Frances in the doorway.

"You do know it was Rodney, then? Where is he now?"

"I recognized the rapscallion, right enough. Rodney Pickett, sure as I'm standing here. I've seen him a hundred times at the store with his mother," Frances said.

"Rod got away," Laurie said. "Poor Rod. Frances came in with Uncle Coley's old bear gun, but he jumped out the window, the same way he got in."

"Couldn't really hit the broad side of a barn," Frances admitted. "Besides all I wanted to do was to stop him from killing you, and the ceiling can be fixed. Fenwick will patch it up later today, temporary, and we can find more of the tin parts out in the barn to put in permanent later on. I just couldn't shoot the boy, when it came down to it."

But where was Rodney?

There was no one at the apartment over the store, the four

268

of them told her. Louis had checked. The Pettengills, who had taken him in after Persy's death, had not seen him, could not find him, and he was not in any of the regular teenage hangouts either in the village or in Cherrybridge. His skiff was in its regular place. He had no car, nor had Persy. Ted Pettengill's father's pickup was in the garage.

"Why did you say 'poor Rod'?" Olympia asked her daughter curiously. Mrs. Potter, weak as she was, could not help seeing that Olympia's hair was newly short, curled in soft ringlets. "You know, Laurie, that he's just attempted to strangle Mrs. Potter, and we now think, Deke and I, that he killed Coley and Regina and Harvard as well."

Mrs. Potter nodded sad assent. "And do you know why?" she asked them. "Not just to get Harvard's place, although I'm sure that had a lot to do with it. Not just for the land and the money. He said they—that *we*—were laughing at him."

"That's what I mean," Laurie said. "Rod lived in his own dream world, Mother. I wanted to tell you about it, but there just never seemed to be a good time. He really *believed* that he came of a noble English family and that he would come into his own some day. And he kept calling me and writing me and sending poems to me about how I was going to go to England with him and be his own *Lady Laurie*."

Olympia turned to Laurie abruptly, and so did Deke. "You mean the lad has been making you a part of his fantasies, too?" he asked.

"Could I have helped, Mother?" Laurie asked. "What should I have done?"

"Laurie, I suppose you were a dream to him, just like the rest of it," Olympia said slowly. "He'd have destroyed you too once he learned you're a real person." She reached a tentative hand toward Laurie, who grasped it quickly.

"Aye, your mother's right on it," Deke agreed. "The poor lad would always be destroying anything real that came between him and his dream of himself. But the thing we must think of now is your own safety, lass, as well as Mrs. Potter's."

"Well, nobody knows where Roddy is, that's for sure," Frances repeated. Alex Whitehead was out looking for him every place he could think of. The Colamarias were out, the Weidners, the constable, both selectmen, Louis Oublette, even Carter Ansdale and Herbert Wyncote.

"Then I think Laurie must stay right here with Frances and Mrs. Potter," Olympia decided firmly. "I'll sleep here nights, too, and Deke will be here, and Fenwick daytimes. Until that boy is found we're not going to take any chances."

"What about school?" Laurie asked. "There's another week, you know, Mother."

Olympia placed a decisive phone call. "For personal reasons," she said, Laurie would not be back in classes for these last few days. However, she expected, of course, that Laurie would have full credit for the term. It would have taken a stronger man than the school principle to deny or even question Olympia Cogswell Cutler.

"And whilst you're here, why don't you let Frances teach you to cook?" Deke suggested. "Part of the time you can go around in the truck with me on the barrens—that'll be safe enough—and we'll keep on with our fishing lessons, but you may as well put your time to good use here in the kitchen. You've got to be a better cook than your mother, that's sure."

Olympia smiled easily, but Frances bristled to her defense.

"No call for Olympia to cook," she said. "Never had to when she was home here, and anytime she wants to move back I'm still willing and able. Of course, I'll teach Laurie if she has a mind to learn, but no talk of having the head of J. R. Cogswell & Son in my kitchen or anybody else's. She's got more important things to do."

This time both Olympia and Deke smiled, a glance of shared amusement and understanding, and Laurie briefly rested her head against Deke's shoulder.

When they had all tiptoed out, leaving her alone again, Mrs. Potter returned to the realization that Rodney Pickett, Persy's beautiful and adored son, with his delusions of grandeur, had been the single force behind all the evil that had befallen Northcutt's Harbor in the past weeks.

Harvard had kindly but honestly told the boy what he knew of his father. Cole's description of Addie Pickett had been equally frank, although tempered with what Cole considered a satisfactory compliment to a teenager. And her own death sentence could have been pronounced on the morning she had smiled with quickly concealed amusement at the striped flannel trousers.

His first real attempt on her life, after the few minor earlier harassments, had resulted instead in the electrocution of her dog. She touched her lips and throat gingerly, remembering how nearly successful the second attempt had been.

It all could have been foreseen, she realized. What she had seen as only the slightly theatrical and amusing vainglory of a young man rehearsing a new role, wearing for the first time a new costume, was in realty a warped and uncertain *me*. And that *me* had been looking for acceptance and recognition, yet fearing (and finding) ridicule in the eyes of an older woman, someone from another world, someone he had reason to respect.

Mrs. Potter recognized her own responsibility. Laurie alone had seen, even in part, the agonies Rodney had been suffering.

She thought again of Harvard. Remembering that awful pressure, the impotence of her own struggles under the strength of that young body, Mrs. Potter remembered Amanda's comment. At least Harvard didn't suffer, she had said. Everything in his chamber was neat as he always left it. So would have been her postered bed here at the Cogswells'. The silken pillow could scarcely have chafed her lips. Would the young doctor have simply given the cause of death as heart failure, due perhaps to too much strain, too much sorrow over the accident to her dog, maybe even the aftermath of the bee stings?

Finally the ultimate horror flooded her mind, driving out all other speculation: Had Rodney also caused the death of his own mother? How, why, could this child have been so monstrous as to lure his own mother to her certain bee-stung death on the blueberry barrens? That evil was too satanic to contemplate. This had to be Curly's doing, Curly's alone.

At that moment, the telephone beside her sounded a muted ring.

"Young Ted Pettengill was the one to drive Rod to

271

Cherrybridge last night," Amanda was saying. "Told him he was just going to give the old girl—that means you, 'Genia—another good scare, the way they did when they threw stones at your house. Ted drove him back to Northcutt's Harbor, let him off at the store. Roddy told him he'd walk back to the Pettengills as soon as he was sure Winks was all right and the store closed up okay. Ted's admitting all this now but swears he hasn't seen him since."

At this point Frances came in with a tray. "You need some food under your belt," she announced. "Fenwick got us some mussels early this morning at low tide, and Fenwick isn't such a dummy as I thought. Anyway I thought Laurie might as well begin on something as easy as a little bowl of mussel soup for you. Eat it up now. Do you good."

The creamy mussel soup was delicious and easy to swallow, even with her still painful and swollen tongue.

"Sip a little rum now," Frances urged. "Just a teaspoonful in the little glass there. It'll help you get to sleep. And don't get out those tarnation yellow paper tablets of yours. I saw what Olympia and Mr. Deke brought for you with your stuff from the Lodge. Just you settle down now and forget all your scribbling. Fenwick's here and he's a good boy, even though I never thought until now he was very strong in the head. I'm here and both the gardeners are back at work outside. Now take your nap."

And so it was later in the afternoon, when Frances returned with a fresh tray—this time with hot tea and a surprisingly welcome addition of hot milk toast—freshly toasted home-made bread with butter and hot milk and a sprinkling of sugar—that Mrs. Potter resumed her thoughts of Rodney Pickett.

No matter what hopes Persey's inheritance had aroused, no matter what an affront she, Mrs. Potter, might have presented, no matter what Rodney's fantasy world might be, it must be that his *real* security lay in his own mother's unquestioning and adoring regard. The day Rodney learned that his mother, human and vulnerable, might be thinking of marrying Curly Gillan must have been the final insult to his precarious sense of self.

THE BAKED BEAN SUPPER MURDERS

Rodney may have corrected her grammar, he may have wished she were not so fat, he may have felt that she did not share a proper preference for BBC television over "Starsky and Hutch," but Persy was still the cornerstone of his existence.

Curly must have seemed the awful, utter, totally *me*-destroying threat to Rodney Pickett's life.

There was another muffled ring of the telephone beside the chaise longue. Giselle Oublette's voice was at first apologetic. "Louis says Rodney would never have known where you were if I hadn't called him on the CB last night," she said. "Louis didn't come home as early as I thought and it never came to my head that I shouldn't call him to say you were safe at the big Cogswell house."

"How could you have known?" Mrs. Potter reassured her. "It must have been only by chance that Rodney was at the store when you called Louis, or perhaps with Ted in the Pettengill truck, in order to overhear the message. Please don't worry. I'm really fine now."

"My Louis got the whole story out of Ted, anyway. He and Rodney fixed up that CB call from the truck when they were driving to school, pretending there'd been an accident and Rodney needed help up on the barrens road. Rodney said there was no way his mother would be able to get out there before lunchtime, and then he and Ted would go out and rescue her. It would make it look like Curly had been trying to get her stung by the bees. Louis says Rodney even had the mother's hypodermic needle with him with her allergy injection ready, just in case."

"So, Rodney was going to be the hero and make Curly the villain," Mrs. Potter said. "Your Louis is a very smart man, Giselle."

"I know, yes," Giselle replied complacently. "I think he will end up the state senator, maybe. Do you think the governor?"

Yes, Mrs. Potter assured her, if he ever appears on TV. With his brains and his looks, no telling where he may end up. And Giselle and their pretty, bright young Cathy will go right along, she thought, and be perfectly at home and at ease, and there will be *plogues* in the governor's mansion.

273

Frances came in with a small radio. The big TV is in the back parlor, she explained, and whenever Mrs. Potter felt like it, it was just down the hall. In the meantime maybe she'd like to hear the news. It wouldn't be in the *Ellsworth American* until it came out next Thursday, but Roddy was all over the air today.

WDEA's announcer had just come on. "And Mr. Rodney Pickett, of Northcutt's Harbor," he was saying cheerfully, "who has been thought to have attacked an elderly woman in a house in Cherrybridge" (Mrs. Potter bristled. Thought to! Elderly!) "has disappeared. Sorrow over his mother's death from an allergic attack is thought to have precipitated his disappearance. It is thought that Mr. Pickett may have joined an international charter flight from the Bangor airport to England, where he is said to have family connections."

A young man wearing blue jeans and answering to Mr. Pickett's description, the bulletin continued, was a last-minute passenger on the plane to Heathrow airport.

"Poor Rod," Laurie said, coming in in time to hear the last of the broadcast. "What's it going to be like for him in England? He's just going to be another grubby American kid, with whatever money his mother had on hand at the store when he took off, and that's all he's ever going to have over there."

Frances returned with another small tray, a chilled stemmed glass and an icy carafe, with the cheering remark that another of Mr. Coley's bombastics was in order. And that Laurie's presence in the kitchen was immediately required if she wanted to see how to poach a whole salmon.

Olympia thought that tonight she wouldn't feel up to joining the three of them, she and Laurie and Mr. Deke, in the family dining room, Frances said. Maybe tomorrow night she'd feel like it, but tonight Frances would again be bringing her dinner on a tray.

"No dinner tonight, Frances," Mrs. Potter implored. "The milk toast at teatime is all I can manage today, and the bombastics are going to put me to sleep—probably before I finish the first one. Thank you, my dear, dear Frances. No matter where Rodney Pickett is tonight, with you and Fenwick

274

on guard—you most especially—and all the family in the house, I'm going to sleep like a baby.''

There were three days of such pampering, of frequent and brief appearances by Olympia or Deke or Laurie, or sometimes of the three of them together.

Mrs. Potter discovered that Regina had a complete collection of Angela Thirkell's novels of English county life, at least starting with *Pomfret Towers* and *The Brandons*. She was rereading them straight through with new delight. ''As much fun as a basketful of kittens,'' she remembered some critic saying. She couldn't wait to get to *Marling Hall* and *Peace Breaks Out* again.

And there were numerous solicitious phone calls. As these continued, Mrs. Potter realized afresh that while Herbert and Teedy, with Persy as a willing accomplice, might have lusted for her land to make possible a real estate development on the Point, their eagerness could never have led to murder. Herbert needed money, Teedy was always dying for a new deal, and Alex Whitehead wanted added local prestige as a landowner or as financier for the group. But none of them would have killed for it. And dear Carter was just that—a dear and amiable friend.

Through it all, Mrs. Potter knew, it had been Rodney, home from school that foggy Monday morning, who had, with Winks as his guide, come to the cottage and miswired the stove. At first, perhaps he thought that removing the ground wire and attaching a hot wire to the stove frame would be enough. Then, remembering his rage and shame on those days when he thought she was laughing at his striped flannels and the new white tennis shorts, he must have decided to add the bypass in the main panel.

''Here's how you take it out, Winks,'' he would have explained, slowly and carefully. ''Just go right in the house after the flash and she'll be woozy and never see you. Nobody's going to get hurt. I'm just doing a job for Curly.''

Naturally Rodney had two purposes: to punish Mrs. Potter for seeing through his uncertain pretensions and to make sure Curly was to be blamed; and to establish himself as an equal

275

in all segments of Northcutt's Harbor society—the village, the resident newcomers, and the summer people alike.

And there was, finally, Mrs. Potter's recognition that when Persy screamed her dying accusations of Curly, she was still, to the last, protecting her child. However she had learned of his guilt (or if she had shared it—would they ever know?), Persy alone must have known that Roddy was the murderer of the three on the Point and Sindhu's executioner.

31

"Wherever the lad is," Deke said at dinner the second night, "we must not rest easy until we're sure he's found. His fleeing to London may be no more than the invention of an eager reporter. Laurie is to stay with me, as I try to instruct her in the blueberry business, or here in the kitchen with Frances, learning to be a proper cook."

"Or possibly with me at the pound, learning the lobster business," Olympia said. "Right now I'm just too busy to keep an eye on her. Later, of course, she's got to know them both—blueberries and lobsters."

"And 'Genia is to be equally guarded," Deke said. "Fenwick remains on guard, making himself useful about the place on a few small repairs I saw needed doing. Jed and Carl are here in the gardens throughout the day, and Olympia and I will both be here at night."

Frances, entering with dessert, announced proudly that she was presenting Laurie's own cream puffs, filled with what had been "her" favorite blueberry cream. Frances's pride in her pupil and her wistful reference—to everyone present, "she" or "her" meant Regina—were clearly mingled.

"Frances said we were to use up the last of the frozen berries," Laurie told them. "I can't wait to try it again with fresh ones, can you, Uncle Deke? And Mother, can you believe I made these cream puffs myself?"

Frances offered the dessert, then placed the remaining serving dish on the sideboard. "For seconds," she said, "for those who can eat another, after what you did to that poached salmon.''

Pausing in the doorway to the kitchen, she added fiercely that if young Roddy Pickett was still around, he better remember that nobody was going to get past her and that old 30-30 of Mr. Coley's. Good thing she kept it in her room in case anybody got cute with her. Oh, and another thing: Was there anything special they thought Laurie should learn to cook?

"Everything, anything," was Olympia's positive reply.

"Did she see how you poached my catch tonight?" Deke asked. "I never had it better, nor better green mayonnaise."

Mrs. Potter was seized with a sudden inspiration. "You know," she said, "I never heard anything much said about lobster pie, all the years we've lived here. And now I hear from Anne-Marie Loeb that Jim, Jim Markham, has a recipe for it."

Frances was slightly affronted. "Lobster pie! Why didn't you say so? I've got an old recipe for lobster pie from the state extension service, if that's what you're wanting. It's fair, I'll say that. But she and Mr. Coley liked their lobsters best just fresh steamed, either hot with melted butter and lemon or plain cold with mayonnaise. Once in a while I'd make a lobster salad for them, sometimes on a cold night a good lobster stew, but not a one of us really fancied lobster pie. Just plain lobster gravy, all it is, in a pie crust."

"I think Jim has something different, a recipe his mother picked up for them at a restaurant someplace," Mrs. Potter offered diffidently. "What would you all think of our having a lobster pie cook-off? Like those flour company baking contests, or those chili con carne contests in Texas? Maybe we could get Jim to come over tomorrow and make his new dish, whatever it is."

Frances rose to the challenge. "Well, if it's a contest, I'm sure I can turn out something better than plain lobster gravy," she said.

"And I'll invent my own," Laurie announced with confidence. "I don't know what a lobster pie should be, but Frances has given me a lesson in plain pastry, so I should be able to *create*—'' (she spoke the word firmly) ''—to *create* my own lobster pie.''

Mrs. Potter was able to reach Jim at the Sportsmans Lodge. Anne-Marie would be waiting tables again tomorrow, he said, but he was out of a job for the moment. Yes, the cook-off sounded like great fun, and he'd be there—at what time? Mrs. Potter thought perhaps four, so that the results could be tasted and judged at dinner. Fenwick would have the fresh lobsters here, and Jim was please to bring his other ingredients and to let her have the bill for them, since she was sponsoring the contest. And so it was arranged.

The next day, although she suspected that there were surreptitious activities going on in the Cogswell kitchen, Mrs. Potter stayed quietly in her room, working along happily through *High Rising* and *The Headmistress*. She managed, without actually rummaging through the desks of her old friends, to locate a sheet of blue paper, a pair of scissors, and three small safety pins.

At four she entered the kitchen.

''The lobsters are already in the pot,'' Laurie told her gleefully, ''And we decided we'd each use three, since they're only one-pounders. As soon as mine are done and cooling, I'm going out to practice my fly-casting. Frances and Jim are going to work here in the kitchen, but they've both promised not to peek at each other, and not to look at something of mine in the pantry.''

''And when are you making your pastry, may I ask, young lady?'' Frances demanded.

Laurie's grin was a joy to Mrs. Potter, remembering the impassive face of some weeks ago. ''You'll see,'' was all she would answer.

''I won't require the pastry board, either,'' Jim Markham told Frances. ''All I need is my steamed lobsters, and I brought the rest of my stuff.''

''Well,'' Frances said rather stiffly. ''Sounds like you two aren't planning a real old-fashioned lobster pie, after all. I thought I'd give a fresh turn to that old extension course recipe, make the lobster gravy a little fancier, but now that I know what the competition is, I'm going to give this another think.''

Clearly, the three contestants did not want, or expect, to be watched by the self-appointed sponsor and judge of the contest. Mrs. Potter retreated again to the joys of Angela Thirkell, only saying that the Weidners would join them at dinner for the judging. An earlier phone call to Olympia had gained approval to this plan, as well as to the inclusion of Carter Ansdale.

''Should there be something besides lobster, do you think?'' Margo had asked, in accepting the invitation. ''Can't I bring something? Chuck is yelling that I ought to bring what he calls my 'Heretical Baked Beans,' which is what I always take to potluck suppers, and maybe a bowl of raw vegetable things?''

Carter's response to Mrs. Potter's call was enthusiastic. ''I'd adore it,'' he said, ''and I want you to know I'm going to find that Rodney Pickett if it's the last thing I do on this green earth. Our firm has British connections and they're working on it.''

Cocktails that evening were in the back parlor, with Frances at the side table preparing bombastics with the same precision, if not the same dramatic flourishes, she had learned from her former employer.

Mrs. Potter offered a toast. ''To friends,'' she said, ''to present and absent friends.''

''And wouldn't *they* have loved this?'' Margo said, a little mistily. ''I know Cole would have had a new limerick.''

Frances interrupted, somewhat brusque in her effort to avoid further sentimentality. ''No appetizers,'' she said. ''You'll see why later.''

When they all went into the dining room, the long sideboard was laden with four major dishes, one lightly covered with a napkin. A printed card (Jim's work, Mrs. Potter thought) was propped up before each. Yet another card in the same distinctive printing identified a large casserole as ''Mrs. Weidner's Decidedly Heretical Baked Beans.''

To everyone's surprise, Frances's entry was a lobster quiche. ''Anybody can make lobster gravy, bake it in a crust,'' she said, "and I made one of those, too, just to show you what it was like. *That's* what's called a 'Lobster Pie.' Looks just like a pie. You could gussy it up a little if you wanted to put your mind to it. But then I figured, if we were getting fancy, I'd show I wasn't behind the door when they gave out cooking smarts."

"Mother got my recipe," Jim said, "when she and some of her garden club friends were in western Massachusetts last month, looking at historic houses at Deerfield. They went to a place a few miles away and they all adored the lobster pie there. If you knew my mother, you'd know she'd end up in the kitchen, getting the recipe from the chef. Of course I changed it just a tad."

(Mrs. Potter and Frances exchanged glances. A *mite* equals a *dite* equals a *tad*. And they all mean a *s'koshi bit*.)

"I mean, who needs to strain a cream sauce if you've got a good whisk and a good arm?" Jim continued. "And I put the whole thing into one big shallow casserole instead of dividing it into four individual ones."

"I'd just like to know what Laurie's been doing, out throwing that line in the backyard until about a half hour before supper," Frances said. "No sign of the pie crust I showed her how to bake."

Laurie answered with certain dignity. "But pastry is tricky, you told me so yourself, Frances. I don't think I have it mastered yet. But I knew something I could make, for sure, and it turned out to be a pie shell, wait and see."

Frances's lobster quiche was superb, a crisp, rich crust filled with a lobster-laden custard, rich with Swiss cheese and enlivened with tiny rounds of sliced green scallions from the garden.

Jim's lobster pie, a sherry-fragrant Newburg sauce with chunks of sautéed lobster, baked under a brown crusty topping, was a winner as well.

Then, proudly, Laurie lifted the napkin that had been shrouding her entry. "Ta *da*!" she exclaimed. "A cream puff shell and a filling of lobster salad!"

The crisp and delicate brown puff, filled with chilled cut-up lobster, sliced hard-cooked eggs, sliced stuffed olives, chopped celery, and mayonnaise, received universal applause. "A few of my scallions," Frances noted, "and also a few of my green peas from the garden, I shouldn't wonder."

Laurie stood her ground. "I just happened to notice some nice tiny green onions coming on," she said, "and I remembered those new peas were very good with the salmon last night. So I just, you know, decided to cook a few of them, very quickly, and toss them in, too."

Anyone who begins a recipe with "I just happened to notice some nice . . ." is destined to be one of the world's good cooks, Mrs. Potter reflected.

Quickly she decided to make her awards. Rising from the big table where they all, including Frances, were sitting—all judiciously and approvingly sampling each dish, returning for seconds, all complimenting Margo on her crazy baked beans—Mrs. Potter produced her medals.

On Frances's bosom, on a prim, flowered cotton print; on Jim's white knit pullover (that alligator again, she thought); and on Laurie's proud, yellow sleeveless top, she pinned identical decorations.

These roughly cut and irregular blue stars all bore the same inscription. On each she had printed "THE GREAT LOB-STER PIE COOK-OFF—GRAND WINNER."

Later she insisted on having each recipe.

Frances returned from the kitchen with a large and well-used looseleaf notebook.

"All right," she said, "here is what lobster pie is supposed to be, only they say you can make it with other things."

1-9 inch double crust pastry shell, unbaked	*½ tsp. salt*
2–3 c. cooked lobster meat, flaked fish, or 1 pint shuck-ed clams	*2 c. fish stock or milk*
	2 tsp. chopped onion
	1 c. cooked vegetables— carrots peas, celery, or a combination
⅓ c. butter	
⅓ c. flour	

Melt butter, add flour and salt, blend until smooth. Add liquid gradually, cook until thick, stirring constantly. Add onions, vegetables, and seafood and heat through. Turn into an unbaked pie shell, top with second layer of pastry, pinch the edges, and bake at 425 degrees until the crust is well browned.

"Extension says, 'ten to fifteen minutes,'" Frances remarked as Mrs. Potter copied the recipe quickly on a lined yellow pad. "I give it longer. Like my pie crust crisp."

"Now for the quiche," Mrs. Potter reminded her, "and I think the old-fashioned pie was delicious. Didn't you notice that there wasn't a bit of it left?"

Frances was clearly pleased. "Not even a smidgen for Fenwick in the morning," she said complacently. "I did save him a little wedge of the quiche, though, so he'd know what it's like."

Mrs. Potter's pen was poised expectantly.

"No need to give you a pie crust recipe," Frances said. "What you do is line your big pie pan with a good rolled crust, and then before you bake it, you mix up these ingredients."

Mrs. Potter wrote quickly:

2 T. flour	2 c. cooked lobster meat, cut up
2 beaten eggs	1 c. diced Swiss cheese
½ c. mayonnaise	¼ c. sliced green onions or
½ c. milk	scallions

"And you bake it in a moderate oven," Frances continued, "for forty minutes or so, until it's done. Suppose I don't have to tell *you* how to test the middle of a custard pie with a silver knife to see when it comes out clean."

Jim had brought his recipe already printed on a neat file card. "It isn't exactly the same as the one Mother sent me," he said, "but this is the way I made it. The restaurant is called 'Bill's,' so I think that's what it should be named, 'Bill's Lobster Pie.'"

"In my book it's going to be 'Jim's Lobster Pie,'" Mrs. Potter assured him, as she scanned the recipe.

"Blend four tablespoons of butter with four tablespoons of flour in a saucepan over low heat. When well mixed, add two cups of hot milk and one cup of hot cream and cook gently for fifteen minutes, stirring often. Strain."

"Mine didn't need it," Jim interposed.

"Sauté a pound of cooked lobster meat in four tablespoons of butter," Mrs. Potter read from the card. "When it begins to turn color, add a quarter cup of sherry, a half teaspoon of paprika, and cook another three minutes. Add a pinch of cayenne, a teaspoon of salt, then the cream sauce.

"Beat four egg yolks," she continued, "blend with a quarter cup of the hot sauce, then stir back into the mixture. Cook over low heat until bubbling, remove from heat, and stir in another quarter cup of sherry."

"The restaurant says to divide the mixture into four deep individual casseroles," Jim interrupted, "but I thought for a party like ours tonight it would be better in one big one."

"Right," Mrs. Potter agreed. "Now tell me what was in that wonderful crumb crust."

"A half cup of coarse, fresh breadcrumbs," Jim said, "a good sprinkle of paprika, a half cup of crushed potato chips, a quarter cup of grated Parmesan cheese, and a third of a cup of melted butter. I increased all of this a bit from the original recipe, to make sure we could really call it a pie."

"Marvelous," Mrs. Potter told him. "Please send our thanks to your mother, from all of us, and tell her I'd love to meet her someday when she comes up this way to visit you."

They all turned to Laurie, who looked as if she were ready for bed.

"Well, you know, about that pie crust," she told them, "I'm not ready to do that yet without Frances. It sounds so easy, but I think it probably takes a lot of practice. Anyway cream puffs, which *look* as if they'd be hard to do, are really, I mean, a cinch."

Mrs. Potter might have written this off as the natural self-assurance of the young—at least of one who could quite naturally and unselfconsciously refer to her "field" of marine biology. However, she also knew it to be true. Much as she wished to be a fine bread maker or a dependable pastry chef she knew her results to be uneven. As a baker of cream puffs, she had never known failure.

Laurie continued.

"All I did was use the regular cookbook recipe—Frances said they were all alike—the one using a half cup of flour and two eggs. Only in place of the half teaspoon of regular salt that it called for, I used a little celery salt, onion salt, and garlic salt instead. I thought it might be a little more lively since it was going to have a salad filling."

Again Mrs. Potter told herself, this is the making of a fine cook.

"And then I spread out the whole recipe flat in a greased pie dish, thinking it would turn into a giant cream puff and I'd split it in two and fill it with lobster salad, as a kind of joke. Instead, you saw what it did? It simply climbed up the sides of the pie dish and made a giant pie crust, still flat and nice as could be in the center. I tried it with a knife point, the way Frances said to do with the cream puffs last night, and it seemed dry and done in the middle. So I just called it, you know, a '*pie*.' "

"And the filling?" Mrs. Potter asked, her pen and yellow pad at the ready.

"No point in bothering with that," Laurie said, in tones as definite as her mother's. "I'll probably never make it the same way again anyway, although if I had a lobster with some coral in it I think I might have frosted the whole top of the salad with mayonnaise and sprinkled the coral over it, just to make it pretty. I suppose you could fill it with anything. Maybe next time I'll try it with a sort of fluffy lobster mousse."

Mrs. Potter mentally revised her awards. They all had said the same thing—Grand Winner—but she now felt privately that on Laurie's lopsided blue star there should be several emerging gold ones, which eventually would shine very brightly indeed.

32

At last came came the morning when Mrs. Potter was ready to try her wings. She had again joined the family at the dinner table the previous night, the night after the lobster pie cook-off, noting that Olympia had assigned Deke to her half brother's former place at the head of the table.

She had been relishing Frances's and Laurie's breakfast trays. Today's had included fresh Maine strawberries, too sweet and juicy to survive travel to commercial markets, as well as a pot of her favorite tea and homemade English muffins.

"One thing Mr. Coley didn't hold with was store muffins," Frances told her. "He said here in Maine they were more like store bread, soft and fluffy. He wanted his made big, a little bit tough, and full of nice big holes. That way when you break them apart with a fork and toast them good and brown, you can slather on plenty of butter."

That's another thing I hope to be able to bake myself someday, Mrs. Potter thought longingly. I'll probably never live long enough to achieve it, as may be true of my dream to make the perfect loaf of French bread.

"I thought I'd drive myself to Northcutt's Harbor this morning while it's still early and cool," she told Frances. "It can't be much after six, but this will be the nicest time to be out today. I just want to take a look at the cottage, and I'll be back in an hour or two.''

Frances, it appeared, had anticipated the suggestion and had already discussed it with the others. Mr. Deke, she said, had said, ''Let her do it if she insists.'' But Fenwick was to go along. ''I don't want her at the cottage or anywhere, alone,'' he said. ''And I want her home before noon.''

Seemed mighty good to have someone taking charge again around the place, Frances said. Even the flower borders looked more the way they used to, with Mr. Deke telling old Jed and Carl what to do. Those Scotch people wrote the book about gardens, Jed and Carl were telling her now, and they were as happy as she was to have a real boss again.

The road down the peninsula was quiet as she headed down from Route 1. Presumably the lobster boats had gone out at first light, but it was still early for cars on the road. The June breeze was fragrant with a promise of heavy summer heat later in the day.

It seemed a liberation to be driving her own car again. Fenwick was an agreeably undemanding and silent companion, after his first remark. ''Never thought I'd be riding shotgun for anybody,'' he said. ''Suppose you're used to it out west.''

They passed the Birdson farm. Ahead, on the right, loomed the gray bulk of the Grange Hall, its gambrel roof sharp against the blue of the morning sky.

The flag flying, at this early hour?

Mrs. Potter braked to a halt, in horror and disbelief.

Hanging from the sturdy pole where the red, white, and blue had fluttered so proudly at the Memorial Day bean supper, there was a flag of another pattern.

Huge pink and white checks hung limply from the yardarm, an enormous enveloping shroud. From the bottom of the shapeless checkered folds hung two limp, bare, and bony feet.

At the top was the twisted, distorted face of Rodney Pickett, his lank body hanging clad in his mother's pink dress, a thin, strong, yellow nylon noose around his young neck.

Mrs. Potter made an abrupt, nearly impossible U-turn on the narrow road, and returned to the sanity of the house in Cherrybridge.

33

"Been hiding there in the loft of the Grange ever since the night he tried to smother you," Amanda announced as Mrs. Potter entered the post office several days later. "I checked up there myself Wednesday morning after you found him hanging from the flagpole. Found a couple of sardine cans, an empty bag of potato chips, an empty six-pack of Cokes."

"If he'd just waited until after Wednesday night Beano, we'd have found him in time," Tillie said.

"My Louis says there hadn't been anybody else up there," Giselle interrupted, "that's for a certainty. The big doors were locked and Roddy had barred off the loose back window where he broke in."

Amanda was unstoppable. "I told you, didn't I? I was right all along. I told you Persy wouldn't ever let Roddy go, and he wouldn't be able to leave her."

"Since it was all Rodney's doing, right from the start—the boat and Harvard and everything," Tillie said, "I hear Curly's thinking of suing the Ellsworth police."

Amanda's recital went on. "Of course, you know all about the note." Mrs. Potter nodded sadly, not breaking the flow of Amanda's speech. "Wrote it on the back of an old Grange bulletin. But I still can't figure out why he signed it with those three crazy names. You heard what he wrote, 'Genia?"

Again Mrs. Potter nodded, but Amanda repeated the words.
Tues June 15

I can no longer live in a world that does not recognize my place in it. I am sorry, Mother.

"And then those signatures!" Amanda continued. "Rodney Addison Pitt-Wyckley! Rodney Pyck-Wickett! Rodney Addison Pick-Wyatt! What do you suppose he meant by all that?"

"I'm afraid he was just trying out names he thought sounded a little more elegant and aristocratic than just plain Pickett," Mrs. Potter said slowly. "Poor Rod."

The subject was closed, another tragedy of Northcutt's Harbor to be accepted and bravely dismissed. This time, Mrs. Potter understood Amanda's courage as she changed the subject. "Now, just between the four of us," she said, "what do you make of the Colamarias? I know they seem quiet enough, but that name sounds a little suspicious to me. He says he writes church music, but does that mean anything?"

She looked at the others closely. "Let me know if you hear anything out of the way. I hear there's an old guy who comes up to visit, pretty classy dresser, and they call him 'El Padrino.' That spells 'godfather' in my book, so keep your eyes open, that's all I've got to say."

Even before reaching the post office, Mrs. Potter had earlier decided to leave the car with Tris to have the oil changed. Concentration on practical, everyday matters was the best way to exorcise that appalling vision—the lank body hanging from the flagpole wearing the pink and white checks as its badge of penance.

She had also earlier decided she would walk to the cottage from the post office. Exercise was what she needed, and fresh ocean air, after her days of being coddled and quiet and of Frances's and Laurie's good food.

Now she walked on slowly down the peninsula road. Her left side still felt incomplete, exposed, without the sleek gray dog beside her.

Poor Roddy, she thought again. How easy for him to feel affronted and belittled by people he also saw as standing in the way of his becoming an important landowner on the Point. Herbert and Alex had fed his vanity, arousing hopes of leaving the world of Pickett's store for the imagined glories of Millstone and the world beyond. Teedy had no doubt added a dash of plain greed, suggesting millionaire status for the owner of First Bite Marina. The boy's own fantasies had supplied the rest. All to be lost in the passion of his jealousy of Curly. Poor Roddy.

Pickett's was closed as she passed the store, but the Colamarias were out in front raking up papers and battered cans. Skip Cooney was helping them and he waved, a wide, open-palm semaphore of friendly greeting.

The road to the pound looked hot and dusty in the mid-June sun. Olympia will go back to fly-casting, she thought, if she ever has any spare time. The three of them, she and Deke and Laurie, will make a very happy family, and C. R. Cogswell & Son will flourish for another hundred years.

Olympia and Laurie and Deke need each other. Deke had excited in her only a momentary romantic flicker of attraction, arousing her need for a friend to confide in, and the old, occasionally recurring need to be looked after, when she thought about Lew. But those needs had never been strong enough to make her think of marrying again, she knew.

They'll buy the Roost from Herbert, which will solve his money troubles. They'll do the same with Harvard's cove, from whichever heirs it goes to, or Tris will hold out for the Maine Heritage. Either way would be fine. Laurie's name will be Cutler-MacDonald (insisting that she has adopted *him* and not the other way around) and Deke will teach them both Scottish country dancing.

She could see them now, Olympia and Laurie, both with pale red hair flying, in long skirts and tartan sashes, whirling in the intricate patterns. She could see Deke's hairy knees flashing below his kilt, and she could hear the bagpipes.

It was all utterly right, and she would love them as neighbors forever.

The road to the Point was shaded, but it was still hot and an occasional mosquito buzzed past her ear. At least we're lucky here, next to the ocean, she thought, not to have black flies.

Then two great ideas came to her, almost simultaneously.

The first was that, if Lyman had not yet done anything about refinishing that kitchen floor, and she was sure he had not, she would call Jim and Anne-Marie, James Markham III and his lady. They'd do it beautifully. And while she had them on the line, she'd tell them that they must insist that Dwight let them take over the kitchen at the Sportsmans Lodge, a proposal to which she would add her own persuasions.

Her second good thought was that it was almost monsoon season at the ranch.

When she had first heard that word *monsoon* in connection with the summer rainy season—the two months or so of the year in which her part of southeastern Arizona received most of its scanty rainfall—she thought it sounded like something out of Kipling or Maugham. Like somebody's writing about tremendous tropical rains and floods and general watery drama.

With her first Arizona summer, she discovered this was to become her favorite season there, and she simply ignored those of her friends who asked her, unbelievingly, "You mean you'd leave Maine in the summer? For *Arizona?*"

Once the monsoons set in (there were recent Arizona dissenters who argued that the Mexican word *chubasco*, meaning thunderstorm, was a more accurate term), the hot dry days of May and early June began to abate.

Each morning from the ranch, she could see, above one or the other of the several mountain ranges visible from her patio, a small handkerchief of white cloud forming. By midday, the brilliant blue sky would be dotted and flounced with big white clouds floating by in innocent patterns that made patches of moving shadow on the pale, rolling, high country beneath them.

By late afternoon, the clouds would be building up into great white towers above the horizon.

Then, if your particular patch of Arizona was lucky that day, one of the great towers might turn dark, a wind would spring up, there might be the sudden coolness that meant hail in the higher mountains, and it would rain. Great, beautiful enormous splashing drops of rain—first only perfuming the dusty soil, then gathering into a flood—would wash red dust and clay down the ranch road, would turn the little dry arroyos into noisy brooks and sometimes even into gushing torrents.

And then it would be over and you would go to the rain gauge to find out how many hundredths of an inch the grateful ranch earth had received, and then it would be time for a swim in the rain-freshened pool, and for a drink and a cool lovely evening. "Rum on the rocks in the rainy season" had been a summertime password at the ranch from the first monsoon season Mrs. Potter had lived there, when she and Lew had first gone to Arizona to stay.

She repeated her two good ideas to herself happily. First, she'd leave everything for Jim and Anne-Marie to handle here at the cottage. Second, she'd be on the morning plane out of Bangor to Boston to Tuscon, and, if she telephoned right now, she'd catch somebody just finishing breakfast at the ranch. They could meet her at the Tucson airport tomorrow evening.

There would be time to pack (not that she ever took much back and forth) and time for grateful and affectionate farewells to Frances, Deke, Olympia, and Laurie. She'd write certain notes from the plane—her regrets at missing the bridal showers, notes to the Weidners and Carter and the Wyncotes, to the neighbors, to Edna and Amanda, to the chancellor and Wendy. She'd be back in the fall, she'd write them, before they had a chance to miss her and just before the leaves started to turn.

The drive back to the ranch would be gorgeous if the air had been cooled by an afternoon thundershower, and if the skies above the mountains were still being lighted with the last flashes of the storm as it faded away.

ABOUT THE AUTHOR

Virginia Rich made her debut as a mystery writer with THE COOKING SCHOOL MURDERS. She was born in Sibley, Iowa, and at one time wrote a food column for *The Chicago Tribune*, under the continuing *Tribune* name of Mary Meade. She has also served as food editor for *Sunset* magazine. Currently, Mrs. Rich divides her time between her working cattle ranch in Arizona and spending some months each year at her home in a small town in Maine not unlike the town where Mrs. Potter appears in THE BAKED BEAN SUPPER MURDERS.

11

MYSTERY
in the best 'whodunit' tradition...

AMANDA CROSS
The Kate Fansler Mysteries

11   TA-75